PRAISE FOR

CHAOS & FLAME

"A gripping fantasy about betrayal, forgiveness, loss,
and loyalty amid a magical war."
—*PUBLISHERS WEEKLY*

"The focus on family bonds and support adds realism, while the
inclusion of prophetic dreams and visions creates intrigue."
—*KIRKUS REVIEWS*

"This fast-paced, action-filled fantasy reads like a mix of *Game of
Thrones* and *Avatar: The Last Airbender*."
—*BCCB*

"Political intrigue, magic, and intricate world-building
will draw in readers."
—*SLJ*

"Gratton and Ireland are no strangers to new and fantastic settings, and this first of a duology should prove to be as enthralling
as all their individual offerings."
—*BOOKLIST*

"An intriguing cast of characters and a diverse, queer-normative
fantasy realm make this novel stand out."
—*SHELF AWARENESS*

BLOOD
&
FURY

Also by Tessa Gratton and Justina Ireland

Chaos & Flame

BLOOD
&
FURY

TESSA GRATTON
JUSTINA IRELAND

putnam

G. P. Putnam's Sons

G. P. Putnam's Sons
An imprint of Penguin Random House LLC
1745 Broadway, New York, New York 10019

First published in the United States of America by Razorbill,
an imprint of Penguin Random House LLC, 2024
First paperback edition published 2025

Visit us online at PenguinRandomHouse.com.

The Library of Congress has cataloged the hardcover edition as follows:
Names: Gratton, Tessa, author. | Ireland, Justina, author.
Title: Blood & fury / Tessa Gratton, Justina Ireland. Other titles: Blood and fury
Description: New York: Razorbill, 2024. | Series: Chaos & flame; 2 |
Audience: Ages 14 years and up. | Summary: Darling Seabreak grapples with her destiny
to reunite fractured houses and bring peace, while Talon Goldhoard, still in love with
Darling, navigates a war instigated by his family, as they both face the challenge of
saving the kingdom amidst dark forces and ancient magic.
Identifiers: LCCN 2023055765 (print) | LCCN 2023055766 (ebook) |
ISBN 9780593353356 (hardcover) | ISBN 9780593353363 (epub)
Subjects: CYAC: Fantasy. | Magic—Fiction. | Fate and fatalism—Fiction. | War—Fiction. |
Interpersonal relations—Fiction. | LCGFT: Fantasy fiction. | Novels.
Classification: LCC PZ7.G77215 Blg 2024 (print) | LCC PZ7.G77215 (ebook) | DDC [Fic]—dc23
LC record available at https://lccn.loc.gov/2023055765
LC ebook record available at https://lccn.loc.gov/2023055766

ISBN 9780593353370

1st Printing

Manufactured in the United States of America

LSCC

Design by Tony Sahara | Text set in Warnock Pro

The authorized representative in the EU for product safety and compliance is Penguin Random
House Ireland, Morrison Chambers, 32 Nassau Street, Dublin D02 YH68, Ireland,
https://eu-contact.penguin.ie.

BLOOD & FURY

BLOOD

The second scion of House Cockatrice was eleven years old when her mother gripped her chin to tilt her face this way and that, studying her hair and eyes and skin and mouth, her posture and her build. *At least you might be beautiful someday,* her mother said.

I'll turn heads with respect and strength, Mother, the second scion answered.

Her mother scoffed. *You can't even paint an empty sky.*

It was true then: the second scion was really quite bad at painting.

And it was just as true now, though Aurora Falleau was seventeen and had struggled for years to learn.

She perched on a stool in the terraced garden of Dragon Castle, protected by ugly mountain peaks that cut off the morning sun and spread cool shade across the summer flowers. This was her older sister's new garden, and it flourished under Solaria's care. Lush lowland roses grew plump blossoms even in the thin air, and the peach tree transplanted from their childhood home at Mount Klevon seemed to thrive. Though they'd only been here a month, the boxes spilled over with sundrops and ruffled bloodwort and Solaria's favorite violets. Solaria had always been gifted with flora, with color and art and beauty.

Meanwhile, the second scion could not even capture the color of light on the pinkshade growing up the trellis beside her. The angle of the curling stem was all wrong, and the brush held too much water so that the green pigment ran. A talent for painting ought to flow through Aurora's veins! She ought to have an instinct for it! Solaria could paint a delicate landscape in her sleep, and she didn't even care about paints or pencils. Solaria preferred living art: sensual gardens and pristine makeup and perfect little desserts she constructed out of spun sugar.

Solaria was born to rule House Cockatrice. They should have kept her and sent Aurora to marry the Dragon regent. Let Aurora join the proud Goldhoard family. She was the one with ambition. She was the one eager for strength. The one who could throw herself into what the Dragons needed her to be. A ferocious match for their ferocious regent.

Aurora had argued as much, but again and again she'd been rejected.

You're only seventeen, Aurora! You don't have a useful boon, Aurora! You aren't as gifted as your sister, Aurora! How can we send an untalented scion, Aurora?

You're not the one Roar Goldhoard wants, Aurora.

Why would she be asked for, when her sister was there to be taken? Her perfect, gifted, beautiful sister.

When the betrothal papers were signed, House Cockatrice hadn't even made Aurora the first scion; they'd chosen a cousin instead, who sang so sweetly he charmed the barnacles off ships and even had a boon giving him perfect pitch.

Aurora had a boon, too. But it was small, nearly useless unless the people she used it on were weak-willed. It did not work on her parents or her sister. She wished she had a better boon. Even if it wasn't strong. A hundred years ago scions of House Cockatrice had glorious boons that let them rule hearts and minds: charm and charisma boons, boons to let them play any instrument, boons that turned their words into illusions or their smiles into starlight. Her grandmother had a prophecy boon so great she could predict anything. Even if it sent her mad, Aurora would prefer the brief flare of power and fame to nothing at all.

Madness was infinitely better than mediocrity.

She lifted the razor off the tray of tools. It was meant for sharpening the edge of her charcoal or trimming her brushes or cutting curls of pigment from the ink sticks. Aurora put the tip to the thin canvas, ready to destroy it, just as she heard footsteps on the finely ground shells of the path behind her. Startling, she hid the razor in her palm and turned with a pretty smile.

Silhouetted by the rising sun so that she glowed, Solaria picked her way to Aurora on delicate silk slippers. Her hair was loose, golden curls falling around layers of dressing gowns of velvet and lace. Solaria held her collars closed at her neck, head ducked to watch her step, except for darting her glance up to Aurora frequently. A tiny blush pinked her white cheeks, and she couldn't keep the smile off her mouth.

Aurora stood slowly, holding the razor against the small of her back. "What are you doing out here?"

The Dragon consort opened her mouth, caught her intended words, and swallowed them with a giggle. Instead, she teased, "Whatever I like. It's my castle now."

Aurora huffed. "It's cold. You're supposed to be in your marriage bed."

Solaria laughed, bright and joyful. She came closer and leaned in conspiratorially. "Roar was summoned by General Sharpscale for some war business, and promised to bring snacks back to bed with him."

Aurora managed to keep the smile on her face despite the rage of jealousy burning in her bones. She was here for support, after all. Support and companionship—and to get her out of House Cockatrice for good.

Solaria's gaze slid to the painting. She stepped around to peer more closely, and her mouth fell into a pretty moue. "Aurora," she murmured.

Aurora braced herself. The painting was fine. She was proficient these days, at least, if no prodigy.

Solaria touched perfect white fingers to Aurora's shoulder. In the sunlight, the soft emotions, the gesture, her unbound hair, and her happiness-flushed cheeks made Solaria into some kind of holy creature, a beautiful work of art herself. Aurora swallowed bile. Aurora was pretty, too; she looked just like her sister, even if their mother called her too ambitious for true beauty. *Beauty is idyllic, inspirational, meditative, yearning, Aurora,* her mother liked to say. *It must be content and humble. If you are desperate, eager, hungry, the art will be thin, the beauty facile.*

So many words for a beauty in service to others. Aurora did not believe service was a requirement of beauty. Passion was. Yearning, yes, longing. What was beauty without desperation? Where could epiphany reside without hunger?

The point was that none of these things that either Aurora or her mother sought from beauty could be found in her bland landscape painting.

"Sister," Solaria said, "you know there is nothing shameful in putting down a tool that no longer serves."

Aurora gasped, and her hand spasmed in offended surprise. A sharp pain bloomed in her palm as the razor blade sank into the thin flesh. Aurora held it tighter. The pain focused her and let her lift her chin. "Is there shame in making art no one admires?"

"Of course not," Solaria said gently, stepping closer. Wind ruffled her hair playfully. She touched Aurora's cheek. "Not if you like it."

"What does liking have to do with art in House Cockatrice? What am I to be, if not an artist?" Aurora snapped. "You are a consort now, practically a queen. In addition to having your art and beauty."

"You have your beauty, too," Solaria said. She moved her hand and tapped the tip of Aurora's nose. "And you're quick and clever; you can make a place for yourself here."

Aurora used her unbloodied hand to remove Solaria's from her face. She held on, willing herself to believe that Solaria believed it. That Solaria wanted her here with her because she believed Aurora could fit with the Dragons. For the Dragons did not create beauty, they protected it. Hoarded it and held it close. Fought for it. *That was passion*, Aurora thought. And the Dragons were surely hungry. Her fingers curled tighter around the razor; warm blood squeezed between her knuckles. Her palm ached.

"Your sister is bleeding," declared the bold voice of Roar Goldhoard, Dragon regent.

Aurora froze, but Solaria turned to her new husband with a glorious smile that only faded as his words sank in. "Aurora!" she cried sweetly, reaching for Aurora's clenched fist.

Allowing her sister to cup her hand in both of her own, Aurora kept her eyes fixed on Roar. He was twenty-five and devastating, tall and broad with luxurious black hair and suntanned skin. Muscular from years of sword fighting. He wore arrogance and strength like a cloak. Now as he stared audaciously back at Aurora, those full lips pulled into a smile lovely but tinged with judgment. He could see Aurora, she felt. See exactly what she was. He liked her, laughed at her sly jokes. But she wasn't the one he wanted. She let disdain into her features as her sister fussed over her wound.

"Let your sister tend to herself. Dragon Castle can provide," Roar said. He held out his hand. "Come, Solaria."

Solaria pouted at Aurora's bleeding hand. "Please do, sister. I'll tidy this—"

"Duncan will," her husband interrupted again, jutting his chin toward one of the Dragon regulars who'd followed him out into the garden.

"Very well," Solaria said.

When Solaria took Roar's hand, he pulled her possessively nearer and seemed to forget Aurora existed. She watched them. Solaria let herself be tucked against him like a favorite puppy.

They left. The soldier Duncan stayed behind, uniform bright green as the ornamental trees surrounding them. Aurora studied him for a moment, then said, "Thank you," and held her bloodied hand away from her dress as she followed the Dragon regent and his consort.

Once inside, Aurora turned the opposite way of the royal quarters. She hurried, injured hand cupped in her other hand until they stuck together with blood. The razor remained embedded in her palm, and as she walked, heedless of her path or anyone around her, Aurora slowly uncurled her fingers. It pulled the skin and muscle of her palm. Tears pricked her eyes, but she blinked them away.

Aurora stood in a dim alcove of Dragon Castle, thick red and green tapestries as still as ice against the walls. It was so quiet but for her own harsh breathing, she might have been alone in all Pyrlanum.

She pinched the razor and suddenly pulled it free. It came easily, and for a moment the cut was clear and visible—a flash of layered skin and red flesh—then blood flooded everywhere, filling the deep slice and pooling. It stretched along the lines of her palm, life line and heart line and all the tinier lines, like the blood sought paths for some distant future map.

Aurora closed her eyes against a wave of dizziness. She planted her feet and breathed carefully. But the air tasted of blood. She smelled it, too, and her vision behind her eyelids flared red red red.

Forgetting herself, Aurora listed sideways, and reached out with both hands to catch herself against the cold wall.

Her palm—her blood—smeared on the heavy bricks of iron-rock, and Aurora felt—

—a pulse.

Aurora's eyes flew open. She stared at nothing but her ghostly white hand, streaked with blood, against the dark gray stone. There was no blood on the stone, as if it had been instantly absorbed. Surely not. Aurora removed her hand and saw blood sinking into the crack between bricks. Sucked in. It was unnatural.

The pulse beat again, up from her feet this time.

Aurora didn't think, but only moved. She headed down. Down to the kitchens, past them to the cellars, through the oldest parts of the dungeons the Dragon regents hadn't used in generations. The pulse came and went, slow as a sleeping monster's heartbeat. It was not a sound. Nor concussive. She didn't see or hear it.

The pulse thrummed in her blood. In the palm of her bleeding hand.

Aurora followed its call to a door that was not a door. Hidden behind a threadbare tapestry covered in woven dragons and edged in tongues of golden fire, the door opened with a grind of stone on stone when she touched it with her bloody hand.

Cold, wet wind licked at her face, and her slippers dampened on the floor of the ancient tunnel carved into the mountain itself.

Darkness surrounded her, but her hands felt old cutouts for candles and boonlight sconces long since snuffed. Far ahead there was the dimmest promise of light. She followed it down.

Suddenly Aurora stumbled into a vast cavern.

Just enough light trickled from old cracks and bat tunnels in the high domed ceiling, and crystals on the hanging stalactites offered their own quiet glow. Aurora stared at the wide black mirror of a still, underground lake.

Walking as if in a trance, she knelt at the edge of the water and dipped her bleeding hand into it.

The shock of cold wrenched up her arm. Aurora felt a crack of power inside her, and she stood with a splash. Something had glowed in the center of the lake, for just a moment. It was more like the afterimage of lightning. With her gaze she followed the ghostly line that pointed in a jagged fork from the lake to the opposite shore. A stone table was carved from the cavern wall, like an altar.

Aurora went to it, but before she arrived, she passed the mouth of a new tunnel. This seemed to breathe sweet-smelling air at her. She stopped, turned, and when she stepped in, she propped herself against the carved lintel with her sluggishly bleeding hand. A boonlight shaped like a crescent moon flashed to life.

It was a ruined workroom. Old books moldered in piles, and half-unrolled scrolls were scattered like pieces of a dragon's nest. There was rotten furniture and mildewed pillows. Melted candles and the desiccated remains of sparrow drakes in travel cages. Their scales glinted dully in the boonlight.

Delight and thrill tingled in Aurora. This was a room no person had seen in decades at least. A secret in the deep guts of Dragon Castle. And it was hers.

Aurora kicked aside trash and went to the desk. On it were more damp books and torn scrolls. Some might be partially restored. In time. But one book looked new.

Lifting it in both hands—both covered in her drying, dripping blood—Aurora smiled at the soft leather binding, and opened it.

This journal belongs to the blood, it began.

No names, not here. The names our parents give us are for them, not for the most crucial parts of us. You will give up much for what I know. I have given up everything. But in return, there is a strength enough to leash and crush Chaos. It is only what we have already done. And if you are willing, it can be yours as it is mine. Power is greater than love.

The words trembled, but only because Aurora's hands trembled. She had not even realized love was what she missed from her family all these years, what she longed for from the chasm of her heart.

But this, this was better.

ENEMIES

THIRTY YEARS LATER

I dream of fire.

It devours me, swallows me whole, until I am consumed by it. My hair, my eyes, my bones, all of it is flame, burning brightly, blinding me, and remaking me into something new. There is pain, but only at first, and then . . .

Then there is only ecstasy.

The fire moves through me, with me, warming, soothing. It whispers to me the history of Pyrlanum, it screams the defeats and despair of the people. It calls to Chaos and Chaos answers in fits and spurts.

The flames whisper that this is the way it should be, that this is right. We are one with Chaos, the flames and me. It is joyous about the future and cajoles me to action. The fire is everywhere, and it knows this land, this country that I call my home. The fire listens to the people, it hears their heart wishes and heartaches, and it shares all of it with me while carrying me through the air, high above it all, a place where there is only truth and freedom. There is no disappointment among the clouds, no pain or regret or fear.

There is only the phoenix.

1

TALON

The water in the shallow stone bowl ripples as the spell-water breaks and Captain Greenspine's wavering face and voice smear away.

"Chaos take it!" I snap, slamming my fist into the table. Teacups and goblets rattle on the thick wood, and the few boonlights we've managed to keep on flicker. I want to push away and throw my chair across the room, hopefully smashing one of the paned windows overlooking the inner gardens, then storm out. It would be so satisfying.

But General Bloodscale would relish such an outburst too much. I can picture the smug smile he'd offer. So instead I carefully flatten my hand and breathe.

"I'll try to get him back, my blade," says Alastair Sevenclaw, the only seer left in Phoenix Crest whose boon is remotely reliable. This mode of communication has always been complicated and difficult even for strong seers, but Aunt Aurora's never failed. I learned to rely on it too much for sending orders to the far reaches of Pyrlanum.

Of course, now I know Aunt Aurora was supplementing her boon with blood magic. She taught me viscerally when she ripped the regent of House Kraken's heart from his chest.

"Don't bother," I say. "He heard my orders. The rest was

questioning the why of them, which should be irrelevant to carrying them out."

General Bloodscale grunts.

"What is it, General?" I ask slowly, hating how my voice sounds silky and dangerous like Caspian's.

"You used to be the first to question commands you found lacking. Why the change of heart, High Prince?"

I grind my teeth. "My blade," I correct. I am not the High Prince Regent, and I never will be. That position no longer exists, was always oppressive, and the last High Prince Regent himself—my brother—wanted it abolished. Though why we should consider the opinion of a prince who lied to us all and vanished from the world is up for debate. But those wishes are one of the reasons we're in this spare office in the royal quarters, not using the Phoenix Hall with its grand sculptures and Phoenix throne.

Bloodscale raises a grizzled eyebrow but inclines his head in acceptance—for now. "My blade, you often suggested that loyal soldiers will be more eager to obey an order they understand."

"These orders have been easily understandable from the beginning. We are stretched thin. The entire land is in upheaval after the—the events at House Barghest last month. Which is—"

"If you—" Bloodscale begins.

"—which is *why*," I say forcefully, "I've commanded the withdrawal to Phoenix Crest and Dragon Territory. As I said in the official orders themselves."

Bloodscale steeples his hand on the map of Pyrlanum. "This remains the perfect opportunity to solidify Dragon control of the south. There's been no word of Kraken leadership, and Sphinx lands are unprotected by the squids. We could even move in toward Furial—"

"General, we are not attacking House Gryphon." I stand, shoving my chair back hard enough it skids on the stone floor. Behind me, flames crackle in the hearth. "They've been our allies throughout the House Wars, and will remain so. The first scion is with us at Dragon Castle—"

"A hostage—"

I lean over the table with my best scowl, desperate to hide the queasy feeling in my guts. Because no matter what Elias themself thinks, they *are* my hostage. Their cousin Vivian would certainly believe so, had we any idea of her whereabouts. "No. Elias Chronicum chooses to be there. And I choose not to conquer Pyrlanum when it is weak!"

Bloodscale grimaces. Finally an argument he can understand. The histories would not call House Dragon strong for taking advantage of the broken Chaos and turmoil of the last month.

I press on. "My brother commanded the war's end before he disappeared. That is the legacy I will chase, not the warmongering and destruction of our father. We will protect what is ours, as Dragons do, but all Pyrlanum is not ours! That is what I am going to do, even if I have to—" *do it myself*, I finish silently. I let my jaw set, fighting back the sharp longing for Caspian, for Darling, for Finn, for anyone, everyone, I want at my side right now.

General Bloodscale studies me, and I wonder who he sees: A fitting scion for our father's rule? Or only the child in diapers I was when he met me? Bloodscale trained me from the age of eleven in warcraft. He is the soldier who clasped an armored pauldron to my shoulder before my first battle. Who wiped tears from my cheeks with rough thumbs after my first kill and said, "Don't let it go, but don't let it stop you, either." He knows me. I don't think he likes me anymore. That's fine.

Before he can disagree, I straighten up. "Do as I command, or depose me."

Alastair Sevenclaw gets to his knees immediately, one hand fisted over his heart. I barely remembered he was here, with all my focus on the dangerous general sharing this office with me.

Slowly, General Bloodscale stands. He puts a fist over his heart and bows. "I will do as you command, my blade."

"Good." I spin and storm out, but manage not to slam the door.

As quickly as I can, I head down the winding corridor to the stairs leading up to Caspian's tower. I shove past that damned doorway carved into a dragon and phoenix entwined in flight, ignoring the sickness pinching up my stomach at the sight of it. He knew so long ago, he knew what he was going to do, and didn't tell me, didn't trust me.

It's hard to know if I should be more furious or grief-stricken, when I don't even really know what actually happened. What Caspian actually did.

I climb the stairs two at a time and burst into his old rooms, eyes darting through the darkness over the paintings of that eyeless girl, my Darling, whom I haven't seen since she burst into flames in my brother's arms and flew away. I can't look at them.

Caspian had a narrow balcony, attached to the nearly hidden back room of the tower where he often slept in a messy nest of pillows and what seem to have been threadbare tapestries. All of it stained with spots of paint and singed by dropped candles. The tall windows push open onto the crescent balcony, and I grasp the stone rail. I grip tightly, wishing I had real talons to gouge the stone, sparking against it. Even using my whole weight to lean in, nothing moves. Nothing shifts.

There's only a wind tearing at my hair, tangling the dark curls. It pulls at my jacket, too, snapping the lapels and tails. The sun is hot, but the wind strips the heat away. This is the highest tower of Phoenix Crest, and I can't hear anything but the roar of wind.

The sun cuts into my eyes from the west, clouds rolling in for a coming storm. The fields and hills spread south from Phoenix Crest, the green and gold of summer bright. A sprawling town peeks out of the trees here and there, too far to be part of Phoenix Crest, too close to be considered separate. The broad grassy field between the fortress and the woods is pastureland this time of year, shared by shepherds on one end and drake herders on the other. But in the past weeks, parts of my army have camped here as they somehow manage to obey my simple commands and withdraw from the south and west. It's slow, but Caspian began it when he introduced Darling as Maribel Calamus at his ball in this very fortress.

Thinking about Darling hurts. The pain coils in my chest, like she has a grip on my heart and might tear it out the way Aurora did to Leonetti. And I want her to; I'd let Darling do it if it meant she was here.

It hardly matters that the thirty-two days since the explosions of Chaos at House Barghest, since I saw her violent eyes, heard her angry accusations, have felt longer than the number of days I knew her. She dug into me.

And then she turned into fire.

She became a phoenix, her flaming wings wrapped around the dark green scales of a newborn dragon, my brother.

They transformed together, then soared into the clouds and vanished completely.

The kraken in the bay raged against the ships—both House Barghest and mercenary—tearing at their sails and crushing hulls, until it sank beneath the waves and vanished, too.

Inside House Barghest, little Darvey Brynson's skin broke and his spine popped and right in the middle of a crowd of angry cousins he turned into a giant black dog and snapped huge fangs at his conniving uncle who tried to steal his House. Then Darvey howled and ran and disappeared.

We heard reports and rumors that Vivian Chronicum, with one attendant in her expansive library, screamed, too, and transformed into a beast of wings and fur, a wicked beak, and gleaming Chaos-purple eyes. She ripped through the ceiling and flew off, gone.

There have been no rumors of a sphinx in the south. No word of a cockatrice anywhere.

No sign of any of them.

Whatever Caspian did, whatever he turned them into, they might not be meant for us. They might never return.

At first I hoped. I assumed. That they would be back—especially my brother and Darling. They'd come tearing out of the sky and land in a courtyard, exhausted and fire-singed. I didn't even care if they returned hand in hand, together, everything about our hearts tangled and changed. I barely cared if they returned as monsters. As long as they came back.

A few hours of hope were all I got before I had to act to stem the turmoil descended upon Pyrlanum in their wake. Because I was the only one left.

Infighting at House Barghest I quashed by force, setting my trusted Dragon's Teeth to command the region. I sent Finn Sharpscale, my second, to take Aunt Aurora and our other prisoners directly north to Dragon Castle. Alone, I went to Phoenix Crest to grab the reins and make the Dragon army submit to me in the absence of my brother the regent.

It isn't going well.

The Dragon army obeyed me for the most part, but they all— not just General Bloodscale—wanted me to accept the regency. "Every dragon needs a head," Bloodscale insisted, and the ministers of work, prosperity, and the hoard agreed. I promised to relay their loyalty to Caspian when he returned, and refused.

I've focused on the logistics of moving a long-term occupying army and the even more troubling need to feed people in the cities and towns my soldiers abandon. The line between total withdrawal and leaving small forces to help with repair and infrastructure is blurry, and made worse by the rumors of the Last Phoenix being reborn, of monsters that might be ancient empyreals returning to Pyrlanum only to judge us and leave immediately.

Everyone blames House Dragon, and I can't even disagree. All this is our fault, and Caspian's especially. Other Houses are certainly culpable—House Kraken never let go of fighting, either, and House Gryphon fanned flames in their own scheming ways. Barghest only cared about individual benefits. Sphinx might or might not have murdered my mother to ignite these House Wars again. But House Dragon took the provocation and devoured everything we could. Always hungry for more. Then Caspian went mad with his wild prophecies and wouldn't let anybody help. Not even people who loved him.

I close my eyes, letting the wind tickle my lashes. I lean down, flexing my shoulders in a stretch.

My boon twinges, filling the black behind my eyelids with a shimmer of violet rainbows. I take a deep breath to tamp it down.

The seer spell-waters aren't the only thing going wrong with Chaos. Boons are falling into hibernation or giving their bearers fevers. Some vanished as completely as the empyreals. Other people, those with no boons in the past, fall to the same fevers, as if their hidden connections to Chaos are being stoked.

We don't even have priests or mystics to truly explain what might be happening. There've been none working for the Houses in a hundred years, not since the Last Phoenix, and the nearest we have to experts are all in House Gryphon. Elias is focused on it, but without resources. In Vivian's absence House Gryphon maintains a chilly alliance with me, neither reacting with hostility nor offering aid. Maybe some folk healers in small villages have a communal memory of what's going on, but they sure aren't going to speak with me.

I wish I could argue it out with Finn. I wish I could spar with Darling so she could tell me where I'm being an idiot and what I'm missing. I even wish Caspian would roll his eyes and tell me disdainfully, *You're doing as well as anyone could expect, little dragon.*

I even want to see Aunt Aurora, despite the gore on her hands, despite her wide-eyed betrayal.

With another deep breath, I tilt my head up to the sky. I look at the pale, flat blue, and whisper, "Please, Chaos, help us."

Only the wind groans at me, twisting around the low, crumbling mountain holding Phoenix Crest.

I look down at the field, and a spear of motion catches my attention: coming from the east, a rider on a war drake, flying the vivid green of the Dragon messenger. The rider kicks up dust, streaking as fast as a drake can run.

Before I realize, I'm off the balcony and making my way down to the main fort. I wave a few soldiers to come with me but don't respond to questions. I lead the small party to the main doors of the Crest. They're pulled open for me, and I emerge onto the marble landing just as the messenger skids to a stop. Her war drake rears its head back and she holds up a hand to me, with a crumpled letter. Her eyes are wide under her sleek messenger helmet. "My blade!" she calls.

"I am here."

"It's the barghest, my blade!"

Everyone's attention sharpens on the messenger. The fist of pain around my heart squeezes. *Darling*, I think. *Caspian.*

The messenger says, "Commander Sharpscale saw it with his own eyes! The barghest has returned to Pyrlanum!"

TALON

It takes five days to get to Finn Sharpscale. By the third day, late afternoon, the four Teeth in my escort and I are racing our war drakes across an open stretch of grassland before the climb toward the darker forests along the Dragon–Barghest border. We're in full regalia, vivid scarlet jackets with white accents, like streaks of blood against the earth. Light scale armor covers my shoulders and straps around my torso, along with a crossed back sheath for my falchions. An armored collar protects the neck and chest of Kitty, my mount. The war drake leans her serpentine face into the wind, teeth bared because she likes the flavor of a hunt, her crest feathers pressed as low along her spine as they'll go. I bend over her shoulders, and let the race turn me fluid as we ride.

The high croak-cry of a sparrow drake draws my attention to the sky. I sit back, signaling Kitty to slow. The Teeth on their equally dangerous drakes slow with me. The war drakes pant and scrape the tall grass into furrows with their claws. They click and purr at each other while I wait for the message.

The sparrow drake is a little dragon with a body the length of my forearm. This one glints with red-gold scales as it spirals down. Its delicate wings are made of long bony fingers with spreading membrane so thin it nearly disappears in the hot sun. The sparrow drakes are as smart as cats, and just about as trusting. House

Dragon has domesticated them over generations, trained them to guard our castles and homes. They dislike leaving their native Hundred Claw Mountains, and so despite being durable distance fliers and willing to be trained, we can't use them as messengers outside our territory.

This red sparrow drake cries out again, heading for the obvious red of our uniforms, but instead of heading for the Teeth soldier who lifts her gauntleted arm to receive it, the drake aims directly for me.

I tilt my head to offer my armored shoulder, realizing this isn't one of the sparrow drakes trained to recognize a variety of signal flags. It's one specialized to the scions of House Dragon. It knows me by my blood.

The sparrow drake lands with a few slick skitters of tiny claws on scale mail, then grips my hair with the little talons of its wing joint. It snuffles at my temple, confirming me. I know the drakes go through a ritual that requires a few drops of my blood, but before this moment I never connected it to *blood magic*. I stare at the pretty red beak of the drake, mildly horrified. I've dealt in blood my whole life. But what Aunt Aurora did to Leonetti Seabreak was so vile, so awful, I don't want it to be related to this seemingly harmless application.

What others of our Dragon traditions are born in blood?

It certainly will go on my long list of questions for Aunt Aurora when I have a chance to thoroughly interrogate her.

"My blade?" one of the Teeth asks.

I grimace at my distraction, and reach for the message tube clipped to the ring pierced through the sparrow drake's ankle. The drake leans into me, chirping at Kitty, who rolls her big emerald eyes back at it.

The message is short. "A specific location for meeting up with Commander Sharpscale," I tell the Teeth. "Two days on. Let's go."

We set out once more, and the sparrow drake stays with us.

It flies overhead or clutches Kitty's spines, hunkered down into a little scaly wart. When we camp for the darkest part of the night, it eats scraps of our dinner and snuggles my stomach.

Finn and his small detachment of Dragon regulars are exactly where he promised. We come to their camp in the shelter of three rugged boulders five times taller than me. The sparrow drake leaps off my shoulder to join its compatriots sunning on the tip of one boulder. I dismount, and Finn grins at me. He puts a fist over his heart and begins to bow, but I grab his elbows and hug him instead. It's inappropriate, but I don't care.

With a huff of embarrassed laughter, Finn returns the embrace, slamming my back enough to knock my breath from my lungs. I'm plenty strong and tall, but Finn makes me look like a scrawny fifteen-year-old. He's a beast with red-blond hair too shaggy to stay where he puts it and a scar bisecting his face. When I step back, his smile has turned grim, and I can tell how exhausted he is. It makes his scar stand out white against his unevenly tanned face, and his clear blue eyes are bruised around the edges.

"Finn," I say.

"My blade. I have word from one of the scouts—they saw Darvey again a mile north. If we go quickly, we might catch him. The scout's waiting at the mark, and with your boon—"

"Let's go," I agree, turning back for Kitty.

Finn mounts up on his ugly bull war drake named, even more incongruously than mine, Bluebird. His drake moves first, with powerful strides, and Kitty takes umbrage, snapping at Bluebird's haunches. I tap her spine in a command to behave.

It's a nice moment of normalcy. These two war drakes have known each other as long as they've known Finn and me—we chose them and trained them together, at fourteen. We were the same size back then, too.

The forest closes in around us, tall blackpines spearing the sky and spindly yews. Pinkshade vines cling to trunks, their blooms half unfurled. As we ride, Finn gives me the rundown of what he's been doing since his official report last week. He headed south to join up with Teeth commander Arran Lightscale in Barghest lands, as ordered, but instead of continuing south toward the Sphinx desert to round up straggling Dragons and unite with his sister, he attended to rumors from a few of the recently freed Barghest indentures claiming they saw the barghest. It was the right call. The empyreals are our next priority. Discovering what happened, what Caspian did, what's going on with Chaos.

"Here, my blade," Finn says, gesturing with his chin to the Dragon regular who steps out from the shelter of a tree. She's in the dull green uniform of a scout, a battle ax peeking over her shoulder and short staff in her hand. She bows and points.

"I saw it here, my blade. A dog larger than natural, its shoulders as high as mine, with a flash of purple in its eyes. I tried to speak to it, but it didn't understand, or couldn't. It ran that way." She indicates north. Toward Dragon territory.

"Good," I murmur, opening my boon as I always have. It's always been an easy clench of Chaos muscles, and I see the shimmering purple trace where the scout indicated. I focus my attention, bring my boon to bear, and suddenly my heart bursts painfully and the trace explodes into an image of a huge, rangy black dog with tangled fur and drooling maw and I see exactly where it is. My head throbs, like it will split open, and—

Kitty sways under me, and I hear Finn's voice, "Tal— *Shit!*"

I don't even feel it when I hit the ground.

I feel it when I wake up, though. My entire body aches like it was crushed under the weight of a whole war drake.

I take a stuttering, painful breath, and as I release, some of the ache fades. But I don't want to open my eyes. The pressure in my skull could pop them.

"You awake?" Finn's voice comes from next to me, gentler than usual.

"Yes," I whisper.

"You've been out for a few hours. Sun set. There's food and water."

I hear the crackle of a fire nearby, the brush of feet on grass and dirt. The whuff of a war drake settling. Night frogs hum from the low trees along the nearby stream. Slowly I open my eyes. Dusk paints everything in gray.

Finn leans over to help me sit up. There's a faint shimmer around him, like an aura. It's his trace.

I lift a hand to rub both my eyes. I wince. The pain has faded, and I only feel slightly hollowed out.

"What?" Finn asks gruffly.

"Your trace. I see it." I look around. Vague lines of traces track and turn in loops around the campsite from all the soldiers here. It's pretty.

"I've had weird dreams lately," Finn admits. "I think it's my boon."

He has a sleep boon: one touch and anyone collapses into sleep. "Any other symptoms?"

"Not that I've noticed, but I haven't been experimenting. Blackspine over there had one of those fevers a few weeks ago, and says her boon isn't working like it used to. She had perfect aim, and now sometimes can't focus, like her eyesight is going. But she sees fine if she's just looking. Blackspine thinks Chaos abandoned her."

I grit my teeth. "Get me some water, would you?"

While Finn obliges, I close my eyes and try to even out my boon. My connection to Chaos feels jagged, raw. It's always been a thin link; that's what most people who describe their boons would admit. Like we've been reaching for blood through a thick scab. But now that scab is torn off.

I breathe carefully to soothe my boon, to tuck it away inside me where it belongs. It's seeping, though, everywhere. I'm hotter than I should be, too.

Finn brings me cool water and a thin vegetable soup with boiled eggs. When I look at him, his trace is gone. I start to eat, and Finn hunkers down beside me. "When we resume tracking the barghest tomorrow, I think we should walk."

I slide him an annoyed look, but don't disagree.

In the morning Finn and I take off alone, on foot. We begin following the direction of the trace I saw yesterday. One of the other scouts returned at dawn to report a village half a day away had a bunch of chickens stolen from their coops so we know it's the right way to head.

We track the barghest all day. I do pause several times to carefully open to my boon. Finn holds my arm like a worried grandfather, but it goes well. The trace is brighter than any trace I've seen before, but thinner, too. Inhuman.

When we find Darvey Brynson, and I have a moment to recover, I'll see if I can trace Caspian—or Darling. I knew both of them intimately enough that if my boon really is changing, maybe it will work. If I have to start on the ramparts of House Barghest, so be it.

The barghest has led us miles north, crossing fully into the rocky forests of Dragon lowlands, by the time it's dusk again.

Finn and I make a simple camp. The sky is clear, the air warm with the approach of high summer. We can sleep without tents or shelter for a night. We don't even need a fire. Out here, it would only attract wild drakes, not keep them away. There's a bend of a stream near us, with a drop-off only a few feet high to create a nice waterfall over smooth rocks, perfect for bathing.

For a few minutes, I can pretend Finn and I are training again. Our mission is standard, low-stakes. There's no countrywide upheaval, my brother hasn't shown signs of intense madness, Finn cares most about having the biggest, best war drake and overpowering General Bloodscale in a spar someday soon. I don't care about empyreals never seen for a century. I've never been in love.

We sleep head-to-head and play an old memory game as the moon rises, a few days past full, looking like a weird shining rock against the pristine stars.

My voice fades as the ache in my chest grows. "Finn," I interrupt.

"My— Talon."

I smile even though he can't see. "When we find Darvey, I'll take him to Dragon Castle. You should keep to your orders and head to the desert to find your sister."

I can't say any more about why: my brother is gone; my aunt betrayed me. Bloodscale challenges my rule even as he obeys. The girl I love turned into fire. I need Finn to find his sister. They've been assigned separately for the last five years. They shouldn't be apart.

Finn is quiet for a long time. Long enough I think he's accepted my suggestion. But then I feel his knuckle knocking against the crown of my head. "If it's all the same to you, I think I'll stick with my War Prince for a while."

My throat closes up. I can't say anything, so I nod. His knuckles relax and he pats my head like I'm a dog.

I start the memory game again, and this time nothing interrupts us but sleep.

We catch the barghest empyreal with shocking ease.

Midmorning I track it to a pool of clear water. We've been following the stream, as the empyreal obviously was. Even without my boon we'd have found him.

But my boon is working well. The trace lights up with barely any effort on my part, and focuses on the barghest instead of spilling into Finn's trace or forest animals. Finn and I move together with the ease of years of practice.

We hear splashing ahead, sounding merry and silly, like a puppy. A giant puppy.

Catching eyes, Finn indicates he'll flank the barghest while I draw it out—our go-to plan, given Finn's boon. But he tosses me a long rope and net, just in case. I'm unlikely to manage to lasso the barghest, but I can distract it. I'd rather not draw my falchion on what is either an eleven-year-old boy or an ancient magical beast. Or a combination of both.

Finn vanishes into the shadows between the blackpines, and I creep forward.

My first sight of the barghest is exactly what I expected: it's a wild-looking, lanky black hound with perked ears and a feathery tail. Its fur is matted and tangled. It's as tall as me. But it's frolicking in the water, diving in, then bursting out with a little yelp. It shakes playfully. I wish I could leave it to its business.

I step out. Rope in hand. "Darvey," I say.

The barghest jerks and turns to me. Its hackles rise and it pulls its lips back into a snarl.

"I'm Talon Goldhoard. You met me. I am here to support you, Darvey."

Its ears go back.

"Lord Barghest," I try instead. "You've been lost to Chaos, but you're back. This is your land. Pyrlanum. Do you remember anything?" Slowly I walk forward. There's no sign of Finn, but I trust he's moving behind Darvey.

The barghest lowers on its haunches. Not to surrender, but to pounce. All right.

I keep moving nearer. I want to control where I am when it attacks.

"Darvey, do you remember my brother, Caspian? He knew you'd be the next Barghest regent, even though your uncle tried to take it. I know something about that." I keep my voice even, calm, stepping carefully forward once and again.

Suddenly the barghest growls and leaps at me, teeth snapping. I dodge, turning to punch it in the side.

My fist connects, and Darvey grunts. He twists with shocking agility, snapping and clawing. I throw the net at him. It tangles, but not enough. I dive down and roll, coming up on my feet on his other side. I throw myself at him, to grapple. Arms around his neck, I lean back and fall purposefully, rolling with the massive dog. It huffs and growls; I growl, too. The momentum brings me up again, and acts to help me fling the barghest to the ground behind me.

It scrambles up. "I'm sorry," I say, just as it attacks again.

This time I grab onto its neck and don't let go.

The barghest falls, ready to donkey-kick me, but it goes limp.

"Chaos," Finn curses. He takes his hands off the barghest's tail. It stays asleep. Finn brushes off his hands. "You're bleeding," he tells me.

I feel it, a warm trickle on my scalp. My left hip and thigh throb with the makings of an awful bruise. "I'm fine."

We look at each other over the sleeping body of the massive empyreal.

"We should have brought a wheelbarrow," Finn says.

It startles a laugh out of me. I kneel beside the barghest's head and think of Darvey Brynson's worried eyes on the day of the power transfer. None of us had any idea what was to come. None of us but Caspian. I dig my hand into his thick fur. He really feels just like a giant dog. I wonder if he likes to be scratched behind the ears.

"We'll figure it out," I tell Finn.

We must.

3
TALON

"I can't wait to sit at one of those big hearths in the castle hall and have a drink," Finn says from astride Bluebird. Beside him, his head level with Finn's shoulder, the barghest Darvey wags his fluffy black tail. The war drake reaches over with a scarred, scaled forearm and tugs at the barghest's ruff.

It's such a strange sight. But I'm glad they're getting along. From beside them on Kitty, I say, "I can't wait to take a nap."

Finn snorts. "I'll put you to sleep, if you don't at least lie down tonight."

"Promise?" I ask with a weary smile.

We're a small party of Dragons making our way to Dragon Castle. Just me and Finn, with three of the Teeth who've been under his command, including two scouts. And of course, the giant rangy puppy empyreal barghest.

It's taken twice as long as it should to travel, after waiting several days for Finn to earn Darvey's trust enough that the beast stopped fighting us. Finn has a soft spot for a good dog. Darvey seems to sense that, even when he's overwhelmed by his beastly instincts or slipping the harness we improvised simply by shrinking to the size of a puppy. He'd wiggled free and bounded away. We'd had to catch him all over again, and during that pandemonium, Darvey grew to the size of a small barn before immediately dropping into something closer to a war drake. He doesn't seem to be able to hold either of the more extreme sizes yet.

Finn finally managed to get the barghest to calm down long enough for a thorough washing, and even I was allowed to help pick tangles out of his matted, tangled fur.

Darvey hasn't changed size in four days now, seemingly content to trot alongside us as we travel.

We approach the castle across a narrow valley that cuts through the Hundred Claw Mountains. Despite the summertime, the mountain valley is cold, and a wind bites at our party as we cross the bridge over the Phoenix Blood River. My war drake digs her talons into the old cobbles on the other side of the bridge as the wind gusts again, bending the towering spice evergreen trees that surround us. Blue-green needles fall like rain, and I hear the crunch of heavy pinecones hitting the ground. It's a sound I've lost familiarity with, having spent most of my time at Phoenix Crest with the southern army. It's been seven years since I lived in Dragon Castle.

Darvey takes the opportunity to skirt around the bridge, splashing across the shallow river with his tongue lolling out. Finn laughs, and two of the Teeth soldiers join him, teasing each other that they also need a bath.

I let them indulge but nudge Kitty on. We should be at the castle within the hour.

Kitty's spines lift in surprise, and her snout lifts sharply in the direction of the bend in the road.

"There, Kitty," I soothe. "This close to the castle, so far into Dragon territory, it's most likely to be friends."

She scrapes her claws on the road again. I gesture at Finn and the others, who fall into line just as a party that mirrors ours exactly in number rounds the corner of spice pines. It's four Dragon soldiers, with the black sleeves of Dragon Castle guards, riding in formation. Two on war drakes, the others mounted on the faster but less powerful racing drakes. Including their fifth: perched on her drake in the center like an honored guest is my aunt Aurora.

My whole body tenses, and Kitty feels it; she barks commandingly and moves forward. I allow it. Her call brings Bluebird and my Teeth's war drakes to attention. Even Darvey bounds after us, hackles raised.

"What is this?" I demand of the guard captain at the fore. I won't address Aurora. She's not bound, her clothing is pristine as befits the aunt of the High Prince Regent, she seems well rested and better than fine—certainly no prisoner locked in a dungeon for the past month!

The captain frowns. "We're escorting our blade Aurora Falleau to Phoenix Crest."

"That woman is my prisoner, stripped of rank and to be held in the Dragon Castle dungeon until I decide what worse will come to her," I say. I will see Aurora explain herself and pay, and if possible, it will be Darling herself or the new leaders of House Kraken who decide Aurora's fate after the murder of their patriarch Leonetti Seabreak.

"My—my blade," the captain begins.

"Talon, darling," Aurora says.

I don't look at her. "Turn around and escort her back to the castle."

"Won't you even look at me, nephew?" she continues.

"Now." I grit my teeth.

"You heard your War Prince," Finn snaps.

At his side, Darvey the barghest bears his huge fangs.

"Oh my," Aurora says, and one of the Dragon guards says, "What *is* that thing?"

"Talon."

My eyes flick to Aurora before I can stop them.

"Let me go," she says the moment our eyes lock.

"I will not," I say, even though I very much want to.

Aurora's eyes seem bigger than usual. She stares at me, and I feel my resolve trembling. I make a fist with my right hand to keep from grabbing my falchion.

"Talon," she murmurs.

I shake my head and look to the captain. "Take her, now. Tie her up, or move so my loyal Teeth can do so."

The captain glances at Aurora.

He kicks his war drake and pulls his sword with a war cry.

Then he attacks me.

I startle, but unsheathe my falchion as Kitty leaps forward. "Get them!" I command, and Finn and my Teeth race after me. I clash with the captain. Kitty tears into his drake, and I only hear screaming war drakes and the clash of steel.

Kitty and I work seamlessly, dodging and pressing in to the captain and his drake. Drakes are good at close combat, with their claws and teeth and solid bodies of muscle and scale. My falchion is made for it, too, and it's an advantage against the captain's longer sword. He needs more leverage and doesn't have it unless his drake disengages from Kitty. I make it quick, cutting under his raised arm where there's a weakness in his armor. I wrench his sword away, then kick him hard. He slumps off his drake. Kitty hisses in its face, and then Bluebird is with us. The two war drakes easily subdue the third.

I look around. The other guard on a war drake has been laid out with a gash to his head. He's off his mount. Of the two guards riding racing drakes, one is dead, the other openly surrendered and is unharmed. But Aurora . . .

The barghest barks for our attention. I see a flash of gold as Aurora leans over her racing drake, escaping into the forest.

I whirl Kitty and give chase. There are boulders everywhere, and the ground is uneven, covered in slippery piles of old pine needles, rocks, and half-rotten undergrowth. I don't know where Aurora thinks she can hide, and she's aware my boon is a tracking boon so I can find her anywhere. This is hopeless for her.

"Aurora!" I yell. "Stop. There's nowhere you can hide from me."

Behind me is a loud growl-yip as Darvey the barghest empyreal lopes to Kitty's side. Just behind him is Finn on Bluebird. "Darvey," I cry, "catch her!" I've seen him race: he's faster than a lot of war drakes, and maybe can catch up with the racer.

Aurora throws her cloak off. It flies at me, but Kitty catches it and tears it to pieces. She stumbles, though, and pine needles scratch at my face as we shove too close to a tree.

I hear the rush of the river. Aurora must think that if she makes it, she can escape without leaving a trace for my boon to track. She doesn't know my boon is changing with Chaos.

"Aurora!" I yell again. She pushes her racing drake harder, and it splashes into the rushing, shallow river.

I'm nearly to her and cut south to crash into the river myself.

But Darvey suddenly leaps forward off the riverbank and collides with Aurora's drake.

They all go down.

Kitty and I hurry toward them. The water rushes hard against her flank and my leg, dragging at us.

Darvey crawls up, but the racing drake doesn't. I see a flash of its bright green scales tumbling in the water.

"Aurora!" I don't see her in the churning river. My chest is tight as I slide off Kitty and land in hip-deep water. It shoves at me.

But there, Darvey has bright skirts in his maw. He pulls at Aurora, and she climbs out onto the bank, bedraggled and drenched. She's coughing, bent over. Her golden hair hangs dark and tangled over her face.

I push through the water toward her and grab her arm. She jerks but lets me help her onto the bank.

Finn and Bluebird appear beside us, huffing with effort. Finn dismounts and lands on the ground with a hard thump. Darvey shakes his whole body, flinging water everywhere—he's grown to fifteen feet at the top of his head.

Aurora turns away from him to shelter from the dog water. She leans against my chest. I almost put my arm around her protectively. I resist, squeezing her arm too tightly.

My aunt looks up. Her big blue eyes are wide and pleading, her pale cheeks splotchy red with effort. I've never seen her look so mussed and helpless. "Talon," she whispers. "Please. Nephew. Let me go."

"There's nowhere to go, Aunt," I say. Kitty climbs out of the river beside me, the dead racing drake dragged in her foreclaws.

"Talon." Aurora lifts her free hand and places it against my cheek. "There's no need for this. Let me go, and just listen. I can explain everything. Listen to me. Trust me," she implores. "I'm your blood. I love you; I've always supported you."

Her words are like a hook under my sternum. I should let her go, obviously. She's my aunt and she loves me. My grip loosens.

Aurora smiles. "That's right. Let me go, little dragon."

I release her. "Aunt, come back with me."

"But everyone has been awful. You want me to be safe, don't you?"

"I do." I nod to emphasize. I want that more than anything. "But I have so many questions for you."

"Such a curious boy," she says and pats my cheek. "I'll answer your questions."

"Talon," Finn says, something frustrated in his voice.

I try to look at him, but Aurora grips my chin, holds my gaze.

"He doesn't matter, little dragon. He'll do what you say. Let me go. You want to."

I nod into her grip but feel myself wincing. I can't let her go, even if I want to. She betrayed me. She murdered Darling's foster father brutally. She lied. But . . .

"Talon, sweet boy." Aurora pats my cheek.

"Aurora . . ." I start slowly. I feel like I'm thinking my way through a dream. There's a pounding sound nearby, big drake feet on stone and earth. Someone is coming—a lot of someones. But my eyes are locked with Aurora's.

Suddenly Aurora drops like a toy whose strings were cut.

She crumples at my feet.

Finn replaces her, staring at me. "What in the pit of Chaos was *that*?" he demands.

"What?" I frown. I look down at Aurora. "Good, you put her to sleep."

"While you—what? Had a chat?" Finn throws his hands in the air.

I stare at my passed-out aunt.

Then we're surrounded by Dragons. Soldiers and drakes—both war drakes and racers—and Darvey's ruff puffs out an armspan. Finn leaves me and pets the barghest as Kitty takes her place with me.

I swallow my discomfort and look up. At the fore of the party of at least twenty Dragons is a tall woman with dark red hair streaked with silver. She wears a golden tabard lined with green scales and belted over a dress dark like old, old blood. A small pauldron gleams on her right shoulder, chained there with delicate iron and stamped with the House Dragon crest. I know her to be the castelaine of Dragon Castle, Annag Mortooth. She helped to raise me, but my memories of her are negligible. "My blade," she says.

"Castelaine." I frown, gesturing down at Aurora's slumped form. "What is the meaning of this? Aurora Falleau was to be locked in the lowest dungeon."

"Yes, my blade." Annag says. Her gaze keeps darting to Darvey. "I will give you a full accounting. But we should return to the castle quickly with the former seer. Word has reached us, intended for you, that the gryphon empyreal has returned as well. Your spies have seen her in Furial. And, if the report is to be believed, the gryphon was in the company of a phoenix."

4

DARLING

I wake, violently, startling upright in a too-soft bed in a too-bright room. Pale walls and bright light all around, sending pain through my too-sensitive eyes.

I will never get used to such a rude awakening.

I swear, long and loud, curses learned at the knee of my adoptive father, and there is movement around me as I shield my eyes. "Can someone please fetch my smoked lenses?" I say, yelling to be heard over the din of rushing feet and panicked voices.

"We are trying, but it turns out—"

"Well, can someone please cover the blasted windows?" I yell. With my anger there is also a sense of warmth, and whoever is with me in the room exclaims and then murmurs something that I cannot quite make out.

The room darkens immediately, a sudden cessation of the assault upon my poor eyes, which water terribly. I blink and give the room a quick glance. I recognize it as the guest chambers from my visit to House Gryphon. A servant in House Gryphon livery, red and embroidered with the house's namesake, bows over the foot of my bed while another quietly tamps down embers on the carpet that covers the floor. But my attention is taken up by the woman stamping the flames, her eyes downcast. I frown at the woman, since there doesn't seem to be a fireplace lit at the moment, the room warm even without it.

So where did the embers come from?

"All apologies, my flame," says one of the other servants, the man who managed to pull the curtains shut to save my poor watering eyes. "We were unprepared. We had thought that your eyes would no longer need the assistance of the lenses in the aftermath of your transformation."

"My what? Why would you think that? Also, what happened to the carpet?"

The man looks from the woman back to me. "Ah, well, you did, my flame."

I try to swallow my confusion and annoyance, and I cannot. I've never been quick to temper, but I feel so filled with anger. But I can't remember why.

I can't remember a lot, in fact. And that only makes me feel even more annoyed. I take a deep breath and let it out. There is something wrong, and it's vexing me something fierce. I frown as I climb out of the bed and begin to stalk around the room. I reach for my blades—old habits and all that—but I am only wearing a shift. Still, the carpet is soft under my bare feet, even if something smells of burning wool.

I realize with a glance down that my feet are *singeing* the rug.

What in the name of Chaos?

"Perhaps we should fetch the regent," the woman murmurs. I don't recognize her, but there is something about her that draws my attention. The wrongness I sense, that is putting me on edge, is *her*. I wave her over.

"You. Come here." I'm curt, and I'm not quite sure why. Something is amiss, something fundamentally left undone, and it chafes in a way that I cannot explain. I need my goggles and to get out of the room where I am. But first, first I must fix this thing within the woman.

However, the wide-eyed look of fear that she gives me startles me a little out of the strange spell that's taken hold. I'm not used to people being afraid of me. Distrustful? Yes. But terrified? That is something new.

"Would you come here? Please?" I add, hoping that a softer tone will accomplish what harsh words did not.

But she shakes her head. "No." Her voice is little more than a squeak.

"Lania," the man begins, and the woman shakes her head. The simple act is enough to annoy me, and I explode toward the woman, a blur of a girl. One moment the bed lies between us; the next I am before the woman, my hands on her arms.

"By the eyes of Chaos," the man whispers, taking a step backward from both of us.

I ignore him. All my attention is for the poor maid I am currently terrorizing with my mere presence.

"Breathe," I tell her, and she does, a quick inhale. I place a hand on either side of her face, and as I look into her eyes I can sense it, the *wrongness*. It's in her. It's everywhere, really, but within the room it's strongest within her. It's like a festering wound wrapped around something wondrous or a bouquet of flowers wrapped in rotting flesh, and once I've made contact with her it's easy to burn away the infection, to cleanse her of the foulness. So I do and let her inner magic run free.

She gasps, and as I let her go, the male servant is by her side. She blinks, again and again, looking at me as though seeing me for the first time. "It's true," she says, and begins to sob. "You truly have returned to us."

"What did you do?" the man demands, but I have no answers for him because I'm not sure. So I climb backward onto the bed, away from both of them.

"Sorry," I whisper, feeling uncertain and small now that whatever Chaos held me has eased up for the moment. I'm ashamed of my brusqueness, my rudeness, but mostly I just don't understand the things I'm feeling. It's like I woke up and my insides have been replaced with Chaos and flame. Turmoil swirls within, a need to do something, but I have no idea how to direct the impulse. And now I am terrorizing chambermaids for no good reason other than because I feel like it.

Some of Caspian's madness must have seeped into me when we kissed. I can think of no other explanation.

The woman, Lania, though, grabs my hand, pressing it to her cheek, her fear completely gone and replaced with something like gratitude.

"Thank you, thank you," she says. And I want to tell her she's welcome, but I honestly have no idea what I just did.

But then the woman touches a wilting bunch of flowers in the vase next to my bed, and the blooms spring forth, fresh and alive as though they were just picked.

The door opens at that moment and Vivian Chronicum, regent of House Gryphon, strides in. She holds my smoked lenses in one hand, and as I jump off the bed to take them from her, she sweeps into a low bow.

"My flame," she says, holding out my smoked lenses. I take

TESSA GRATTON & JUSTINA IRELAND

them with a sigh. As Vivian straightens, she smiles over at Lania.

"Ah, it's as I thought, then?" she asks, directing her words at the servants.

"Yes," the man says with a grin. "Lania's boon is . . . improved."

"What are you talking about? And what is this 'my flame' nonsense?" I ask. "Is it something that Caspian has decided we're doing now?" I pull my lenses into place, securing the glass over my eyes. These are not the pair I lost the night I fought Talon, but they are well crafted and less ostentatious than the pairs Caspian kept having sent to my rooms. They are familiar in a world that feels strange, and the agitation in my chest calms somewhat.

Vivian freezes, a small frown on her face. "You don't remember?"

I blink, and try to think about the last thing I remember. There was House Barghest, and my adoptive sister Adelaide's small fleet in the harbor. But then it all went wrong, and Caspian—

"Ah, there it is," Vivian says with a smile. "It was the same for me, my flame. The empyreals and their influence is stronger than even I could have expected with my years of study."

I blink; my memories are impossible, like a fever dream come true. It seems that life has thrown me yet another surprise. "So, it is true, then?"

"Yes," Vivian says with a bright smile. "Welcome back, dear phoenix."

The maid is effusive after whatever I did to her, and I am embarrassed by her abject gratitude. Vivian decides it's probably best to give Lania and Merle, her partner, space to compose themselves, so Vivian leads the way through the house, the household staff bowing incredibly low as I pass, so much that I worry that they'll injure themselves.

"Ignore them," Vivian says. "It's a wonderful time for our house, historic times! They're as excited to see you as they are fearful."

I say nothing, but try to smile at the next person I pass. But I'm pretty sure that Vivian is wrong: there's no excitement here, only dread.

What did they see to make them so afraid?

"You're probably starving—I know I was—but don't worry, there will be plenty of food where we're going. I've been taking my meals in the library as I try to find some new references to explain what happened at House Barghest and to the rest of us. Thus far I've been working from secondhand reports and rumor, so I'm very glad you're awake. I'm hoping you can shed a bit of light in the darkness. How are the legs? Steady? Good?"

"Yes, surprisingly so."

"One of the benefits of the empyreals was a limited amount of healing and of general good health. I've noticed it myself. I cut myself recently, and the injury sealed itself back up immediately. I've been meaning to run a more detailed series of experiments but just haven't had time. Ah, here we are."

Vivian has led me to the library. But I pause on the threshold when I see the crew of workers and massive scaffolding.

"What happened here?" I ask, taking in the construction. It looks as though the tradesmen have been at it for a while, and I frown. It wasn't that long since I was here. A week, maybe two.

The memory of Caspian demanding a ladder and scampering up to secure the House Gryphon relic is too fresh. "Wait. And how long have I been away?"

The work looks near to completion, entire walls patched and repaired. When Leonetti had decided to build a new wing of House Kraken for the orphans he'd adopted, it had taken years to finish, the work a tedious routine of measuring, sawing, and hammering that had seemed like it would never be done. Unless the carpenters and stonemasons in House Gryphon far outclass those hired by House Kraken, this looks to be weeks' worth of work.

"To answer your first question: what happened was that I was standing here when Chaos took me and changed me to an empyreal," Vivian says, beaming with pride. "The crew have been slowly patching the hole, but I think we may do stained glass instead, to mark the occasion. It's just lucky that I managed to change in a place where there were no rooms overhead. The only casualties were a few of Scanlon's *Ruminations on Poetry*, which, while difficult to replace, were very, very dated."

"And as for your second," Vivian says, her smile softening, "we were missing for nearly a month after Chaos's Return. It's been over two months since the regent of House Barghest died."

I stumble a little at that, and Vivian grabs my arm, steadying me. "Yes, I had a similar reaction. It's not much farther, and then you can fortify yourself while I recount the events you've missed."

I nod and Vivian lets me go. When it's clear I'm able to walk just fine, she leads the way to a nook within the library. House Gryphon is a confusing mess of corridors and switchbacks, and the library is no different. I don't recognize this place she's led me to, and I realize that on my last visit I only saw a fraction of the house. I get the sense that this alcove is Vivian's private space. There are small paintings of brown-skinned children and personal correspondence littering a desk. Ancient tomes and scrolls cover another nearby table. A window made of stained glass, depicting a gryphon in contemplation on a mountaintop, casts colored shards into the space, which is dimly lit by boonlights, a consideration of my sensitive eyes that I appreciate. But my attention is for the platter of meat, cheeses, and fruits spread across a sideboard. Small crocks have been arranged near the platters, and when I pull the lid off one, I find a hearty tomato bisque, still steaming, the scent of it causing my middle to roar like a pack of wild drakes.

"I apologize in advance for my manners, but I am absolutely starving," I say, tipping the crock back and drinking the soup. It's hot, but I don't mind. I rather like the way it burns down my throat.

Vivian simply gestures toward the food, and I take that as my cue to eat my fill. I finish the soup and fill a plate with food while stuffing bread and cheese into my mouth. It's probably a ghastly sight, and I don't care. I need food. The last time I was this hungry, I was chasing sand rats through the sewers of Nakumba.

These accommodations are far, far better.

Once I have a mountain of meats and cheeses on my plate, I perch on a brocade wing chair that looks very uncomfortable but enfolds me in a way that has me sighing and sinking into the material. Vivian pours tea for both of us, and I gulp it down like the soup before going back to my plate of food.

"So, hot foods no longer bother you," she says, studying me. "Have you noticed any other changes?"

"I singed your carpet with my feet," I say, swallowing a mouthful of meat and cheese. "I'm not sure how or why, though."

"Hmm. Interesting. I've been experimenting with controlling aspects of the transformation. For example." Vivian holds up her hand. A look of concentration comes over her face, and her nails grow into long, curved talons dripping a viscous liquid.

"Poison," I say. "The gryphon dagger had it as well. It's fast if you ever need to use it." The memory of Caspian slicing the dagger across my hand is suddenly fresh, and I pause as events rush back, fast and hard, leaving me desperate and angry all over again. I push the emotions to the side. I have bigger issues than the nonsense House Dragon brought into my life, although I do wonder where Caspian and Talon are.

Mostly Talon. My heart quickens its beats as anger and longing war within me, and I stuff a piece of sausage into my mouth in annoyance. I might be a bit lost, but I will never forget the sting of his rejection at House Barghest. Or the feeling of his body against mine the night before that. Chaos take it all.

"Yes. I've been trying to grow wings while in my human form, but I've only been able to manage a few feathers," Vivian says, pulling me back to the conversation at hand. "It seems it could be useful to effect a partial change that allows me to remain in control, more so than when I am the gryphon."

"Okay, so what did I miss? Tell me everything," I say around a mouthful of food. Vivian finds all these returned abilities fascinating, but as I satisfy my hunger, my thoughts are for the people I care for. Adelaide and Miranda, Caspian and Talon, Chaos take them both. And Leonetti. The last I remember, he was dragged out, still in chains, his gaze proud as his eyes met mine.

We've already lost so much. I may have gained a few abilities, but what have I lost in the meantime? I'm almost afraid to ask.

"So, what I know is mostly from my scribes. The day of Chaos's Return, I was in the other wing of the library with my head scribe, looking for additional information on the missing boons per a request from Elias. I remember something strange, a feeling like falling, and the next thing I knew, I woke in a retainer's field. The scribes say I transformed before them, destroying the room you saw and taking to the sky. Reports are that the other empyreals disappeared as well, and we all reappeared around a month ago. The barghest, and I have to assume us as well. As for our story: I awoke, and once I had my bearings, I was able to send out a search party for you. It was quite spectacular, honestly. You were in a nest made of glass on one of the nearby cliffs. Our scholars have dubbed it Phoenix Ascendant. People have already begun making pilgrimages to the site."

I vaguely remember hunting wild drakes in a scrubby mountain area, the feeling of flying low and plucking the creatures off the side of a mountain, their carcasses little more than charcoal as I swallowed them down. "Wait, how did you release yourself from the change?"

Vivian shrugs. "I have a memory of flames and you calling my name, and from the few eyewitness accounts I've heard, we battled, you won, and I changed back to my completely naked human form."

I shake my head. "I don't remember that."

Vivian leans forward. "We have accounts of the phoenix attending the coronations of every house to 'mitigate the distress.' I believe that is the historian's way of discussing the potential to become trapped in the transformation."

I nod. "What about the other houses? Kraken? Is Leonetti released from his imprisonment?"

Vivian shakes her head. "No one has seen or heard from Leonetti. There was a kraken sighted in the bay on the day of Chaos's Return, but whether that was Leonetti or someone else . . ." Vivian shrugs. "I don't have enough information to guess. No one has seen any members of House Kraken. Even their safe houses on the mainland have been abandoned. They've either taken to the seas or retreated to their islands. I'm sorry, I don't know anything more than that."

"So I've been gone for two months, and Leonetti is nowhere to be found. Has the kraken been sighted since?" There's a feeling in my chest, a panicked worry. If Leonetti isn't the kraken, then Adelaide is, which means Leonetti is dead.

I will not consider that he might be gone. It's just too much to handle all at once.

"Not that we've heard, and we have connections within every territory in Pyrlanum. But I have the feeling empyreals are not found until they want to be. My house sent scouts to ride to the edges of our territory, but there was no sign of me. What I do know is that a few days after my rebirth, the first of Talon's missives was received in Furial."

"What did they say?" I ask, my stomach twisting at Talon's name.

No, I have to forcefully remind myself. *He isn't for me. Not anymore.*

I will never be able to forget the way he turned away from me in House Barghest, off to do his aunt's bidding. He made his choice. He is a Dragon, and that is all he will ever be. And as much as I never wanted to believe that all Dragons were bad, I have to wonder if perhaps my foolishness is part of why things turned out so terribly.

I should've known better. And perhaps, just maybe, I should've listened to Gavin.

Vivian is still speaking, so I pull my thoughts away from my own regrets and listen to her.

"Talon has gone through with Caspian's final wishes and has been drawing down House Dragon troops, withdrawing them from other lands and placing locals in charge once more. My scribes say it isn't going especially well, mostly because there has been some infighting within House Dragon, but it is happening. But perhaps you should tell me what you know. I have the feeling that Chaos's Return is partially thanks to you."

I nod, and around mouthfuls of food I tell Vivian about the wake, the botched Naming ceremony, and Caspian's strange ritual and kiss and the sudden change that swept over me. I leave out Talon's betrayal, because why tell the only ally I have that I was a lovesick fool? It still hurts too much that after everything we shared, and after everything we promised each other, he could turn his back on me so easily.

"That matches the reports I've received. Elias sent a missive in the first few days after the Awakening, but I haven't received any response to my more recent letters. I suspect that the Dragons are intercepting them."

I put my plate to the side, the worst of my hunger sated and the current conversation demanding my full attention. "What did Elias write?"

"Much of what you told me, and something else besides: apparently the newly anointed regent of House Barghest was nearly eaten by his nephew, little Darvey Brynson, when the boy transformed into a massive, slavering hound. The man survived, though. Most unfortunate."

"I suppose we now know who the true heir to House Barghest is," I say. And then I snort. And laugh.

The next thing I know, both Vivian and I are laughing hysterically. It's a relief, that kind of mirth, sparked by the near death of a terrible man, but mostly just an outlet for the sheer insanity of the past few months. It's the kind of mirth I haven't experienced since Adelaide and I once braved a summer storm and nearly died. She'd gotten us through the currents okay, somehow managing to keep the boat upright despite the strong waves and the wind. After we'd looked at each other, each soaked, and Adelaide had deadpanned, "Well, I guess it was supposed to rain today, after all." It had cemented our friendship, that day.

Now, giggling with Vivian over the nearly murdered regent, one who was obviously deemed unfit by Chaos, I find myself sighing again, my sides aching just as they had on that long-ago day.

"What are we going to do?" I ask, once I've gotten control of myself. "This is just so big."

"I have an idea, but I figured I would lay it out for you first. You are the phoenix, and the lore tells us the phoenix was the heart of Pyrlanum, the lifeblood of the land."

I remember the blood of Caspian's ritual and the still-beating heart he held in his hand, and I sigh. Vivian has no idea how right she is.

"And?"

"You have the closest ties with House Kraken, so we should definitely align with them first. But in the interim, Lania was one of the many members of House Gryphon struck with the fever that spread across the land in the aftermath of Chaos's Return. I suspect that the fevers are less an actual sickness and more boons trying to manifest in adults. We have reports that boon fever used to strike children before their twelfth year, which is when boons usually appeared. I think your return is causing people to get ill later in life. I'd be honored if you would take the next few days and meet with all those in the house who had the fever. Just to test my theory."

"That sounds fine. What else, though? I suspect that you're going to ask for something else as well."

"I think you should also take the time to work on controlling Chaos. To wait until you have some control of the phoenix before searching for your House Kraken family."

"What do you mean, control Chaos? What are you talking about?"

"Lania. Oh, sorry. One of the abilities I've discovered since I was changed is that I can see the hidden—it's been highly useful in researching—and Lania had a boon that was, well, frustrated. Before, it was weak, only able to keep things from spoiling for a few days with a simple touch. But now—well, you saw what she did with the flowers."

I consider the memory and swallow thickly. I can sense the truth of what Vivian has said, and when I close my eyes, I can feel more of that festering rot. It's like getting a whiff of a foul scent and becoming nauseated, and the more I focus on the feeling, the worse it gets. There are smaller tendrils, like what I felt in Lania, but the strongest sense of something that needs to be fixed comes from outside House Gryphon. If I were to close my eyes and start walking, I am willing to bet it would lead me somewhere in the nearby hills. But to what?

Either way, without a goal and without a kraken to search out, I am at loose ends. And Vivian is right. Before I do anything else, I will need to learn how to control my new abilities. Because if Talon is trying to hold his house together, there is no telling what Pyrlanum will face if things fall apart once more. I've had enough of war. I'm finally in a position to stop it.

I put my plate to the side and take a deep breath. "Well, if we're going to commune with Chaos, I think this is probably something best done outside. After all, books are highly flammable."

Vivian's grin is infectious, and despite everything else being thrown to Chaos, I have to appreciate that at least I've gotten an ally out of this whole mess. I'm glad the phoenix found her first out of all the empyreals.

I can only hope that Leonetti is somewhere beneath the waves, waiting for me to find him as well.

TALON

There's a life-size mural of Darling on the stone wall of Caspian's
bedroom in Dragon Castle.

I forgot, or I never knew. We haven't lived here since I was a
child, since our father conquered Phoenix Crest and moved the
center of his rule there.

Annag Mortooth had me shown here to rest and bathe before
dinner, making assumptions I'd rather ignore about my status.
These are the Prince Regent's rooms. That's still my brother. But
I'm tired and cranky, so I let them put me here for now. I'll move
in the morning.

Caspian's rooms here are not as impressive as his gilded suite in
Phoenix Crest, or the tower filled with his scrawling, wild paintings. These are warm with dark pine and a hearth that opens onto
both the sitting room and sleeping room. Layered rugs on the floor
and a few drake skulls on the walls give the quarters an old, rustic
feeling. His bed is low and crowned with green silk hangings. He
hasn't lived here in years, either, and there remains almost nothing
of him. There are still dust covers over the bookshelves and low
sofas in the sitting room. A servant hurries to clean out the fireplace, and another goes into the bathroom to check all the fixtures
and functions and run the bath.

I can't look away from the painting. Caspian had to have been only thirteen or so when he created this. So young. Did he already know what was to become of them both?

I close the distance until I could brush my finger along her cheek, but I don't touch. She's a painted scrawl of brown and black, with wild, spinning pits of fire for eyes. Fire, like the phoenix she's become. She stands there, emerging from darkness. It's her. The shape of her face, amateurishly wrought, but recognizable.

Nearly two months ago I kissed her. She pinned me to the grass of the Barghest gardens and loved me. I can hear her laugh if I try.

Being without her now is an open wound that seeps through its bandage again and again.

I close my eyes. I reach out to place my hand against the cold stone wall, fingertips where her lips would be. I open myself to my boon and think of her.

My boon flares hot and I grip onto it, despite its new volatile nature. I hold. I focus. This painting has no trace, but I know Darling. I know what she looked like to Chaos, the pattern of her trace.

Then—I *can* hear her laughter.

A dim room. Darling wipes her mouth on the back of her hand. She's eating a mountain of food.

She wears plain smoked lenses and turns her head. Her lips move. She's speaking to someone.

Scars drip along Darling's hairline—burn scars. There are pale painted walls behind her, a curtain that is familiar. Books and scrolls everywhere.

Gryphon Manor. She's there.

With her is Vivian Chronicum. The regent of House Gryphon. They speak, share a pot of pale tea. Darling laughs.

I open my eyes.

It was no firebird I saw. No monstrous empyreal. Darling is herself. So is Vivian Chronicum.

Quickly I turn my mind to Caspian.

Suddenly—*bright sunlight, a snap of wind, pebbled green-black scales rippling into a tail. Blue sky, mountain peaks, then blood and the scream of a herd drake, the hot gush of meat—*

I grunt at the pain slicing my skull apart. I lean my forehead against the cool stone wall. With every beat of my heart, the pain throbs. Sweat breaks out along my spine. I take several long breaths.

"My blade?"

"I'm all right," I say without opening my eyes. "Can you bring me some water?"

"Yes, my blade. Is it . . . your boon?"

Startled, I turn. "It is." I study her through pain-narrowed eyes.

She curtsies. "We have a fever-reducing tea. Healer Elias developed it for boon-related fevers."

"Is it already brewed? Can it be taken cold?" I don't want hot tea.

"Yes, my blade. We have it prepared, unfortunately."

I nod. Too many boon fevers, too much unhinged Chaos afflicting people across Pyrlanum. I hope Elias has some answers for me.

Dinner is informal, held in one of the smaller dining rooms near the main kitchens. Clean and fever-free, I stride in to find Finn and Darvey already there, the latter curled into a large ball of fur beside the crackling fire. Finn sits near, alongside Annag Mortooth, her daughter Sheena, and Elias.

They all rise upon my entrance, murmuring "My blade," except for Elias who is silent.

"Is Aurora secured?" I ask Annag.

The castelaine nods. "In a small dungeon, bound and gagged, with several guards, all of whom are instructed to only approach with wax stopping their ears. She remained under the sleep when I left."

"Good." Annag had explained to me on the ride to the castle that although Aunt Aurora had been faking her prophecy boon with blood magic, it seemed she did have a boon, and it was one of the older, uncommon House Cockatrice boons of persuasion. It absolutely had not been strong before the return of Chaos, or Aurora could have convinced anyone to do anything. But now she was powerful. Only Annag could resist. The older castelaine had said with a wry smile, "For a long time I thought I had no boon, but it turns out that's because my boon is immunity to boons."

I go to sit at the dinner table, but Elias remains standing, long brown fingers steepled against the table with some urgency. I turn to them. They're wearing green, which is strange to see, but it's the most common color in Dragon Castle. Elias's brown eyes are filled with a strange hope when they look at me.

We've never been friends. I sent for the Gryphon physician a few years ago, intending them as a personal doctor for Caspian, because they had a reputation for understanding boons and boon afflictions better than anyone. They hadn't been able to help Caspian, much to my displeasure. But they'd grown devoted to him.

Indeed, the first thing Elias says to me is "No word on the Prince Regent?"

"He's in the mountains."

Finn says, "He's been spotted?"

I shake my head no. "Sit, let's eat, and I'll explain."

Annag nudges her daughter to alert the servers to bring in our food. Sheena obeys, a light flush on her pale cheeks. She glances at me every once in a while, and I suspect I know why: she's always wanted to join my Teeth. She wrote me a long, pleading letter over a year ago that I never answered. Teeth earn their place through the army ranks. If Sheena wants in, she just needs to prove herself to her commanders—but it looks like she's not even a soldier.

I take a long drink of cool water, ignoring the wine Finn pours. Once the plates of roasted chicken and a potato-leek soup are left for us, I say, "I'm a hunter by my boon, and since the resurgence of Chaos, it's changed, as have many."

Elias leans toward me. "Expanded? Most that have changed have grown more volatile, strengthened. Others are experiencing fevers and strange sensations, as if hidden boons wish to erupt themselves."

"Yes, expanded. You have theories?"

"I studied the remnants of Caspian's ritual at House Barghest, and I believe he was not summoning or recreating empyreals and the phoenix, so much as releasing them."

I frown. Finn says, "They were imprisoned?"

Elias's smile turns to a wince. "In the blood. That is why Darvey here became the barghest, not his appalling uncle. The potential may be in anyone from each House, but Chaos chooses direct lines. Bloodlines."

"This all comes back to blood magic?" I ask. I set down my knife, unsettled.

"I don't know exactly. There must be a difference between the Chaos magic of the phoenix and the methods of blood magic, especially in how it relates to empyreals, though empyreals were never my research specialty. However, the key I believe may be in the ritual we use to invest a new House regent, which is derived from the more ancient practice when the regents were always empyreals."

I frown, thinking through the simple anointing ritual: shared drink and vows just about covers it. Except, the name— "The shared blood of Pyrlanum," I say. "That's what the drink is called."

"Exactly. We use a honey liquor with specific herbs now, meant to boost a regent's boon and gather the blessings of Chaos. But it used to include blood of the empyreals, thinned with human blood, and then also an herbal honey liquor."

"Perhaps," Annag says lightly, "my blade, my quill, we can discuss blood magic after we've eaten?"

I huff what could generously be called a laugh. I glance at Sheena, who looks rather green around the mouth. "Good idea, castelaine. Thank you."

Finn snaps his fingers. "Darvey, wake up, come eat."

The barghest lifts his head, ears perked. He gets up with a loud puppy groan. His yawn is massive, showing off curving fangs and a lolling canine tongue. Then he trots over to Finn. Standing, his head is level with the sitting, but also huge, Finn. Finn scratches under his chin and offers him a piece of chicken.

Elias clears their throat. "You were going to speak of Caspian."

First, I take a drink of the thick soup. It's spiced perfectly. "He's in the mountains. I saw him with my expanded boon. I no longer need to trace someone from an origin point—or at least, not always."

"He's alive, and . . . well?" Elias asks softly.

"He's alive. A dragon. Anything else, I don't know." I nod at Darvey. "Darvey is aware of some language, and seems to have retained his intelligence, but I'm not certain he knows who he is. We can't say more about Caspian until I get to him."

Elias absorbs my information, their face lowered to look at the rough scores on the table. It must be incredibly difficult being in love with my brother. Caspian is changeable and strange, and even though I think he loves me, and feels desires, how can a person love someone they can't grasp hold of?

Hard enough loving someone you can't keep. At least I caught Darling in my hands for a little while.

"When will that be?" Elias asks.

"As soon as possible," I promise.

Darvey makes a slavering noise that draws all our attention as he swipes more chicken from Finn's plate. Finn laughs, then pushes the boy's giant barghest head away.

"There's more," I say. "I could see your cousin, too, Elias. And I saw Darling. Not the gryphon empyreal, nor the phoenix. But them. They're themselves again—human."

The silence that drops suddenly is disturbed only by Darvey chomping through bones.

"They can turn back," Annag says, relief clear in her voice.

"I may know how," Elias declares, standing.

In the past month, the Gryphon physician has made a home in one of the long storage rooms in the Dragon healers' level of the castle. They chose it because the room came equipped with shelving and plenty of storage, as well as scales and measuring tools for the castelaine's people to prepare and disseminate supplies to all parts of Dragon Castle. Now, it's transformed into a laboratory.

Elias leads me there, with Finn and Darvey behind. Finn has his arm on the simple harness made of rope he's been using to help guide the giant puppy. I should request that Annag find something nicer for him, since Darvey is a guest regent from an allied house.

"Make yourself comfortable," Elias says absently as they light several candles, then immediately turn a dial built into the work-table that lights a small fire in a bowl. They search the shelves for a moment and begin laying out supplies: packets of herbs, a glass vial, a tiny knife, a shallow bowl. As I watch and Finn follows Darvey sniffing along the floor toward the wall—after mice, I assume—Elias mixes a few herbs in the vial, then adds a little bit of honey wine from a small corked bottle. Then they pick up the tiny knife and bowl. "I need some blood."

"Blood magic," Finn says contemptuously. His tone makes Darvey's head come up, and his fluffy black tail wags anxiously.

"Blood magic is *wrong*," I say. I know I sound cold, but it's the only way to push off the brutal memory of watching my aunt drive her hand into a living man's chest to tear out his heart for her blood magic ritual. I swallow nausea. I'm glad I barely ate.

Elias meets my concerned gaze. "Technically this is blood magic, yes. But the recipe for the blood of Pyrlanum ritual drink is centuries old. It always has blood in it, just a touch. Human and empyreal. It's only that we haven't *had* empyreals in a hundred years."

Finn snarls, then says through his teeth, "You can't take this kid's blood, Elias Chronicum."

"Do you want him to remain a beast forever?" Elias snaps.

Darvey butts his head against Finn's shoulder, big puppy eyes moving from Finn to Elias to me and back.

"It's all right, Darvey," Finn says, his demeanor shifting. He scratches behind Darvey's drooping ears.

"Do it," I say. "And then use mine for the human portion."

Finn glares at me but doesn't protest again.

Elias approaches Darvey quietly. "It won't be much, or hurt much," they say gently. Darvey leans away from them. Finn pets his head and nose.

"Go on, Darvey," Finn soothes. "It's all right. You're fine. Nothing to fear."

Swiftly, Elias cuts at the base of one of Darvey's ears. The barghest flinches and presses closer to Finn, nudging Elias away. The physician pays it no heed, but leans to catch the blood in their little bowl.

When Elias turns away, Finn immediately presses a cloth to the wound. I doubt it will take long to heal.

I unsheathe my falchion as Elias comes to me. "How much?"

"A few drops," Elias says.

After undoing my left bracer, I toss it to Finn and roll up my sleeve. Holding my hand over the bowl, I put the razor-sharp edge of my falchion to my soft inner wrist.

"For the love of Chaos, the back of your wrist," Elias scolds. "I don't need to pause and tend to an arterial bleed."

"I'm better than that at judging a cut," I say, but do them the honor of obedience. I slice shallowly into the back of my wrist. It seeps blood immediately, then a few thick drops gather and fall.

Finn comes to me, trailing a whining Darvey. He wipes the blade of my small sword, then takes my wounded arm to clean and tend it.

Elias lets a stream of the mingling blood drip into the vial of herbs and liquor. They use the delicate forceps to pick the vial up by the neck and slowly stir it by tilting it in gentle sunwise circles. "Possibly there is, or was, a boon specific to this process," they say, eyes on the golden-brown liquid. "But there had to be a reason for it, and a way to keep the empyreals from being locked in one form."

"It might not work even if you have the exact recipe," I say. Finn grunts, wrapping my wrist with a bandage. He secures it efficiently with a knot and tuck we're taught in field training.

"Just so," Elias says. They pour the vial back into the bowl and bring it around the table to Darvey. "If you would, young lord," they say, offering the bowl.

Darvey cocks his head. Finn says, "You can do it, Darvey," in a voice that is equal parts big brother and pack leader. He takes the bowl from Elias and brings it right to Darvey's nose.

The barghest empyreal dips his tongue in once, twice, and a third time; then the whole thing is swallowed. He tips his head back and licks his thin black lips. Then Darvey lets his tongue loll out, and sits. He wags his tail against the floor like a broom.

We're all staring.

Nothing happens.

"How long?" Finn asks.

Elias shakes their head. They set the bowl down and pick up a handkerchief. They don't do anything with it but twist it between their hands. "Faster," they finally say.

Darvey thumps his tail, clearly just fine. But just as clearly not transforming back into an eleven-year-old boy.

It didn't work.

"There must be a different means of returning the empyreals to us," I insist. "Darling and Vivian are themselves, and Darling wouldn't use blood magic. How could they, even if willing?"

"There's a blood witch we could ask," Finn says darkly.

I meet his blue eyes. He doesn't look happy about it. I'm not. But there is so much we need to know. I need to know. "Yes. When she wakes up, I'll ask Aunt Aurora about—everything."

DARLING

I hate waiting.

I'm good at it. All Barbs are. So many of our missions were bloodless, sneaking behind enemy lines to observe and report, or following the path of a unit of Dragon soldiers as they moved from one town to the next. But even when we weren't waiting for something to happen, we would wait for the moment to strike. We were always outnumbered—conscription will do that—but we were smart enough to pick the moments that mattered.

And now, I find myself in the same place, biding my time for news of the kraken to make its way to House Gryphon.

When I was a Barb I would spend hours—sometimes days—lying next to a crossroad or a bend, the perfect place for an ambush. But all that time in the tall grass and brambles was infinitely easier than the time I spend moping about House Gryphon. Even if I've only been returned to myself for a couple of days.

"Only fools rush in, especially when we're talking about Dragon territory," Vivian says with a laugh before we retire for the evening, and it's so near to something Leonetti once said that my heart seizes. But she's right. Of course she is. And even if Vivian didn't know, the gryphon would. Her house has shared a border with the serpents far longer than anyone else, and they also bear the honor of being one of the only houses never conquered by House Dragon.

And not for lack of trying, if Vivian's histories are to be believed. So even though I want to throw a handful of things into a satchel and take off in a run across the mountains, I bide my time and concede that perhaps a plan is in order.

I spend the first day after I wake eating and sleeping, since I am exhausted in a way I have never felt, my muscles weak and jelly-like, my footsteps dragging when I move between rooms. It's a luxury to lie about in the gardens eating my fill of excellent House Gryphon cooking and reading a book of poetry that I only half understand. A few of the servants are those with the frustrated boons like Lania, and when they get too near, I wave them over and release their Chaos. At some point in the day a shadow blots out the sky, and I look up to see the gryphon soaring overhead. One of the gardeners sees the sight as well and points it out to me.

"Isn't it beautiful?" he says, voice soft in reverence. I think he might be crying.

It's a fine way to spend my first full day back, but I am built for action, not leisure. Too many more days lazing about the garden, and I might go mad.

Luckily, when I wake the next morning, ready to meet with those in the house who may have boons, Vivian instead leads me to a small nook in the library.

"As happy as I am that you wish to help my house, I think you need to prioritize controlling the phoenix. And before we work on trying to transform, I think you should read up on the nature of the phoenix," she says. "I have the sense you are not entirely comfortable with being an empyreal, and we think maybe knowledge will help you move past some of your trepidation."

"We?" I ask, and Vivian smiles.

"The gryphon and I."

I blink at that but just nod. Because how can I argue with an ancient being made of Chaos?

While I relaxed, Vivian had her scholars comb the archives for anything related to the phoenix and used it to set up an unoccupied nook in the library. This one is much smaller than Vivian's, but it has no windows, so the area is dim enough that a single boonlight is all I need to comb through the materials.

I thank Vivian and immediately begin reading.

Most of the materials are conjecture. It seems that perhaps the phoenixes have traditionally kept their knowledge to themselves, a fact I find interesting. There are no firsthand accounts of being an empyreal from past phoenixes, although I suppose that might be because those are kept within Phoenix Crest. Instead, most of the materials seem to be more general knowledge about the empyreals. Even so, I devour them, happy to have some information, even if it's mostly just flowery suppositions.

There are scrolls and scrolls that posit that the origination of the empyreals was to protect the island from outside threats, and then there are the artistic renderings, skilled drawings of a gryphon in repose or a barghest enraged. They make very little sense, and most of them contradict one another. But it is fun to spend a morning eating pastries, fruit, and tiny stuffed eggs and reading the dusty tomes. I can understand why one would want to pledge themselves to House Gryphon. It seems like quite a satisfying life.

For the most part I read the material and put it to the side. But there is a section of one philosopher's argument that seems useful: the abilities of the empyreals.

There is a chart and an outline of each empyreal along with their noted abilities. The gryphon's poison talons I already know about, but the rest are incredibly fascinating. The barghest seems to have the ability to shift its size from very small to extremely large, bigger than a fortress, if the illustration is to be believed. The dragon bears indestructible plate armor, which makes sense since Caspian's house treasure is an armored breastplate made from a dragon scale. The cockatrice is apparently able to paralyze with sound, and the sphinx can create a "miasma of confusion," whatever that means. The kraken can manipulate tides and currents, which makes me think of Adelaide's ability to sail a ship faster than anyone else. Is she able to access her empyreal abilities even before she can access her kraken form?

Most interesting to me is that of the phoenix, for obvious reasons. My body has become strange to me since I woke, the same and yet not, and it feels safer to try to understand these abilities by way of a third party's testimony than through trial and error. Mostly because I am terrified that I will lose more weeks of my life, and when I wake again things will be even worse.

The treatise, though, is mostly vague on the abilities of the phoenix. It states that the phoenix is as immutable as the flame, which seems kind of a strange thing to say. I think of the singed carpet in my room, relocated to the House Gryphon archives because of its value, my footprints now historically important. But I also think of the way I found myself on one side of the room and then the other. And then I read a sentence that chills my skin and has me standing and pacing in agitation.

"The phoenix is the heart of Chaos and can access the deepest wells of that strange and fickle power."

The phrasing haunts me until lunch, when I begin to feel a tug, like I am being physically pulled in a direction by an invisible hook lodged under my ribs. I ignore it and spend the rest of the day tending to those who have recovered from what Vivian is calling a boon fever. All the people I meet with have boons that have improperly manifested, and I spend hours touching them, like I did Lania when I first woke. The more boons I awaken, the stronger the tug becomes, but by the time Vivian and I retire for the evening— dinner an in-room affair—I'm mostly able to ignore it.

The next morning Vivian and I meet in the central courtyard before dawn, when the sky is barest pink. It seems odd to think a few months ago I arrived in this same courtyard in an ostentatious carriage with Caspian and Talon. Now, Caspian is a dragon, and Talon is my enemy once more.

It's too easy to remember the look he'd shot me when I disembarked, when he'd thought I was trying to seduce his brother. Oh, to have such troubles once more. It was much easier to navigate Talon's moods when they were petty and personal.

Unwittingly my memory goes back to the last afternoon at House Barghest, how Talon turned away from me when I called to him after Caspian flounced from the Naming ceremony, how Talon refused to release Leonetti despite knowing I was right. He pledged himself to me and my cause—the cause of House Sphinx— and then promptly abandoned me in my moment of need.

How can I forgive him for turning his back on me when I needed him most?

"How are you feeling about trying to transform?" Vivian asks. She wears a simple robe and I have a matching one as well. Over a small pot of tea and pastries—me yawning and wishing the tea was something stronger—Vivian explains the process of transformation, how she basically just lets go of her human form to assume that of the gryphon in her blood. I nod and drink my tea, but I have no idea what she's even talking about.

"If you want to watch, I can—" Whatever else Vivian is about to say is cut off as something physically pulls me across the courtyard. The insistent tug has become an urge I cannot ignore, and before I know it, I'm running across the courtyard and bursting into flames.

The phoenix demands its due.

When I return to myself, I lie in the middle of a field, shivering. My smoked lenses are gone once more, and my eyes water in the early morning light.

"Miss? Are you okay?" a voice calls.

I squint to see a person approaching, their outline haloed in bright light. "Yes, I'm fine. Just getting my bearings. Can you tell me where I am? I'm sorry, I can't see."

"You're on Sunstone Farm; I'm Meredith, the matron of the farm. I saw you streak across the sky like a falling star before you crashed here. Would you, ah, like a blanket or something? No offense, dear, but you are as naked as the day you were born."

I realize for the first time that I have no clothes. Instead I am covered in what feels like soot. Most likely the remains of the robe I wore. Vivian mentioned that the transformation was hard on clothing.

"I would be grateful," I call back, not moving from where I sit in what feels to be a patch of clover. "Pardon my ignorance, but am I still on House Gryphon lands?"

"Aye, but just barely. Wait here and I'll be right back." There's the sound of footsteps running away, and then I am alone once more.

The pull I felt earlier is gone, replaced with a sense of rightness that I know belongs to the phoenix and not to me. Vivian had referred to herself and the gryphon as "we," but I don't feel like the phoenix and I are two parts of a whole. Instead, I'm wondering why the creature took hold of me, forcing a transformation and bringing me where I am.

And how in the name of Chaos am I supposed to get back to Furial?

The beat of wings interrupts my thoughts, and something heavy comes to land not far away. I try to squint at it, but the sun is now full up, and without any kind of cloud cover or shaded lenses, my eyes are useless.

"Well, that was quite the display," Vivian says. I feel her settle onto the grass beside me. "I have a few riders on the way. They'll bring you an extra set of lenses for your eyes. Oh, and clothes for both of us."

"I think a person who lives here is bringing me a blanket," I say. I yawn, but it ends in a sigh. "What happened?"

"After you decided to burst into flames, I shifted and followed you. I'm not sure what you were doing, but the phoenix flew to a small ridge just outside Furial and exploded it."

"'Exploded it'?" I echo, confused. "I . . . how did the phoenix explode it?"

"I'm not certain. All I saw was you diving toward the location, changing the entire area to glass. There is a crater there that I am certain scholars are going to have a field day with. The glass left behind looks like flames erupting from the earth. It's quite pretty."

I swallow and try not to feel like the world is spinning out of control. I am mostly successful.

"Do you know what was there? I don't understand why the phoenix would take over like that." I also feel deeply uncomfortable about my body not being my own. It's one thing to have limitations and to know what they are, but it's quite another for those limitations to belong to someone else entirely.

"I don't, but I am sure we will know by the morning. Also, I have a missive from House Dragon that was sent along. There have been a number, in fact, but we've been avoiding sending a response. I haven't read it yet, but would you like to see it when I do?"

I shake my head a bit too fiercely. "No. Burn it. We will deal with the Dragons when it is time and not a moment sooner."

Vivian looks like she wants to argue, but her expression evaporates as someone strides toward us. "Ah, it looks as though the person you spoke to is returning. Hello, Meredith! How are the children?"

It turns out that Sunstone Farm is a safe haven created for war orphans, and the information makes me think of Leonetti. Where is he? Where are Adelaide and Miranda, and all the rest? My heart aches, and a deep melancholy settles over me. I miss them.

Meredith settles a blanket over my shoulders, and I remain where I sit while Meredith and Vivian discuss local news. It turns out we're half a day's ride from Furial—flying as a phoenix is faster than even the fastest drake—and Vivian and Meredith help me navigate the landscape so that I can sit inside. I am left alone in a shuttered room so that I can see while Vivian takes a tour with Meredith, but I mostly just wait in the gloom and think.

I have to get control of the phoenix.

Singeing carpets and chasing maids with frustrated boons was bad enough, but this? This makes me want to claw the empyreal from inside my body. I will not let myself become a puppet of Chaos.

"I'm in control here, you understand?" I mutter out loud to myself. "You will not do that again, not without my consent and not without my agreement."

But I'm alone in the room, and neither Chaos nor the phoenix see fit to give me an answer.

For the first time I understand just how Caspian must have felt the entirety of his life.

7

TALON

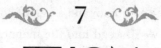

Three days after arriving at Dragon Castle, I receive a report that the kraken empyreal has appeared off the coast of Dragon lands. It is churning the waves and occasionally destroying a pier, chasing off fish and ruining the livelihood of Dragon fishing villages.

I intend to see to it myself, driving it off if necessary, but first I need to interrogate Aunt Aurora. The problem is that she has yet to wake up.

"This has never happened to me before," Finn protested the fifth time I asked him what was wrong. "I did everything the same way. She should have woken up naturally. That's always how it's worked. You remember when we brought that damned Barb to Phoenix Crest, I had to put her back to sleep every six hours."

I accepted it, but we can't wait any longer. I sent a letter to Darling and Vivian at Furial, asking to set a meeting soon—at their convenience. I need to have as many answers as possible by the time I hear back. We've still no word of the kraken, sphinx, or cockatrice empyreals. When I look for them with my unreliable boon, I only see blurry images. Elias agrees it's likely I can't easily see someone I don't know personally. Given time, I might train my boon to find people I have no trace of, but for now, it's too hard on my body to keep giving myself fevers and headaches.

Today I've dragged Finn to the dungeon with me. He's going to try to wake Aurora up.

We've got Annag Mortooth and a handful of Teeth and castle guards with us as we descend into the mountain. The air smells of wet stone and smoke. The narrow corridors should be lit with boonlights, but we've resorted to torches and candles while so many boons are volatile—even basic light boons. A Dragon with such a boon exploded the stairs in one of the west wings of the castle yesterday, merely trying to light a chandelier. He's alive, but concussed. There's significant damage to that level's infrastructure.

Aurora's cell door shrieks as Annag unlocks it with a key on her belt. We file in, just the three of us.

My aunt sleeps on a cot in the wrinkled dress she drenched in the Phoenix Blood River. Her tangled blond hair flares across the threadbare pillow. She has water and a bucket should she wake, a single chair, and nothing else.

Annag brings in a handful of candles and lights them from the torch outside the cell, sticking them on the two stone shelves on either side of the door. It's dark, but it will have to do.

"Be ready," I warn Finn as I scoop Aurora up against me and carry her the two steps to the chair. I put her down with more gentleness than she deserves and let her head loll back. Finn stands behind her.

Aurora hasn't awoken.

Finn puts a hand on her hair, a hand on her shoulder. He closes his eyes. We wait.

In the flickering light, my aunt looks young, abused, and vulnerable. I clench my jaw and refuse to feel pity or sympathy. She raised me, loved me, and lied to me for my whole life.

Nothing happens for a long moment. Finn frowns. His eyes move behind his lids, as if he's looking for something—or dreaming himself.

Aunt Aurora's entire body jerks.

Finn's eyes snap open. "Chaos," he whispers. "I think . . . I think I saw her dreams."

At the hushed tone, I brace myself.

Annag says, "Sweet Chaos."

"What did you see?"

"Blood," he says softly, staring at Aurora's head like he can still see into it. "I'm not unfamiliar with violence, but this was . . . It felt good. I felt powerful, and I saw her killing people. And animals. I saw her kill Darvey, Talon." Finn's face blanches as he makes an awful grimace. His scar on his cheek stands out like a crooked worm. "His . . . she took his heart."

Like she did to Leonetti remains unspoken.

My skin goes cold. I lower my gaze from Finn to my aunt, and I step closer, hand going to the hilt of my falchion. I should drive it through her neck right now. Stop her before she wakes, Chaos take her information. She won't help us.

"Yes," Finn hisses, sensing my intent.

But I stop, clenching the grip of my blade. I can't. She betrayed me, but she murdered Leonetti Seabreak right before my eyes. Justice belongs to House Kraken, and Darling.

Aurora groans softly. Her head lifts.

Finn has a knife at her throat instantly. Aurora's eyes flutter open; she gasps.

"Aurora," I say in my hardest voice. "That is a blade at your throat, and the hand at your shoulder can push you into sleep again in an instant. Here with me is Annag Mortooth, who is immune to your boon."

Aurora looks at me. "Talon," she croaks. She winces and swallows.

"The moment Finn or Annag even suspect you *might* be influencing me, they will act, and you will be asleep again—if you're lucky. Then gagged and bound until your execution. Do you understand?"

Her vivid blue eyes water, but Aurora nods.

"Good. Now." I crouch in front of her, elbows on my knees, and glance up. "Tell me about blood magic."

Aurora frowns, a cute expression she uses to pretend confusion. "What about it, nephew?" she asks, sounding helpless.

"You know what happened at House Barghest? About the return of the empyreals?" I know she has. The soldiers she persuaded with her boon to help her escape gave complete confessions. I want to know if Aurora will admit it.

"I heard," she says. Good.

"What does blood magic have to do with the empyreals?"

Aurora laughs softly. "I see." She sounds normal already, despite her filthy gown, the blade at her throat, and the eager Dragon behind her.

"Answer me, Aurora."

"Why should I?" Her eyes flash. "If you're going to execute me, why?"

"It's the right thing to do," I snap. "Our world has been given over to Chaos, and we don't know why, or how to fix anything. Blood magic has everything to do with whatever's happened. You're my family—a Dragon! If you care at all for that, for me, for anything you ever said to make me think you weren't a depraved villain, give me answers!"

Aurora is silent. She studies me.

Finn shifts behind her, but I ignore it to focus on my aunt. I can't have feelings about this, but I loved her. I trusted her! I let my fury and grief show, until my eyes burn with tears. Then I bare my teeth at her. "You're alone," I choke out. "If you don't want to die alone, answer me, Aurora."

My voice breaks on her name.

Aurora sighs. She blinks back tears of her own; I wish I believed them. "There is a cavern below this castle, little dragon," she says. "And the private study of a blood mage. A long time ago, that blood mage, a Dragon regent, and a squid worked to suppress Chaos. We were held back by the phoenixes, oppressed by their power. It was time to break the ancient promises of the empyreals, the reign of the phoenix, and so our ancestors made it so."

"Impossible," Finn says. "Dragons and Krakens don't work together."

"That's what you question?" Aurora rolls her eyes up toward him.

"What did they do?" I interrupt. I'll worry about what I believe later. We already knew our great-grandmother was responsible for the murder of the Last Phoenix.

"A massive blood array. It was complex."

"Explain it to me in little words."

Aurora narrowed her eyes. "I spent your whole life learning to wield blood magic. Most of my notes and the books I've managed to gather are locked behind a trap in my office in Phoenix Crest. Unless you can bring me there, I have little to offer."

"I cannot. Try harder to explain."

"It isn't that I don't want to, but I'm afraid blood magic on the surface is simple: one uses blood to add power to sigils, arrays, and spells—blood that opens gates directly to Chaos. I simply invoked

Chaos I otherwise had no access to. Blood magic is a great equalizer, Talon."

"That's what you call what you did to Leonetti Seabreak?" I stand. "It was disgusting and cowardly, Aurora. *Not* the work of a Dragon. He was my prisoner, a father, a leader! Not a—a chicken to slaughter for your soup."

Aurora shrugs, but Finn presses on her shoulder, and she glares. "He was a necessary casualty. I remember what I saw, Talon. Tell me, is Caspian dead? Did your Darling betray you, too? Is that why you're truly so upset? She kissed your brother and he died, in my vision. My true vision."

I swallow. I don't let myself look away from her. "Your vision was not true," I say. "They kissed, but they didn't die. Caspian flies wild in the mountains now, a newborn dragon empyreal. And Darling?" I lean closer to my aunt. "Darling is the Phoenix Reborn."

Aunt Aurora gasps. "No."

"Yes. Tell me how to get to this cavern under the castle."

"You don't want to do that," Aurora says. "Talon, stay here, keep talking to me. You can't leave me—"

Suddenly Aurora slumps, passed out.

I blink.

Finn withdraws his knife. "She can't say things like that. Commands, imperatives."

"I . . . yes." I nod. "You're right."

Finn hauls the unconscious Aurora to the cot. He wipes his hands on his jacket. I haven't moved, staring at her, my mind whirling.

I wonder if I can use my boon to trace a hidden door or find a cavern. "I need to find this cave."

Annag smiles grimly. "I have an idea where to begin."

Annag has lived in this castle for all forty-some years of her life, worked in it and loved it, and for at least a decade has ruled it in the stead of the absent Dragon regent. Every report of someone going missing, of strangely cold rooms, or of drafts that cannot be found and stopped, eventually find their way to her. Annag easily suspects the best place to find a secret or ancient passage in the bowels of Dragon Castle.

Once we've re-secured Aurora, Annag leads us into the cellars. There's a particular storage room they stopped using in her mother's time because food spoiled or froze, or people vanished when seeking this or that supply. The shelves are rotting in place, with nothing stored there any longer. The ceiling is bare rock, and the walls seem to be the same.

I stand in the middle of the room and open my boon. Finn curses softly behind me, and grips my shoulder.

Instead of tracing a door or passageway I've never seen—that might not work, because it never has in the past—I recall Aurora's trace. I imagine her standing before me, walking to the mechanism or handle, whatever it is that reveals the passageway.

My body heats. Like a flush of embarrassment or shame. I embrace it, allow it to happen. The pain follows, spiking my skull. I hate that my boon is so unreliable. It's like losing my sword hand but needing my blade.

Chaos tears at me, in popping bubbles: Aurora, younger, a bloody hand, the wall pushing back, someone I don't know falling through the wall, closed in, trapped, Aurora again, rushing out from the dark corner, panicked, and then—then—

I open my eyes and I walk directly for the far corner, and I hit one stone in the wall. It aches up my arm, but the wall groans. A door appears. I step forward, but someone catches my arm.

"Talon, you're sweating; your cheeks are pink," Finn says, his grip bruising.

"I have to follow it." I pull free. "Stay here and hold the door open. People have been trapped before."

"Talon—"

"Do it!" An unfamiliar rage heightens my voice.

Finn falls back. Behind him, Annag's face is a pale, floating ghost.

I turn and follow the dark passage, assuming they will wait for me.

It cuts down sharply, the walls rough, wet, cold. The air grows colder and wetter as I descend. I can't see anything, but I continue. One step, then another.

Finally it opens into a dim cavern. There's the quiet lapping of water on a bank, and my eyes drink in dim light. I have no idea how it exists here, the light. I see a broad black lake, still as a mirror. It should either be still and silent, or rippling, but not both.

Across from me is a broken altar.

I stand and stare, but am unbalanced. I should go back and get Finn. Anyone else. People with torches or boonlights. Elias might know what to think of this place.

Instead I continue walking.

I walk around the edge of the lake, pulled by something inside me. My boon, or Chaos itself, I cannot say.

Near the opposite bank is an arched doorway, and through it, a tidy room caught up in dust and mildew. A study, recently cared for and organized. Desk, chair, bookshelves with ordered books. Nothing on the floor but puddles of water and tattered remains of nests.

On the desk is a candlestick, a quill, and a single book.

I walk to it and pick it up. It smells like tempered iron and leather.

Cradling it in one hand, I turn open the binding. On the first page it reads,

This journal belongs to the blood.

8

DARLING

The trip back to House Gryphon from Sunstone Farm is a quiet one, and Vivian seems to understand that I need space with my thoughts. I ride back to the castle with her house guards while she decides to fly back. One moment she is there; the next she is a fading blot in the sky. The look of rapture on her guards' faces sours my stomach.

If only they knew how terrible being an empyreal truly is.

We don't ride past the place where I destroyed part of a mountain, but one of the guards, a broad-shouldered youth named Anders, tells me all about the spot.

"We rode past it on the way to find you, my flame," they say, their eyes alight with wonder. They wear their hair close-cropped, and for some reason they remind me of Elias, although much friendlier. Perhaps they are a cousin. "The hill is now a brilliant sculpture of glass that would make any artisan of Cockatrice swoon," they confidently pronounce, and I know they are trying to pay me a compliment, but all I can think of is that once again I have lost time.

I cannot keep living half a life, the phoenix doing what it will. I have to find a way to control the beast living in my blood.

When we arrive at House Gryphon, the hour is late and I take myself to my rooms. Food is sent up, and I gratefully accept it before asking for privacy for the remainder of the evening.

Exhaustion weighs on every part of me, and I eat quickly before throwing myself into the luxurious bed.

And . . . I can't sleep.

In the aftermath of the phoenix seizing control, I find myself unable to rest.

I toss. I turn. And every single time I close my eyes, all I see is the landscape zipping by. A memory that isn't mine. The phoenix has even taken my rest.

I sit up in bed, taking a deep breath. I close my eyes and reach down deep inside myself. I can sense where the phoenix rests, as though the creature has built a nest in my gut.

"If this is going to work, we have to work together," I say to the slumbering phoenix. I can feel it, a strange warmth that doesn't belong. Or perhaps, even worse, does. It's as though I have suddenly realized that a limb was sleeping and now it has woken in a prickling, tingling discomfort.

"I will help you with whatever you need to do," I say, swallowing a yawn. "But you have to let me be in control. I need to understand what we're doing, and why. Otherwise, I will have myself locked in a House Gryphon dungeon. Or worse." I think back to the ritual Caspian did on the top of Castle Barghest. "Someone was able to keep you from manifesting for over a century," I murmur. "I am certain the ritual could be repeated."

There's a burning in my middle, sharp and swift, followed by . . . amusement? An effervescent lightness. The phoenix doesn't speak, nothing so helpful as that. But I can feel its emotions and it is not quite so impressed with me, either.

"Well, it seems neither of us are very happy with the current turn of events," I mutter, "but we will have to make do."

That seems to mollify the empyreal trying to slumber within me, and my own exhaustion finally takes hold and I fall into a deep—and dreamless—sleep.

When I wake the next morning, House Gryphon is abuzz with activity, people rushing this way and that.

"Vivian has asked you to meet her in the courtyard," Lania says when she sees me wandering down toward the library. "She says you should dress for travel and bring anything you might need for a few days away."

That news makes me hurry back to my room, where I throw together a few trousers and tunics for the road. They aren't Barb blacks, but Vivian has been great at acquiring clothing that suits me. It makes me wonder where Caspian might be. He must be trapped somewhere as a dragon. How is he faring as an empyreal? He was always so petulant that I cannot imagine him taking well to the change.

I push the thought aside, because that line of thinking invariably leads to Talon, and that is not a path I wish to travel at the moment. As long as I don't think about Talon, his betrayal won't hurt.

I arrive in the courtyard, but I am the only one there, with the exception of a few workers. When Vivian finds me pacing across the cobblestones, she gives me a tight smile.

"I have good news and bad. Which would you like first?"

"The bad news. Always," I say, slowing my steps until I stand before her, adjusting the straps of my pack.

"The kraken has been sighted, but along the coast of Dragon territory. There are reports of a unit of Dragon regulars harrying the kraken. So far they've done little to provoke the beast, but my strategists believe the War Prince himself will attend, as he did when the barghest appeared."

My heart hiccups at the mention of Talon, my emotions too close to the surface, and I take a deep breath to settle my them. There will be time for that much later. "Can he hurt him? Leonetti?"

Vivian shakes her head. "I don't think so. But there are House Kraken ships following behind, and there is a risk that in his haste Talon could reignite this war. The embers of conflict burn even months after Caspian's declaration of peace."

"Okay. So what's the good news?"

Vivian grins brightly. "I can fly us there," she says, gesturing to what looks like a huge market basket being dragged into the courtyard. It's large enough to fit a person, with a small door in the side to allow easy entrance and exit. My stomach drops as I figure out her intent.

"No. Vivian, no, this is incredibly unsafe—"

"Nonsense! I found this in the archives, and we've spent the past couple of days putting it together based on the designs. After yesterday, I figured you would be hesitant to transform, so this will get us there quickly, and without you having to attempt something risky."

I'm still shaking my head even as she pushes me toward the basket, the door unlatched so that I can climb inside. "I know you mean well, Vivian, but I just . . . This seems unwise."

"Nonsense. Traveling overland will take too long, and this

will hopefully get us to the coast before the Dragons. You are the phoenix," Vivian murmurs to me. "You must do what others cannot, even when it feels too hard."

Vivian moves off to give herself space to change, and a nearby guard bows as they gesture toward the basket. There is a small chest in one corner and a stool in another.

"Please, my flame," the guard says. "We follow your spark."

His words send a chill down my spine, and in my middle the phoenix preens a little. They recognize the sentiment even though I don't.

I nod absently, but before I can enter the basket, my attention is pulled to where Vivian stands in the midst of the courtyard, removing her robe and handing it to her head scholar, who stands nearby.

And then Vivian gives herself over to the gryphon.

I had expected a sickening shifting of body, to watch wings spring forth from Vivian's back as her body twists into a new shape. But her transformation is anything but grotesque. She stands in a wide-open space, her eyes closed, and there is a sort of sigh. It's the only way I can explain the way the world seems to inhale around her, a strange pressure building. A breeze begins to pick up, swirling around where Vivian stands, and brown feathers and fall leaves join the maelstrom, growing in number until Vivian is no longer visible. The swirling vortex, brown and red and beautiful and chaotic, grows in diameter and height, becoming stronger, until there is a high-pitched scream and it all falls away.

And there, standing in the courtyard, is the gryphon resplendent.

I find myself walking toward the creature—it's hard to resist getting a closer look—and as I do, the creature spreads its wings and resettles them. It watches me with a shining black eye, more animal than person, but I can sense that Vivian is in there, the same way I could sense Lania's frustrated boon. Perhaps this is what that dusty scroll meant about "pools of Chaos."

I have never seen a gryphon in real life, and judging from the hush around the courtyard, this has not been a regular sight for the house, either. It's the size of a farmer's cottage, and if the courtyard had not been so sprawling, the creature would have been cramped. It strikes me that this is probably exactly what the space was built for: to accommodate a large creature with a massive wingspan.

"You are beautiful," I say, and the creature ducks its head so that I can scratch the spot where the black beak meets the rest of the feathered head. I'm not sure how I know it would enjoy such a caress, but it does, making a sound like a cat's purr deep in its throat.

The gryphon has four feet, massive wings, and an eagle's head with feathered ears. It's sleekly muscled like a hunting cat and covered with what looks to be a combination of feathers and golden fur, the front feet those of a bird of prey and the rear feet cat paws. But despite the merging of two distinct animals in one form, it is symmetrical and perfectly proportioned.

I am suddenly immensely jealous that it's so easy for Vivian to shift into her empyreal form. What must it feel like to give herself over to the entirety of her nature and not feel like something is being stolen from her?

She is right. I need to be braver. I used to be, but so much about all this is too big for me to process. I keep thinking of the pain when Caspian unleashed the change. I still bear the scorch marks along my hairline, the skin twisted and thickened into burn scars, one more mark of Chaos upon me, if one counts my eyes. It doesn't bother me, but it is a stark reminder that there is a price for all this.

"Let's be away," I tell the gryphon, and it shrieks in agreement.

I run back to the basket, slamming the door and securing the latch. Then there is the rush of wind and the soft thunder of beating wings, and we are off.

It's a weird feeling to be carted through the air by a creature I'd always thought was a myth, another way for people to try and make sense of the world we live in. At first my heart slams against my rib cage, panicked and scared. I try to think what I would do if the gryphon drops me or the basket somehow fails. And I realize that I would just have to try and turn into the phoenix. Not that I'm sure how to do that. But I'm hoping that fear of death will unlock that knowledge.

After a while, I take a deep breath and tell myself it isn't worth worrying about. And once I give in to the pointlessness of the fear, it dissipates, leaving me to enjoy the trip. And there is much to enjoy.

What would have been a week-long journey takes mere hours by air. We soar over mountaintops and homes, the people below tiny specks of humanity. Rivers run silver across the landscape, and I try to figure which clusters of rooftops might belong to places I've been. Seeing Pyrlanum at this altitude loosens the dread and anxiety that has been knotting my middle since I awoke. It's cold at the higher altitudes, but Vivian has thought of it already, a thick fur blanket tucked in the wooden chest along with a few rations. I wrap myself tightly and try to settle into the ride, eating a hard cheese and a palm-sized loaf of bread when my middle begins to complain. When I yell up at the gryphon, asking if it wants to stop to eat, I understand the answering chittering sounds to mean that she will eat when we get there. I try not to dwell on the strangeness of having a shouted conversation with a gryphon and instead just enjoy the view.

Soon enough the coastline is visible. Ships in a Kraken honor guard formation sail slowly along the coast. A few leagues ahead of them is a group of riders, most likely the Dragon regulars Vivian mentioned.

"Head south and then drop me on the ship flying the House Kraken flag," I shout up at the gryphon. There is a *ka-ree* of agreement before the beast angles its body sharply away from the riders, heading down and around to the south. We fly up the coast, skimming lower to the ships. And then I am falling through the air, hundreds of feet above the lead ship, the gryphon taking my request entirely too literally.

I grip the sides for a moment, heart pounding. The basket is hurtling toward the deck of the ship, and I realize that it and I will both strike the ropes and the mainsail long before we hit the deck. I only have one choice.

I have to fly.

I leap out of the basket, flipping myself backward, ignoring the shouts far below. I'm not quite sure how to become the phoenix; none of the dusty old tomes I read had an instruction manual, but it's unnecessary. The phoenix has taken my late-night plea to heart and helps without fully taking me over. One moment I'm falling, and the next I'm landing on the deck, softly, nimbly. I blink, every single deckhand on the ship staring at me, too stunned to draw their swords. I have no idea what they all just saw, but judging from their expressions it must've been impressive.

"By Chaos. It's true. You're the phoenix."

I spin around to see Miranda, my adoptive older sister. For a moment I'm afraid I'm going to have to argue with her, convince her to let me help turn Leonetti back into a man, explain my absence, and apologize for everything. But she holds her arms open, just a little, and I know none of that is necessary. She knows.

I run into her arms with a sob, hugging her and holding on for dear life.

We're both crying, hugging each other, and blubbering apologies. I have so many questions, but there's no time. I pull back and wipe away the tears from where they've puddled under my goggles.

"Where's Adelaide?" I ask, and Miranda's face is stricken.

"You don't know?" she asks, her voice a murmur.

"Know what?" I ask. But in that moment, I do. She doesn't even have to say it. I can feel it.

"Adelaide is the kraken," Miranda says, and my world shatters. Because there is only one reason that Adelaide would be the kraken.

Leonetti is dead.

I come to the realization just as Vivian drops onto the deck, naked and shivering.

I want to fall apart. I want to scream and cry and curse Chaos. Leonetti Seabreak, the best of us and the only father I have ever known, is gone, and I don't even know how or why.

But Leonetti was the one who taught me how to be a soldier, a leader, and my training snaps into place. "Quick, fetch the chest that's in the basket," I call to the sailors cutting the basket free from the rigging. It falls to the deck, landing with a heavy *thunk*, and a woman I don't know grabs the blanket and wraps it around Vivian, before running back to grab clothing from the chest.

"If you'd told me I would end my day today watching a gryphon drop my sister onto my ship, only for her to turn into a human flame and flicker in and out of existence onto the deck of my ship, I would've sent you to the brig to dry out," Miranda jokes, trying to lighten the blow of her revelation, and I manage to dredge up a smile.

"I came to help Adelaide. But first . . ." That same kind of Chaos bubble exists in several of the soldiers on the deck, including Miranda, and when I put my hands on either side of her face and free it, she gasps.

"What did you do?" she murmurs.

"You had a partial boon. You should have free use of it now. I . . . it should be stronger. So be careful."

Miranda nods, although the expression on her face is less enthusiastic and more resigned. "What now?"

And just like that, it's like I never left.

"We have to get closer to the kraken next time it surfaces. I'll talk to her, try to get her to break out of the shift on her own. And if she can't . . ." I trail off and shrug. "I'll figure it out."

Then I walk over to the nearest deckhand and begin releasing boons.

Because work is easier than acknowledging the millstone of my grief.

9

TALON

Kitty stretches her legs and lopes fast across the hills toward the coast. I've brought two of my Teeth with me, and their drakes flank me, easily keeping pace. Traveling this way, it's just over a day to the edge of Dragon land, where we expect the kraken empyreal to appear next.

We ride all day and into the night before I let us make camp some two hours from the sea. Kitty goes hunting with one of the soldiers and the other two drakes, while the remaining soldier cares for the tiny flock of sparrow drakes we've brought with us to send any emergency messages. They perch on a drake tree, built of sturdy wood with branches enough for all five of them to have their own. The base rests in a stand when we're camped, and hooks into a loop in one of the war drake saddles. When we ride, it rises like a flag, and the little sparrow drakes cling like red, gold, and green pennants.

The red sparrow drake Finn sent last week is one of them, and it keeps looking at me. Occasionally it leaps over to land on my shoulder and comb little claws through my hair. Because it knows my blood.

I'm even less happy about how the sparrow drakes are trained than I used to be, after finding the old blood magic altar and study. Instead of paging through everything in that dank cavern myself, I gathered up the strange blood book and a few extra scrolls and dumped it all on Elias's desk. It's their job now to go through everything and continue trying to understand. I didn't want the task. Elias did, but I'm slightly concerned about how eager they were to take it up.

As we set up camp near the coast, I build a fire to boil water and rehydrate our dinner. Once everyone has eaten, including the sparrow drakes who nibble pickled robins' eggs and the scraps from the war drakes' hunt, I settle against Kitty's bulk. She's nestled in the fallen pine needles like a huge, scaly duck. I instruct my Teeth not to worry about me unless I haven't opened my eyes for several minutes, then I sink back into my boon.

This time, I hunt the kraken.

I don't know what Kraken scion became the massive squid, and I might not be able to see it. But I have to try, despite Finn's concerns. I can handle a fever.

I reach for the sea, and for the trace of an empyreal. I hope knowing how Darvey the barghest traces, maybe I can find the kraken instead.

The heat comes, and the headache, but I see it:

It dives through the churning sea just off the coast, exactly where we'd expected. I see it curl arms around a seal and crush it, then draw it toward its hungry beak. It rises to the surface, where the half-moon reflects on the water, to slap at one of the Kraken naval ships trailing behind it like an honor guard.

I open my eyes to the warm fire, blinking at the echoes of red flame like the sleek gray-red of the kraken's skin. I wish I could use my boon to widen my vision, to see how many ships float behind it, and where it might be going.

Both of the Teeth watch me with interest. Their names are

Maise and Pol Scaleguard, cousins from the same secondary Dragon family line who worked separately to earn their places in the Dragon's Teeth. Maise has been in longer than me, and Pol joined the year after me. I've known him since I was fourteen. I like them because they fight hard and are disciplined enough to treat me formally most of the time, only indicating our distant relation at the right moments.

I meet Maise's dark green eyes, then her cousin Pol's. "You have questions."

Both Teeth nod their heads. Pol speaks first. "Do you know where the High Prince Regent is?"

"In the peaks of the Hundred Claw Mountains." I glance up at the black crown of pine trees surrounding us, and the stars beyond. As if he'll be there, soaring. "I saw it happen. He is the true Dragon regent once more."

Maise sighs contentedly.

Pol reaches to scratch the eye ridge of his war drake.

For a moment, I lean forward, ready to ask if they've named their mounts. It was Darling who named Kitty, and inspired by her I named Finn's Bluebird. I close my mouth. I don't want to speak of her.

Another one of the sparrow drakes drops from its perch on the drake tree, landing at the sooty edge of the fire. It shakes its tail and crawls over to me. Like all drakes, it has only four limbs—true dragons, as Caspian has become, are the only ones with six limbs. The sparrow drake's wings are the same as its forearms, the elbows and little fingers spreading long enough to stretch skin and tendon between. This one is bright gold, with beady red eyes. It shuffles to my boot and picks at one of the stitches. I bend to lift it up into my lap and rub at the dry scales under its chin. It purrs.

"At dawn, send one of these ahead to alert the battalion tracking the kraken up the coast that our arrival is imminent," I command quietly.

"Yes, my blade," Maise says.

We retire shortly after that. The war drakes hear and smell better than any human, even asleep, so there's no need for a watch.

Midmorning, I see the glint of sun on the ocean before I hear it.

It's too late in the day for dawn to be in our eyes, but the light feels harsh.

The Scaleguards and I ride to meet with the battalion of Dragon soldiers, commanded by a veteran soldier named Rosalind Wing. She's got a hundred regulars and three Teeth on loan from the group I left at House Barghest with Teeth Captain Aaron Lightscale. They've been mirroring the kraken's progress up the coast for the last several days, attacking only when the beastly empyreal harries the coastline. Rosalind Wing has a section of skilled archers she deploys when the kraken is out in the water harassing fishing boats.

She's a decade my senior, with a war drake of her own, and dismounts to salute with a snap. I remain on Kitty and acknowledge her with a nod. "What do you have to report?"

Rosalind puts her hands on her hips. She's got dark hair and ruddy suntanned skin. Her uniform is regular soldier green, but she's wearing the copper scale mail of a commanding officer, spilling off her shoulders like wings. "The Kraken fleet is seven ships strong, and two new ones arrived overnight. One now flies a House Gryphon flag. They've stayed back from the rest, but we don't know their capabilities. It remains a Kraken ship, my blade. The kraken itself has vanished under the waves since sometime after midnight, and has yet to reappear. We have a guard set up to keep eye on it resurfacing, and a rotation schedule so most of the soldiers are at the ready. Here we're a few miles from any villages, so there shouldn't be rogue fishing vessels, and the bay below us has no infrastructure. If we engage, it's as good a place as we can hope for."

"Let's keep your current arrangement," I say. "I'll join the lookout up on the overhang." I nod my chin at the tall hook of the nearest cliff. The sea has cut beneath it, turning the overhang into a dramatic-looking claw of land.

"Yes, my blade," Rosalind says. She glances out toward the narrow bay. "And your orders for the beast itself?"

"Harry, harass, drive it back for now." I narrow my eyes, following her gaze to the water. "Better not to murder any empyreals at the moment. But if it's between you and your soldiers' lives, pick Dragons."

"My blade!" she snaps, and the soldiers arrayed behind her repeat it.

The title echoes up to the bright blue sky.

With their voices ringing behind me, I turn Kitty toward the ocean.

Staring out, I can't help but think of the western coast, the bay of Lastrium where I and my Teeth fought to defend the city and its stores of fossilized venom from the Kraken navy. They attacked thinking they could retake their captured leader, Leonetti Seabreak. Darling's adoptive father, whom my aunt murdered. That fight is where I met Darling, the eyeless girl my brother painted madly for years and years. The girl I fell so quickly, so strongly in love with.

I don't let myself close my eyes and seek her with my boon. Not now.

Instead, I turn my attention to the sea, to the enemy navy, to what I will do today.

Rosalind leads me to her command tent, and inside I sit at her low desk to write a brief message. *Kraken captain, in honor of the return of our empyreals, meet me on shore for a meal of peace. House Dragon will not fight you today. Invite your Gryphon representative with you. Talon Goldhoard.*

I stamp it with an official Dragon crest, and roll it tightly enough to fit into one of the gilded messenger tubes the sparrow drakes are trained to carry and deliver.

Rosalind holds back the flap of the tent for me to emerge once again. I offer the tube to Pol Scaleguard. "Send that to the Kraken ship flying the Gryphon flag. Let's go to the overhang."

I lead the Teeth and Rosalind with a handful of her soldiers up the grassy incline to the edge of the cliff. From there, Pol instructs one of the sparrow drakes on its mission—they're intelligent, and the ones we use for messages know basic commands and a few signal words.

From here, the ships loom along the deepwater line, five of them and the one hanging back with the Gryphon flag. I can't see people from this distance. If I knew who was onboard, I might use my boon to see more clearly.

Just as Pol looses the sparrow drake, the huge kraken empyreal bursts from the ocean below us.

The crash of waves startles me, but I lean forward. Its reddish tentacles reach and curl, splashing sea-foam and spray in all directions.

Several Dragons behind me exclaim. Its long head shines with water, and it turns, seeming to crawl along the surface of the ocean toward the Kraken ship with the Gryphon flag.

The ship slowly shifts, its sails billowing, and heads inland.

Coming to meet the kraken.

"Archers," calls Rosalind. I hear the creak of bowstrings behind me.

The other Kraken ships move, too, falling into place around the kraken like an honor guard.

Something flashes on the Gryphon flagship.

It's closer now; I can see movement of people on the deck.

A sudden instinct, sharp enough I suck in a quiet gasp, hits me. I close my eyes, feet firm on the cliff's edge, and I reach out with my boon for Darling.

Instantly I see her: at the rail of a ship, yelling something to the sea. Spray splatters across her dark brown face, and she rubs at her bulbous goggles to clear her vision.

"Darling," I say softly.

Her head jerks around, as she looks in a new direction. Toward me.

As if she heard me.

"Fire!" Rosalind yells.

The twang of bowstrings tugs me back to myself. I frown at Rosalind, but she's staring at the kraken.

It's attacking the ship.

Its huge arms shoot out, one of them coiling around the spar at the prow of the ship.

Our arrows arc high, and a few of them land against the kraken's shell, but it doesn't even flinch or seem to notice. I stare hard. Darling is on that ship.

Rosalind commands another volley.

They loose the arrows. A crack like thunder sounds as the spar breaks off the ship, and just then there's a bright explosion on the deck.

My lips part. I know what that is. I've seen it before.

A bird of brilliant golden and red feathers, sparking with real fire, leaps off the ship.

Arrows rain down at it.

"Stop firing," I command.

"My blade," says Rosalind.

My attention is riveted to the phoenix. Darling.

It dives for the kraken. One coiling arm reaches for it, but the phoenix dodges. She is brighter than the sun.

I can't breathe.

Then the phoenix drops right onto the kraken's head.

Fire spreads, almost like the water itself is ablaze.

Then the kraken . . . disappears.

The phoenix skims along the water, circling. She bends her neck and lets out a scream of triumph.

"My blade?" asks Rosalind.

"Leave it. The kraken is subdued."

The other ships of the Kraken navy pull nearer to the spiraling phoenix. Something is in the water beneath Darling. A person. Swimming.

A cannon booms.

One of the Kraken ships is firing on us. It slams into the cliff a long way away: a warning, not an attack.

"Retreat," I say, backing off.

We withdraw from the cliffs. But this is Dragon territory, and we won't go far. The land is ours to protect.

I don't know if that kraken disappeared because it chose to, or if Darling did something. I want to talk to her. I continue watching from farther ashore, eyes stuck on the brilliant glow of the phoenix. Sparks trail from her long tail feathers and scatter from her wings.

She soars, and I know she can see me. I wait, chin lifted. I want her to come. To land beside me. Just looking at her makes me feel cold. I need that fire or I'll freeze.

But Darling does not come. She circles again, then flies out to sea, with the Kraken navy following in tight formation behind.

10

DARLING

When I return to myself, I stand on the deck of Adelaide's ship, my sisters hugging one another and crying. Vivian holds goggles and a robe for me, and I shrug into the robe before pulling on the goggles. I watch Adelaide and Miranda but don't approach them, not yet. I want to give them space. It's been months since we've seen each other, and the stares of the sailors pretending to be busy around the deck are not evoking a feeling of confidence.

"It's a strange transition," Vivian says, holding out a sandwich once I've slipped into the robe.

"Yes," I say, because it's hard to explain what it's like to be me and then someone else.

I hadn't wanted to turn into the phoenix. My plan had been to just get close to the kraken and sort of talk it into changing. But once I saw it thrashing in the water, I could tell that I needed to be other to do the job at hand.

The phoenix had hesitated, as though wanting to make sure I wanted the change. Perhaps all my muttering got through to the creature, because the transition was slower this time, so that I could sense myself changing. I'm still not entirely certain what I did while the firebird, but at least I was myself, unlike before.

And I understand a bit of Vivian's awe over being the gryphon now. It was exhilarating and terrifying giving myself over to the change. Losing control isn't something I enjoy, but there is something in becoming the phoenix that feels right. I find I want to soar again, even though I am tired and hungry.

I take a bite of the sandwich, and chew as I consider my feelings. Vivian places a warm hand on my arm. "Once you've recovered, we should talk. All of us."

I nod as Vivian moves off. I finish my sandwich, and then I make my way over to where Adelaide leans heavily on Miranda, as a sailor I don't recognize relates the story of how the kraken destroyed much of the coast.

"And then you smashed the Barghest ships like they were little more than kindling! It was awesome," he says, his words raising a chorus of agreements and a few laughs from the rest of the deckhands gathering around.

"Adelaide," I say in a low voice once there's a moment of quiet. The sailors see me and for the most part they scatter, but a sun-baked girl with blond-streaked braids hangs back.

"I heard you were helping people get their boons," she says.

I nod, and she swallows, her expression nervous. "Do you see anything in me?"

"Chels, not now," Adelaide whispers, and I hold up my hand.

"Not everyone has a boon," I say. "I think . . . I think Chaos is still getting itself sorted out. But you . . ." I can sense the same soap bubble in her middle, same as so many others, and it's a small matter to motion toward it, freeing the magic. The more I do it, the better I'm getting at correcting the imbalance, and I wonder if it would be possible to fly over an area and release more boons instead of having to meet with people one at a time. The hand-waving is already better than grabbing strangers, most of whom are terrified already, so I make a note to ask Vivian if there's anything in the House Gryphon archives about the phoenix releasing boons. I doubt it, but it would be nice to be able to help more people quicker.

Chels grabs her middle and gasps. "Oh," she says, "oh."

She sort of stumbles away, overcome with emotion and wonder, and Adelaide turns a lopsided smile on me. "So what, now you're just walking around performing miracles?"

I sigh, too tired to laugh at the joke. "I've always been a miracle worker. Remember that time I convinced you to dance with Lyle Breakwater?"

"Ugh, don't remind me. I can still feel each and every ill-timed kick," she says with a sad smile. It fades and she watches me while I return the regard. "Are you good?" she whispers. "Are *we* good?"

I blink away sudden tears and nod, and Adelaide throws herself into my arms. Something in me flares at the contact, a feeling that belongs more to the phoenix than me, and I hug her back before stepping backward. "I think . . . the phoenix isn't exactly comfortable with such close contact. I get the sense it has history with the kraken? And not a good one?"

Adelaide steps back as well, a frown twisting her tan brow. She pushes her dark hair, still damp, back and places her hands on her hips. "Yeah. I . . . When I was in the ocean, I could hear it call to me. But there were other thoughts as well. Memories of people I didn't know, feelings about places that weren't mine."

"There is a treatise that states that the empyreals persist even when their regents perish, and I think they carry much knowledge with them," Vivian says, coming over. "I'm sorry to interrupt the family reunion, but there is much to be done, and it's clear that we aren't the only ones trying to find the remaining regents. Is there somewhere we can talk?" Vivian asks, and Miranda steps forward.

"The captain's quarters. Why don't I stay here and oversee the repairs to the spar while you all do political things?" Miranda says, humor twisting her lips.

Adelaide reaches out to give her one last squeeze, and as I walk past, Miranda pulls me to the side. Vivian turns but I wave her on.

"What's wrong?" I ask.

"Chels isn't the only sailor who's been asking if you can help them. Do you think . . . I don't want to intrude, my flame."

I jerk at Miranda's using the formal address, and anguish is sharp in my middle. "Don't call me that."

She releases me and takes a bit of a step back. "I didn't know. One of the sailors spoke to Vivian and—"

"Miranda. You're my *sister*," I say, voice low. "Nothing will change that. Not even Chaos. I don't care what the lore says. I'm still me. I would be happy to help whoever feels like they'd like to try. Like I told Chels, Chaos is still not what it used to be, but it grows stronger every day."

"You say that like you can talk to it," Miranda says, and I shrug.

"I think I can. Call it forth, at least. I'm not sure. Honestly, this is all so new and . . . it doesn't matter. I will help any who want it. And maybe even those who don't," I say, realizing the truth of the words as soon as I say them. "I'm sorry I didn't ask before freeing the remainder of your boon."

Miranda smiles sadly. "It's fine. I think I was just taken aback by the strength of it. It's actually a good thing."

I want to ask Miranda how her boon has changed, but I get

the feeling that there is something else unsaid between us. Vivian is also right. We have much to do, and so I am left with pulling Miranda into a quick hug before jogging to catch up with Adelaide and Vivian.

When I enter the captain's quarters, Adelaide has already claimed the captain's chair, and I smirk at the way she and Vivian stare each other down. The tension in the air is nearly palpable, and I sink into the remaining chair with a sigh.

"Adelaide, Vivian. Vivian, Adelaide," I say, making introductions. They both look at me in surprise. "Great, now we all know each other and we can stop with the posturing."

"House Gryphon's spies were responsible for revealing the location of my father's safe house the night he was taken," Adelaide says.

Vivian nods. "We were. And House Kraken has destroyed countless rare manuscripts in its time ransacking House Gryphon libraries across Pyrlanum."

"And the war is over," I say, my voice low. "We can fight about who has wronged who, or we can move on and hope there is a Pyrlanum left to rebuild once we've sorted the rest of the empyreals out."

"I'm not doing anything until I know what happened to my father," Adelaide says.

Vivian looks to me, and I can almost hear her thoughts. There is no easy way to share the news, but for the information about Leonetti to come from Vivian might fracture the tenuous peace I'm trying to build.

Before I can answer, Adelaide slams her hand on the table. Lightning crackles around her palm. Looks like that dusty old scholar might have missed a few other abilities as well.

Adelaide doesn't notice the crackling energy, her anger holding sway. "What aren't you telling me?"

I clear my throat. "Leonetti is gone," I say, the pronouncement triggering tears. I lift my goggles and dash them away. "I'm sorry, but he's gone. That's why you're the kraken, and not him."

"Well, technically the regent is chosen by Chaos—" Vivian begins.

"Not the time for a history lesson, Vivian," I snap, and she inclines her head in apology.

"So. The Dragons killed him," Adelaide says, shock making her words little more than a whisper.

"We don't know that," I say, because we don't. "It could have been someone from House Barghest. The castle was in turmoil that last day, and I'm sure that Talon would've tried to keep him safe. He has too much honor to slaughter a man in chains."

"I'm going to ignore that you're on a first-name basis with the War Prince," Adelaide says. "But we should know something. Someone has to know something."

"We have to talk to Talon. He'll know. Not because he's the War Prince," I say, meeting Adelaide's sneer at my familiarity with him. What would she say if she knew we were briefly engaged? That is not a conversation I am ready to have with her. "But because he's one of the few people who witnessed the events inside the castle. If anyone can pinpoint how Leonetti died, it'll be him."

"Talon Goldhoard has sent missives insisting he wants a peaceful meeting, but that can't be the priority right now," Vivian says. "I am very sorry to hear about Leonetti, but by my count there are two other regents in play, the dragon and the sphinx, and we need to find them and release them from their form before Talon captures them."

"He'll go for his brother first," I say. "So we should head south."

"What makes you think I'll help you?" Adelaide says. Vivian shakes her head in disbelief, and I gape at her.

"Why wouldn't you?" I ask, and she shrugs.

"I'm not sure where your loyalties lie right now."

The statement cuts me to the quick. It's exactly what I feared, and when Vivian makes to argue I hold my hand up to halt her words.

"Vivian. Can you give us some privacy?" I ask, and she inclines her head respectfully before standing and leaving the room. When the door closes, Adelaide springs to her feet, rounding on me.

"Why didn't you kill them like Gavin asked?" Adelaide says, getting right to the heart of the matter. She's never been one to mince words or bide her time. And as much as I love her, I also won't lie to her. I want her assistance finding the sphinx, but I don't think I need it.

"Because it was a stupid idea that would've gotten me killed."

"No one would've traced it back to you—" she begins, and my snort of laughter cuts her off.

"You cannot be serious. A member of House Kraken kisses the Prince Regent and he drops dead—of course it had nothing to do with her! It's just an unhappy coincidence. Is that really how you and Gavin saw that going?"

My emotions simmer too near the surface, and I shoot to my feet. Adelaide watches me with her arms crossed, her expression stormy, but she says nothing, just glares at me.

I've been waiting to talk to her for months, and I'm not done with what I have to say. "You asked me to do the impossible when I had no options, no help. Gavin and I could have walked out of there at any moment with his boon, but you wanted me in the Dragons' nest because . . . what? You thought you were finally going to show Leonetti you were the *best* of us? The most ruthless of his Barbs?"

Adelaide winces almost imperceptibly and some of my anger dissipates. "So that's what it was about, huh? Your insecurity."

Adelaide stands. "You don't understand—"

"No, I don't." I slip my fingers under the straps of my goggles and rub my temples. "You're my sister, Adelaide. And you put your own goals above my life. How am I supposed to feel about that? And the irony is that it didn't matter in the end, because no one can deny you're the best of House Kraken now, not with the empyreal within you. None of this had anything to do with me, and now Gavin is dead and Leonetti as well, and you want to make that my fault?"

I shake my head, a feeling of defeat coming over me. I worked so hard to win a peace that would work for everyone, and now it's gone.

Flames lick up my arms, intermittent flickers, and I realize that if I stay in the captain's quarters with Adelaide any longer, I will explode. And there is nothing more dangerous on a ship than a fire.

"You are free to make your own decisions. Help me or not. But when I saw Leonetti across that room at House Barghest, he was proud of me. Would he have felt the same about using poison to effect an assassination?"

I spin on my heel and slam out of the captain's quarters. Miranda sees me first, hurrying over as I stride across the deck, taking deep breaths. Vivian is nowhere to be found, but then I glance up. She's become the gryphon again, and she circles high above the ships.

"Darling, is everything okay?" Miranda asks.

"Adelaide is throwing a tantrum, but why is the gryphon circling?"

"She sensed some kind of threat. Not sure what. We've already left Dragon territory and we're almost past the part of the coast that Barghest controls. It won't be long until we reach the Teeth Islands, and we'll most likely pull in there to resupply. It's been a hard few weeks."

I nod. The Teeth Islands aren't far from Nakumba, a few dozen leagues across open sea, and Vivian and I could definitely cover that distance on our own. "I don't think Adelaide is inclined to help me," I tell Miranda. "Which is fine. Why don't you have any of the sailors who want to try unlocking their boon come see me, and then Vivian and I will take our leave when we hit the Teeth?"

Miranda frowns, the expression marring her pale skin. "Maybe I should talk to Adelaide."

"No. She's already in a mood, and you'll just draw her ire." Leonetti was the only person who could ever dampen Adelaide's temper, and he's gone. Remembering that causes my heart to seize all over again.

How am I supposed to do all this—be the phoenix, help heal a country always at war with itself—with my father gone?

Did I tell him I loved him? Did I ever tell him how he saved my life, how I respected him more than anyone else in the world? I don't know that I did, and now he has gone, returned to Chaos as we used to say, and the chance is lost.

He will never again tug playfully on my goggles or laugh at one of Adelaide's terrible jokes. When Gavin died, my grief was tempered by anger at his utter foolishness. But with Leonetti, all I feel is an ever-widening maw of despair, waiting to swallow me whole.

I shake my head, refusing to give in to the sadness that threatens to overwhelm me. There will be time for grieving once things have calmed down. For now, I have to find the remaining empyreals and bring peace to Pyrlanum. Maybe then Adelaide will see that there are things worth fighting for.

"Why don't you go grab those sailors and I'll get to work unlocking boons?" I say. Miranda nods and strides off, and my gaze is drawn once more to the gryphon soaring high above us.

Peace is still worth fighting for. And nothing else, not Talon's betrayal or Adelaide's anger or even my grief, will matter until the House Wars are finished once and for all.

11

TALON

I want Caspian back.

I need him to explain things to me, because even though it would be easy to blame everything that's happened on dead regents from a hundred years ago, on Aurora or Darling, I know it's my brother's fault. He planned this for years, with a prophecy boon that gave him the gift to paint Darling. Over and over again he painted her, drew her. He didn't see the future, he saw *her* future. Maybe it was fate that the Dragon scion would receive such a boon from Chaos. The Last Phoenix was murdered by my great-grandmother, then the Dragon regent, so the phoenix was tied to our bloodline. Caspian, the current Dragon regent, resurrected the power within Darling.

When we reach the crossroads half a day from Dragon Castle, I order Pol and Maise to continue and make my report to Finn.

"Where are you going, my blade?" Maise asks.

I look north, to the distant, misty peaks of the mountains. "To speak with the Dragon regent."

Neither one of them protests, though more questions settle behind both their eyes. I reach my left hand toward the sparrow drake perch hooked into the loop on Pol's saddle. "Sparrow, here," I command the sparrow drake on the highest branch.

The sparrow drake chirps and launches itself off the tree. It spreads its reddish wings to glide onto my bracer. I nod and bring my arm down, nudging until it hops off and takes up a perch on the curved horn of my saddle. It grips with its tiny claws, curling its tail down and around one of the rein loops. This one is deep red with burnished copper edging its crest scales and tiny horns.

Kitty ruffles her head feathers, and twists her neck to glare at the sparrow drake with one big emerald-green eye.

To the Scaleguards, I say, "I'll send this one with news if I need to. Otherwise, tell Finn I expect to be back at the castle in a week, if not sooner."

"Chaos bless your mission, my blade," Pol says. His cousin nods sharply in agreement.

"Protect the hoard," I answer, using the first part of the Dragon motto.

I guide Kitty along the northern road. This stretch links the broader main route to the eastern road leading from the coast to Goldvein, our capital city in the heart of the territory. I'll follow it to near Goldvein, then camp and use my boon to seek Caspian's exact location. Hopefully he's not moving around too much.

Alone, Kitty and I move with an ease of long partnership. I let her have her head, and shift easily with her loping gait. At first the road leads us through close, tall pines, twisting down along a foothill to a small river valley. From there we travel alongside huge boulders, with a shallow drop into the rushing river. I have always loved this part of my work: the cross-country trips. Moving with a whole army is cumbersome—though not as bad as escorting Caspian's and Darling's royal carriages on their tour. But since I became commander of the Dragon's Teeth, even though I officially handed the command title to Finn, I've had more opportunities to travel with only a handful of equally fast and ruthless soldiers and war drakes.

Alone with the wind in my face, Kitty's long legs eating up

distance, and my boon relaxed to note any coming danger, my thoughts quiet. I feel expansive. Unhindered.

The only other time I've felt anything like this was when Darling kissed me.

Brooding over the loss of a lover and maybe-friend is not how I want to spend my precious time, though.

The little sparrow drake clings to Kitty's saddle, and when Kitty climbs us out of the river valley to a section of road that stretches straight across a low rolling hill, I signal her to run.

Kitty bounces once, and that's all the warning I get. I lean down, low to her sinewy scaled neck, and curl one hand protectively around the sparrow drake.

I keep my eyes open, squinting into the wind, and let myself grin.

We pound across the hill, toward the dark edge of the forest again, and suddenly jutting cliffs.

Kitty skids to a breathless stop—breathless on my part, at least. Kitty opens her jaw and huffs out a long hiss of pleasure. Her green and black feathers flick in quick, delighted gestures. I sit up and release the sparrow drake; it scrambles into my lap and clings, cheeping its displeasure.

"I don't think you could keep up, if I let you fly," I tell it, rubbing its head crest. "Let's go, Kitty. We'll cross the main trade road ahead, then stop for a snack."

Kitty trots on, and in less than an hour I slide off into the lee of a huge black boulder. I remove the saddle, hanging it over a fallen pine branch, and rub Kitty down, then loose her to hunt something while I feed the sparrow drake an egg.

It feasts, then makes itself a nest of dry pine needles. It's asleep almost immediately.

I should give it a name.

I have a snack myself, then sit against the boulder to open my boon.

Eyes closed, I take a deep breath, and press the Chaos inside me just enough to track my brother.

Caspian.

I find him.

He slams into the flailing body of a small herd drake. In the next instant his wings pump hard and he takes off, the drake clutched tight in one rear claw. Its blood falls in rivulets to the grassy earth, leaving a trail until Caspian is too high and the blood just dissipates.

Caspian flies to an outcropping of stone jutting from a nearby mountain. He drops the very dead drake and turns to land, facing the rest of the world as he tears through the drake's scales and plate armor to the sweet, hot meat below.

It's his feelings, not mine. My stomach twists and I focus to hold on to the vision. I need to locate him.

As soon as I think it, I know where he is. Or rather, I feel how distant he is from me, as if there's a tether connecting us.

Northwest, only a few hours as the dragon flies.

It takes me another day and two nights to reach my brother.

The way grows steeper and more fraught, but nothing Kitty can't handle. For the most part the roads are in good order, but when we get high enough into the mountains, where there's no need for anything that can support wheels, we reach a few places where Kitty is climbing. She loves it; I can tell by the eager ruffling of her feathers and how she sometimes clacks her fore claws together like pleased applause.

We're high enough the air thins, and both dawn and dusk arrive quickly and last a long while. Peaks surround us, and I'm very glad I know exactly where to look. Caspian has ranged along this stretch of triple mountains the whole time, returning every few hours to a specific bowl lake embraced by rangy short trees and wildflowers. It's where he's sleeping, and I've seen the shadow of a cave beyond the crystal blue water.

Kitty suddenly throws her head back and stops. Her head cocks as she listens. The sparrow drake falls still, too, having learned to understand Kitty's behavior. Mine, too. All I hear is the distant soughing of wind through the trees below us. We're above the growth line, surrounded by rough stone and thin dirt, scrubby grass and surprisingly beautiful violet and white flowers. I think the lake is on the other side of the ridge ahead.

I quietly say, "It's all right, Kitty." I dismount and unhook the loose bridle we use for control. "Stay near."

She lowers her face so I can scratch her eye ridge the way she likes.

The sparrow drake follows me as I take off myself. There's no path here, and I'm careful with my footing. I don't have any mountain gear, but I shouldn't need it. I've seen in my boon visions there's a way into the lake. I have to use my hands a bit, to pull myself up and over the ridge, but then the bowl lake spreads below me, water glittering with the afternoon sunlight.

And there he is.

Caspian lounges by the lakeside, sunning himself. His dark green wings are stretched fully out, the membrane between each long bone thinning to a spring green, with darker veins like tree branches. His scales are green so dark they might be black in places, and there are a few edged in silver in a pattern that reminds me most of goldfish. Horns curl from his head, near his temples, and smaller horns grow down his snout to a wicked-looking hooked mouth with teeth that show despite his jaw being closed. His tail is longer than his body and neck, thick and spiked, too, with a forked end point. His claws are black and even from this distance look sharp.

I slowly make my way down the ridge.

The sparrow drake sees the great dragon and stops flying so abruptly it drops a foot in the air before snapping its little red wings out and veering around to flap back over the ridge. I hope it's returning to Kitty.

I try to be quiet, as Caspian is clearly asleep and I don't want him to fly away before I can speak with him. I have no idea if he'll even understand me. But Darvey seemed to, some of the time.

I can't know if Caspian is sleeping so deeply that he doesn't notice me, or he's so confident of his draconic invulnerability that the little rock slides my boots cause and the scuff of my steps don't penetrate his doze. I get to the lake itself, and casually strip off my gloves to wash my hands in the ice-cold water. Thank Chaos it's summertime, so this is just the chill of a great height, and the only snow streaks the peaks, where it never melts. If it were closer to winter in either direction, this whole valley might be covered in snow too deep for me to wade through.

I pick around the bank. Wind gusts and the water laps at the tiny pebbles of the narrow beach.

My brother sleeps on a wide flat rock, scoured clear of grass by wind or maybe Caspian himself. The moment I set foot on it, Caspian's eye snaps open.

He doesn't move otherwise. That one huge eye tracks me slowly. It's black, except for a sheen of Chaos purple and green flecks. And that eye is as large as my entire head.

I stop. "Caspian," I say, calmly. Not calling for him, but as normal as I can make it. "It's Talon, your brother. Do you know me?"

The dragon pulls his wings in with excruciating slowness, letting the claws at the knuckles and tips drag against the stone; they grate and cause tiny white sparks to fly. I settle my hands behind my back, wrapped together in a soldier's resting pose, and wait. And wait.

When Caspian's wings are folded, he sits up in a fluid motion that disorients me.

He's just so big.

His head is longer than my body is tall, his claws the length of my legs at least. And now he arcs his wings up over his head, and they do not blot out the sun: they block the entire sky.

My lips part but I can't speak for a moment.

A dragon.

A real, living, great, intelligent dragon.

It hardly matters he is—was?—my brother. This is the Dragon regent, an empyreal of legend.

I sink to my knees and put my fists over my heart. "Regent," I say this time.

Caspian relaxes his wings, tucking them back much more casually, and tilts his head down to look at me with both eyes at once. The way they're positioned, to either side of a crest and his snout horns, means he has to consider angles if he wants them both trained in one place. He opens his mouth and touches his sinuous black tongue to one of his fangs. Then he makes a rumbling sound that reverberates up his chest.

It sounds like a deeper version of Kitty's purr.

I sit back on my heels and smile. "Caspian."

The purr strengthens. Caspian shifts onto one rear hip and folds his forelegs together, linking the claws like they were hands. It's a curious pose I've seen him take before, reclined on a settee, waiting for me to get on with it.

I laugh once. I am *so* glad, it's making me giddy.

"Come back to Dragon Castle with me," I say.

Caspian stops purring.

"Caspian, you're the Dragon regent. The first dragon empyreal in a hundred years! We need you."

The dragon looks away in obvious displeasure.

"I need you," I say. "Can you turn back?"

He doesn't respond.

"I have the barghest empyreal, and I've retained control of Dragon and Barghest territory, and Phoenix Crest, of course, but the future is uncertain. I saw Darling—"

Caspian's head snaps around and he leans down to stare at me with one eye, barely an arm's length away. My spine goes rigid, but I don't back away.

"I saw her," I say more quietly. "She was herself, and then she burst into flame again, and I watched her fly. She has the kraken empyreal. I need you."

Caspian snorts. He lifts his head away, removing his intense stare. He looks up at the bright blue sky. Only wispy clouds mar the sapphire dome.

"House Dragon needs you," I add. I get to my feet. "Please."

Then the great dragon actually rolls his eyes at me. He gets to his feet, too.

I crane my neck to keep looking at his Chaos-black eye. "Caspian, you can't just abandon us! I know you struggled for a long time to bring this about, but your work isn't over, it can't be!"

Caspian flares out his wings.

"Caspian."

Suddenly he lowers his head again, and pushes at my chest with this curved beak of his upper jaw. I stumble, but he purrs again. Affectionately.

I reach out, to touch the warm green armor of his face, but Caspian rears back.

"Caspian!" I call.

He ignores me, and with a single great pump of his wings, leaps into the air.

Wind and dust blast me back. I nearly step into the lake before I regain my balance.

The sound of his wings is like thunder as he climbs high and higher.

"Caspian!" I yell again, with all my might.

He soars up, banks north, and the sun gleams against the long curve of his tail as he disappears over the peaks.

I yell his name until my voice gives out.

12

DARLING

I spend the rest of the afternoon and most of the evening helping to unlock boons and avoiding Adelaide. At one point I find her watching me across the deck, and I'm half hoping she'll throw a knife at my head when I'm not looking, a return to her usual self. But there's no blade forthcoming, just sharp glances and even sharper answers whenever anyone tries to talk to her. So I go back to my work, finding the little wells of Chaos within each soldier and calling them forth when possible.

There are, of course, people who have the wells but pulling them forth would be dangerous for them, like picking an unripe fruit before its time. If it weren't for the infection or whatever it is that interferes with boons, they would come forth on their own. And perhaps one day they can. To those people I simply say to come and see me in a couple of days, giving both of us time to find a way forward. It's strange to know things and not understand how. It isn't logic or experience, but just a deep-seated sense of truth, and I wonder what other things will spring forth wholesale in my mind. I know this is the phoenix's knowledge, and while I'm glad to have it, the disconnect is still a bit jarring.

It's weird not to know myself. I am me but I am also something else, and I still don't know how I feel about that.

It doesn't seem to be bothering Vivian, though. Or Adelaide. A little before dusk, she walks out onto the prow of the ship, strips naked, and dives into the sea, transforming as she goes. I don't watch for her to come back; I can sense that she's hunting a school of fish that passes by. I can also sense when Vivian is tired and ready to turn in for the evening, but there's no such knowledge for the sphinx, barghest, cockatrice, or dragon. I wonder if I'm limited by distance or if the connection is because I restored Vivian and Adelaide to themselves. I'm not sure it matters. Chaos seems to have its own plan, and I have the feeling that it doesn't matter what I do, I am a cork trapped in a current, cursed to follow the stream wherever it leads.

Miranda gave Vivian and me a crew room to share, the hammocks clean if a little musty. But neither Vivian nor I are comfortable in such close quarters, most likely the empyreals making their thoughts known. I'm much happier sleeping on the deck, as is Vivian, so we find a small space behind a few coils of rope and claim it for our own, using the furs and clothing from Vivian's trunk to make ourselves as comfortable as possible. It isn't glamorous, but at least it doesn't stink of salt eel like the hold.

"Do you want to talk about it?" Vivian asks once we've settled in for the night. Miranda decides to anchor and give everyone a break when Adelaide doesn't return as the sun sets. The sound of singing comes from one of the other ships, the sailors clearly enjoying some strong drink, but our ship is as quiet as a tomb. I have a feeling that my presence has put a damper on any possible festivities.

"There isn't anything to talk about. Adelaide asked me to assassinate Talon and Caspian in a cowardly way, and I didn't. So now she blames me for Leonetti's death. But I still can't believe Talon would kill a prisoner." I stare up at the stars, and they remind me too much of the last night Talon and I spent together, in the shadow of the everbloom bower. I roll onto my side and then back onto my back, suddenly uncomfortable. "I have to talk to him, find out the truth of that day. I know it was Aurora's treachery that led to the entire day going sideways, but I'm not sure what she thought to gain. Talon wouldn't want to be the High Prince Regent. He would do what he had to, but he would hate every moment of it."

"Aurora has never cared for Caspian, and vice versa," Vivian says. "It seems pretty clear that she was trying to depose Caspian in favor of Talon, who has always been biddable when it comes to his aunt. Perhaps too much so. She was eager to step in and raise him after his mother died."

"Do you think she killed Talon's mother?" I ask. There is a tone in Vivian's voice—a subtle disdain for Aurora that I cannot help but share—that makes me think she does, and when she sighs heavily, my suspicions are confirmed.

"We've always suspected it was her or one of her handmaidens, but there was never any proof, and by that point the old Dragon was mad with grief, threatening violence to any who opposed his slightest whim. We figured it was best to keep our own counsel. But now, I wonder what would have happened if we'd been more honest."

I wonder as well, and the morose topic of conversation sends me into a funk that keeps me awake too long. I want to talk to Talon, to ask him how he could choose such an odious woman over me. His betrayal at House Barghest still stings, and when I think too long on it, flames dance across my skin.

So I close my eyes and listen to the drunken singing on the next ship over, and finally fall into an uneasy sleep.

The trip to the Teeth Islands should take about a week and

a half, but with Adelaide's abilities we make it in five days, even though we anchor every night. And I feel every single minute of those five days. By the time we sail into port, I am eager to escape the ship. Adelaide still isn't speaking to me, and Miranda looks pained whenever she sees me and Vivian. What I'd thought would be a happy homecoming has become something fraught and disappointing. I was House Kraken for so long, but now I am something else. What, I'm not quite sure. As far as I know the phoenix holds no house.

I'm not sure which I am sorrier to lose: my sisters, or the house that welcomed me and made me who I am. Especially since I am forced to grieve Leonetti all by myself, giving myself over to tears in fits and spurts when the grief becomes too heavy.

Even Vivian finds the atmosphere on the ship unbearable, and she has taken to spending more and more time in her empyreal form. Miranda watches Vivian explode into the gryphon, the sailors tightening ropes every time Vivian shifts, her transformation not well suited to a ship.

"Is that normal?" Miranda asks after a couple of days of both Adelaide and Vivian changing and spending most of the day in their empyreal forms.

"Who knows?" I say with a harsh laugh. "It's all new to me."

"But you don't change," Miranda says, looking worried.

"I am always the phoenix, no matter how I appear," I say, the words not quite my own, but true all the same. At some point I'd considered the phoenix other, a separate entity within me. But over the past few days, unlocking boons and sensing the little bit of Chaos that is the spark of life within every living thing, I've started to sense the will of Chaos, and it feels a lot like what I want as well. Strange, but not awful. I'm guessing Vivian and Adelaide are experiencing the same merging of consciousnesses. We should be documenting this for future generations, and I make a mental note to talk to Vivian about assigning a scholar to conduct interviews with each of the empyreals once things are something like normal.

Assuming that even exists.

The Teeth Islands are beautiful: white sandy beaches, clear blue water, a temperate climate that is warm without being too humid. A gentle breeze chases away any insects that might decide to harass us, and the dock master is only too happy to let the House Kraken ships into port. This is their territory, after all.

Making landfall cheers the sailors as well, and when Chels comes up to me and presses a small carving into my hand, I am as surprised as I am delighted.

"This is for you, my flame," she says. Most of the crew have taken to using the honorific, even the few sailors I know from my time in the house. It's just another part of the tension on board the ship that I'm eager to escape. I miss just being one of the Barbs, a soldier and not a myth.

I turn the carving over and it's beautiful. It's a piece of driftwood, rendered into an incredibly complex phoenix. I can almost see the flames flickering off the edges of the wings, and I want to ask Chels if this is what I look like when I transform. But I don't, because I know it is.

"Chels! This is beautiful."

"My boon," she begins, before clearing her throat and dashing away sudden tears from her eyes. "You unlocked it, and now . . . I don't think I'll be a sailor much longer."

I nod in agreement. Artistry like this belongs in Cockatrice. Once upon a time people moved houses based on their gifts, but that flexibility is one of the many things we lost with the phoenix.

I hope we can get it back.

Someone calls Chels and she sketches an awkward bow before running off back toward where a group of younger sailors are disembarking, skipping and laughing down the gangplank. I wish I could join them on whatever mischief they're about to get into.

I suddenly feel a thousand years old, and I swallow a sigh and go to find Vivian.

She is sitting on her trunk, eyeing the basket we used to travel from House Gryphon to the ships. "Do you think we'll need it?"

"I don't think so, but shifting into our empyreal forms does provide the singular difficulty of trying to find something to wear on landing." A headache has started behind my eyes, and I take off my goggles to get some relief, rubbing my temples while my eyes are squeezed shut.

"Yes, that is what I was thinking. Maybe we should think about hiring a boat instead. Are you okay?"

"Yes, I just . . ." I blink, and suddenly I am running down the gangplank after Chels and the other sailors, sunshine burning my eyes, my goggles dropped somewhere on the deck behind me. The younger sailors see me and startle, standing to the side so I can get past them. I don't know where I'm going; my eyes are watering and I'm basically running blind, but something is pulling me through the busy docks and to the center of town, where the market stalls crowd together and the good-time parlors ply strong drink and delights of the flesh.

I'm past it quickly, my running pace much faster than anything I could accomplish on my own. When I slide to a stop, I stand in front of a school, children playing in the courtyards. Standing in the shade of a frilled palm, I can see a bit, and the children fill me with a sense of happiness. But the school isn't why I'm here.

The Chaos is.

I can feel it, humming just under the surface of the island. Small pools of boons and something bigger, more fundamental, like finding a spring that's been dammed for too long. It's all coming from a strange shrine tucked in the trees. There is something ugly and terrible about the shrine, and I want it gone.

No. The phoenix wants it gone. Wants it *burned to the ground*.

I burst into flame, and then there is only instinct. It's better this way, and I'm not sure if the feeling is mine or the phoenix's, but I agree. I fly high, until the flames on the tips of my wings gutter and try to go out. It's not high enough. I need more height or else I won't have enough speed to punch through.

And then there is nothing.

When I return to myself, my eyes water and I cannot see a thing. I'm naked, of course, but someone has placed a blanket over my shoulders, and I clutch it tight. Someone presses my goggles into my hands. "You dropped them on the ship," they say, a voice I don't recognize. "I followed you. My boon is speed, and the others couldn't keep up with you."

When I slip the smoked lenses into place, a stunned-looking woman wearing Barb blacks stares at me.

"It really is true. The phoenix has returned."

I turn away from her and look around, trying to piece together what took hold of me. I stand next to a glass bowl. A crater, really. The small temple is gone, along with most of the trees surrounding it. All around me, people are shouting and celebrating and crying, but none of them are where I stand. They are all giving me a very wide berth.

"What happened?" I ask the woman, because she seems to be the only person who wants to talk to me.

"You . . . I think you gave the people back their Chaos," she says, frowning. "Just like you did with those of us on the ship. But, bigger."

"Darling! Are you well?"

I turn to see Adelaide and Vivian running up the hill, Miranda far behind them. Adelaide slides to a stop and stares at the crater. Vivian is less stunned, but then again, she's already seen the handiwork of the phoenix.

"What . . . was that?" Adelaide asks.

"It was wrong," I say.

"The temple of the moon," Vivian says. "It was a blood cult from long ago. I didn't think there were any of their altars left." At my raised eyebrow, Vivian gives me a half smile. "I did a bit of research after you decimated that ridge near Furial. That's the only thing we have on any of the maps, and for some reason it was removed by our cartographers a couple of centuries ago. I didn't even know it was there, but the phoenix did."

"It's bad for Chaos," I say. "I don't know what happened. I knew there was something rotten here on the island and I . . . lost myself."

"You flew into the sky," the Barb with the speed boon says. "You were so high, and then there was a sort of an explosion, and then you dived into the old temple, melting it all into . . . this," she says gesturing. "I've never seen anything like it."

"And you're not likely to again," Adelaide says. "Let's get back to the ship and get you some clothes."

I nod, and Vivian wraps an arm across my shoulders and hugs me close as we walk. "I think this is what the literature meant when it said that the phoenix is the heart of Chaos," she says. "It seems to me that releasing the boons and freeing the empyreals is all about fixing Chaos, so to speak. You have to return Pyrlanum to how it was before the Last Phoenix went missing."

"Murdered," I say. "She was murdered." I feel the truth of it, and it's almost like my own memory, but I don't have time to dive into the past. The present demands too much of me.

There is a sudden twinge of awareness, and when I focus on it, I smell hot sand and feel the sting of dry desert winds. "We have to get to Nakumba. The sphinx is close. I can feel . . . her."

"We'll leave as soon as we resupply. We'll take a skeleton crew and one of the smaller frigates," Adelaide says, not looking at me. There's a strange rolling gait in her walk. Not sea legs, but something else. Is the kraken with her the same as the phoenix is with me? It seems like it.

"So you've decided to help me?" I ask, and Adelaide shrugs with just a single shoulder.

"You're the phoenix. I don't think I have much choice."

It isn't a win. But it's as close to Adelaide saying sorry as I've ever heard, and I decide to take it as a sign that she can't stay mad at me forever.

"Well then. On to House Sphinx," I say, just as my stomach

groans, loud enough to be heard over the din of the marketplace we pass through.

"Perhaps lunch and then heroics," Vivian says, and I cannot help but laugh in agreement.

These are strange times. But at least lunch is a constant.

I'll take what I can get.

13

TALON

The first to greet me upon my return to Dragon Castle is the dark red sparrow drake. I sent it ahead of me when I began the climb down Caspian's mountain so that the castelaine and Finn would know to expect me.

Kitty huffs and snaps her teeth at the sparrow drake. She's irritable from exhaustion, and needs a hot spring bath, fresh meat, and her nest to sleep in for a day or so. I pushed her because she seemed as eager as me to return.

The sparrow drake squeaks and lifts higher on a gust of wind. Then it alights upon my left fist, chittering at me.

Darling would give it a grandiose name, I think, because it's so little. Emberwing, or something like that. "Ruby," I say, unable to bear calling it something in Darling's voice.

The sparrow drake tilts its head, maybe preening a bit.

Then Finn is here, hands on his hips, in full Dragon's Teeth regalia. Behind him are Annag Mortooth and her daughter, and the second Dragon in command after Finn, Hendry Fallwing.

They greet me with fists against their hearts, and I'm grateful to hand Kitty over to Hendry for proper and immediate care. Finn passes me the key and knife without any fanfare, and leads me inside. I thank Annag for meeting me, and say I'll take a meal with Finn. Finn asks her to let Elias know where we are. They have a blood magic report for me.

Finn leads me to his room, not mine, through a bustling castle. I suppose the bustle makes sense, for a summer afternoon. Light streams in from thrown-open windows, and the ceilings here are as high as possible to allow for light and air. The castle is built with rooms situated so that hearths pile on hearths and every wing shares a vast system of fireplaces. Most of it is lit by boonlight, however.

We take a route longer than I expected, and when we turn up stairs I've never used, I shoot Finn a questioning look.

"We're avoiding the section of stairs being rebuilt after Fior's boon blew up."

"How is he doing?"

"Well, though he'll have some scarring."

I frown.

"Scars will get him better marriage prospects," Finn assures me. That draws a weary smile from me.

Finn's rooms are below mine, in a curving tower with windows overlooking eastern ridges and a sheer drop that's carved with terraced pleasure gardens and a few medicinal herb gardens. The sun glares through puffy clouds as it heads out to the distant sea.

There's hot soup steaming on the square dining table in his common room, with mulled wine and a little cauldron of drake herb tea. The stringent smell is comforting, because it reminds me of my childhood. My mother made cauldrons of tea like this. I remember suddenly Caspian overturning one into Aurora's lap shortly after Mother died.

I unbelt my falchion and hang it over one of the extra chairs, then pour both of us tea and wine. I hold the teacup close to my face to breathe it in. Finn drinks his right away, watching me. "Eat,

Talon," he says in a rumbling low voice. "Better get that done with before Elias shows up to turn our stomachs."

After I have some tea, I sit in front of one of the soup bowls. It's a rich yellow chicken broth with root vegetables and a few green leaves. When I dip my spoon in, I find soft, fat grains at the bottom. Finn eats, too, after pinching some pepper into his. He's eyeing me, but clearly trying to let me eat before he outright glares.

Fine. I dig in, and let the soup fill me up with warmth and sustenance. Despite the afternoon, and the high summer, the breeze wafting in is cool. Mountains are like that. I longed for afternoons like this when I was serving with the Teeth in the hot southern territories.

All my memories of this place are shadowed with Caspian—overhearing people gossip about him, even before Father restarted the House Wars when Mother was murdered. Caspian was always the strange one. Dreamy, as if he never quite woke up, or teasing inappropriately, or suddenly quiet as a hunting drake. He always sketched, but I don't remember anyone caring until after Mother died. Before then, it was more of a game, something to keep his restless hands occupied while Mother let me weed her garden with her. That was enough for my hands. Pinching encroaching violets out from between the sundrops and miniature peonies. I don't remember Aurora in any of those moments.

I can't eat anymore. My throat closes up. Luckily I'm near enough to the bottom of my bowl that Finn won't say anything.

He does uncover another tray, and ignores the serving tongs to toss me a bun with his hand. I catch it. It's warm, and heavy enough it's got to be filled. Probably my favorite: spiced mushroom and pork.

Before I tear it open, there's a knock and Elias sweeps in. Over the green and black they've found one of Caspian's old embroidered robes. But no—it's my mother's. The spring green silk is crusted with glass beads at the hem, like snowdrops.

"Elias," I say.

"Welcome back, my blade," they answer, gesturing to the empty chair. I nod and they sit.

"Did you find him?" they ask immediately.

I pour them tea. "Yes."

"But he's not here with you."

Obviously. I sip my own lukewarm mulled wine.

Finn gusts out a huge sigh. "Does he even want to come back?"

Elias flattens their hands to the table and doesn't meet my gaze.

I say, "I don't know, but if he does, it would be as a huge dragon. He won't fit in here at all. Not in most of the gardens. Maybe on the great tower's crenellations. Maybe just in the fore yard." I grimace at the idea of the Dragon regent sleeping with the sparrow drakes and blacksmiths, on a pile of hay. It makes me think of all the waste a real dragon must generate, and I squeeze my eyes closed and try to think of something more pleasant.

But only Darling appears in my mind's eye. She'd laugh in surprise at the turn of my thoughts—not offended at the idea of empyreal shit, but that I'm the one worried about it.

Finn gives me a rundown of what messages and intelligence we've received. Elias is convinced Vivian will want to maintain our alliance, for the sake of peace, but not at the expense of the Phoenix Reborn. The Kraken fleet withdrew to unclaimed waters and are heading south. Possibly toward Sphinx territory, or just to loop around the cape back up to their own islands.

I say, "They have the phoenix, gryphon, and kraken. We have the barghest and presumably dragon. Though neither is capable of returning to human shapes." I take a moment to tear open my bun. The innards steam pleasantly. "Any word on Sphinx or Cockatrice regents appearing?"

"Brigh sent word from Nakumba that the sphinx has been seen near the city."

"Good. How is Darvey? Any sign of returning to himself?"

"Much the same. He's been bouncing between Elias and me. Training and hunting with me, meals and napping with Elias in either the library or Elias's workroom."

"And General Bloodscale?"

"He's holding Phoenix Crest with no difficulties at this time."

"He won't like letting go of the fortress. But Phoenix Crest never belonged to House Dragon. We stole it."

"You're just going to hand it over to the Phoenix Reborn." Finn says it like an accusation, not a question.

"Phoenix Reborn," I murmur, ignoring his tone. Darling. It feels so right to me. The title, Darling as the heart of Pyrlanum. She's already so much of mine.

"Yeah," Finn drawled. "Your Darling is making a mess of everything. I knew she would."

"Finn, you wanted her dead."

"Don't be so quick to put that in the past tense," he snapped.

"Finn." I glared.

"She did have poison, Talon. She wasn't on your side, even after you made it clear you were on hers."

"My aunt murdered her father, and further betrayed us. Darling was not wrong to mistrust House Dragon."

"Caspian is not a villain," Elias suddenly interrupts.

I snap my mouth shut hard enough my teeth click. Finn scowls. "We don't think he is," I say.

"Darling trusted him, in the end, and she was right to. He did all this. He awoke the phoenix—we should be thanking him. Celebrating him." Elias raises dark eyes to mine. Their expression is ferocious.

I nod slowly. "All right, Elias. Tell me what you've discovered."

Finn pours more wine. I hold it, but wait to drink.

Elias takes a moment to gather their thoughts before saying, "The books and scrolls in that place are old, mostly ruined. Aurora must have taken the most useful of them to Phoenix Crest, as she said. The book that supposedly 'belongs to the blood' was written by a blood mage at least a hundred years ago—possibly the very mage who helped the regents of House Kraken and House Dragon bind Chaos."

"Bind Chaos?" I say, incredulous. That sounds not only impossible, but horrible.

They pull their lips into a line. "I know how it sounds. There is little detail in that book—it speaks mostly in dramatic metaphor. I believe they found a ritual, or an array—a large, complex design of symbols and letters—that could dampen, or . . . trap Chaos. They murdered the Last Phoenix, and that is where her heart came from, why it was preserved."

Finn taps his wine cup on the table a few times, thoughtful. "The Prince Regent undid their . . . array?"

"I don't think so." Elias frowns. "I think he punched a hole in it—or rather, burned a hole in it. He forcibly returned the phoenix to Pyrlanum, and everything that has happened since is the messy result. Empyreals dragged in the phoenix's wake, but haphazardly; boons awakening here and there, or trying to and failing, or suddenly expanding. One of the reports from Furial is that the phoenix burned an old altar of the moon so hot it became glass. I hypothesize it was one of the places that blood mage must have put an anchor for their spell. There will be more. The array is broken, but remains. At least in pieces."

It's such strange information, I hardly know what to do with it. I know battle and tactics, I know logistics, but not magic. Not history and prophecy. "Did any of what you found give insight into why Darvey remains in his empyreal form?"

"No, though I have some additional ideas for how to adjust the tincture."

Finn frowns mightily, and I start to protest, but Elias lifts their hands. "I will not experiment on that little boy. In any case, I think the best way to revive him—and Caspian—is for the Phoenix Reborn to do it."

Oh. I lean back in my chair. It makes complete sense. If Caspian brought her back, and she's reborn, but the empyreals were dragged with her, as Elias eloquently put it, then of course it must be the phoenix.

Why hasn't she responded to any of my offers to meet? I glance at Elias and wonder if his cousin Vivian could be keeping us apart. And if so, why.

Darling might not want to speak with me, but I know her: she'll do it for the good of Pyrlanum. We're going to have to do this together, eventually.

I'm not such a fool to think she'll *want* anything I have to offer, but I hope I have what she *needs*, at least, when the time comes.

I go see Aurora. Finn insists on going with me, but I wouldn't have protested. I need him to be a proper threat to her. As we head down into the mountain, I wrinkle my nose at the mildew smell, and Finn tries to distract me by inviting me to join him playing fetch with Darvey in the back gardens to relax. I wonder if he should be more respectful since Darvey is not only the regent of House Barghest now, but also a sacred empyreal. But Darvey is only eleven, and besides, I don't have any intention of treating Caspian any differently if I ever get to speak with him again.

The scent of the caves shifts, and I pause, recognizing it immediately: blood.

I dash forward, falchion out.

The guard at the door is dead. Blood sticks his hair to his head, and a smear of it spreads down the rock wall, as if he fell back and slid down as he died.

The door itself is ajar. I kick it back, ready as I can be, but the prison is empty. There's only a mussed bed and a table with nothing on it. Behind me, Finn is roaring commands for guards.

My heart pounds, and I open my boon.

Aurora's trace is easier than ever to find. Not just because my boon is stronger now, but because I know her.

"This way," I say and follow it back the way I came, frustrated I didn't notice it before. A group of soldiers pounds down toward us, and I command, "Lock down this castle. The prisoner has escaped. Pass this order from the first scion: kill Aurora Falleau on sight."

She's too dangerous to talk down.

I don't know if one of my soldiers or an old resident of Dragon Castle betrayed me again, or if she used some blood magic for the opportunity to influence her guards. Either way, she has to die.

The soldiers run off first, sounding the alarm. "Go find Darvey," I tell Finn. He hesitates, knowing his place is with me, but I see him remember the dream he related to me: Aurora going after Darvey's heart. He nods sharply and runs.

I focus on Aurora's trace. I half expect her to turn for the underground lake, for the old cracked altar. But she goes up.

Dragon Castle bursts into loud activity as soldiers snap into duty and start kicking down doors, scouring the place.

I keep quiet and focus on the trace. A few soldiers join me, weapons ready and quietly going along at my flanks. The trace is strong, easy to see. I barely feel like I'm taxing my boon as it leads toward the rear of the castle, up to one of the cliff rooms, and out into a garden.

The rear garden, where Finn said Darvey likes to play.

My entire body goes cold.

It's my turn to run.

I burst into the rear garden, which is a long sloping lawn with gravel paths and small evergreen trees shaped into teardrops and flames. The sun blazes reddish twilight, and the long shadows of the western peaks and castle towers cut eerie stripes across the yard.

A small bark gets my attention, and I turn. "Sir," says one of the soldiers. I see them.

Aurora has Darvey the barghest backed into a stone wall. He's small, like a regular dog, and he whimpers. My aunt is in tattered clothes, with boots too big for her and her hair a tangle of old braids. A knife drips blood in her left hand. A rope dangles from her right.

"Aurora," I yell, sprinting toward her. "Let him go."

She turns to me, elegant despite how tired and dirty she looks. She smiles pleasantly. "Talon," she says. "You don't want to stop me."

"I do," I say, but it's a lie. It shouldn't be. I slow down. I have nothing to stuff my ears.

"My loyal nephew," she keeps going. "Put down that knife. Let me go."

"Stay back," I order my men. I don't know if she can command them to hurt me, but I don't want to find out. "So you can't hear her. One of you go for Finn. Another, Annag Mortooth. Block your ears."

Aurora turns to Darvey. "Be a good boy," she says. "Come to me. I'm perfectly safe, and you will have an easy time with me."

Darvey's fur stands on end, and he has his mouth open, but he's panting, not growling. He's just a kid.

"Be quiet," I tell Aurora. I step closer. It's easy. I adjust my grip on the falchion. I can just decide to stab her and that will be that.

"Talon, you love me," she says.

I do.

But I can still kill her.

"You don't want to hurt me."

Her words tremble through me. I clench my jaw and take another step. My fingers ache. "I don't," I admit through my teeth. Relief washes down my spine. Agreeing with her feels good, but it doesn't free me. I don't want to kill her, but I *will*.

"You will not hurt me, you can't. What would your mother

think? My dear sister? How can you even imagine it, Talon?" Her voice is soft and smooth, but so strong.

I nod. "I know." I do. Sweat breaks out on my neck and chest. I have to focus. I don't want to hurt her. I don't.

Darvey whimpers.

With a hoarse gasp, I leap forward and slash out with my falchion. For her gut.

Aurora spins and reaches out for me.

I falter, I twist my arm so the blade cuts along her shoulder but doesn't kill her.

Aurora grabs my face. "Talon, stop, you won't hurt me. I know you, and I know who you are, what you're willing to do. You won't kill me. You love me."

"I will," I hiss. It's the best I can do. Her hands on my face are cold, her gaze bores into me, and she will *not stop talking*.

We're surrounded by Dragons. I hear the creak of armor and sliding blades. The wind moaning down the mountain. Finn yells my name. It all sounds like I'm deep underwater.

"You're my best little dragon, Talon; you won't hurt me. You'll let me go. You know you want to, and you must. It's the best way to keep everyone safe—to keep me safe. Don't move."

As she speaks, Aurora reaches with one arm around my waist and takes my claw off its holster. She presses the curved blade up under my jaw. "You're helping me," she murmurs. "You'll be fine, just help me, little dragon. My sweet Talon, you would never hurt me."

Her boon shakes through me. I know in my gut that I can't fight her because she's right: I don't want to hurt her. I don't want her to die. I love her.

I'm not strong enough to fight this. I think tears fall hot down my cheeks. I have to fight this. She—she's awful, she's a murderer. I can see the chunk of Darling's father squeezed in her hand. I shudder and I lift my falchion.

"Stop." Aurora presses the claw to the soft skin under my chin. Then she yells, "Everyone else get out of this yard or I will kill him."

My soldiers move even farther away. They're reluctant, but she has my own claws bleeding me. It stings; I don't care. My whole body is trembling, down to my bones.

Aurora keeps talking, to me and to the soldiers, until they're gone. We're alone. Except Finn, my best friend. He says, "Give me the barghest, and I'll go."

Darvey huddles near the wall, a little ball of fluff. I have no idea what she said to him to make him so afraid.

"Take him, then," Aurora says.

Finn whistles and I hear Darvey scramble. I take a deep breath. I can break this.

I say, "You disgust me."

"I'm used to Dragons being disappointed with me in this garden, Talon. Dragons and everyone else." Her big blue eyes widen in false innocence. "But you—you are strong and good. Your mother would be proud of you."

It makes my insides shudder to hear. Aurora commands me to walk with her, drawing me deeper into the garden. Then two Dragons in full armor appear from the shadows.

I glare at them, but they look coldly back at me. They greet *her* as "my blade," and I know they aren't under her thrall. They are betraying me. Who knows how long they've belonged to her. Years, probably. Maybe since Aurora first came here, when my mother married my father.

Aurora pats my cheek and says to one of the traitors, "Take this."

The traitor puts his sword to my neck, and Aurora uses the claw to cut open her own palm. I hiss. The sword presses against me, digging deep enough to break skin.

"Talon," Aurora says, a little sadly. She touches my forehead with blood, and I flinch away. "None of that."

The traitor soldier leans in, puts another knife just under my ear. I have to hold very still.

Aurora draws something on my skin. It burns.

Then she says something I don't understand, and I fall to my knees, and know nothing more.

14
DARLING

We anchor the frigate a league off the coast. We've made good time thanks to Adelaide and her control of the currents. The frigate normally holds a complement of about fifteen sailors, but true to Adelaide's word, we pared our crew down to the bare bones, leaving us with only ten people total, including me, Miranda, Adelaide, and Vivian. It turns out with Adelaide's abilities the sailors don't have much to do. The currents carry us where we want to go with very little intervention.

After my stunt back on the Teeth Islands, I feel a bit more myself, but it's hard to ignore the disconnect between me and the phoenix. I don't like the feeling of being at the whims of Chaos—I've started to think of it as more of an entity since Miranda pointed it out—but I also don't feel comfortable talking to Vivian or Adelaide about it. Adelaide for obvious reasons, but Vivian because she seems to enjoy her time as the gryphon, taking the shape of her empyreal at least once or twice a day. Adelaide as well. She will stride out of her quarters and dive into the ocean without a word to anyone. For them, the transformation seems normal and enjoyable.

But every time I become the phoenix, I lose a bit of myself. I dislike the feeling of not knowing what I'm about. Chaos seems to move in much the same way as Caspian did, and I cannot know if what I am feeling is real or a byproduct of that indomitable force.

And I so very much do not like being a puppet.

Asking others what's happened feels shameful and embarrassing, and my memories of my times as the phoenix are scattered and haphazard, images and feelings rather than concrete events. I want to know if it'll always be like this, but I also don't have time to hole up somewhere and figure everything out.

Luckily, the sphinx gives me the gift of time.

I can sense the sphinx, but the gryphon's constant flights over Nakumba and the surrounding areas reveal nothing. When I speak to Vivian, she's clearly frustrated by her lack of insight, and I share her frustration. A week passes before I realize that I cannot leave this to Vivian.

I will have to find the sphinx myself.

I sense that she isn't far away. It could be that this empyreal is keeping itself hidden, waiting for Chaos to tell it when to appear. That means I will have to become the phoenix on purpose, and I'm not looking forward to that.

So one day, after yet another unsuccessful scouting mission, I decide I will have to figure out how to remain more myself. I watch as the Barbs pull up anchor, grunting with the effort of working the winch. Perhaps if I ground myself more fully in my human form when I change, it will allow me to better control the change. An anchor, so to speak, so that my human mind does not drift while fully merged with the phoenix. It seems like the right answer, and I wonder if perhaps I read it somewhere in one of the endless tracts Vivian furnished back at House Gryphon.

I stare out at the city of my birth, pondering the issue as we set sail.

Adelaide has taken to moving the ship every couple of days, and it feels like every time we must move locations, her temper grows shorter. I debated leaving the ship—there has to be somewhere that Vivian and I could camp—but Adelaide will hear nothing of it. And so, every third day we weigh anchor and move a few leagues down the coast, following the shoreline.

But this has been the first time we've sailed close enough to the port that I can see the city itself.

Nakumba. Sunbaked and merciless. The city crouches on a cliff over the ocean, the desert at its back. It's hot here, the sun is punishing, and Adelaide stands next to me and scowls at the desert.

"How is it you found me in the sea, but you cannot find the sphinx in that little bit of sand?" she grumbles.

"You don't have to stay," I say. It's hard to talk to her. She wears her anger like a funeral shroud, and I refuse to apologize when I'm not sorry. Miranda watches us with a worried expression, her brows furrowed and her lips a moue of displeasure. I've already told her that she doesn't have to choose. I get the feeling I'd lose if I pressed the issue. But I won't pretend I regret not using the Kiss of Death Gavin slipped me. I wouldn't have been able to live with myself if I had.

"Why wouldn't I?" Adelaide snaps back. "Where else would I go?"

"Anywhere but here. It's only going to be worse for you once the sphinx is spotted. Because there is very little water, and the sphinx is outside the city," I say. If I close my eyes, I can sense her movements through the desert. I open them back up. "But if you're willing to leave the sea, I would welcome your company." She says nothing, and I sigh. "I know you don't believe it, but I always had Leonetti in mind. Winning his freedom and Pyrlanum's peace." It's not an apology, but it's as close as Adelaide is going to get.

"I'm still mad at you," Adelaide says, her voice small. "But I'm equally mad at myself. I let Gavin convince me assassination was my best bet, and I was wrong. And I don't like being wrong."

I nod, because her statement requires no answer. Then she grabs me up in a hug. "I'm glad I didn't lose you," she says, and I hug back just as hard.

"It turns out I'm incredibly hard to kill," I say with a laugh.

When I pull back, Miranda stands nearby, and I wave her in for a three-way hug. She wraps an arm around each of us. "No more fighting. You're both brats," she says, kissing us on our temples.

And for a moment, all is as it should be.

I wake at dawn the next morning with a scream trapped in my throat.

In the dream I was being chased through the desert by a strange creature, one that wanted to devour me. Only when I finally had nowhere else to go, the monster bearing down on me, the monster turned into a wide-eyed girl a few years younger than me.

"Help me," she croaked, before falling to her knees and turning to dust.

I don't know if the dream is portentous or not, but I definitely need to find the sphinx.

The dream drives me out of the nest where I sleep on the deck, Vivian snoring nearby, and across the warm wooden boards. The sky has barely pinkened with the dawn before I am stripping off my clothing and climbing to the crow's nest before I can second-guess myself. I swallow hard at what I am about to do, but I can see no other way to find her, because I am now certain the sphinx is a brown-skinned girl, scared and lost in the desert.

Chaos showed me that.

I take a deep breath and leap from the crow's nest, reaching for the phoenix as I do. The change is instant, as though the firebird was waiting for my invitation. The creature tries to wrest control and I have to fight to maintain my shape, my consciousness.

We must work together, I think, but the phoenix isn't interested in listening to a human. Why would it? I am small and breakable, and the phoenix is eternal.

Mostly eternal, I think back, but the great bird ignores the thought.

Still, I don't lose myself this time, but I am wholly unable to take control of our flight. It hardly matters, though. The phoenix careens over the city, flames licking the sandstone structures, and there a little outside town is the sphinx.

It runs along like an oversized kitten, gangly and strange. I get the impression of hair and a human face, before the phoenix wheels backward, away from the creature. I struggle to take control, to turn back to the desert, but the phoenix resists. A sensation like fear sings through me, from the phoenix. It doesn't want to confront the sphinx just yet.

But I am unsure why.

The firebird turns back to Adelaide's ship, and I am released from the change a few feet above the deck. I slam onto the boards before quickly stamping out any wayward sparks that may have found their way onto the ship. The sun has fully risen, blinding me, and so I fumble toward where I slept until someone drapes a blanket across my shoulders.

"Here." Miranda hands me my smoked lenses, and I pull them into place before grabbing my clothing and getting dressed.

"Thank you," I say. I feel unbalanced, but now I know for certain that there is a way to talk to the phoenix within me. Now I just have to convince the empyreal to listen.

"I saw you climb into the crow's nest earlier," she says. "Is everything all right?"

I nod. For the first time in weeks, I feel like I finally understand what I am doing. And I am loath to relinquish the sensation.

"The sphinx. She's in the desert. We have to go get her. Now."

15

TALON

Nakumba is the capital city of the Sphinx territory, or it was when there was a Sphinx regent. It's been more than a decade since House Dragon, led by my father, marched south and massacred the entire family.

Situated between the desert and the sea, Nakumba is a sprawling, flat city of pale brick with plentiful rock gardens and seasonal gardens that bloom in one way or another for most of the year. That is what I've heard, at least. Of the six great Houses, Nakumba is the only one whose capital city I've never seen with my own eyes until now. Even the capital of House Kraken has hosted me—in battle, of course, but I remember the waterways that made up their streets and how difficult it was to assault. Which is why House Dragon ultimately failed to conquer Kraken. Even when we starved them out, they took to their ships and islands, where we couldn't trap them again.

I walk through the bright, sunny streets of Nakumba without attracting much attention for once. I'm not in uniform, and nobody here would recognize the War Prince by my face. Instead I wear a paler green-and-black jacket with short sleeves and a linen tunic beneath, with loose pants tucked into boots. It's hot in Sphinx territory, but I won't give up my boots for the woven sandals many locals wear. I have my falchion at my waist, but left my distinct claw weapon a day's ride north, with the bulk of the small team of Teeth who accompanied me here.

The claw makes me churn with guilt to look at. I let Aurora go. Even though I understand I had no defenses against her boon, it chafes. It *hurts*.

I let her go. A murderer, a traitor, an unpredictable blood mage. I have no idea what she wants. But I do know the lengths to which she'll go to get it. I've tried seeking her with my boon, but I can't. Elias suggested it must be thanks to whatever blood magic she performed upon me, blocking her to my boonsight. We have soldiers scouring the countryside for her, and sent an urgent missive to General Bloodscale. But after discussing with Finn and Elias, we decided the likelihood of her going after another empyreal the way she went after Darvey is high. And right now, the lone sphinx is the most vulnerable.

I want to find the sphinx empyreal to keep them safe, and I want to have as much advantage as House Dragon can get, but mostly I want to be here if this is where Aurora is headed. Capture her. Kill her. I'm not sure how to face Darling if I can't.

This kind of work is what I'm supposed to be good at. Military tactics. Hunting. Planning.

I know the sphinx is near Nakumba because of rumors and my boon, and now that I'm here, I need local aid.

Or as close to local aid as Dragons are wont to use.

I check the markers the people of Nakumba use as addresses while I cross a broad avenue with gangly desert vines planted in the center. They're vivid fuchsia, crawling along an arched trellis. I smell dust and a crisp floral that reminds me of the jasmine that grows in the foothills near Phoenix Crest.

The inn I'm looking for is called Lion's Rest, and the address was passed to me via a series of clandestine arrangements. I find it easily: the forecourt is filled with people resting in the shade of umbrellas and spiky palm bushes, speaking quietly in the hot afternoon as they drink cold teas and rose ice. I stride in and note the person I'm here to meet sitting with her broad back to the corner of the building. She's leaning on the wall, one sandaled foot up on the neighboring bench, and from her location she can see in three directions: behind her is the inn itself.

I wind through the other tables and sit with her. "It's been a long time, Brigh."

The incredibly muscled young woman grins—exactly the way Finn would grin if his face hadn't been bisected by that scar when he was barely fourteen. Brigh is Finn's older twin sister: she's technically one of the Teeth as well, but more specifically, she's the commander of my intelligence. She's been down here for three years, convinced the Krakens weren't where the real threat to House Dragon waited. I'm glad of it, since she knows Sphinx territory in and out, and in a way, she was correct all along: the Phoenix Reborn came from Sphinx. If Darling is a threat to anything, she's a threat to the rule of House Dragon.

Brigh has the same red hair as Finn, but she wears it shorter than him, shaggy around her face and ears. Her cheeks are tan from the southern sun, making freckles like little embers shine down her neck. She's easily as large as her brother, and honestly, maybe her muscles are even thicker. She could toss me over her head if she cared to, though I guess I'm faster—that's the only way I beat Finn when we spar anymore.

"You're taller," Brigh says. Then she leans in, her green eyes sparkling. "My blade," she whispers.

"Not as tall as you."

Brigh shrugs. She's been this big since she was thirteen. If she hadn't pursued spycraft, she'd have been able to marry into any Dragon family with her strength and humor. Even mine. Brigh waves over a server in the loose robes of Sphinx, and orders me a taste of their local fermented sweet milk. "Trust me," she says.

"Food, too," I instruct the server. "Your favorite that complements the milk."

The server nods and hurries off, answering calls from neighboring tables.

"So, there have been rumors, but also semi-official news, that she's harassing farms and goat herds mostly in the southwest and west of the city," Brigh says.

"For three weeks?"

"Give or take. It took a while for rumors to start. I think people thought she was a regular lion for a while."

"Any information about where she came from?"

Brigh shakes her head. "I assume one of the cousin families, some third branch or something, survived. It's agreed she's a *she*, but otherwise, nothing. She doesn't look old, but she looks like a winged lion, so." Brigh shrugs.

"It's unlikely she's more than fifteen or twenty. Or her name would have been recorded somewhere." I wonder if this Sphinx regent is the real Maribel Calamus, the name Caspian inflicted upon Darling when he was trying to sell her to Pyrlanum as the Sphinx regent. Though it's possible Caspian's declaration was true—Darling *is* Maribel Calamus, and the new Phoenix Reborn came from House Sphinx.

Wouldn't it be lovely to ask him. And receive a truthful answer.

The server brings our order, and pours the sweet milk for us into narrow, tall clay flutes. The food he brings is a tray of salted, roasted roots and soft cheese. Once he leaves, I lift the milk. We salute, and sip. As advertised, it's sweet with the sharpness of fermentation. I like the tacky sensation. We taste the thinly cut purple carrots, and then I ask, "What did people think of Maribel Calamus?"

"They were looking forward to her return," Brigh says immediately. She's peeling crusts of toasted skin off a thick white radish. "Nakumba was eager for a regent again. It would have been a good balance. Not everyone believed, but they wanted to. They wanted the wars over."

I nod. "So do I."

"It would be a nice new challenge to spy in peacetime," Brigh says with a grin.

"Do you have the same boon as Finn?"

She shakes her head. "No boon, though our mama used to say my boon was growing as big as my brother." Brigh snorts. "I think that's just our father's influence, and hard work."

"My boon is a tracking boon."

"I've heard boons have suddenly grown in strength, since the reappearance of the empyreals."

I knock back the rest of the fermented sweet milk. "Not only grown, but exploded in some cases. I used to have to be near someone to track them. To sense their trace, in the immediacy of their passing by. Now, I can hunt anyone I know of. That's why I need you."

"Oh?" Brigh looks suitably impressed.

"I can see where the sphinx empyreal is, but I need someone familiar with the area to help me pinpoint her."

"That I can do." Brigh laughs and finishes her drink, too.

An hour later I find myself in Brigh's rented rooms: the second story of a long, low boarding house for single people. The proprietor gave me a dirty look, but Brigh explained I was her brother's boyfriend, and the old man didn't seem much mollified but did let us pass. With a warning about the building curfew.

Brigh's quarters are one large room, with a sleeping pallet and storage closet on one end, an open bowl hearth that is common in Sphinx territory and shelves of supplies on the other. It's simple, low-ceilinged, with a few rugs layered on the floor, and a single window looking out over the street. Brigh flicks open a starter stick and gets the coals in the bowl hearth going. "Tea?"

I nod and kneel beside the hearth. "I'm going to start. I'll describe what I'm seeing to you, and you identify any landmarks for me."

"Simple enough."

"I hope so. It's likely I'll develop a boon fever, but it will pass." To the quick sounds of Brigh heating water and opening little clay jars of herbs, I settle into a comfortable position and close my eyes.

Carefully, I open my boon. Instantly, heat rises up my neck, and I ignore it as best I can. I look for a sphinx, an empyreal that feels like Darvey and Caspian—their Chaos-riddled traces are like mirrors to each other, and using that as a signpost is how I saw the sphinx once before.

And now:

A sand-colored tail, curled around a furry body, in shade. The earth is dark orange, gravelly, but there are boulders and a few trees that look like a desert juniper variant.

I speak slowly, falling into the vision.

The sphinx stretches, yawns. I can't hear anything.

A vulture circles overhead, a second, a third, but they drift on the summer wind, uninterested in the sphinx. She stands. Her human face is pretty, warm brown, with eyes too large in proportion to human features. They are pale brown, shot through with the ivory of House Sphinx.

The sphinx rubs her back along the boulder, pausing to scratch her hip. Then she startles, turns, and runs off.

To the sphinx's left is the distant outline of the city: a long wall, gleaming white, and a tower.

"Is there a colored flag on the tower?" Brigh asks.

I focus, trying to see the distance, but the sphinx is moving away. "Red, I think, or orange?"

"The southeastern gate is marked with dark orange. You're sure it's not blue or white?"

"Yes."

I sink back in.

She lopes down an incline covered in pale yellow grass and a green ground cover like some kind of clover. More boulders. And there—the sphinx hops up onto one boulder, and there's the shine of running water. A thin creek.

"I know where that is, south of the city," Brigh says.

Slowly, I open my eyes. I rub my cheeks to return fully to my body. Tiny sparks of Chaos blink in my vision.

Brigh sticks a cup of tea in my face. The steam is sharp, maybe oversteeped, but it helps. "Let's go," I say, and knock back the burning liquid.

We're joined by three regulars in Brigh's local network: Dragons all, though two of them have lived and worked in Sphinx territory longer than Brigh, she tells me. The third transferred to Brigh after a sea battle gave him persistent nightmares and the Dragon military doctors decided he needed a new line of work. I'm surprised spying is less directly stressful than outright battle, but Brigh says he's thriving.

This time of day, Nakumba is wide open, without any curfew or requirements for coming and going since the army began the official withdrawal last month. Even before then, after Caspian announced Darling as the Sphinx scion, Caspian had been pulling our forces back, preparing for their returning regent. The city is run by locals now, but there remain Dragon soldiers at the gates. Brigh gives me a wide-rimmed sun hat to duck beneath in case I know any of the guards. I don't. I didn't coming in to the city this morning, either. If I had, it would be fine: I'm allowed to be here. But I'd rather not be noticed. Since the massacre of House Sphinx, we've been a constant presence, but a light one. Sphinx had no means of fighting back, and House Dragon left them alone, except for taxation and the occasional sweep to clear out any Krakens or other enemies.

Our meeting point is a quarter-mile south of the southeastern gate, just off the road markers. It's a well-used watering hole for beasts of burden, with herd drake troughs and posts for tying racing drakes up before heading into town. Luckily for us, it's empty, and we can see for quite some distance.

When Brigh introduces me, the soldiers fall to a knee, showing their surprise. I have them stand. "Have you hunted like this before?"

They have not, though two of them have hunted the desert

cats we have that are not true lions, but close enough. The soldiers brought weapons to take one down. I tell them we are here to capture, and under no circumstances will they cause harm to the sphinx. This is an empyreal, a regent, and she deserves our respect. They nod, and also have ropes and a heavy net. Lastly, I warn them about Aurora and her boon, and I pass them the wax earplugs that are the best option for resisting her. "For Aurora Falleau, you can and should execute her the moment her identity is confirmed."

The soldiers seem surprised but don't question the order.

I take a moment to check my boon again. It connects instantly to the sphinx: she's close. Playing with a tumbleweed, like a huge housecat. I smile through the sharp headache that cuts behind my eyes.

Then I get to work. We head out, toward the southwest, since that's the angle from which I saw the city wall originally. I leave my boon sense open, looking for traces. Not many people walk off the road in this part of the land, not this near the city. It's rocky and the ground uneven, with a lot of ragged trees and evergreen scrub, easy to twist an ankle. Brigh points in the direction of the creek she knows, and that's when I find it: the actual trace of the sphinx empyreal.

"Here," I murmur.

The trace shimmers like a ghostly line in my sight, a path created as the sphinx moved. It's delicate violet with a rainbow overlay—like mother of pearl. That's the color of Chaos to me: in my dreams, in a trace, in Darling's stormy black eyes.

I follow it, motioning the soldiers to follow me quietly.

We sneak, the only sounds the wind and our boots shifting gravel, and the occasional cackle of a ground bird.

The trace gets stronger and I crouch behind a boulder. The soldiers imitate me, readying ropes and the net. I peek around the boulder, and there is the creek, spilling along a shallow bed. The sphinx pounces for something, splashing with all four of her wide lion's paws. Her mane curls and kinks around her face, like hair and a long beard. She's strange-looking, but gorgeous, as all magical creatures must be. Even the barghest has a strange beauty to him when he looks at me a certain way, for all he is eleven years old and a big shaggy dog.

I step out from behind the boulder.

The sphinx freezes. Her brown-ivory eyes widen at me.

"Lady Sphinx," I say calmly. I bow without taking my gaze from her.

The sphinx sits back in the water, and flares her wings. They've been tight to her spine before, but now they spread to either side, flicking water with the long primary feathers. They are speckled tan-brown-ivory, with a shimmer of blue-purple in places where the sun hits right. She stares at me.

"I am Talon Goldhoard, First Scion of House Dragon," I say. "I would like to help you."

She frowns. The rumors were correct: her human face is youthful and girlish. Pretty.

I understand her skepticism, assuming she understands me. *When was the last time a Dragon helped anybody?* Darling sneers in my mind.

I step forward slowly. "I won't hurt you," I say.

The sphinx snaps her tail and a wind gusts in my face. I hold a hand up to block the dust, and hear a grunt from one of the Dragon soldiers trying to spread out and flank her.

I look and I don't see the sphinx. She's gone.

Stepping forward, I open my boon again: there is the shimmer of her trace. It leads directly to her. She's barely moved, crouched lower to the water, her wings down like crescent dinner plates, trying to hide her.

She did something to confuse me.

"Where did you . . ." one of the soldiers says, obviously confused, too.

"I can't see you," says another. They don't have my boon to help them.

The sphinx doesn't move. There's a glitter of Chaos in the air.

I frown, but I can see her just fine with my boon, and concentration.

"Be still, focus," I tell my soldiers.

"My blade," one says.

The sphinx snaps her tail again. That's not good. I peer at her, my boon holding strong. She peeks out between her primary feathers: one big eye finds me.

The rest of my Dragons are stumbling away.

"Someone's coming," Brigh says suddenly behind me. Her hand clasps on my shoulder.

I keep my gaze on the sphinx. "I'm Talon, Lady Sphinx. I'd like to be your friend. I'd like to help you return to your human form, remember your name, and take up the mantle of Sphinx regent. Do you understand me?"

Her head tilts consideringly. I'm not sure if it's because she does or does not understand. I hold out an empty hand, palm up. Offering. "I'm not here to hurt you."

I hear the approach of a dozen footsteps. The sphinx seems to tense: I think she's going to leap into the air and fly away. My soldiers are not prepared with their ropes and net.

The sphinx suddenly rears back, head snapping toward the newcomers. She bounds up the bank, away from me.

"Stop!" cries a new voice.

It's my turn to snap my head around.

She's standing gloriously in the sunlight, curling hair tangled around her head as if torn free by harsh winds, one hand thrust out, and wide round goggles over her eyes that suck in light like black holes.

Darling.

16

DARLING

We move quickly once I've confirmed the sphinx is prowling the outskirts of Nakumba.

It's a not a mission everyone needs to attend. I truly only need Vivian and perhaps a helper to find the sphinx again, now that I can feel her presence, and after a long afternoon and evening of discussion we opt for a small rowboat to take us to the shore. It will be faster than docking, and has the additional benefit of avoiding any remaining Dragon forces that might still remain in Nakumba.

I'm not sure what Talon knows just yet, and I want to avoid that uncomfortable situation for as long as possible.

Miranda decides to remain with the ship while Adelaide, Vivian, and I go ashore with a couple of soldiers from the Barbs. Adelaide asks for volunteers, since every sailor on our ship also happens to be one of House Kraken's best soldiers, and I'm surprised when every single person raises their hand and Adelaide is forced to choose. I know one Barb, Penna Shorebreak, but the other, Len Nigma, I've never met. He's older, weathered, and with deep brown skin and a kind smile that is made cruel by a scar that goes from his ear to the corner of his mouth. When we climb into the rowboat, his gaze upon me is a bit distracting, but when I turn toward him, he gives me a nod of respect. "You probably don't remember me, but I was there the day old Leonetti pulled you from the sewers."

I blink. "You used to have long braids."

"Aye, that I did. I was House Sphinx before the lizards burned us to the ground with their lies. I pledged my skills to Kraken in the ashes. All that to say, you now have my blade, my flame."

"Mine as well," Penna adds. "You unlocked my sister's boon, and I've never seen her so happy. That's worth fighting for. You are worth fighting for."

I smile, their heartfelt declarations making me feel tired and overwhelmed. But it won't do to seem ungrateful. "I thank you, but we're all fighting for the same thing: peace and a Pyrlanum where every voice is heard."

"Hear, hear," Vivian says. When we get settled into our seats, Vivian sits next to me. "Did you mean that last part, about every voice being heard?"

"Of course. Why?"

"I have some treatises—don't make that face, you'll enjoy these. They're about alternative ruling systems. Anyway, I think you might find something of value in their discussions."

"Later," I say. And Vivian must sense my growing unease, because she simply pats my hand and says nothing more.

The ride to shore is a short one. Adelaide is able to steer and propel the tiny craft with just the currents, and after a few bumpy minutes we make landfall a little south of where the city lies.

Once we've landed on the rocky beach Adelaide turns to me. "What now? It's best to avoid the city. It's probably still crawling with Dragons and not the safest place to be."

I reach out for the sphinx, Chaos all but pulling me to her. "Wait here. I'll find her and change her back. She's close."

I slip out of the clothes I wear, Len turning his back to give me some privacy, before handing my goggles to Vivian, who takes my clothes as well. And then I take to the air.

I try to hold on to myself this time, not lose myself to the will of the phoenix. An anchor, Vivian had said, and my thoughts immediately turn to Talon.

The pain and anguish I feel whenever I think about him grounds me, and I mentally pick at the scab of my heartache. I hate remembering how alone I felt when he turned toward his aunt, when he ordered Leonetti taken away in chains. But the painful memory works. There's a moment of struggle as the great empyreal tries to take hold, but it relents, and then I am me but also the phoenix, soaring across the desert.

I feel free and alive. But most of all, I am coherent and in control, and that is the best sensation of all.

I dip my wings and circle the space where I know the sphinx to be. The creature splashes in a creek, and I swoop low, intending on releasing her from her form. I don't see the creature so much as I see the Chaos of the empyreal, tangled like a child trying to tie sailor's knots, poorly. But before I can get close enough, the sphinx hits me with a strange wind. And I am lost. My wings dip and I am plummeting to the ground.

I have forgotten how to fly.

I arc my body back, away from the sphinx and back toward the coast. But I am falling, too fast, and when the water comes into view, I angle my body into a point and dive deep under the waves.

When I surface, sputtering and choking on the salt water, back in my human form, a current picks me up and carries me to the shore. Penna wades in, lending a hand, and I quickly pick myself out of the waves and back onto the beach.

"What happened?" Vivian asks as I get dressed.

"Confusing wind. That parchment you handed me back at House Gryphon said something like this might happen, but I didn't know . . . She must not have truly seen me when I scouted her yesterday. We'll have to get closer to her, and someone will have to distract her so I can unlock her Chaos . . . I'm actually pretty sure I can do it without changing into the phoenix this time."

Adelaide and Vivian nod, and Penna and Len heft their packs on their backs, their blades gleaming in the hot sun.

"Well then, let's find us an empyreal," Len says with a grin, and we set off to find a path up the cliffside.

Our trek through the desert is grueling. The clothing we wear is ill-suited to the climate, so we end up stripping off pieces as we walk. By the time we sight the small stream where I last saw the sphinx, we are drenched in sweat, and most of our water is gone. Penna and Len look fine—they're Barbs, after all—but Vivian and Adelaide have wilted considerably. I especially feel sorry for poor Vivian. I doubt she's ever undertaken anything so strenuous while being the studious regent of House Gryphon. But she doesn't complain.

No one does. We are more focused on our goal.

I can feel the connection between the sphinx and me, so I lead our group. A few times the terrain forced us to detour, but we adjust our trajectory and trudge on. Despite our many detours, judging by the sun, it's only been a couple of hours since I last saw the sphinx when the sounds of conversation filter to us.

Not just any voice. Talon.

"Look!" Vivian says. We approach on a well-worn animal track, even with the streambed. Talon and a number of people, most likely House Dragon soldiers from within Nakumba, stand nearby with nets and swords. He's trying to trap the sphinx, but for what purpose, I have no idea. And I am not inclined to give him the benefit of the doubt.

After all, the last time I saw him, he wasn't exactly on my side.

"Vivian, can you stay here and shift, distracting the sphinx?" I ask in a low voice.

She nods, and then I point to another nearby path. "If the rest of you go that way and make a lot of noise, we may be able to split the sphinx's focus. Her wings can cast a wind that will confuse you. But I don't know if she can focus it in more than one direction at a time."

"As you wish, my flame," Len says, Penna echoing his response. Vivian gives me a curt nod, and Adelaide grabs my arm.

"Be careful," she says.

And then I am running up a small incline to a nearby ridge to get a better view.

I'm only a few feet above the streambed, but it's enough to be able to take in the entire scene. Talon has his hands out, trying to placate the sphinx, but it's clear from her body language that she isn't buying whatever he's saying. Rather, she looks ready to pounce.

Talon has no clue that he could be lunch.

"Stop!" I yell, and Talon freezes, turning toward me. I can tell the exact moment he sees me. His face telegraphs every single emotion, wide-eyed wonder melting into childlike delight before he averts his eyes in shame. It seems I am not the only one who has remembered our final moments together too much.

I drag my gaze away from him and turn toward the sphinx, her wings up, ready to loose another dizzying spell at us.

I rip off my goggles. "Now, Vivian!"

I can't see the moment Vivian begins to shift because my eyes are tightly closed against the too bright sunshine, but the wind that buffets my skin is all I need. Adelaide and the Barbs begin to hoot and make a racket, and I give myself over to the phoenix.

There is freedom in the empyreal. The phoenix urges me to let go of my pain, my heartache, my uncertainty, but I hold fast to it, the anchor made easier by seeing Talon looking up at me, awe on his face. It's too much like that night under the everbloom bower for me to think of anything but him as I dive over the sphinx, distracted by the gryphon behind her and the people making a racket on either side. With her attention elsewhere, it's a simple thing to angle my body so that one fiery wing brushes her back, singeing the fur but releasing her from her empyreal form.

I land deftly behind her, releasing the phoenix form so that I am once more naked. Luckily, Penna rushes over with my goggles and an overdress that I quickly drop over my head.

"That's inconvenient, my flame," she says, and I laugh.

"Yeah. As though always searching for my goggles wasn't trouble enough." I actually don't care about being nude in front of others, which is definitely a recent development. I have to wonder if that is because it keeps happening, or if the empyreal is working some effect so that I don't die of embarrassment every time someone gets a glance at my nude form.

Adelaide has taken a blanket over to the sphinx, who is young and wide-eyed and looks a lot like me.

Her abundant curls have been hacked short, but her skin is the same deep burnished brown as mine. Her face is rounder and she's half a head taller, but I've never met someone before who could have been my cousin. It's a strange sensation, like looking into a warped mirror.

She also looks like maybe she was hit with her own confusing wind. "I . . . who are you?"

"My name is Darling Seabreak," I say, not bothering with the pretense of Caspian's House Sphinx name. "I'm the Phoenix Reborn. You're the House Sphinx regent, which is why you've spent the past few weeks in your empyreal form."

The more I talk, the more panicked the girl looks, and Adelaide pulls her gently toward the footpath.

"My name is Adelaide Seabreak. I'm the regent of House Kraken. Why don't you have a drink and a bit of food, and I'll explain everything," my sister says as she leads the girl back the way we came. As Adelaide passes she jerks her head behind me, and I turn to see Talon standing a few feet away.

"Darling."

"War Prince," I say, and he has the grace to wince.

"So we're back to that."

"It's who you are, first and foremost," I say, not bothering to keep the bitterness from my voice. I want to rush to him and rain kisses down on his face. But I'm still too angry for that to happen. And I need to know what happened to Leonetti before I can even consider unlocking the Talon-shaped hole in my heart. "You showed me that at House Barghest."

He swallows hard, and it's easy to see that the past weeks have been hard on him. He's lost weight and there are hollows under his eyes. There's stubble dotting his cheeks and his hair is too long, and despite everything, I would give my left wing to be back with him under that everbloom bower in the moonlight.

Leonetti, I remind myself. The pain of his loss steadies me in my resolve.

"My flame," Talon finally says, dropping to his knee and fisting his right hand over his heart. "You have my blade, and my life, should you desire it. House Dragon swears its allegiance to the Phoenix Reborn."

The rest of his soldiers fall to their knees as well, and I walk past Talon to an incredibly large woman who looks familiar. She is gorgeous, well-built, but there's something about her that makes me frown. And it's not just her boon, all twisted up and weak.

It's then that I realize she looks just like the brute Talon considers his best friend. Ah, well. The bastard was bound to have family members.

It's clear that she doesn't like bending the knee to me—I can't think that anyone in House Dragon will be thrilled to concede a war that they were winning—but it doesn't stop me from placing a single hand on top of her head and freeing the Chaos lodged within her. I then do the same to the remaining soldiers, eliciting a few gasps and sending one large man into tears.

When I turn back around, Talon still kneels on the ground, and I realize that he's waiting for my command to rise. Chaos twists in him, too, but it feels different. I can't bring myself to touch him yet. "Stand, all of you. There will be no more groveling and kneeling. It's silly and unnecessary," I say.

Talon turns toward me warily, and I walk back to where he stands. "You have the barghest?"

"Yes," he says. "He's safe."

"Where's the dragon?" I ask. I can't call Caspian, former High Prince Regent, by his first name. I'm angry at him as well, for pulling me into a scheme and giving me no warning. The entirety of House Dragon is made of schemers and plotters, and I have very little patience for it. Whatever honor they once had clearly has been eroded by time.

No, the phoenix has very little affection for the dragon. I have a feeling there is a story there. I wonder if I can ask my empyreal.

"Roaming Dragon territory." He bites his lip, and I know there is something he wants to say, but it doesn't matter.

I have a task to do, and Chaos won't let me rest until it is done.

"Fine. We need to go to Dragon territory. War Prince, your people are free to accompany us or not, as you wish. But you will follow my rules. Adelaide, your ship?"

"At your command, my flame," she says with an extravagant bow, the poor sphinx girl looking on in wide-eyed confusion as though she is still waking up.

When Adelaide straightens, she is barely holding back a laugh, which is how I know she's enjoying my sudden responsibility entirely too much.

Her gaze lands on Talon, and her mirth dies on the vine, replaced with something much more deadly. Leonetti's only biological daughter will not let her father's death go unavenged. I hope whatever knowledge Talon has of that night can give us all closure, but most especially Adelaide.

"Sail to the port at Ethlaugh," Talon says with a fist over his heart, dragging me back to the matter at hand. "I will be there to escort you into the mountains."

"Great. We head to Dragon territory at sundown. But first, I have work to do in Nakumba." I can feel the annoyance of another one of those shrines, frustrating and clogging the flow of Chaos. Vivian circles above us, and I realize she is waiting for me. She must sense the work I still need to do, seeing what is hidden.

Penna steps forward, and I hand her my goggles and yank the overdress over my head. My back is toward Talon, and I have a perverse thought that I hope he enjoys the view.

And then I am in the air, thinking about Leonetti being dragged away in chains, and wondering how I will stomach spending time with the man who broke my heart.

ALLIES

17

TALON

Pushing as fast as the war drakes can go, Brigh and I manage to arrive at the Dragon port of Ethlaugh before the kraken empyreal's ship. I summon Rosalind Wing's battalion of regulars and arrange for an escort befitting the Phoenix Reborn all the way from here to Dragon Castle. It should take four or five days, depending on how quickly everyone can move.

I'm in a hurry to find Caspian, so Darling can use her Chaos to bring him back, but at the same time I'd rather linger in this space where nothing is certain.

When the Krakens arrive, the gryphon flies over the ship, sun on her bright golden fur and feathers. She screams and it seems to rip through the sky. I don't begrudge my Dragons their gaping mouths.

I greet Darling again with a complement of six Teeth and twenty regulars, and on my cue, we bow to the Phoenix Reborn. "House Dragon is ready to escort you, my flame," I say. The soldiers on both sides, Teeth and Barbs, and the Dragon citizens who live in Ethlaugh can hear it from my lips again and again if they need to. The wars are over, just as our High Prince Regent Caspian Gold-hoard declared months ago.

Much has changed since then, but not this.

Darling doesn't look comfortable, but she nods firmly, sun shining on her smoked lenses. She calls me War Prince. It hurts, but I understand. It's my title, it's all I can be to her now, and it's what I must be for the rest of Pyrlanum.

The gryphon drops onto the long pier, transforming into a naked Vivian Chronicum before one of the Kraken Barbs throws a robe around her shoulders. She's going with us.

Brigh steps up and gestures for the phoenix and her party to follow up the rocky bluffs into the town proper. We have an inn ready, and meals. We leave in the morning.

I fall into step beside Darling. She eyes me as unsubtly as ever. "How is Gianna?" I ask. The young girl who'd found herself regent of House Sphinx had seemed frightened when I saw her last.

"She's on the ship with Adelaide. They won't set foot into Dragon territory at the moment."

"I don't blame them," I say.

Darling snorts.

I say, "When Caspian is returned to us, and Darvey, we should have a meeting of all known empyreals."

"Not in Dragon Castle," Darling says.

"Phoenix Crest," I offer quietly. She's so close, our hands could easily brush together as we walk at the end of the line of Dragons and Krakens and solitary Gryphon.

Darling huffs a breath that is not quite a laugh, and definitely disbelieving. But she nods.

I let Brigh settle them into the inn, while most of the Dragons return to their temporary barracks and the military camp outside the town on the highest bluff.

The innkeepers eagerly serve the meal, and I take a few Teeth to care for our war drakes.

When I return to the inn, most of the Dragons and Barbs have settled down, but Darling sits with Vivian. I remain standing as I join them. With a bow, I say, "We can be ready to leave at first light, if that suits you."

Darling grimaces, but nods. Vivian gives me a long, knowing look.

I excuse myself before I can be embarrassing.

In the morning we move out, a few of us on war drakes— including Darling—and the rest marching alongside. The gryphon empyreal soars overhead.

It's a few days to Dragon Castle, though I'm of a mind to take Darling straight up into the mountains after Caspian. I have a difficult time not staring at Darling. The war drake she's on is slightly smaller than Kitty, with vivid green scales and a feather crest of brilliant blue-black. Darling already named him Bunny. He's got a choppy gait that reads as eagerness. She didn't tell his name to me, but to one of her Barbs who looked askance at the drake. Darling wanted him to relax.

There is so much I need to tell her. Even though it won't make anything better between us, I owe her explanations. But not now, not surrounded by so many others. Tonight I'll make my report to the Phoenix Reborn. My confession to Darling.

I ask, "Can you sense the cockatrice empyreal?"

Darling turns her head, so I assume she's looking at me. Those goggles are as disorienting as they've always been. She's pulled her curls back into a puffy tail, and her clothes are simple and practical. She's probably glad to dress herself. I remember the diaphanous layers Caspian inflicted upon her with a twist of bitter nostalgia.

"No," she says after a moment, as if she'd debated answering me at all. "Or yes, but it's as if the distance is so vast that the feeling is too broad. Directionless. I don't think I could follow it," she admits.

"When I look, there's nothing but a . . . void. It could be distance. It could be worse."

"Death?"

I frown. "Except death isn't supposed to stop it. If a scion dies, it passes on."

"I guessed it would be your aunt." Darling's voice is casual, and Darling can't lie that well.

Cold washes over me, from the crown of my head to my guts. She doesn't know Aurora killed her father.

Darling must know the previous Kraken regent is dead. Because Adelaide is the kraken empyreal now. But how he died, we've kept those details tightly guarded.

I slowly draw a breath. I nod, frowning at Kitty's feather ridge. Tonight. I'll find a moment for us to be alone. Surely she'll allow it.

Darling says, "I clearly sense we're going in the right direction for both the barghest empyreal and . . . the dragon."

"I've seen him."

"Caspian?" she says, voice slightly higher than usual.

I look at her again. Her mouth is set, her face pointed ahead. Maybe she won't allow me to speak with her privately. Maybe we lost that chance at House Barghest, when she followed Caspian, and Aurora murdered her father under my care.

Taking a deep breath, I let it out slowly and scratch gently at the base of Kitty's neck spines. She preens a little. "I spoke with him, too. I think he understood me but wasn't interested in what I had to say."

Darling laughs once.

I let myself smile wryly. She always seemed to like it when I smiled. But I don't look at her again. She's thinking about my brother, Caspian, who kissed her and changed our whole world. They both became something greater than they were, and . . . flew away from me.

That night we stop deep in Dragon territory at one of our military waystations.

The waystation is like an inn, but without a staff. There's a couple who live there and maintain it, making sure it's stocked with firewood and feed for our mounts. This couple are Dragons, of course, and they're respectful to me. They seem in awe of Darling. When Vivian drops out of the sky and transforms into a naked woman in a gust of wind, they nearly fall over each other to bow. Darling herself puts a robe around Vivian's shoulders.

The couple keep their eyes lowered as they point out where the war drakes can rest, where we can rest. Darling immediately gathers her Barbs and leads them to one of the small wings of barracks. She doesn't even glance my way.

Fine. We aren't allies. We certainly aren't *engaged.*

My Dragons and I bed down our war drakes. I care for Kitty and Bunny both. Brigh seems to waver between irritation at Darling's dismissal of the Dragon scion and amusement at my uncertainty. Every look she casts me drips with an elder sibling's judgment, and I simply take it. I've weathered worse. Brigh arranges a night watch schedule, and cheekily calls across the courtyard to tell the Barbs they needn't worry about it and can sleep like babies.

I don't quite have to break up a fight, but it's a near thing.

We eat separately, and I barely manage to choke anything down before I withdraw to the yard to run through sword forms. The sun is low, fading shadows around me. I try to sink into the work, the familiar stretch and pull.

But Darling appears suddenly. She watches me pose in a high and tight form. I lower my falchion and tilt my head in an invitation. We've sparred on the road before. It was *good*. I always felt better after we laid into each other that way.

Darling's goggles are pinkish-gold in the final twilight, like tiny twin suns glaring at me. My chest tightens. She's considering it. I need this contact: even if it's violence, it's something we were good at doing together.

"We have to talk," she says.

So it will be that kind of violence instead.

I bow slightly, gesturing toward the thick trees.

Darling picks a direction and takes it. I follow. The blackpines stand tall, their branches spreading only once they reach at least twice my height. Below that level, the red bark is marked with stubs of old branches that have fallen away. It makes the forest here soft underfoot: old needles rotted into layers of ground cover, mixed with small tangled flowers here and there, brambles like early blackberries, and some thorny brush roses. Nothing is blooming yet. I wish Darling could see this forest a month from now, when the late summer flowers thicken it with color.

After a few moments, Darling pauses, then reaches up to unhook the leather strap of her goggles. She tucks them into a pocket on her long vest. My fingers itch to rub at the line they pressed into her temples. It must be tender. Then Darling does it herself, wiping her hands over her brow and eyes.

I step beside her, and study her face as she blinks and adjusts. There's just enough light it's easy for both of us to see, now.

On her left cheek and temple is a wavering burn scar. I've seen it already, but not without the goggles hiding most of it.

"How can you burn?" I murmur.

Darling sucks in a soft, quick breath. She looks at my chin, my lips, my ear. Not my eyes. "This has been here since the first—the first transformation," she says to my shoulder.

Everything in me wants to close the distance and tip her chin up. I want to look into her violet-rainbow Chaos-churning eyes. I clench my jaw and keep my hands to myself.

"Caspian knew," she says as she starts walking again. Not quickly, but a meandering wander. Darling puts her hand on a blackpine, patting it as she passes. Like greeting a friend.

"He made it happen, I guessed." I walk just behind her. I can see her ear, the line of her cheek, and her lashes on this side. "But he didn't tell you anything?"

"Never," she says, almost a snarl, except it's a little bit fond, too. "But he—he had this entire thing planned out. Gathering the House prizes, that was the real purpose of the tour."

I stop, stunned. But it makes sense. "The House Gryphon dagger. The jeweled eye from House Cockatrice."

"Yep. He used them for the . . . the ritual to wake up the phoenix. It was all about that. Always."

It's the same conclusion Elias reached. I wonder when Caspian foresaw it. Probably years and years ago, since he's always dreamed of his eyeless girl.

Darling has walked on into the twilight, and I catch up in three long strides. "Darling."

"Talon."

"Darling . . ."

She laughs once and looks at me, eyebrow quirked up. But when she sees my face—frowning, worried, I barely know what expression I'm making—her amusement fades.

I step closer, but still don't touch. I don't get to do that. "I have to tell you something."

Darling has always been so expressive, and she grimaces now. She shakes her head, her Chaos-tinged eyes narrowed at me, almost pleading. Then she hardens herself: I can almost see the phoenix lowering around her like a fiery mask.

"Leonetti's dead," she says harshly. "We know. I've known since I realized Adelaide was the kraken empyreal. He died right there, while Caspian was setting up his ritual and—and kissing me."

I remember that kiss. It gutted me for a split second—then it upended the whole world.

The light is dimming, dark purple and reddish here under the forest canopy. "He was murdered. Aurora—did it."

"That bitch," Darling spits. "I am not surprised by that."

"She . . ." Why is it so difficult to say? To report?

"I'll never understand how you could choose her over me," Darling says. Now she's bitter.

"I didn't," I snap. "I never did."

Darling studies me, a look of almost disgust on her face. "She told everyone you were the rightful Dragon regent, and you went to her side. You kept Leonetti, you—you gave my father to that monster, and she killed him. I wanted you to free him. I asked for weeks!"

It's all true. And that's not even the worst of it. I can't get anything past my teeth. I can see the blood, the wet chunks of heart, and if I open my mouth to tell her, I'll throw up. My shoulders heave as I take a huge breath. I hiss it out. I take another.

Darling's eyes narrow. They glint violet-black. She won't help me. I have to say it myself.

"Aurora killed him for blood magic," I say very quietly. I realize I'm furious. At Aurora, at everything. "She took him from me while I was rallying my soldiers, and then it was too late."

"Blood magic? *What?*"

"She was faking her prophecy boon with blood magic."

Darling turns away and puts both hands on the nearest tree. Her fingers dig in. She might start bleeding. But no, the bark beneath her hands begins to smoke, then blacken.

I stop breathing.

Darling's head bows. "She . . . you're telling me . . . she . . ."

There's a flicker of flames through her fingers.

I put my hand flat between her shoulder blades. "Darling. The tree."

"Tell me, Talon!"

"She killed your father and used his blood to make herself see a prophecy."

"What did she see?" Darling yells, spinning back to me. "Was it *worth it?*"

"You, Caspian. Kissing. Dying." My mouth is dry. There are charred handprints on the bark of the pine tree.

Darling's Chaos eyes shimmer with tears. "Close, but not quite accurate, was it?"

I don't say anything for a moment. I want to hold her. Would her hands burn me, too?

Darling looks away, out into the darkening shadows of the pine forest.

I say, "I imprisoned her. I wanted to save her for you. For House Kraken to choose her justice."

"Justice," Darling whispers.

I can't help but put my arms behind my back. Stand at attention. She's the Phoenix Reborn. When she turns to me again, her mouth is open to speak, but she stops. Stares at me.

"Wanted to," she says. "You wanted to save her for me. But you didn't."

"Aurora escaped," I say. It's a report. I'm delivering a very bad report to my superior. "We're scouring the territory for her, but we don't know where she'll go, what she wants. She can get anywhere."

Darling puts her fist against my chest and shoves. I step back, and she keeps coming. "Aurora Falleau escaped from *the War Prince*?"

I grab Darling's fist in both my hands. "She was faking her prophecy boon. Her real one is the most dangerous thing I've ever encountered." I can still feel the blades of my claw pressed up against my chin, feel the tremble of how badly I wanted to obey my aunt. I squeeze Darling's hands, hoping to impress upon her how serious this is. "She can . . . command. Persuade. With her voice. She speaks and you have to listen, to do as she says."

Darling closes her eyes. "And you can't find her with your boon."

"I've tried. My boon is greater than it was, but also gives me fevers and—"

She tugs her hand away even as I nod. "Come on, Talon. We have to explain this to Vivian, and then we'll see what I can do about your boon."

18

DARLING

We find Vivian in the common room that's been set aside for us. Apparently when you see a woman turn from a gryphon in front of your inn, special concessions are made. I asked the Barbs—even though Vivian says they became Flames when they pledged themselves to me, but whatever—to make sure that the innkeeper and his wife are compensated, and they returned saying that they only wished for me to unlock their grandchildren's boons, should they have them. It seems that word of my exploits has traveled faster than even Adelaide's tide-driven ship.

It is odd to be known. But I'm also happy to agree. Each boon unlocked is closer to—something. I'm not quite sure what, and neither the phoenix nor Chaos seems inclined to enlighten me. Hopefully I am not pushing us ever closer to our doom.

That is a problem for another day. Right now, I need to find Aurora so she can be brought to House Kraken justice.

And my best chance to do that is to figure out why Talon can't find her.

Vivian has a piece of parchment that she is drawing upon, and I realize that it's a map. When we approach, she looks up with a smile that dampens somewhat when she realizes Talon is right behind me. I understand how she feels. I am both repelled and attracted to Talon, my emotions seesawing from one moment to the next. I love him. I still do. But I'm so angry that it hurts to look at him.

"Vivian," I say, taking charge of the conversation before Talon can say something and ruin any chance of Vivian helping. I don't think she's quite over Caspian stealing her family relic, even though she is now in a position to create her own gryphon claw dagger. "I need your help."

"As long as you aren't planning a murder, I'm happy to assist," she says.

"You can see what is hidden. We need to find Aurora Falleau, the former Dragon seer. Can you feel where she's hiding?"

Vivian shakes her head sadly. "My ability doesn't work that way. I can't find her, not from a distance," Vivian says, standing with a frown. "But I can sense that something has been done to the War Prince's boon." She approaches Talon, walking around him as though inspecting a hog for auction. "It seems as though it's been hobbled. But you should be able to tell better than I can."

"I can't sense the boon itself at all," I say. "The Chaos is there but the spark of the boon . . ." Talon frowns, not liking that answer.

"I still have it, though," he says. "When I search for Caspian, I can still find him, even after whatever Aurora did. And that's how I found the sphinx, too. It does still work, only not on Aurora."

"What did she do?" Vivian asks, her expression mild but a note of emotion riding her voice. I don't know her well enough to sense it, and her face gives away nothing.

Talon explains once more how she escaped, and something that she did with a sigil and blood, and Vivian inhales sharply.

"Blood magic," she says, spitting on the floor like a superstitious peasant and not the head of a house. "That would explain the nausea I feel whenever I look at you. But why are you looking for her? What did your aunt do?"

"She killed Leonetti," I say, my tone flat. At some point the grief will overwhelm me, I can feel it waiting its turn, but for now I am more interested in finding Aurora and delivering her to Adelaide and Miranda. They deserve to give the woman House Kraken justice. "That's why we need to find her."

Vivian sits back down slowly and shakes her head. "You Dragons," she says, her voice low and full of rage. "How much more pain will you inflict for your selfish whims?"

Talon visibly hardens himself. "You say that as though House Gryphon wasn't supporting our actions every step of the way." Talon's tone isn't as icy as it should be, but he does hold Vivian's gaze.

"There is a ritual I read about," Vivian finally says. "It was about strengthening boons, but half of it was missing. One of the necessary items was a phoenix feather, even though the creatures have been extinct for centuries."

"I have feathers?" I ask, and Vivian shakes her head.

"From what I understood of the parchment, there were actual animals, phoenixes, fiery birds that nested in and around the central mountain range. Like the wild drakes that harass the countryside. But like the wild gryphons, they're long gone."

I tap my finger against my chin. "Perhaps the phoenix knows some way to unlock your boon," I say to Talon.

"You talk to your empyreals?" Talon asks, looking from Vivian to me.

"It's more feelings and impressions," Vivian says with a shrug. "But that's probably your best bet for finding the murderer. After all, her connection to Talon isn't just through his boon, but also by blood. If you can somehow unlock whatever she's done, it should be easy enough to track her."

Vivian stands and stretches, and gestures toward the table. "I'll give you two some privacy. Good luck," she says, picking up her map and leaving us alone. The innkeeper comes in as she departs.

"Good evening, my flame," he says bowing low to me. "War Prince. Can I bring you two something to eat and perhaps a refreshment?"

"Yes, whatever you have on hand," I say, and Talon inclines his head in agreement. I sit at the room's table and close my eyes, the sound of a chair scraping the floor a sign that Talon is doing the same.

I wait until the innkeeper has come and gone before I open my eyes and blow out the nearest candles. Before us on the table is an urn of a hearty stew, as well as soft white bread and a salad of dressed greens. I dig into the food, but Talon says he's eaten already. Fine. A sweet juice that I cannot quite recognize goes along with it, most likely a berry native to Dragon lands. I could ask Talon what it is, but we aren't in a place for casual conversation just yet, so I hold my tongue.

There is nothing but the sounds of my eating for a long moment, and when I've had my fill, I sit back and close my eyes once more. This time I am reaching for Chaos, or at least I think I am. I can sense the wells of it—in me, in the people in the main room drinking and whispering, and in Talon. But his is dim, muted, and I stand suddenly, startling Talon.

"I think maybe I can try and free your boon the same way I have for others," I say. "Are you willing to try?"

"Anything to find my aunt," he says.

I gesture for him to stand before me, and he does, an arm's length away. The phoenix is annoyed by this, urging me closer, and as I step forward, flames leap from the front of my body to lick over Talon's chest, the fire appearing from nowhere. I jump backward, eyes wide with alarm.

"Are you okay?" I ask, and he laughs.

"Yes. They weren't hot. It was more like a caress," he says in wonder. He raises a hand toward me but then thinks better of it and drops it back by his side.

The phoenix is not happy about that. And so I let the empyreal do as it pleases.

I step forward, nothing in my mind but finding Aurora and delivering her to justice. A strange cool fire erupts around us both, shading from orange to blue and finally a deep purple-black that seems to shimmer.

"Chaos," Talon says in wonder.

I place my hands on either side of Talon's face, the Chaos flames licking up his body. We are pressed together now, and it's hard to focus on what the empyreal and Chaos want me to do, because all I want to do is kiss him.

So I do.

Talon goes deathly still as I lower my lips to his. It's the kind of connection that sizzles every single nerve ending and leaves me feeling too warm and weak in the knees. I try to tell myself that this is to find Aurora, that I'm still angry with him, that nothing has changed. But my heart is a traitor, and calls me a liar.

With our lips connected, I can feel the Chaos of him, even that poor injured spot. It's like a spot of mold on his boon, a creeping poison. Not as bad as the frustrated boons I've seen across the land, but similar. Whatever Aurora did, it's bad.

And it's inexorably linked to her.

That is when the Chaos flowing around us reacts, poorly, and I am thrown backward across the room, slamming into the wall with an echoing boom, like artillery on a battlefield.

"Darling! Darling, can you hear me?"

I come back to myself slowly, and Talon helps me as I sit up with a groan. He kneels next to me, unmoving and watchful.

I swallow dryly. "Is there any water?" I ask, my voice hoarse.

"Brigh," Talon says, and there's the sound of running feet. "Are you hurt?"

"No. Just . . . angry," I say, because Chaos very much does not like what Aurora did to Talon. He yelps and dances back, and I realize that I am beginning to flare up. "I felt that one," he says with a small grin, and I find myself smiling back.

A cup of water is pressed into my hand, and I calm my fire enough to take it and swallow it down. The innkeepers stand in the doorway, and I hand the cup back to Brigh. "Thank you. Talon, could you, ah, help me to my room?" I say. My legs are weak, and as he helps me to my feet, I realize asking for help was a good call. Whatever happened when I tried to reach out to his boon has left me shaky.

The innkeepers stand in the doorway, their eyes tear-filled. I'm not sure what has upset them so much, but then I look down at the floor. The tables and chairs have been thrown against the walls, most of the furniture ruined and little more than kindling. But most grievous of all is the floor. The wood has been burned, the outline of a fiery bird still smoldering in bright spots that twinkle deep purple. It doesn't seem to be spreading, but then I realize that's because it's pure Chaos.

"I'm very sorry about your floor," I tell them. "I'm, uh, not sure it will go back to normal."

They shake their heads. "Don't be. It's an honor to host you, my flame," the woman says with a bow, her husband following suit awkwardly. I nod and Talon helps me past them and up the stairs.

"I—do you think you could compensate them for the room I just destroyed?" I whisper to Talon. "I'm sorry to ask you, but I have no gold, and I don't want to try and explain this to Vivian."

"Darling, you realize that you just made them incredibly rich, don't you?" he says incredulously. "They will be selling tickets to see the Mark of the Phoenix for generations. You gave them a gift."

I sigh. "Well, I'm glad something good came out of that. I'm sorry I couldn't unlock what Aurora did to your boon. Whatever it is, Chaos hates it."

"It's okay," he says, as we take the last few steps to the landing to my room. "Are you sure that you'll be all right, my flame?"

I look at him, trying to parse what he means by that. I realize that this is him telling me that every step we take will be my decision. Despite the kiss we shared—my lips tingle just thinking of it—he isn't reading anything into our embrace.

Somehow, that makes me love him a little more.

"I will be quite fine," I say. He hands me my goggles and I open the door to my room. "Good night, War Prince."

"Sleep well, my . . . phoenix," he says.

And then I close the door, and wonder how I am going to resist throwing him to the ground and loving him until Chaos devours us if we are ever alone again.

Neither the empyreal nor Chaos have an answer, either.

19

TALON

Darling and I agree to send Vivian and the rest of Darling's Flames with Brigh and the rest of the Dragons as an escort to Dragon Castle. I take Darling directly to the bowl lake where I found Caspian. I'm too anxious for him to return to us, especially after Darling revealed that Aurora actually damaged my boon with her blood magic.

If she hurt my boon, the wound could fester or grow until I can't find Caspian, or anyone.

I do my best to hide my fear from Darling. She doesn't need additional burdens. There is so much on her plate, and I know how to play my role. I'm the War Prince, commanding House Dragon to serve the phoenix. That's everything I can be for her right now.

I tuck fear away with the memory of her red-hot lips brushed against mine, and the feeling of her power pouring through me.

It rains for most of the first day we're alone, delaying us, but we make up for it by resuming before dawn. I think Darling is as eager as I am to find Caspian, to bring him back to himself. Or not Darling herself . . . but her phoenix. This is part of the Phoenix Reborn's mission, and it must be seen to.

It's disconcerting, but I try not to be jealous. If anything, Darling and Caspian's relationship is even more complicated than ours. And not in a good way. Especially now that they're both more than human. That's something I can't share with them.

The sun flashes between thick, fast-moving clouds when we leave the war drakes at the base of the ridge and climb onward. I go first, more experienced, and Darling takes my hand when I offer it to pull her up.

I realize, when she skids a little on a loose rock and squeezes my fingers, that she could have just flown over.

Maybe she's not used to being the Phoenix Reborn.

Maybe she wants to climb at my side, a small voice considers. I quash it.

We make it over the ragged tip of the ridge to find the valley empty. The lake glints painfully even to my eyes, and we slowly slide-climb down toward the soft patches of grass.

Darling puts her hands on her hips to look around. There's not much, just the lake, the scrubby grass and spindly evergreens, and the cave.

"He's near," she says, softly enough it's snatched away by the sharp wind.

I resituate the bag we brought over my shoulder. "The cave?"

Darling nods and starts for it. The ground is uneven, but not a treacherous incline. I'm drawn into the silence again. There aren't any birds up here, or the whisper of trees, or creaking of harnesses. Just our footfalls and the quiet lapping of the lake.

The cave entrance is triangular, its peak reaching very high and narrow, and only large enough at the base for the dragon empyreal to squeeze in. Barely, I think. We have plenty of room.

Gravel marks the threshold, giving way to smooth granite. It's totally dark beyond the reach of the sunlight, and smells like clean water and wet rock. I don't hear any dripping, but a very subtle rush. Maybe there's a spring in the back.

Darling removes her goggles almost immediately. I set the bag on a dry patch of rock and dig out a fire starter. But I don't get a light going. It would disrupt Darling's vision. Instead, I follow her, sticking close. Besides, Darling could just light up the whole cave with her phoenix fire if she needed it.

As my own vision adjusts, I can see the dim gray-blue of the cave farther in than I expected. There are piles of . . . things. Rubble, maybe, and what looks like a broad swath of tattered cloth, or a tapestry? I peer harder. There's an old trunk, half-rotted, and what spills out is shiny.

"I think that's . . . jewelry," Darling says, starting toward the old trunk.

A pole leans against the cave wall, hung with several pennants, dull now, but they must have once been bright red and green.

Darling crouches and touches the jewelry. It tumbles away under her fingers, sounding like coins and rocks.

"A hoard," I breathe. A very old one. Maybe untouched since the last dragon flew these skies.

Darling laughs a little. "Back there," she gestures toward the deeper shadows, "are some newer things. There's a statue, I think, and curtains, or . . ." She falls quiet.

"Darling?"

"He's coming back." Darling stands and brushes off her knees. She heads for the mouth of the cave again, replacing her goggles.

I go, too. If she manages to change Caspian back, I'll have other opportunities to explore. Maybe with my brother beside me.

The dragon is dropping out of the sky right onto us. He snaps his wings out, and the wind knocks me back. Darling manages to keep her feet.

Caspian fills the whole sky.

His rear claws touch down first, almost delicately, for all that his legs are as wide as the oldest red oaks on the western coast. He folds his wings back, and barely puts his foreclaws to the ground. I back up, toward the cave mouth, but Darling stands there, so close to him, even though compared to the dragon she looks tiny for the first time ever.

Caspian twines his neck, and brings his head down to stare at Darling. One huge violet-black eye pins her in place; then he twists his head to look at her with the other eye. Darling parts her lips to take a deep breath, but still refuses to give ground.

I can't stop staring at them, even when I notice Darling's hands flicker with her phoenix fire.

Then Caspian huffs a breath, and roars.

Darling flings an arm over her face. I wince.

Caspian throws himself back into the sky, wings beating hard.

Darling curses, tears off her goggles, and throws them to the side before her entire body ignites.

She's in the sky then, too, chasing after my dragon brother.

Just like before.

The two of them chase each other in high spirals. They vanish over the ridge, then burst back into my field of vision: distant, but they are a massive dragon and a tiny sun, spinning out from each other and back again in a dance.

Caspian flees, then wheels back as if he can't quite bring himself to leave entirely. Darling is right there, spinning around his tail, herding him closer. Not quite touching him.

Good, if he falls from that height—can she catch him without burning him, if he's a man again?

I can hardly breathe. I'm glued in place, helpless. My neck aches from bending back to watch. I can feel my pulse in my skull.

Caspian swoops down over the bowl lake, and I yell his name.

Darling makes her move.

The Phoenix Reborn cuts around, grasping at the dragon with fiery talons.

It happens so fast.

One moment: a dragon.

The next: empty sky, and a pale human form, bent and plummeting for the water.

I run.

Caspian splashes down.

I'm stripping off my coat and splashing into the water before I realize what I'm doing. I fling it back to shore, and follow it with my uniform jacket and shirt. There's no time for anything else. I push deeper and dive.

It's not too deep of a lake, and it's crystal clear. I swim, kicking hard, and have to go up for air. I dive again and see him: Caspian floats, limbs loose, naked, his long hair tangling like seaweed. No—he's sinking.

I swim for him. My lungs are burning; I should have left this to Darling—she was raised a squid, for Chaos's sake!—but there, I've got a hand in Caspian's hair. I grab it, pulling. My eyes sting, too, but I get an arm under his shoulder, and drag him up. I burst into the air and heave for breath.

I drag Caspian with me, holding his head above the water.

The shore is close: Darling, a girl again, waits with relief clear on her face.

When we're near enough, Darling helps me haul Caspian up.

He immediately groans and turns over, coughing up a little bit of water. I get up, shivering immediately. I head for the bag and fling it open, pulling out the clothes we brought, and the blanket. There's also food and fire supplies, but I push those aside and return to my brother.

Darling is helping him sit. His head is lowered, his hair dripping over his face and down his bent back. He draws his knees up and leans around them. Coughs again. I crouch back beside him. "Here's a blanket, and some clothes."

Caspian shoves Darling away, and glares at me. "Why did you do that?"

I frown. "Save you from drowning?"

His glare shifts, and for a moment I think he'll agree with me. But he merely sneers and says, "Turn me *back*."

I blink at him. Wind brushes my bare shoulders, and my whole body breaks out in goose bumps. I shiver. "Get dressed, Caspian."

Caspian mutters something that sounds really rude in response. He pushes Darling away, hard enough she falls back and lands on her hip. She makes a scoffing sound.

This is going great.

I stomp over to my shirt and uniform jacket, pooled on the ground like blood. I use my shirt to wipe water off my body and squeeze my hair. Then I put on my jacket and find my coat. My pants are soaked, my boots the same.

Darling is talking to Caspian, but I ignore them. I squelch around, gathering up some detritus and sticks, which aren't common up here. I take them just inside the cave and start making a fire. There's plenty of old cloth in this hoard that should burn just fine.

When I turn back, Darling is in the cave, too. I've found

something that will do as a blanket-skirt while my pants dry, and something easy to tear up into fuel. Darling uses her phoenix fire to light the fire.

Caspian stands at the mouth of the cave, gangly and exhausted-looking, wrapped in only the blanket. He's got the clothes bunched up in an arm, pressed to his chest. I can't see his expression as he's backlit.

I plop down and start the arduous process of removing my soaked boots, then prop them one by one near the fire. Then it's time for my pants. I pause for a moment, staring at the bright fire. Caspian slowly shuffles nearer, recalcitrance in every gesture.

Then I get up and back away, but not too far. Just to the edge of the light before I strip off my pants and underwear. It isn't like this is anything they haven't seen before, if either of them decides to look.

Darling busies herself taking out some of the food we brought, and then stomps off to get water for the pot.

Caspian sits and stares at me. I wrap the musty blanket around myself and join him.

The crackle of the fire is the only sound.

For nearly three months I've wanted to talk to my brother, and now I don't even know what to say. I stare back at him. His eyes are human green; maybe the pupils flicker with Chaos, or maybe it's just the fire between us.

Darling returns and plops the pot directly into the fire. "You two idiots," she says. "We don't even have tea or anything, but you're going to drink some hot water."

"Thanks," I say.

Caspian turns his ire to her, lips pressed mulishly.

Darling reaches over and shoves his shoulder. "You're welcome."

"I didn't thank you, nor shall I," he says, drawing himself up with all his arrogance. Even mostly naked, wrapped in a blanket, it works for him.

"You think I'm happy with this entire fiasco, Caspian Gold-hoard?" Darling snaps. "You did this to me, without asking me; you used me, used all of us, for your own purposes, and now you think you get to just walk away?"

"Fly away, preferably," he says primly.

"Oh, Caspian," Darling says slowly, and it sounds like she's really ramping up to lay into him.

He deserves it.

"You're the one who should be thanking me," he says, leaning into her anger. "*Phoenix.* Tell me, are you lauded as the heart of Pyrlanum? Are you our savior? Do people throw flowers at your feet yet, or feathers or something? Matchsticks?"

"Are you joking about this?" Darling's fists spark. "It's been a disaster. No one knows what to do—and you could have warned us! We could have prepared! People drowned! That barghest nearly *ate someone.* I set fire to half a forest!"

Caspian smiles.

I grip Darling's forearm. She startles, looks down at my hand. Then slowly uncurls her fists. She doesn't look at me.

"What's your plan now?" I ask my brother.

"Plan?" He turns wide eyes to me.

"You're the only one who knew, or at least guessed, this out-come. So you must have a plan, or seven."

"I don't have a plan, little dragon," Caspian says, quietly. His face drains of all expression. "I didn't think past the ritual."

"Yeah, right," Darling says.

A sad smile turns up the corner of Caspian's mouth. "I didn't think I had to."

Dread curls in my gut, and I tighten my hand around Darling's wrist.

Caspian glances at my hand. "I was supposed to die," he murmurs. He blinks, like he's seeing something we can't.

Maybe he is.

"What?" Darling stands up, snatching her arm from my grasp. "Who did you think would be the dragon empyreal?"

Caspian flicks his gaze to me, and draws the blanket tighter around his shoulders. "I knew I was bringing back the phoenix, Darling. I thought it would cost me my life. A heart for a heart."

Everything Caspian said to me leading up to the fiery ritual falls into place. Things like *I'll never be old* and *not your time, still mine, for a little while.* "Caspian," I say, and even to myself I sound strangled.

"I knew you'd be a good Dragon regent," Caspian says. He reaches out and pats my arm. "And really, you should still do that. When I recover my energy, I'll just . . ." He waves his hands in a vague flapping motion.

"That's not how it works," Darling says. She thumps back down beside me. "You did this; you're just as stuck with it as we are. You have to come back to Dragon Castle and wade into these dirty waters with the rest of us."

"What if I don't want to?"

He sounds like a spoiled child. But anxiety and affection curdle together in my stomach. He gave so much up for this. He thought he was dying. For Pyrlanum. For the phoenix to return. I can feel myself forgiving him more with every breath he takes.

Darling ignores Caspian and fishes the pot of boiling water from the fire with her *bare hands*. "Well, this needs to sit a minute before you try to drink it," she says, wincing.

I say to my brother, "You don't have to rule." I clear my throat. "You don't have to. Just . . . come back with us, and be there. You're an empyreal. A regent. Just . . . help me, for a little while. When we get everything worked out, it's all right if you come back here. If you . . ." The words are too thick in my throat. "If you stay."

"Talon, you—" Darling gapes at me.

"I can do it," I promise Caspian. I don't want to. It's never been something I wanted. But I can. For him.

Caspian groans. He leans back, arching almost inhumanly, then slaps his hands over his face. I stare, confused.

Then my brother gets up, awkwardly, and folds himself back down around me. His arms wind around my shoulders. "You're the worst," he whispers. "Why are you like this? Who taught you to be like this?"

I grip his wrist in both my hands, pressing it to my neck. I squeeze my eyes closed.

"You're the one who's the worst, Caspian," Darling mutters.

His arms tighten around me.

I feel something brush hair back from my temple, there and gone. Maybe Darling, I don't know. The fire flickers heat against my face, and I hold on to my brother. He's coming home with me.

20
DARLING

I'd almost forgotten what a brat Caspian can be.

He is sullen on the trek down the mountain to the ancient castle that is the seat of House Dragon. I wasn't expecting him to be so unhappy about being able to release his dragon empyreal, even after the stupid chase he led me on. When I try to explain to him that the dragon isn't gone, he roars at me, more empyreal than man, and I respond by flashing a few of my flames and yelling back at him, the phoenix's scream. Talon has to jump aside at the flaming wings that burst from my back, but the display goes a long way toward quieting Caspian's sulk.

As does Talon's quiet declaration that Elias will be delighted to see him.

Actually, it's probably more the mention of Elias than anything I do. The phoenix is also unhappy with the dragon, the same irritating, scraping emotion I felt when I freed Adelaide. I wish I could speak with the phoenix, a real conversation, not the strange impressions of emotions and urges that I currently have.

Our arrival at House Dragon is a solemn affair. The barghest comes bounding out of the main gate, a fearsome, slavering hound. Talon shouts for him to wait, but I know what he needs, and I run forward to greet him as well. He skids as he realizes who I am, a momentary fear, but by then I've already grabbed him and released his empyreal form, Talon shrugging out of his jacket for the boy who suddenly sits on the ground, shivering and dazed.

"You could've at least waited to warn him," snaps a too-familiar voice. Finn stands at the gate with the castelaine, which is what Talon told me the woman who maintains the house is called. House Kraken had no such titles, but I suppose that is because the manor house was never left empty to take over another seat of power. All the Dragons' names run together in my head, and I am reluctant to enter the place. I find the castle cold, gloomy, and unwelcoming. It is more a place of defense than any other house seat we've been to, and here in the mountains, it's hard not to remember that Talon's people slaughtered mine. The Dragons are too much like the inhospitable land they call their own.

"I find it's best to get it over with quickly. Unless you have first-hand knowledge of being the phoenix?" I say as Finn steps forward to bow to Caspian and Talon as we continue into the castle.

Finn's jaw tightens, the barb landing home, but he doesn't respond. He hesitates for a moment but then grimaces and gives me a bow as well. "My flame," he grits out. The bow he makes in my direction isn't as sharp or deep as the ones he gives Talon and Caspian, but it is clear that it pains him to show even that modicum of respect. I wave him away. I'm not interested in petty grievances at this point. I have much bigger concerns. Besides, the castelaine gives me a kind smile as she inclines her head in respect. It's a less ostentatious gesture, but at least she means it.

Vivian and Elias greet us just inside the main gate, Elias rushing to Caspian and then holding themself back as they remember that their relationship is an open secret.

"High Prince Regent," Elias says, sinking into a low bow, and Caspian shakes his head.

"Not any longer," he says, an edge of annoyance riding his words. "Why don't we just stick with Caspian for now."

"Well, Caspian, the least you can do is acknowledge Elias. They've practically wasted away to nothing waiting for you," Vivian snaps, clearly annoyed. Caspian huffs, and I put my hands on my hips.

"Enough," I say. "Caspian, go find something to wear. Vivian, are Adelaide and Gianna here yet?"

"The kraken said they would be here by the dinner hour," Elias says, even as he casts baleful glances at Caspian.

"Any sign of the cockatrice?" I ask, even though I already know the answer. I can't sense the last empyreal at all, and that is a problem. It's like a missing tooth, and the lack is an annoyance. It isn't a problem for now, but I have the sense that it could be. The phoenix is adamant we need every empyreal to anchor Chaos, whatever that might mean.

"None. We've even tapped into our spy networks," Finn says, reluctantly giving me the report. Darvey, the barghest, now in little-boy form, stands a little behind Finn, his shadow. The kid is a terrible judge of character, but what can be expected from someone who grew up where he did? House Barghest was a terrible place run by terrible people.

"As soon as the creature rears its head, I will let you know," Finn says. And then, after Talon gives him a sidelong glance, he adds, "My flame."

I sigh and rub my temples. The cockatrice issue is an annoying one, but there's something calling my attention in the castle. "I have to take care of something, and then I want a bath. And a nap in a real bed. Since Adelaide won't be here until the evening, why don't we reconvene then?" I say, and then I turn and leave without waiting for an answer, the phoenix and Chaos both pulling me toward something crucial.

"Darling," Talon says, running after me. I don't slow my steps, and I give him only the barest of glances.

"What's wrong?"

"Nothing, I just . . . are you okay?"

"Yes, but there's something here . . ." I stop in the corridor and back up. The walls are lined with tapestries, some of them old enough to have been made in the days before the first empyreals, and it's just such a tapestry that I stop before. "There's a door here."

Talon nods. "How did you . . . no, never mind," he says, pulling the material back carefully to reveal a small wooden door that looks as though it were made for a child.

"Where does that go?" I ask, because there's no lock.

"The root cellar," he begins, but I'm already shoving the wooden door to the side and tearing off my lenses as I descend into the gloom. "Wait, that's not all that's down there. I'll take you, but you should be careful."

"It's down here, whatever . . ." And that's when I feel it, the same urge to just *explode* that I felt on the Teeth Islands.

"Get back!" I tell Talon, before setting off into a run. There truly is a root cellar, but there is something else besides, a rot that must be cleansed.

And whatever it is fills me with anger and annoyance that I fully understand is not my own.

A chill wind runs down the corridor, the draft coming from in front of me, and I skid to a stop and I realize that this is much more than a root cellar—it's also an escape route. Light from up ahead casts the path before me in grayscale, but it's still too far away to see the doorway. The tunnels bend and twist, and I'm sure there are any number of traps I could be setting off.

"Darling, let me get a boonlight and come with you. I've been this way recently. There's a lake and something like an altar—"

"No," I say, my voice ricocheting off the stone walls so that my response sounds monstrous. "It isn't safe for you." I don't want to worry about Talon's safety, now that I know I have something bigger to handle. "You won't survive what I'm about to do."

That seems to mollify him, and I go back to following the path through the mountain. There are times when I lose myself, and I realize that it's possible to use the phoenix to move great distances in the blink of an eye. But I'm careful to go only as far as I can see.

The path finally widens, and I get the sense that we are far beneath the castle. The path through the stone has opened up into an amphitheater of sorts, a large area with an underground lake, the kind of place a house could hide out during a siege and easily defend. There are other entry points along a far wall, and I make a note to ask Talon if he knows where they all go. Dragons. So predictable.

The lake in the middle is what draws my attention, and as I step into the icy water, my boots immediately soaked since I don't bother removing them, I can sense the horrible things that happened in that spot.

A dragon, old and cunning, hatching a plan to rid the land of the young, newly risen phoenix with the help of a blood mage and the kraken.

A ritual, bloody and awful, the phoenix lured under the mountain by falsehoods and a too-trusting demeanor.

And a heart, imprisoned in flame, scale, and seaweed so that a new phoenix could not be reborn.

But worse than all that, Chaos, at the bottom of the lake, stoppered and unable to flow without a phoenix to call it forth.

I dive, going down, farther down than I have ever dived in my life. But the lake is bottomless, and I will drown before I get to the source of the problem.

And so I call forth the phoenix.

I am righteous flame, and I am angered by an ancient betrayal. But more than that, I am saddened. Chaos beckons, and when it reaches out to me, I reach back, a beloved parent welcoming me home.

And then I am nowhere and everywhere all at once.

I walk, shivering and naked, across a scrubby meadow. The sun shines, but this far north it's more of an idea of warmth despite the season. I consider shifting back into the phoenix and flying back to House Dragon, which looms in the distance, but I am exhausted and I'm pretty sure I might crash right into a turret. Still, I'm debating doing it anyway when there is a shout.

"Lady Phoenix," someone calls, and I turn to see a freckle-faced girl with pale skin running headlong toward me with a blanket, her pale braids flying out behind her. She runs too fast for a normal person, and I smile. "The War Prince said you'd be here after you ordered him not to follow."

I accept the blanket and wrap it around my shoulders. "Did you have that boon before, or did you just get it?" I ask.

She hops from foot to foot. "Just got it! Fergus won't be able to pull on my braids now."

I laugh. "Would you be so kind as to run back and tell the War Prince that I'm fine and I'll be there shortly?"

"Mm-hmm!" And then she's gone, a retreating form sprinting back across the meadow.

I walk toward the castle, each step slow and deliberate. I just want to sleep for a week. Even the phoenix agrees with me. It's the first time the empyreal hasn't urged me on to another task.

Puffs of dust begin to rise, and riders approach. Talon sits upon Kitty, and Finn rides alongside, leading a third mount. Once, the war drakes frightened me. Now, thanks to Talon, I know how to coo and scratch them to make them more amicable. Although part of me wonders if that's the effect of the phoenix as well.

"What did you do?" Finn demands as they draw even with me.

"I freed Chaos," I say.

"It's not that," Talon says. "The people . . . you've given them something . . . special."

"It's easier to fix Chaos than each person," I say. "Safer for everyone. In the Teeth Islands, there was a structure . . . I've been sensing them all over. I think they're the reason that the phoenix disappeared and the boons weakened at the same time. But can we talk about this later? I am tired and hungry, and no offense, but I will eat a drake if I have to." At Kitty's askance look I pat her warm scales. "Not you, friend."

I climb onto the drake, whom I decide to call Violet because of the purple streaks in his feathers, and we ride. Talon only speaks once, to tell me that when he was near the lake, he found an old study belonging to a blood mage. He gathered what he could, and Elias has been researching. It is, of course, where Aurora learned. Talon says there's more in Phoenix Crest. I let his words roll through me, but try not to absorb too much. The phoenix and I are too tired to deal with this right now.

The rest of the ride to the castle is silent. When we arrive, a bevy of women help me off the drake and take me up to the room I've been given.

"Hurry back down," Talon calls. "Everyone is here and unhappy."

I nod, intending to rush, but when I get to my room, I realize that there is no way I can pass up the bath waiting for me in the center of the room.

Talon will just have to keep them distracted.

A fire blazes in the hearth, the flames climbing higher when I near. The tub of steaming water is far too warm for just about any-one else, but it is perfectly delicious for me, and I have to swallow a squeal as I climb in. I never want to leave.

Especially since there is a dining room full of angry empyreals somewhere beneath me.

I doze in the bath while one of the women helps get the tangles out of my hair with a familiar-smelling pomade, and when I turn around, I realize it's Miranda. "I didn't know you were here," I say, feeling drowsy and relaxed. "But I didn't really think that Dragons knew anything about coca-nut oil."

"I told Adelaide I would hurry you along. She knows how you like to luxuriate in the bath."

"It's hard work fixing Chaos," I mutter. "I can at least take a ten-minute bath."

Miranda gives a breathy laugh. "I wanted to get a few moments to talk to you without Adelaide around as well," she says, the comb tugging rhythmically as she picks knots out of my hair just like she did when I was little. "I want to stay with you and serve at Phoenix Crest when Adelaide goes back to the sea."

That wakes me up, and I sit up in the bath, water sloshing all over. "What? I mean, I would love to have you, it's just—are you sure? I cannot imagine Adelaide will be happy about that."

Miranda puts the comb to the side and grabs a nearby pitcher and pours a measure of the concoction before handing me the cup. "Drink."

I glance at it and laugh. "You aren't trying to poison me, are you? You should've done that before I was an empyreal."

She doesn't even smile, and so I take a drink. It's a strange blend of things, cactus pear and some fruit I know but don't recognize, herbs and a spice that makes my tongue feel a little numb. But more than that, as soon as I drink it my fatigue melts away and I feel brand-new.

"Whoa, did you make this?" I ask, and Miranda nods slowly.

"My boon. I always knew how to make poisons, things that would hurt people. But now, I can fix people as well. I think I should be somewhere I can share my recipes with as many people as possible."

"You can do that on a ship," I say, and Miranda shakes her head.

"No. I can't. Adelaide is, well, she's not handling Leonetti's death."

"Will she be a problem?" I ask, voice low, and Miranda shakes her head.

"No. But I think maybe she needs space. She's so angry. She

yelled at a deckhand the other day, and one moment she was fine, and the next there was lightning flying off her in strange little bolts. I just need some time. On my own." Miranda closes her eyes for a moment before opening them. She's so pretty, but there are dark circles under her eyes. "I'm so tired. I just want a break."

I nod. "Miranda, I love you. You're my sister. But Adelaide is going to be hurt if you leave. Talk to her first. And I support whatever you decide."

"I know. Now, let's get you dressed before they all kill each other."

When I enter the main dining hall, Miranda is closer to the truth than either of us realized. Caspian slouches at one of the tables while Elias watches him from another. Vivian and Adelaide are arguing about something while Gianna, the new sphinx, looks on with crossed arms and an expression of dismay. Darvey Brynson, our Barghest regent, hides under a table, Finn kneeling nearby and trying to convince him to come out and sit at the table like the boy he is, and not a hound. Talon watches the havoc before him like a man drowning, and somehow it is his lost look that provokes my ire.

"Enough," I shout, and there is a *whoosh* as flames erupt around me before receding once more. Everyone in the room falls silent, and I stride into the room. I'm not wearing one of Caspian's extravagant concoctions, not anymore. Instead I wear a simple dress of purple and black. The colors of Chaos. I like it, even though I am pretty sure the phoenix chose it.

"The war is over," I say. "And the longer you all keep bickering or refusing to acknowledge it, the harder it will be to convince the rest of the continent to lay down their arms. Adelaide, House Gryphon isn't your enemy. If you want reparations for grievances, make a list and we will address them. Vivian is reasonable. Vivian, you will also be making reparations to House Sphinx, so that Gianna can reestablish the house. Same with House Dragon. Get me a list of assets seized from House Sphinx in the past decade and begin the transfer of ownership. Wrongs will be righted."

The room is deathly silent in the wake of my pronouncement, and for a moment I wonder if I've overstepped. But the phoenix preens. *Never*, it says, and the voice is so unexpected that I hesitate before moving on.

"Darvey. Come here," I say, gentling my voice. It's clear he doesn't want to listen, but he's an empyreal, and he can't resist scampering out and creeping close to me, to the Chaos that I am.

"You need to reestablish your house," I say to him. "Is there any-one you can ask to help at House Barghest?"

He shakes his head, wide-eyed. "My father said that they were nothing more than a nest of vipers." He's so young, so small, and I think of the massive hound he was just moments ago.

"You need a second-in-command," I say. "Think upon who you would like—"

"Finn," he says, looking back at the scarred mountain of a man, and I sigh.

"Think about it," I say, my words for Darvey, but my gaze upon Finn, who looks like he's just discovered a talking drake. "Finn is House Dragon and would need to be released from his duties here to swear fealty to another house."

"Is that a no?" Darvey asks, looking like he might run back and hide under the table.

"No, it's a 'talk to people before making decisions for them,'" I say. "Talk to Finn. And Caspian, since he is head of the house, and then let everyone know your decision tomorrow."

"Oh, so now you care what I think?" Caspian says, and when I shoot him a sharp look, he presses his lips together.

"Are you returning to Phoenix Crest, then?" Vivian asks. "General Bloodscale will be difficult to dig out."

"He'll obey if he wants to remain a Dragon general," Talon says coldly.

I take a deep breath, and begin to pace as I talk. "We have before us the unenviable task of ending a war none of us started," I say. "We are all going to make mistakes, and that includes me. When the phoenix is rested, I will leave for Phoenix Crest and subdue any remaining resistance to peace that stands before us. Caspian, can you please send a missive to your general, warning him that if he continues to wage war, he will have to face the wrath of the phoenix?"

Caspian gives me a messy salute. "Anything else?"

I give a short nod. "Enjoy your dinner. I am tired and will be taking the evening meal in my room."

I spin on my heel and leave, hands fisted so no one will see them shaking. As soon as I leave, the room erupts in conversation once more, voices raising in a way that indicates more arguing. I decide that it can be someone else's problem for the moment.

How in the name of Chaos am I ever going to be able to lead this thrice-cursed country?

And do I even want to?

21

TALON

The sun has just risen, but hides behind the eastern peaks of the Hundred Claw Mountains. They rise black and jagged silhouettes, the sky behind them pale blue smearing into gilded gray and yellow. Lines of fire highlight a few long, streaking clouds. I watch the color change from the highest lookout tower of Dragon Castle, trying to clear my mind of everything else.

There's a covered coffee service beside me, thick and brewed sweet as I've always liked it. When I prepared it in the upper kitchens, I realized I have no idea how Darling likes to drink coffee, or if she likes it at all. It's been rare to find in Pyrlanum during the last few years of the war.

Last night everyone was given honored guest quarters, and ushered into their own spaces after Darling left so dramatically. Annag is good at hosting, thank Chaos. I'm not, and Caspian doesn't even try.

It was something Aunt Aurora did for us.

Caspian fled to his own rooms and locked himself in. I assumed he had plenty of alcohol, and hoped that Elias would join him, though Vivian's expression made her seem intent on keeping her cousin with her for the night. I tried to relax with Finn and Brigh in their rooms instead, listening to them drink and tease each other, catching up as they haven't been able to do in more than a year. Darvey fell asleep in a pile of blankets near the hearth, and once the boy passed out, Brigh immediately laid into her twin for adopting a son when she wasn't looking. Finn poured himself more liquor and insisted Darvey was more like a baby brother, but without any heat and avoiding my gaze. That's how I knew Finn was considering Darvey's request to be his second.

Finn will be a good second—I know, because of how long he's been mine. I won't keep him from leaving House Dragon.

Realizing it made me maudlin and childish. I hadn't even had a drop of wine. They were selfish feelings unworthy of the First Scion of House Dragon. Of the War Prince.

When I said good night, it was late, and I wandered past the rooms Annag had assigned to Darling. I closed my eyes in the hall-way and nearly reached for her with my boon. But if I had, she might have noticed and come out, and then what would I have done but kiss her and try to share something I didn't have any right to any longer?

Instead I left Darling alone. I asked the Dragon soldier stationed in that wing to pass a message to the Phoenix Reborn, asking her to join me on the parapets in the morning to make an attempt to-gether to locate the missing cockatrice empyreal.

I've been waiting here since the first light paled the sky. I expect it might be some time more. Darling is not the dawn riser I am. I do know that much. I know what she's like, her courage, her vicious defense of justice, her laughter. It's the details of how she would live her life if she could choose that I don't know. Coffee sweet or bitter? Favorite soup? Does she eat breakfast early? Prefer to spar in the morning or evening? Does she read for pleasure? Do I even know how to do that? Would we be friends if we'd met as regular people?

There are no regular people in times like these. Everyone has been forced to choose sides.

And now she's the Phoenix Reborn.

The sun breaks over the long side of Scar Scale Peak, and I have to look away.

When I finally turn my back to the morning, Darling is there. She stands in the dim shadows of the stairway, her goggles mirroring the sun as tiny pupils of fire against the round black lenses. She leans her shoulder lazily against the stone arch. Her curls are pulled back into a simple knot, a few broken free already around her face.

"Darling," I say.

She smiles, and it turns into a yawn. She covers her mouth with the back of her hand.

I love her.

It's incredible to me that half a year ago I didn't know her name. She was only a strange, frightening figment of my brother's wild mind. There was an empty place for Darling with me, with us, for as long as I can remember, and she just wasn't in it.

Now she is. But the shape of it is so different from anything I could have guessed.

"Come have some coffee," I say, managing to sound normal, I think.

Darling nods sleepily and drops down onto the cold stone floor beside the dome covering the tray. I crouch and pour, handing her a cup. There's no steam anymore. "I assume you can heat it again?"

She smirks. But just swallows the coffee directly, and holds out her cup for more.

I oblige. There are a few breakfast snacks, too, cakes with dried fruit, and we eat a little in silence. As the light grows, a few sparrow drakes chirp at us from the barren cliffs beside the tower. They hop around in their morning routines, eating little bugs if they can catch them. Two dive to land on the crenellations beside us, heads cocked in curiosity. A green one chitters at us. I toss it the end of my cake. Its dark blue friend snatches the cookie and they're off, snarling at each other playfully as they fight over the snack.

Darling is sitting straighter by the time she's had half the coffee. "You think we can find the cockatrice together?"

"I wonder if, because you have a connection to the empyreals, that would be enough of a trace that I can stretch my boon to follow it."

Darling hums thoughtfully. "It's possible. But we have to be careful. We don't know what Aurora did to you."

"It's worth the risk, to find the cockatrice." I clench my jaw, glancing away. I tried again to find my aunt after the weird wave of Chaos that Darling unleashed yesterday—it woke several boons, and caused the castle foundations to tremble. I hoped whatever she unlocked had burned away the blood magic inside me. But it didn't work. I can't see Aurora.

"Ready?" Darling says, brushing her hands together to shake the crumbs away.

"Yes."

We situate ourselves facing each other, cross-legged. Our knees could press together if either of us shifted slightly. "If it's too hot," she says, "you can back up."

"Last time when you did this it felt good." I glance at her lips then away.

Darling takes a deep breath. "I'll try and focus on the phoenix's link to the cockatrice. What do you need to see it?"

"I'm not sure. I've felt your power before . . . and other times. I think I can concentrate that way."

"All right." She doesn't sound convinced, but neither am I.

I offer my hand.

Darling takes it. I curl my fingers around her wrist, and she does the same.

Then I close my eyes and open my boon. Immediately my head aches, starting in the back where the spine meets skull.

"I feel that," Darling murmurs. "I'll start . . . looking."

I ignore the pain and focus on Darling's trace. It's different than it was weeks ago. It licks with flame, like a spill of white-hot fire. I see it, and I feel it like it's part of me, too. My fingers tighten on her wrist as I let my awareness of her trace open up to what I know of the cockatrice empyreal. The imagery I've seen: a large rooster, with scales and feathers, angry emerald eyes. Darling once teased Finn that the war drakes looked more like cockatrices than dragons.

Darling's hand in mine isn't just warm, it's hot. I'm hot all over. Sweat breaks down my back.

The cockatrice's trace is there, I see it, I feel it. But I cannot grasp it. Like a road of stars, fading into a horizon because the sun is coming up. Darling is that sun, her trace overpowering the link to the empyreal. Impossible to follow.

I hold my boon open; I strain to make out the edges of the path, the direction. East, east, that is the best I can do.

Darling's trace pushes into me. Claiming control. My eyes open of their own accord. Her goggles are gone, dropped in her lap. Her eyes are closed, and her skin is shining, like she's made of embers, a banked fire.

Her skin is so hot under my fingers. It will burn me.

I can't look away. I can't let go. She's so gorgeous.

Then fire licks up her forearms. Dancing like little butterflies. They appear on her cheeks, too, iridescent orange and gold, with sparks of blue. The fire grows, springing in arcs of flame-feathers.

It's too hot. My whole body sweats. My hand hurts. I don't let go.

I grit my teeth. I hope Darling can use my boon better than I can.

The pain in my hand sharpens. I must make a noise.

Darling's eyes fly open.

She instantly flings back from the morning light shining behind me, crying out.

The fire extinguishes.

My vision is hazy with after-images of my Darling, the Phoenix Reborn, surrounded by beautiful, perfect fire. "Darling?" I say. I can barely see, but I reach for her.

The movement makes me grunt, then hiss.

Darling scrambles to get her goggles back in place, grimacing and cursing under her breath.

"Anything?" I ask, bringing my hand to cradle gently near my lap. It's burned, but not too badly. I don't see blistering, but the cold wind that soothes my headache makes the burned skin hurt sharply.

"The same. Except, maybe I saw she's . . . young. Very young? I can't be sure."

"I only know they're east of here. Maybe over the sea, where House Cockatrice fled."

"East. We'll have to send someone."

"You can't leave, but it also has to be—" I frown, working out our options. I wince at the growing pain in my burned hand.

"Talon!" Darling lunges for my hand. She stops herself right before touching it.

"I'll be all right. We have salves for this. Elias will help and get it wrapped."

"Let me," Darling says. She reaches slowly for my hand. I don't move. She touches the wound gently; it's soothing.

Surprise makes my hand twitch.

"I'm sorry," she says quickly.

"It's fine," I say. "Is that part of your power? Healing."

Our heads are so close the breeze brushes one of her stray curls against my temple. "Maybe. Yes. Everything is still unclear. I wish I could spend more time with the Gryphon library. Or maybe there's still something to find here. Dragons hoard, after all."

"You should speak with Elias. They're supposedly the expert on boons, before this."

"We're meeting later this morning to talk about blood magic, too."

"They studied what Aurora did to me, as best they knew how." I look down at my hand. The ache is deep, but no longer sharp. Darling slowly cups my hand in both of hers, fingers soft as they pet the tender skin. Around her, little flicks of ash mar the tower stone, in swirls like feathers. "Darling, what is it like to fly?" I ask.

Her head comes up and I feel pinned in place by her goggled gaze. I wish it was dusk, or I could swathe the sun in heavy clouds, so she could look at me with only her Chaos eyes. Her mouth opens, just a bit.

"Talon!" My brother's voice whips between us.

We jerk apart, jarring my burned hand.

Darling whirls on her knees. "What is it, Caspian? We're busy!"

I carefully get to my feet and tuck my burned hand behind my back. It's a habit to hide my weaknesses, especially from Caspian, if I can.

Caspian strides toward us from the stairway. His hair is loose, and his embroidered robe hangs off his shoulders, the hem dragging behind him. But he's fully dressed beneath it, for once, in daytime clothes even, dark green and dragon-leather accents. Except his bare feet.

I end my sweep at his face and freeze.

Caspian's expression is pinched and cold, his lips pale as death. His eyes seem luminous with absolute fury.

I have to steel myself not to step back.

Darling moves between us. "What in lizard shit is wrong?"

Without breaking his glare, he firmly shoves Darling aside and uses all the height he has on me to loom over me. I've never seen him like this. He looks so angry. "Why," he says in the coldest voice I've ever heard, "didn't you kill Aurora Falleau when you had the chance?"

I settle my stance and release my clenched jaw. "She was awaiting trial. There was a lot going on."

"Trial?" Caspian curls his fingers in the lapel of my uniform jacket and twists. "What does she need a trial for? You know what she did; you know exactly what she did."

"It was more complicated than that." I grab his wrist with my uninjured hand and squeeze, shoving him back.

Caspian draws his lips back from his teeth and it looks ugly. "I trusted you to take care of her! I—" He closes his eyes. Says through his teeth: "And you let her *escape*."

"Caspian," Darling says.

"And you," he whirls. Points a shaking finger in her face. "Did the War Prince describe how your father died? The way Aurora shoved her hand into his body and tore out his heart?"

Darling swallows. She sucks in a breath but can't answer.

"Caspian, stop," I step forward and grab his shoulder. "She'll die. She'll pay."

Caspian laughs. He doesn't stop. He backs away from us, hands on his face. His whole frame shakes with his hysteria.

I look at Darling; she looks back at me. I shake my head. She does the same.

Caspian crouches suddenly, his knees poking out like grasshopper legs, his back bent over. He moans through the laughter, shaking his head. He digs his hands back into his hair and pulls tight.

I leap forward and try to stop him before he rips his scalp bloody.

"Caspian," Darling gasps, and helps me.

Together, we get him seated. His legs sprawl. Darling pets his hair back, taking his hands in hers.

"Don't use your phoenix magic on me," he spits, pulling away from her.

I get him a cup of the cold coffee and put it to his lips. Caspian drinks messily, rolling his head to look at me. His eyes are wide and sad now.

"She was supposed to die," he whispers.

"Who wasn't supposed to die?" I say. I don't want Caspian like this, mad with his expectations. I'll never forget him saying *he* was supposed to die. Better yesterday when he was being a brat.

"Talon," Darling chides this time. "Stop. And Caspian, pull yourself together. Kraken and I are the aggrieved party, and we will take care of her justice."

"Death," he insists.

"Maybe!" Darling flings up her hands. "I'm—the phoenix isn't like that. It can't always be death. Besides, I thought you were tired of war and killing. I thought you wanted to be better than the people who came before."

Caspian looks at her and smiles. "You think better of me than I deserve. Naive. I thought my baby brother was the naive one. I suppose you're well suited."

Caspian closes his eyes again and leans his head back against the tower wall.

Darling moves her head and brow, so I know she's rolling her eyes. Nausea has settled in my stomach.

Suddenly Caspian sits up. "You're wrong," he says. "I'm the aggrieved party, if that's a game you want to play. I demand Aurora Falleau's death."

"You're the aggrieved party?" Darling drawls. "Do tell."

Caspian leans toward her and his smile becomes downright vicious. "She killed my mother, and framed House Sphinx, which was subsequently wiped off the face of our island."

The tower beneath me tilts. I might say something, but there's a roaring in my ears. I shake my head.

Mother. Aurora. It's impossible. I can't believe it. I'm shaking my head. A hand grips my wrist, then another. Darling is before me, her mouth moving, her hands on my wrists. My right hand throbs.

I see my mother, her long pale hair, her hands pinching weeds, showing me where to pinch, too, my tiny fingers in the dirt. She laughs at something—me, maybe, or Caspian, I don't know.

It's my last memory before she died.

"Caspian," I finally manage. I hold on to Darling, but I look at my brother. "What—what happened?"

"She poisoned her. I don't know why." Caspian sits there, almost relaxed. He pours the last of the cold coffee and pouts when nothing more drips out of the pot. "I saw her die. I saw the poisoned cup. I painted it," he says so quietly. His lashes flutter. "I didn't know what it was. And I saw Aurora pour the tainted tea." Caspian drinks the last coffee, knocking it back like liquor, and leaves his head hanging back, his neck long and vulnerable.

"You painted it," I say. My voice sounds hoarse, like I've been screaming. "But Darling wasn't . . ."

"Oh, little dragon. I didn't start painting Darling until that day. I think that's what made your fate, Darling." He lowers his head to smile. "Aurora's actions. I suppose you could thank her. We all could. She started the course of events that would return the phoenix to Pyrlanum."

Darling reaches for her own coffee cup. She flings it at Caspian, and an arc of leftover coffee splatters his face. He blinks, shocked. Then grins.

He says, "If you don't want to thank her, let's go slit her throat."

"No."

Caspian whines, "Darling. Everything I've done since I was eight years old has been to make Aurora pay for taking my mother from me."

My jaw feels permanently fused, but Darling scoffs. "I don't believe that," she says. "You might want her dead, and I understand. I do, too. But that isn't why you set yourself on fire. You didn't play mad and lie to everyone you cared about for revenge. You did it to bring justice back to Pyrlanum. For everyone. For me." Darling punches Caspian in the shoulder. "You're such a jerk. But you want what we want. We're going to make this place better than our ancestors could."

My chest is warm again, finally, the nausea pulling into something like faith. Faith in Darling, in the Phoenix Reborn.

But Caspian studies her for a moment, chin up, arrogant. "You do that. I'm going to kill my aunt."

Then he glances at me. He stands. And he sweeps away, leaving us there without a reply.

22

DARLING

It feels odd to depart the ramparts in the aftermath of Caspian's tantrum, but I have my own tasks to take care of, and at the end of the day, his whims are no longer my problem. Maribel Calamus, scion of House Sphinx, was beholden to Caspian Goldhoard, High Prince Regent. Darling Seabreak, Phoenix Reborn, is not.

Besides, Caspian isn't the only person unhappy with me.

Adelaide and Gianna leave early, shortly after breaking their fast, the sphinx staring at me a bit awestruck, and Adelaide looking like she wants to take me out to sea and throw me overboard.

"I suppose Miranda spoke to you," I say, and Adelaide responds by angrily throwing her pack in the back of the carriage that will take her and Gianna back to the port where the Kraken flagship is docked.

"You took my two best Barbs, and now you've taken my sister. Anything else you want to steal away before I head out?" she says. The attitude isn't like her. She's usually playful, laughing and joking, mostly at others' expense. I don't know what to do with this version of Adelaide.

So I do the only thing I can think of. I pull her into a hug, even though she's stiff and won't hug me back. "I miss him, too," I say, before releasing her. Her expression of shock is quickly smoothed back into a scowl, and I give her a small smile. "Fair winds and following seas."

She doesn't say anything, just climbs into the carriage.

Gianna lingers a bit, and then finally comes over to grab one of my hands with both of hers. "I never thanked you," she says, voice soft.

"No thanks needed. I couldn't exactly leave you as a sphinx forever."

"Oh, not for that," she says. "For restoring my house. My grandmother used to tell me stories of the First Sphinx and the great acts of our people. I never imagined I would get to see it for myself." She lowers her voice, her gaze sliding to the doorway behind us, but we're the only ones in the courtyard. "Nakumba has a future now, a real one not ground beneath a dragon bootheel." She laughs. "So, thanks."

"How does it end?" I ask Gianna. "The story of the First Sphinx. I know House Gryphon's version; what about yours?" It makes me ache to realize that House Sphinx was never really mine. It was always an idea of a home, a family, a place where people cared for me. But for Gianna it was real, and even though I am a little jealous, I can't begrudge Gianna her happiness.

"We're going to miss the tide," Adelaide snaps from inside the carriage, and Gianna looks at me in alarm.

"Next time," I say. "I'll see you both in two weeks at Phoenix Crest."

Gianna nods and scrambles into the carriage, and then they are gone, the wheels clattering as they leave the packed earth of the courtyard and begin their trek down the mountain.

"She won't be mad at you forever," Miranda says, appearing from wherever she was hiding.

I snort. "And yet, I notice *you* didn't bother seeing her off."

Miranda shrugs, her expression coy. "Someone had to tend to Talon's burned hand. You'll be glad to know he's right as rain."

I smile at Miranda and tilt my head. "I suppose this means I should give you a fancy title. The Balm of the Phoenix."

"I better get a fancy title. You should've heard the way Adelaide laid into me last night."

"She'll come around. And if she doesn't, you can give her a drink to sweeten her disposition." I pause. "Wait, can you do that?"

"I'm not sure," Miranda laughs, "but it might actually be worth a try."

For a moment it's like the past few months didn't happen and I feel light and free. Then Len and Penna approach, and the feeling dissipates.

"What are you wearing?" I ask, fighting to keep the dismay from my voice. Their normal Barb blacks have been replaced with purple tunics embroidered with bright orange flames, the trousers still black. But I cannot stop looking at the flames on the tunic and feeling that maybe they're a bit much.

"They're Flames now," Vivian says, appearing with Elias. "You need to remember who you are, Darling. Especially when it comes time to deal with Bloodscale. Despite what Talon says, the man is bloodthirsty, and he was instrumental in planning the attack on House Sphinx. He won't be an easy one to win over."

I glance at Len and Penna, expecting them to argue. But they look proud of their new uniforms, and so I force a smile.

"They look great," I say, even though I hate all these silly trappings of power. But Vivian is right. If I want people to believe I'm in charge, then I have to act like I'm in charge.

Deep within me, the phoenix preens a little. It missed this.

"I was wondering if you'd join us for the midday meal," Vivian says, giving me a small bow even though I keep asking her not to. I've never met a person so enamored of protocol. "Talon has set aside a small room for us to speak privately. I have some thoughts on how you can begin laying the foundation for your rule."

I exchange a glance with Miranda, her amusement writ large on her face. She's enjoying my discomfort, and I sigh.

"Why not," I say. "I suppose this is my job now."

"Great, if you'll follow me?" Vivian says, and I frown.

"It's a little early to eat," I say, and Elias sighs heavily.

"It will take most of the morning to go through the information we've collected," they say, and inwardly I groan.

"You enjoy your, uh, study session," Miranda says, disappearing just as quickly as she arrived. My Flames stay where they are—of course they do. They're my shadows now.

I force a smile and hold out a hand before me. "Fine. Let's go."

For the first hour Vivian and I talk ruling philosophies as we wait for the midday meal. She is highly interested in what I will do, and has even collated a list of sources—philosophers, generals, and people who apparently spend all their time thinking about government—that I should read to learn about governing people. I pretend to be interested, but it's all so boring that by the time the servants arrive to lay out lunch I'm tempted to jump up and lend my assistance. But I can already hear the lecture on appearances and procedure I would get from Vivian, so I remain where I am.

Once the food—a meat pastry of some sort with greens dressed in a mixture of vinegar and oil—is set and everyone has filled their plates, I clap my hands like Leonetti sometimes did, getting everyone's attention.

"Enough about politics—what do you know of blood magic? Aurora is our most pressing issue, and our best bet in finding Aurora is to undo whatever it was she did to Talon's boon. I can't fix it, not without risking killing him, at least. So, thoughts?"

The sudden silence in the room is deafening, and it actually feels like a chill descends.

"Not supposed to talk about blood magic," Penna says, suddenly uncomfortable.

"My mother once told me that my father had paid a blood mage to curse his brother after a bad business deal, but I always thought it was a lie," Len says in his gravelly voice, tearing apart a piece of bread at the memory. "But perhaps it was truth after all."

"The Last Phoenix was killed by a blood mage, a Kraken, and a Dragon," I say. When everyone begins to speak at once, I raise my hands. "I saw the memory last night when I destroyed the—I don't know what it is. Chaos stopper?"

"It was an altar to the Temple of the Moon. A blood cult," Elias says, leaning forward. "But what I want to know is how the phoenix knew all that. Can you explain it?" A strange light has entered their eyes, and it takes me a moment to realize it's excitement.

"The memory? I'm not sure. It was like the phoenix remembered and showed me."

Elias shakes their head vehemently. "No, the shrines. You can find them?"

"I think so. But why is that important?"

"When I was researching boons for Talon, I came across a story.

It was presented as myth, so I read past it, but it talked about how in the days before Chaos touched the land, blood mages would make sacrifices on altars tied to Chaos. That in the moment of death, Chaos would flow and they could manipulate the force as they saw fit. Seeing the future wasn't one of the things mentioned, but shape-changing, cursing others, a lot of really awful things," Elias says. They seem to realize that maybe blood magic isn't something to be thrilled about and they temper their excitement, but just barely. "When Talon found the blood mage's journal a couple of weeks ago, I went back to my earlier notes and realized that the myth I'd read was most likely true."

"So what are the shrines, as you call them?" I ask. It doesn't feel like the right word, but I also don't have another word for what they are. Something bad. *Graves*, I think, and that feels more correct, but still not true. They were places where Chaos went to die, but it was more than that; the death was slow and depraved, like a slow torture.

"The shrines were places where blood mages could do large spells," Elias says, pulling me back to myself. "Control the weather, call earthquakes, level cities. There was a passage about Gunjaro sending a fleet of ships to the Teeth Islands. The blood mages flattened the fleet and leveled the nearest cities in Gunjaro, and that was the last time someone tried to invade Pyrlanum."

"The first empyreals were summoned by powerful blood mages," Vivian says, and I freeze, because what she's saying feels right. But only partly.

"Is that something you or the gryphon knows?" Elias asks, analytical even in their excitement.

"No, I know it. I read it in Gregory Calamus's history of the houses. His belief, based on sources no longer available to us, was that the first empyreals were tied to the most powerful blood mage lines in the country. They struck a deal with Chaos and asked for permanent access to Chaos in the form of the boons. The price they paid was a bit of their humanity, so that the children of Chaos could exist in this world."

"So the empyreals anchor Chaos to this world," Elias says with a nod. "I read a treatise that said that the boons were tied to the empyreals and that the phoenix was the heart, keeping houses from fighting and preventing violence. The phoenix was strongest, and selected from the population at large, not just the blood mages."

"If that is the truth, that means the three who killed the phoenix were just blood mages going back on their word," I say. No wonder I felt so much rage from the phoenix and Chaos whenever I was in those places. It was less about the empyreals and more about what those bloodlines did to the children of Chaos. "Okay, so technically you should be able to use blood magic, Vivian. Does that mean you have answers as to how we stop Aurora? Or at least free Talon?"

"I don't know. We do have some forbidden archives in the library that contain blood magic rituals. I can have one of our more senior scholars research anything about the empyreals in there."

"I have the journal that Talon found," Elias offers, "but there isn't anything but a lot of puffery and self-important rhetoric. There definitely aren't any instructions. Talon thought that those might be at Phoenix Crest in Aurora's workroom there."

"Well, until we can gain access to Phoenix Crest, the House Gryphon archives are probably our best place to start. Talon said Aurora wanted Darvey for some reason. If she's been pulling from these taboo practices, she might be up to something big, like her ancestors before her," I say, pushing my plate away. The phoenix is beginning to vibrate under my skin, delighted I finally understand that the work we're doing is important. It's distracting. "But destroying these shrines is even more important than I thought. I don't suppose there's a map of them somewhere?" At everyone's head shake I sigh. "Okay then, new plan. Vivian, please send an inquiry to your house about any possible defensive spell against blood magic, and I'm going to let the phoenix show me what other shrines are in Dragon territory that can be destroyed and level them before we leave tomorrow."

"Won't that cause boons to begin to waken across the land?" Elias asks, and I nod.

"Yes. It's going to be bedlam. Before I head for other territories to do the same, it might be worth sending an alert somehow to the various governors and mayors so that they know why things are happening. I know that Talon spoke about sending a missive declaring the return of the phoenix; let's use that same network to share the return of Chaos. I have to destroy all the shrines I can. The last thing we need is for Aurora to find one of these and cast something awful."

I'm not happy about the shrines, but I am pretty excited to have something to do that isn't trying to corral a bunch of empyreals. I've never shied away from leadership, but I barely know who I am right now. There will be plenty of time for philosophy and government after Aurora is secured away from everyone.

"Do you really think a single blood mage can stand against empyreals?" Vivian asks, doubt riding her words.

I snort. "They've already managed to kill one phoenix. I'd like to avoid being next."

We finish quickly after that, everyone anxious to get to work. Penna follows me out to the courtyard, and I quickly strip. I've already ruined so many clothes, I'm loath to lose the few remaining ones I have.

And then I let go, taking to the air on fiery wings, determined that Aurora will not take another life.

I will burn her to the ground, first.

23

TALON

Darling is leaving today.

I catch her an hour before her party's departure. She's in my mother's terraced garden with Darvey and Vivian, all of them human, and sharing breakfast. The garden has become somewhat of an empyreal sanctuary. None of them love being under the heavy roofs of Dragon Castle.

Darvey stands up and waves when he sees me. I appreciate his enthusiasm. Since Darling woke him back up to his human form, he's been even shyer with me. At least he trusts Darling as he should, and Vivian indulges him like kin.

She still treats me coolly. That might have more to do with Caspian's tantrums than with me specifically. They were friends for years, and he used Vivian as much as he used the rest of us. Plus Elias isn't going with her today, but staying here with Caspian. If I was her, I'd hate that, too, given Caspian's temper.

Darling stuffs a few more bites into her mouth as I approach. She must still be recovering from the flight the phoenix took yesterday afternoon, and well into evening. I was told Darling flew the expanse of Dragon territory, destroying every blood altar she could find. Of course she's hungry. The smoky lenses of her goggles seem dull in the morning shade of blossoming fruit trees. Apples, I think. I don't remember exactly. It's been a long time since I've been here in late summer to find out.

The three of them eat at a circular stone table with four place settings. I wonder who ditched them. Probably Caspian. He hasn't bonded with the other empyreals, to say the least. Darling said the empyreals she sensed in the memories of that underground lake were Dragon and Kraken, and I wonder if that has anything to do with Caspian and Adelaide being more antagonistic to the rest of the empyreals. It could just as likely be their charming personalities.

"You need something?" Darling asks.

"Hungry?" Vivian asks without Darling's morning grumpiness.

"I ate, thank you." I nod to her, then smile at Darvey. "Finn was looking for you, something about morning exercise."

Darvey bounces on his toes. For a moment he almost seems to grow taller, but it might only be his little-boy hair standing on end like his barghest ruff does. "I'll find him!"

The Barghest regent dashes off, then screeches to a halt and spins. He bows to Darling. "Oh, I—I'll see you at Phoenix Crest! I promise I'll think about what you said, and, and try my best."

Darling grins at him. "I know you will, kid."

With that he's off again.

"Darling, I was hoping for a word before you leave," I say.

Vivian gestures for a few of the Dragon attendants to come clear the table. She says, totally ignoring me, "I will finish my tea, my flame, and see you at the gates."

Darling stands and brushes her hands together. "Sure." Then Darling finishes her tea and lifts her eyebrows at me. I gesture for her to walk with me to one of the lower terraces. She does. We go quietly, crunching on the pale gravel path to the stone steps curving down. This terrace is a half-moon lawn partially shaded by trees on the upper terrace. It has an intricate water work edging the terrace, creating a waterfall down to the next. The pretty trickle is constant and soothing.

I walk toward the edge, to the smooth stone of the bank, speckled with tiny droplets. The rising sun hasn't quite lifted over the peaks, so the water is a cool, soft blue despite the stripes of pink and gold on the clouds. "I have something for you," I say as Darling joins me.

"A gift?" She sounds equal parts surprised and skeptical.

"Not exactly." I turn to her, arms crossed. I'm nervous, and it feels better to hold myself back with such a pose.

"What, then?"

"Spar me for it."

It startles a laugh out of her.

I look at her mouth, the laughter warming my chest.

"Talon, I don't know if you remember, but I'm a phoenix now. I'm faster and stronger, and I can literally set you on fire."

I smile slowly. "Then you should win your prize easily."

Darling laughs again. She wrinkles her nose in that adorable way. "I don't even carry a sword anymore."

"I brought two." Reaching behind me, I unsheathe the extra falchion strapped to the small of my back. I offer the hilt to her.

She's shaking her head, but amused, I think. "I was wondering about those."

"My flame," I say, maintaining a slight bow until she takes it. She's careful not to brush our fingers too much.

I step back, unsheathing my own falchion with a flourish. Since yesterday, Miranda's tonics and Darling's initial healing have brought my burned hand to a place where it's usable and barely hurts.

Darling attacks.

It's refreshing to leap into action, and I block, backing up. We dance around, give and take. At first we're darting close and apart, again and again. The blades clash, sliding, like ripples of the sky. Darling doesn't use her power, so I don't trace her with my boon. It's a friendly spar, easy, almost relaxed.

But Darling twists fast then, and I cut out, spinning, too. I flip my falchion so it aims backward along my forearm. This way I can block and get much, much closer to her. Or I can hook with it in long swipes. Darling pivots, keeping away from me, turning on her toes, around and around. Faster and faster. I pick a moment and step in, cutting.

She blocks me with a little grunt, throws me back. I charge her again, and we hit together hard, locked up, blade to blade. The heels of her boots are very close to the water.

"You aren't even trying," Darling hisses. Having fun.

It's one of the first things she said to me, all those months ago in Lastrium.

You aren't trying to kill me.

I don't want you dead.

I smile and press into her.

Darling sparks with fire, startling me away. She laughs. I stumble but recover quickly. She moves suddenly: she's before me, then gone. I fling around just in time to catch her falchion descending to my unguarded back. She's so strong I'm forced to use my left hand, too, putting it to the unedged side of my blade to hold her off.

I gather my own strength and shove.

She falls back, then instead of the expected swing, she kicks out at me. I dodge, and swipe to catch her ankle. We both miss. We stand there, panting.

This time I attack first. But Darling leaps into the air, her whole body flaring fire-hot, and it's not quite flying but an inhumanly high jump. She uses my surprise and her height advantage to kick my falchion back. I turn, but she's too fast: she hits fully against my back, an arm around my neck.

I don't even know how she did it, but she's got her falchion point against my cheek as she wraps her legs around my ribs. She's burning up, not quite on fire, but holding onto me much more like a squid.

"I win," she says delightedly in my ear.

"Yes, my flame," I answer, turning my face to look at her. We are so close. I can feel her chest against my back as she breathes hard, and the strength in her thighs. And the heat waves radiating off her.

Darling suddenly lets go. She hops down, landing softly.

I give myself a moment, just breathing, too. Then her hand is on my waist. I freeze, but Darling sheathes her falchion at the small of my back with a little slick metal sound. I smile at myself and turn, sheathing the other blade.

"My prize?" Darling says with sharp sweetness.

I nod, but for a moment only stare at her. Her brown skin almost glows in the first real sunlight over the peaks. Her dress is more of a vest with four long panels for skirts, easy to move in, and bright purple. Beneath it she has a cream and brown tunic and pants, and there's a short leather jacket tight around her ribs that's close to light armor. I want to touch her, especially now that we've sparred, that she beat me so easily. I want to *keep* her.

But I unbutton a pocket on the vibrant red skirt of my own uniform jacket. Before I can remove her prize, Darling makes a tiny strangling sound.

"Darling?" I step closer, worried.

She's biting her bottom lip as if to hide a grimace or frown. Darling shakes her head, and says, "You actually have something for me? I really thought you were going to kiss—"

Before she finishes I kiss her.

Her lips are hot, and I barely have a chance to notice before she pulls back.

I swallow. I didn't mean to do that, though I've wanted to— badly. Darling is clearly staring at me, even though I can't see her eyes. She doesn't back off. "Talon," she murmurs.

"Darling."

This time, I lean in more slowly. It's a question for her. Darling puts a hand on my chest. Not holding me away, but inviting.

I kiss her again, just a brush of our lips. She smells like tea and sweat—and fire. Not smoke or ashes, but a stringent, clean smell. It's just itself. I let myself taste her, and it's the same. Darling tastes like fire now.

She deepens our kiss, tasting me back. I try not to think of anything but how it feels: her hot hand a pressure on my chest, the summer mountain breeze, the chitter of sparrow drakes, Darling's fire lips moving slowly against me.

It doesn't last. Darling sighs; I murmur her name. She leans her forehead against mine, on her tiptoes. I cup her elbow for her balance.

Slowly, Darling sinks down to her heels. I keep gentle hold of her elbow. I wish I could see her eyes. But the sun peeks down at us, too bright. It's such a strange thing that this vibrant phoenix must hide part of herself under the only other thing in our world that shines like she does.

"I want," I start to say. I stop. I know I can't have what I want.

She touches my lips with the tips of her warm fingers.

"You," I murmur.

Darling's hand drops.

I have so many arguments for why she should keep me. It would be good for Pyrlanum to see House Dragon serving the Phoenix Reborn, at her side. Like her friend Miranda will do from House Kraken. I'm meant to be a first scion; she can remake the War Prince into her own weapon; we can make peace together. I love her. Once, I made her happy for a few hours. Happy enough she agreed to make me her consort. Doesn't she want to chase that? Can't she let herself chase *us*?

"House Dragon can't have the phoenix," she says.

"That's not what I meant."

"It's what it would look like."

I shake my head. I remember kneeling to her. I'll do it again, when we're all together at Phoenix Crest. "Darling," I say.

"You can't have Darling, either," she says. "The last time I said yes to you . . ." Darling steps away from me.

"I know." I don't reach for her, even though her lips tremble before she presses them flat. "I know," I say more firmly. "But it's still what I want."

Darling hugs herself. I can't tell if she's angry or upset or hurt. Maybe all three. And not being able to tell is part of our problem.

"I also know that House Dragon has a lot to make up for—to the phoenix. Not only to the people of Pyrlanum, but . . ." I cut my gaze away but force myself to look back at her. This is something I can't shy away from. I might want Darling, but my family, my house, hurt her personally, hurt the phoenix, hurt the entire land, and ruined Chaos for a hundred years. There are so many reparations to make.

Politically, spiritually, personally. "I will do everything to earn a place with you. To make House Dragon deserve your trust."

Even though I can't see her eyes through the goggles, it's obvious her whole attention is locked on me. But she only says, "I have to go."

"Wait." This time I get the gift out of my pocket without interruptions. The glass lenses are cool in my hand, the simple straps untangled. I hold them out in my palm.

"Oh Chaos, my . . ." her face tilts up to me. "You kept these this whole time?"

They're her goggles, the smoky lenses she wore the night we met. We fought, and she killed some of my Teeth. She poisoned Finn. She mocked me and stabbed me in the shoulder with a table knife. When she passed out, I took the goggles and kept them. On me, most of the time, but occasionally in one of the carved boxes where I keep my favorite things. "I did," I admit.

"You big stupid hoarding dragon," she says, but she's laughing as she takes them in both hands. She angles the lenses to catch the sunlight. "I can't believe you."

"Caspian made you enough replacements."

"Those were so delicate and floral—these I made myself, for fighting and practicality." Her hands close around the lenses.

I wait, watching her. She caresses them once more with her thumbs, then tucks them into her vest.

She looks back up at me. "Why now?"

I look away, out over the terraces and across the narrow green valley. A pocket of beautiful pleasure gardens in the hard heart of Dragon Castle. "They aren't mine to keep. I don't—I won't—" I shake my head ruefully. "I've taken enough away from you."

We're quiet again, with the wind and chattering sparrow drakes.

Then Darling slips her hand into mine and presses something there. I glance down. It's the goggles. "Keep them."

"Darling—" I start to turn, but she stops me with a hand on my shoulder.

"I have to go, War Prince. I'll see you at Phoenix Crest."

I nod, and remain facing the cliffs as her footsteps move away. Only when I can't hear her do I look, just in time to see her vanish between apple trees on the terrace garden above me.

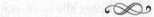

Almost everyone is there in the yard to see the phoenix's party off.

Finn hugs his sister Brigh, the two of them like red-headed bears, Finn vivid in Teeth scarlet, Brigh in the green and brown regular uniform. She's leading the Dragons in the phoenix's party, with an official letter of surrender signed by me to be handed to General Bloodscale. He's to turn Phoenix Crest over to the Phoenix Reborn and leave nothing but an honor guard. He'd better comply. No matter how little he likes it.

Vivian prepares to transform and fly, but first she and her cousin Elias speak in soft tones just to the side. Elias is mostly listening, their eyes continually going to the sky. I'm glad they're staying to work in Aurora's old rooms for a few more days, hoping to find some kind of blood magic counter before joining my own party. We're heading to Barghest territory first, to reintroduce Darvey and relieve my Teeth soldier Arran Lightscale of his temporary command. Then we'll go to Phoenix Crest, too, for Darling's official investiture. I hope Brigh's spies will have located Aurora—or that she'll make a move to reveal herself—before we're all together. But all the reports are frustratingly lacking in evidence. The only place we know she's spent time in the past fifteen years is here at Dragon Castle and Phoenix Crest. She's not in either, and I'm afraid to find out who she's influenced or hurt to hide.

Darvey waits at my side, a shaggy black dog nearly as tall as me. He doesn't quite lean, but I can feel him vibrate with wanting to— eyes darting between Finn and Darling as she goes to join Vivian and Elias.

I have her goggles hanging from my belt, hooked in the knots that hold my sheaths in place. Like she's at my back.

Finally Finn backs away, and his sister orders her Dragons into formation with the wagon. Several of the Barbs are riding within, along with attendants and belongings. Darling herself has Bunny back for when she is tired of flying and destroying the blood magic shrines—she still refuses to ride in a carriage—and the war drake is clearly happy to see her. Happier than war drakes usually get.

Elias kisses their cousin's cheek, and they too come stand with Finn and Darvey and me.

The only signal for leaving is Vivian's dramatic transformation and her scream as she shoves hard off the ground. The war drakes cry back to her, a layered shriek. Darling winces.

Then Darling lifts a hand to me. I bow to her.

That's it. They pull out, through the massive gates of the castle wall, over the empty fire moat. I watch until the last trailing Dragon is gone.

Elias says, "Talon, where's Caspian? He should have been here."

Finn sighs and scratches Darvey's ruff.

I close my eyes and open my boon.

Instantly I find Caspian. Dragon empyreal, wings wide, soaring over boulder-strewn foothills. The sun glints on his green-black scales.

"Flying," I say as I open my eyes again, with only a small headache today.

"Pouting," Finn mutters.

Elias looks at Finn. There's deep worry when they change their gaze to me. "He left me abruptly last night, and I don't think he spent the night in the castle."

"He'll come back," I promise. But doubt wiggles in my stomach. I don't know what Caspian will do. I never have.

FURY

24

TALON

The knocking on my door is insistent.

With a frown I stand from my desk. The room is too dark; the sun has set and I barely noticed, not lighting any candles or calling for boonlights. My shoulders ache from hunching. I've spent each night writing letters to spread out to every territory, every Dragon commander, and every non-Dragon leader in charge of cities and towns in all the reaches of Pyrlanum, in my own hand and marked with my personal seal. Not only is this an announcement of the phoenix's return and an invitation to the celebration at Phoenix Crest, but I'm reinforcing my promise that House Dragon is standing down from war, and warning them of the blood altars Darling is destroying and what to expect from the sudden, vivid return of Chaos to their people.

I cross the small study and the sitting room to the door. I put my hand to the wood and close my eyes, reaching with my boon.

This is a new skill I've noticed since Darling tried to expand my boon: I can use the boon to trace around corners or through doors and see who's there, even if I don't know who I'm looking for. As I practice, my headaches decrease. At least, for these smaller efforts.

The trace on the other side is familiar, though, and I see a flash of Elias's face. They're holding a pitcher and cups, without a jacket, but only a flowing pink and green robe over loose trousers. I think . . . it's Caspian's robe.

With a small sigh, I open the door.

It's been two full days now since Darling departed; we leave to-morrow midmorning for Barghest, and Caspian has not returned.

Elias pushes in immediately. "Have a drink with me," they say, lifting the pitcher. It's the narrow-necked kind suited to long pours of pretty, clear liquor.

"I'm not Caspian," I say, closing the door behind them.

"Obviously," Elias says with a sniff. They go to the low table near the hearth and plunk the pitcher and cups down. Kneeling, they poke at the embers with the iron, turning coals over. Then they reach into the kindling box and toss some in.

I watch for a moment, then close my eyes and search for my brother with my boon.

He's flying. When I look for him, he's usually flying. Tonight he drifts low over a setting sun, toward a wide, flat rock. South of here. I think I recognize the chimneys and trees of the village beneath his jutting rock. Ashroot Village, a town three days' war drake ride from Phoenix Crest. Caspian lands, spreads his wings, and roars. Probably scaring the people trying to have their dinner.

I frown. To Elias I say, "He's being a menace near Phoenix Crest."

"So, like usual," Elias murmurs.

"I'll be right back," I tell them, then I head for the kitchens, nodding to the soldiers and castle attendants I pass. Everyone is mission-focused in Dragon Castle, so it's easy to get to my destination without being stopped. The kitchen workers pause at once to put their fists to their hearts, but then get back to prepping morning dough and cleaning the day from surfaces and pots. I ask for a tray and whatever they have to spare, only to be gently chided by the kitchen boss. She reminds me I should let her arrange for regular deliveries, and I remind her I'm leaving again in the morning. She huffs and extracts a promise I'll let her have her way when I come home to stay.

Home to stay is such a foreign thought.

Laden with a flask of sweet coffee, heavy rolls and cold chicken and a root salad, I trek back up to my rooms. Elias sits bent over the low table, their fingers drumming against the lacquered green wood, staring into their very nice fire.

I set the tray down, and Elias watches me in turn as I remove boots and jacket and loosen the collar of my tunic. I join them at the table, and see they've already poured liquor into the cups. Lifting my cup, I meet their brown eyes. Elias does the same, and we nod, then drink. I sip, while Elias knocks theirs back.

They squeeze shut their eyes and breathe harshly, then immediately pour another. This time, Elias sips. I pick at the sweet root vegetables, beets and turnips and oddly colored carrots all baked and glazed and salted. They're good.

Elias eats a small chunk of carrot. Then drinks again. Then they say, "You're just going to nurse that while I drink?"

"Yes. If you want someone to get drunk with, you should go find Finn or Annag's daughter or one of the off-duty Teeth."

"But you are the one who knows," Elias says with a sigh. They pour another drink.

I frown, concerned enough I almost reach out to cover their cup. It's not the strongest liquor, but if they drink the whole pitcher, they won't be able to travel tomorrow. "Knows what?" My voice sounds gruff from worry.

Elias laughs once. "What it's like to love someone you can't have."

The food turns to rocks in my stomach. "Chaos," I mutter. I don't want to have this conversation. Not with anybody, and certainly not with my brother's depressed lover.

"I used to think it was enough to just be with him," Elias laments. "At his side, helping him, taking his attention when I could."

I grimace. I've had all those thoughts.

"But since he's returned, since the—the *Awakening*," Elias says it bitterly, "he doesn't give me any of that. He left me behind when he died."

Swallowing back the chill I feel whenever I think of Caspian expecting to die, I reach out and swipe the liquor. I set it down on my other side, out of Elias's reach. "You shouldn't be telling me this."

"Why not?" They pout with their whole face, and I remember suddenly that Elias is not much older than me. We're hardly grown up, barely adults. Me, Elias, Finn, Caspian, Darling—not to mention Darvey and that young sphinx, who are literally children. Vivian is the oldest of us, and she's what, not even thirty? Our parents certainly did not do well by any of us.

That makes me think of Aurora, who loved me, raised me, but killed my mother. Plotted against us, me. Wanted Caspian dead, too. Murders for blood magic, for power.

I pour us both another cup of the clear pink liquor. Elias takes it with a sour smile. We touch our cups together, with a pretty ceramic click, and drink. The liquor is gentle, but tingles as it courses down my throat, reminding me of Darling's phoenix fire, and when I finish, I immediately pour cold coffee into my cup. No more for me. Elias can do what they want.

I wash down some chicken with the coffee. I don't mind the coffee cold. It's still sweet and thick, comforting more than refreshing at this time of night. Elias is sipping another cup of liquor, holding it in their palms against their chest. Which is definitely covered in one of Caspian's elaborate robes. This one is vibrant pink, embroidered with dark green pine boughs and tiny painted robins and bluebirds. The collar looks heavy with soft silk. Elias drinks, the equally heavy cuff falling away from their bony brown wrist.

A small spot of dark rust brown mars the edge of the cuff.

"Is that blood?" I frown again, even deeper.

Elias's gaze flicks down. They finish their cup and nod. This time they put the cup upside down on the table and close their eyes. "I grow more convinced every hour that the only way to counter blood magic is with blood magic."

I grab their sleeve and pull it back to reveal three small cuts along their upper forearm. "What did you do?"

"Experiments," Elias says dismissively.

"Elias, research is one thing; I don't want you doing blood magic." I think my voice is shaking; I can't get the splatters of blood from Leonetti's heart out of my head, the smell of blood, the slick feel of it when Aurora painted it on me and knocked me out.

The look Elias gives me states very clearly what they think of anybody getting what they want.

I release them and rub my forehead as if I could wipe out the phantom blood sigils. My boon could be permanently damaged from blood magic.

Elias follows my movement and says, "I drew a version of that mark on your head. Since the phoenix awakened my boon to a new strength, it's like I can tell the truth of some things. Words, intentions, but also if I concentrate, it's as if I can guess the meaning behind something like that sigil. I understand this is a common House Gryphon boon. Regardless, I'm convinced she used something meant to be a simple spell for forgetting, but altered it so that you didn't forget her, but your boon did. She erased herself from Chaos's tracking awareness through you. I've considered some possible experiments to prove it, but I don't know the intricacies and wouldn't like to hurt someone."

"Good."

"Yes. But . . . it might be the only way. I've done all the research I can here." Elias's mouth curls in distaste. "Blood magic is *disgusting,* and I don't like having this all in my head. But it's better than Aurora whispering in Caspian's ear for him to slit his own throat."

I swallow. I look into the fire, wishing I could see what Elias was searching for in those glowing coals. Darling could reach directly in and pluck it out, alight and bubbling, if she was here.

Elias sighs and lists to the side.

"He'll come back," I say quietly.

"To me?" They sigh wistfully. "I feel like a fool, but you love him, too; you know what he's like."

"Impossible," I say, thinking of the times Caspian has pushed me away. Lied to me, held back, schemed as if what I did wouldn't matter. "I'm sorry. Maybe if you go back to House Gryphon, you can move on."

"Ah, my blade," Elias snorts. "I don't want to do that. What could be better than loving Caspian Goldhoard, dragon empyreal and prophet?"

"If he loved you back."

"Does Darling love you back?"

The question startles me into a gasp. My throat feels tingly still from the alcohol. "I . . . think so."

"Does that make it better?"

I draw a long breath and hold it, wondering.

Elias says, "I do understand. You love each other, but there are more important things right now. That used to suit me. Or at least settle me. Caspian has always had something more important than me. Paintings, frolicking. I believed the peace I thought he was chasing *was* more important than me, but the rest . . . now? He's been through this incredible event and survived, and he's a *dragon*." Elias smiles at me, and I know why Caspian is drawn to them, to the charm there, the wit and brains. I nearly ask if Caspian ever drew Elias, but I know the answer.

Elias's smile fades. But the drinking makes them very talkative. "It's worse now. He isn't behaving so erratically, as if being the empyreal soothes the jagged edges of his Chaos. I'm not sure he even sees prophecy any longer. But even still, he won't take a moment to relax. The other night, when we were together, I saw the truth." Their voice fades as they continue, "It's a terrible boon. To know he doesn't love me. He cares about one thing right now: killing Aurora. He's single-minded."

"Being single-minded is how he changed the world . . ." I murmur, trailing off as I realize. My eyes widen. "Aurora. What happened when he left? You said he left the night before Darling and her party?"

Elias pouts again, tilting to lean their elbows drunkenly on the table. "He kept talking about Aurora, about how frustrated he was he couldn't have a vision of her to paint, to find her. Angry that she slipped through your fingers, that she should be dead. He raged. Threw a goblet in the fire. He wanted to know why I couldn't figure out how to stop her, and we talked about how the boons have changed, about hers, about everything I've cataloged, including

Finn's, and he was momentarily very distracted by the idea of Finn falling into a dream. Then he stared at me, and he—he kissed me, and he swept out like he'd never been there, except for the broken goblet."

I stare at Elias, who's not looking back at me after that monologue. But they're right. I do know my brother. And he *is* dangerously single-minded. He flew off after that rant with Elias, and every time I've looked for him, he's been circling low, roaring, and stealing sheep. Making a ruckus. Somebody will try to slay him sooner or later. And I know who he wants it to be.

"Elias," I say, getting to my feet. "We can't find Aurora, so Caspian is trying to bring her to him."

25

DARLING

Our entrance to Phoenix Crest is a somber one. We arrive in the evening and stay at an inn Len knows from his time running intelligence missions for Leonetti. It's neutral ground, the kind of tavern that has sworn no allegiance to one house over the other, a rare thing after so many years of war.

Originally Vivian and I had spoken about just flying to Phoenix Crest and taking control. After all, there isn't much anyone can do against an empyreal. But the addition of others to our travels had made a more professional arrival more realistic. Plus there was the small matter of not having clothes, should there be any conversation required. I'm not sure how the old phoenix did things, but I cannot imagine arriving naked and demanding control of the castle would go over well, firebird or not.

Vivian also thinks it prudent to give General Bloodscale time to react to the missive Talon sent. He sent one by sparrow drake, but Brigh carries another copy, and while Vivian and I wait at the inn with my Flames, she takes her soldiers with her to deliver it. Everyone thinks it's more politic to give the man time to receive the information and react before we land on his doorstep.

I'm not sure it will matter. General Bloodscale is a violent man used to being in charge, and a Dragon, besides. Surrender will leave a bad taste in his mouth. I think it far more likely that we'll have to take the castle by force.

I'm going to need an army. Not only Talon's army and my Flames, but regular people willing to fight for the phoenix. It seems utterly unbelievable to me that people would be willing to do such a thing, which leaves me right back where I started.

How am I supposed to fix this broken country when I have no idea what I am doing?

In that moment, I think of Leonetti, and how he'd always joke, "You know how you eat a whale? One bite at a time!" The joke had always made Adelaide and me groan, while Miranda would smile politely. In that moment my grief is raw and jagged, and by the time I dismount from Bunny, I'm blinking away tears.

Was he scared in his final moments? Did he know he was going to die? Or was it a surprise?

Like everything else—Adelaide's anger, Caspian's petulance, Talon's heartfelt declarations—I put it to the side to be dealt with later. I have a whale to eat, and not much time for anything else.

The inn is a fine establishment, and thanks to Len, the owners are expecting us. The men, husbands who bought the inn when the previous owner died, are more than excited to see us. They are *overjoyed*.

They bow and scrape, and "my flame" the end of every sentence. I finally just sigh.

"Would you like me to burn something into a wall somewhere? I won't do it unless you ask, just because it seems rude," I say, tired from my exploits across the land, freeing the Chaos trapped under shrines. I found three in the journey from House Dragon to Phoenix Crest, and there are at least two more within a day's flight.

I had to urge the phoenix to patience. I have the feeling it's better to release Chaos slowly, and allow people to react to the return of boons. We passed through a few towns and found people laughing and giddy as they climbed up walls, grew trees overnight, and any number of other things. I can only imagine what kind of havoc would ensue if the entire country suddenly discovers their hidden abilities all at once. More incidents like that exploded staircase at Dragon Castle.

"If you would not mind, my flame," the taller man says, his name escaping me. A mixture of hope and greed flashes in his eyes. But it's a pure, honest emotion, and I don't mind it.

I put my hand on the door to the main common room and let go. I've learned that becoming the phoenix is less about forcing a change and more about releasing the sense of myself. It's like letting go of a long-held breath, and when I relax, my hands flare immediately, the one pressed to the door charring the wood. Only it isn't a handprint left behind, not like the burns we saw in House Cockatrice from the First Phoenix. Instead it is a stylized bird, wings held aloft and flames licking all around. I've been leaving these marks everywhere I've stayed.

Apparently the story of the firebird I left the night I tried to strengthen Talon's boon has traveled faster than we could. The door continues to flicker even after I remove my hand, and I half wonder if the embers will ever go out. I get the sense that when they do it will have more to do with my death than with the flames dying.

"Now," I say, clapping my hands and mustering a smile at their awestruck expressions. "Might we have food and a room to rest?"

They put us in a well-appointed back room with soft, brocade chairs and beautiful end tables. A buffet of cold meats, hard cheese, fruits, and savory spreads is quickly set up, watered-down ale set aside to wash it all down. We all fill our plates, Len and Penna eschewing the ale in favor of water. This inn is on a main road that links all the different territories in Pyrlanum, so I'm unsurprised that it seems that they do well. I wonder how their coffers will grow when people come to see the flaming phoenix embedded in the common room door.

"You should start charging for that," Len says, popping a bramble-berry into his mouth, and I kind of agree with him.

"I could probably feed all the hungry people in Pyrlanum if every innkeeper wants to pay me for a burning handprint," I say with a snort.

"Taxing businesses to help the poor is one of the central tenets of Larkin's generosity theory," Vivian says. She's been teaching me all about different forms of government, and I've been mostly bored until she mentioned a system that would require the people to decide who rules them. I like that. It would be impossible to undo the house system right away, but a central committee where everyone is chosen by the people in their local vicinity seems like a nice idea, sort of like Leonetti's council of advisors. A voice for every group.

It makes me miss him, deeply. I can only imagine what Adelaide is feeling, and I wish we could talk about it. But I have a feeling it will be a long while before Adelaide and I talk like we used to.

We wait in the inn when there is a knock at the door. I stand to open it and find the innkeepers on the other side.

"Ah, my flame, I'm sorry to bother you, but—"

"Is that her?" someone yells, and the man is pushed to the side as people crowd into the hallway. I don't recognize any of them, but they all have the hard look of soldiers, and when they see me, they stop.

"Are you the Phoenix Reborn?" asks one man, stepping forward and removing a hat I recognize as belonging to Dragon regulars.

"I am," I say. The man looks like he's about to argue, so I release my flames just enough that they warm the small space. The man takes a step backward and a dark-skinned woman with a close-cropped halo of white curls steps forward.

"I am Niore Clem, and I wish to join your guard," she says, dropping to her knee. Soon every other soldier crammed into the hallway does as well, and I clear my throat.

"Len?" I call, and he's immediately at my side.

"I do believe you have some, uh, recruits," I say. There are at least twenty people in the hallway, and I have no idea how skilled they may or may not be.

Len grins though, the gap where he lost a tooth in a bout of fisti-cuffs making him look mischievous. "And you were worried about trying to raise an army."

He steps around me and waves toward the door that leads to the attached stable yard. "All right, you lot, outside. We're going to start taking names and talking skills. Penna?"

"Aye," she says, striding out to stand next to Len. "This is almost enough for a platoon. Well done, Ferg," she says to one of the younger men in the crowd.

"You started recruiting?" I say in disbelief.

Len leans in close. "I asked about trying to raise a fighting force the other night, and you said, and I quote, 'Yeah, probably a good idea, but I don't have time for that now.' I took that to mean you wanted me to do it, my flame."

I swallow my groan and nod. "Well done, Len. I suppose that means you're the captain of my guard, now, with Penna your co-captain."

"Aye," they say in unison, grinning from ear to ear, and then they turn back to our recruits as I wave and slip back into the quiet of the common room.

"'And so the phoenix was the lifeblood of the land, and the land gave its lives for her,'" Vivian says quietly. "It's a passage from Jorgen's 'Lament of the Firebird.' Beautiful song if you've never heard it."

"I have the feeling that I will have many chances to hear it," I say. I can already feel the galas and dinners and luncheons that I will have to attend as I step into a leadership role. I groan. Why isn't there some way to change things without having to be a show drake?

General Bloodscale takes his time. Two days pass with us cooling our heels in the inn, Len and Penna training the new soldiers, before we hear back from the powers that be at Phoenix Crest.

Vivian and I are reading when there is a sharp knock on the door. The person on the other side doesn't wait for an answer, and Brigh strides into the room, dropping to a knee before me. Even though I sit, she is almost as tall as me. I quickly gesture her up as I stand.

"How'd it go?"

"Bloodscale is a tough old dragon. His words were, and I quote, 'Phoenix Crest belongs to House Dragon. Get me the Dragon prince in person, because I don't believe a word of this.'"

I nod. "Well then, that seems simple enough. Take your soldiers and station them at the Dragon inn at the main gate, since I doubt he'll let you back into the castle. We're going to have to get Caspian and Talon and bring them here ahead of schedule. Vivian?"

Vivian stands and follows me out to the yard, where Penna and Len are taking down names and skill sets with pieces of parchment and small stubs of pencil. Every morning a fresh group of hopefuls has flooded the courtyard of the inn, and while our hosts seem a bit dismayed by the crowd gathering, they are also savvy enough to keep it to themselves. It seems there is some benefit to being the phoenix.

When I walk out, though, all conversation ceases and all eyes are on me.

"Who here has worked inside the castle? Phoenix Crest," I clarify, and two or three hands go up.

"How many people are inside right now?" I ask, and after a moment of murmuring, a younger man with tanned skin, dark hair, and startling blue eyes answers.

"I was a guard there, and we counted a thousand souls, including household staff."

"That's what I thought. Thank . . . wait, come here."

The young man grins, and when he comes forward, I place my hand against his cheek, feeling the Chaos all twisted up in him. "You have a boon, but it hasn't been freed by the destruction of the shrines," I say. "Why?"

He blinks and tries to pull away, but my hand on his cheek holds him fast, Chaos connecting him to me. I can sense a darkness there, woven up right along with the Chaos, and that's when I realize what I'm feeling is the same taint I felt with Talon. It's weaker, but it's there.

"Blood magic," I murmur, but the words are no sooner out of my mouth than the man's expression changes, his smile disappearing.

"For Lady Aurora," he yells. A blade appears in his hand out of nowhere, and he plunges it into my middle. The pain is instantaneous, sharp and cold, and the phoenix is quick to react.

The man explodes into flames, ignited by my hand still cupping his cheek, and when I step back, all that remains is greasy ash.

I bend over in pain, pulling the blade from my middle. Penna and Len are immediately on either side, and when I straighten, I groan.

"I'm okay," I say, the wound already healed. I turn back to the other recruits. "Is there anyone else who's here under false pretenses? If so, you can save us all some time and just confess now. As you can see, a phoenix is not so easy to kill. And it would be nice to not have to incinerate anyone else."

I reach out toward the rest of the recruits, and none of them have the feel of blood magic on them. Which is good. I smile, and there are a few sighs, whether of relief or something else I'm not sure. "Now. Was his quote about the number of people in Phoenix Crest correct?"

There are a few "yes, my flames," and I nod and turn back to Vivian.

"We have to head back to House Dragon and bring Talon and Caspian. I won't put innocents in danger."

"Nor should you," Vivian agrees.

I turn back to Len and Penna. "Keep up your recruiting. I'll return in two days. If the innkeepers have any issues, tell them the phoenix appreciates their generosity and will repay it in kind."

I look down at my dress, which has a long rip and is now soaked with blood. So much for keeping my clothes nice.

Without another word I give over to the phoenix and head back to House Dragon.

Hopefully someone will have clothing to spare.

26

TALON

It takes days to get to Ashroot, though I left before dawn the morning after realizing Caspian's plan. Just myself with Elias clinging to my back as we ride double on Kitty. She's faster with both of us than we'd be with inexperienced Elias on their own war drake, and I need them with me to work their blood magic. We barely stop to rest, too desperate to get to Caspian before Aurora.

Finn argued hard, but I ordered him to stick to the plan, and take Darvey and our Teeth to House Barghest to collect Arran Light-scale and half his battalion before joining us at Phoenix Crest. He must get used to serving Darvey. Then I told him to send a sparrow to Darling to let her know what Caspian is doing, and where I'll be. Once Phoenix Crest is the Phoenix Reborn's fortress again, we'll be in her territory. And Caspian must believe Aurora is near Phoenix Crest, or he'd have chosen a different location for his rampage.

My fury and fear keep me alert even as the days pass. *Why can't he ask for help? Tell me, or if not me, then Darling, his plan. Let us help! He doesn't have to do everything alone. Look how it turned out last time! And now he's the empyreal of House Dragon—he can't risk himself like this! We need him. I need him. We could have set this trap together.*

I'm seething on the third night, unable to sit still or sleep, twitching constantly with the urge to keep going. But Kitty needed to hunt and rest for a few hours. We're in a small grove of towering blackpines, and Elias sits near the fire sketching something in their slender book of notes. Every once in a while, they press the fresh cut on their forearm and use blood to draw something. I'm fairly sure Elias summoned a breeze with one such sigil, but despite the necessity I don't want to think about it.

But Elias suddenly stands, walks to me, and with a grim smile reaches out to press a small scrap of paper to my forehead. It's cool, slick. I have time to realize *blood* before I pass out.

I wake up in rays of sunlight filtering through the pine needles.

With an ugly gasp, I sit. Kitty snorffles, and clicks her fangs at me.

"You're up," Elias says. "It worked."

I refuse to speak to them until we're packed and mounted, and Kitty's loping stride devours the road beneath us. After an hour under the clear morning sun, I turn my head and loudly ask, "What did you do?"

"I thought I could use some of the old seals to figure out a sleeping spell. And," they say just as loudly in my ear, "I hoped I could use the paper to transfer it immediately, to avoid mistakes. I was right."

"Can you find a way to shield me from her boon?"

"I think so. It will be crude. I'm not practiced enough, nor do I have enough time to experiment, to make it specific to boons, or her boon. I worry it could block all boons, or do something permanent."

"I understand."

We ride with only the rush of wind and Kitty's delighted growls as I let her take whatever speed she likes. Then Elias squeezes me and says, "We should stop slightly early tonight so I can practice the spell before we find them."

"Elias—"

"Will an hour make a difference?"

"Maybe! It only takes a moment to kill."

Elias is quiet for a long moment, then they say, "Caspian took this risk. I won't risk you unnecessarily, too. He wouldn't forgive me."

I hate it, and my instinct is to deny Elias this comfort. I won't forgive myself if we get to Caspian only an hour late.

"Talon," Elias says. I turn my head so I can see their profile. "The dragon empyreal is indestructible."

I tense suddenly enough Kitty startles, too, but continues running. She glances back at me for command. I pet her ridge feathers and force myself to relax. "Indestructible?"

"In dragon form, at least. His scales. They can't be damaged."

The heart shield treasure of House Dragon is a shield made from the chest plate of the First Dragon. I tried to nick it once, under my father's orders, and couldn't, even with my sharpest dagger. "If he stays a dragon, she can't hurt him," I murmur too softly for Elias to hear.

But they seem to know. They nod.

We ride.

The landmarks north of Ashroot Village that I recognized in my boon visions of Caspian appear mere hours after sunrise on the fifth day.

I pull Kitty to a halt and look at Elias. It's time.

They dismount and dig into the bag hooked onto the rear of Kitty's saddle for their notes. We practiced this last night, and it was uncomfortable, but it worked. Elias prepared a series of blood sigils onto scraps of paper that will activate his spell, and some to deactivate it.

I take a deep breath and listen to the wind, the huff of Kitty's breath, and the empty forest. When Kitty is near, even the birds tend to be still and silent.

Then I wait for Elias as they cut into their arm again. I offered my own, but Elias said I need to be strong to fight. This is what they can do. When they have the blood they need, they meet my gaze for a moment, and nod. I nod back. Elias takes a paper in each hand and puts a drop of blood onto the already drawn sigil. They press one to each of my ears, just in front of the shell. They whisper, and my skull fills with the sounds of the ocean.

It's disorienting. All I hear is my own rushing blood, overpowering the sounds of wind, Kitty's chuffing, and even Elias's words as they face me and yell. I think I can tell what they're saying by their mouth alone, but I can't hear it. I nod.

Once Elias deafens themself, we set out again. We rely on taps and touches to communicate, though there's little to say. I'm glad about the long relationship I have with Kitty that allows me to feel her eagerness through my seat, and recognize the signals in her spine feathers, since I can't hear her small chirps and growls.

When we reach the ridge overlooking Ashroot Village, we dismount. I tell Kitty to stay unless I call for her with the signal whistle. She knows my commands.

Hearing my voice muffled in my own head is strange, but no stranger than everything else.

Our plan is to find Caspian to make sure he's safe, then help with his trap. If he refuses, I'll simply do what I want anyway. And remind him that's the trick I've learned from the Dragon regent.

The first sign of Caspian is a vibration in the air, and wind pushing at my face and the trees all around. I think he must have roared and beaten his wings. I get out my falchion and dash forward.

The second sign is a handful of Dragon regular soldiers, in full uniform and armor, waiting at the edge of the tree line.

I call out to them: "*Dragons*," and they turn, startled. I'm in my uniform, too, vivid red and white of the Teeth. "*Stand back*," I say, the words like loud cotton in my head. "*I am Talon Goldhoard.*"

One, the captain, bows with her fist over her heart and speaks, shaking her head.

I ignore her and move through their line. She reaches for my arm but stops. In my reproachful glance, I see her mouth make my aunt's name and I understand.

These Dragons are here with Aurora. She's nearby.

"*I am your War Prince. You will obey me, not Aurora*," I say.

The captain is startled, but thankfully salutes again.

Not traitors, then. Something more complicated. I don't have time to find out. I dash beyond the tree line just as Caspian slams down before me, hard enough the ground trembles. His scales glint green-black, his tail swipes for balance, and his wings are rampant. His toothy maw opens and he roars loud enough it shakes the air.

He isn't roaring at me, but at Aurora, who stands at the cliff.

She braces herself against this loud onslaught, hands out, and she's talking at him—I can't hear, but her face is determined, strained.

Caspian stomps and roars, but he doesn't advance. His wings tremble, and the shadows they make on the wide expanse of rock waver.

I stride forward, falchion drawn.

I'm going to cut her down. Without hesitation.

She sees me, and immediately yells at both of us, a smile on her face, forced. But somehow her eyes warm as she looks at me.

But when I keep coming, when I angle my falchion to point it at her chest, her expression breaks into panic.

The roar of my blood feels like a rush of willpower and strength. Aurora is pinned against the cliff's edge, far below the grazing fields and Ashroot Village's spread.

The heat of Caspian's dragon breath shoves against me, and the shade of his wings. I won't let myself feel anything else, but I hold her wide gaze. I won't feel. Won't stop.

Her mouth moves and she holds out her hands, pleading.

I step in, pushing the tip of my falchion toward her heart.

Brilliant fire explodes in my vision, and a heat wave knocks me away.

27

DARLING

Vivian and I are flying back to House Dragon when I feel it. It's no more than a sense of wrongness—like a dish out of place—but the phoenix tilts its wings and changes course, the gryphon following without question. They most likely feel it as well.

It's not long before I realize what I sensed. Blood magic, the taint of it. It's like the shrines, like smelling a pile of dung before stepping in it, and I scan the land to see where it's coming from. It's not too far from a village, and the red jackets dotting the landscape are unmistakable, as is the green-black dragon with its wings spread.

And that's when I see them, Talon and Aurora. His blade is drawn, and I have no doubt he will run her through if he can.

He is the War Prince, after all.

I circle lower, and as he makes to thrust, I beat my wings once, strongly, sending him stumbling backward. Aurora takes that as her chance to flee, but it's a small matter to throw a little phoenix fire toward her. It encircles her, trapping her where she stands, and she stares up at the sky with wide eyes as I circle once more and come in for a landing.

When I come back to myself fully, Talon is waiting for me with his jacket and my smoked lenses, the ones I told him to keep back at House Dragon. I shrug into the jacket and put on the goggles, grateful. It says something that he's taken to carrying my old lenses with him, but I shy away from delving into the thought too deeply.

"What are you doing here?" he asks, his voice strange. I sense the recent blood magic clinging to him, weaker than the manipulation of his boon, and I clear it away. It's a bit like running my hand through a spider's web, and neither phoenix nor Chaos like the sensation.

"Bloodscale refused to surrender without one or both of the Dragon princes in tow, so I flew back to get you and Caspian. But it looks like someone had their own agenda," I say, giving Caspian, the dragon, really, a pointed glance. He huffs in my direction, and I sigh, turning back to Aurora. The Dragon soldiers who stand nearby are confused, but I don't sense any of the entangling blood magic that tainted the assassin back in Phoenix Crest. Still, as Aurora calls to people nearby through the fire, I can feel the power of her boon, warping and cajoling. But it doesn't pass through the phoenix flames, and the soldiers stare at her in confusion.

I wonder if I can take her boon from her.

Vivian is by my side, draped in yet another soldier's coat. "I read a treatise that the empyreals were known to take the boons of those who misused them," she says. She knows exactly what I was thinking. Her tone is mild, as though we're discussing the weather, and I laugh. What would I do without her? She's the next best thing we have to a primer on empyreal behavior.

I step toward Aurora knowing what I need to do.

I let Talon's jacket fall, no doubt giving the soldiers behind me an eyeful, but I've become accustomed to being naked in public, and I am more focused on my task. I step through the flames until I stand before Aurora. Her eyes glint with a terrible light, and she grins.

"Well, didn't you manage to claw your way out of the sewers," she sneers. But I don't have time for witty repartee. I have a country to fix.

And she is one of the many things standing in my way.

I reach out, and she tries to back away, but the flames behind her, my flames, flare dramatically. She freezes and I touch her cheek. When she flinches, I smile, because although there aren't any flames, she isn't going to like what comes next.

I find the Chaos within her, tainted and twisted up with her blood magic, and I flare.

Her screams are instantaneous and she falls to the ground, sobbing. I tamp down the flames around me and Talon is there, wrapping his uniform jacket around me once more. I lean into him, inhaling the scent of sweat and something that is indefinably Talon: part war drake, part mountain pines. I ache with wanting him, the memory of the kiss we shared making my lips tingle. He squeezes me once and releases me, not taking advantage of the moment, and it only makes me want to find a place where we can spend an afternoon away from the world and all its problems and just *be*.

But the Dragon soldiers are picking a sobbing Aurora up from the ground and putting her into restraints. This is a matter I have to deal with, so I place my heart back into the cage I've built for it, Darling fading away and the Phoenix Reborn appearing once more.

Just in time, as a naked Caspian storms toward us, Elias chasing after him with an ornate robe he must have carried with him just for Caspian.

"Why did you stop Talon?" Caspian demands. "Why didn't you let him kill her?"

"Justice is not for House Dragon to decide," I say in what I hope is a voice that comes across as regal. "House Sphinx and House Kraken have suffered the most because of Aurora Falleau's lies and deceit, and they will decide her fate. Whether she lives or dies is up to them. We'll take Aurora to Phoenix Crest and have a real trial, and then decide what to do with her."

Caspian draws himself up, but I turn on him, all phoenix, and he wilts. "Fine. It's your funeral," he snarls, spinning on his heel and stomping toward the nearby village. Most likely off to find a tavern.

Elias runs after him, calling his name, and I turn back to Talon with a small smile.

"I don't suppose there's anywhere in the village to get some clothing for Vivian and me?" I ask, and one of the Dragon soldiers steps forward, sinking down on her knee before me.

"My mother is in the village and is a seamstress, my, uh—"

"Flame," Talon says, and the soldier's confused expression melts into relief.

"My flame," the soldier says. "It would be a great honor for her to clothe the Phoenix and Gryphon Reborn."

Vivian smiles. "Well, you can never have too many clothes."

"Not when I keep incinerating them," I agree with a sigh. I realize the soldier is still down on her knee, and I gesture for her to stand. "That sounds fantastic, thank you. Is there also some place to eat in the village?" I'm starving after our flight and working the Chaos.

She nods, and a few of the other Dragon regulars come over, giving advice and falling over themselves to help, dragging an unconscious Aurora along behind them.

"What are we going to do when she wakes?" Talon asks, and I shake my head.

"I took her boon," I say. "She can't manipulate people anymore. Well, at least not like she did before."

"I cannot imagine Chaos granting such a terrible gift," Vivian says.

"The gift was charm, not manipulation. At some point she used blood magic to strengthen the boon, and this was the end result when Chaos was unleashed." A sharp pain stabs my middle and I groan. "Okay, food, now. Conversation, after."

The nice thing about being the Phoenix Reborn is that when I say things, people listen. I'm not sure if that's the effect of Chaos and the phoenix riding me, or a measure of respect for stories about rulers long gone, but it's less than an hour from my request until I've been stitched into a very nice dress by Rhoda, the local seamstress, and am sitting in the ready room of the village's lone tavern devouring a roasted game bird paired with a salad of bitter summer greens.

Talon watches me eat with an expression of amusement. Elias and Caspian have gone off who knows where, and Vivian sits with us, quiet as she ponders something besides the full plate before her.

"My flame," she finally says, and I don't quite manage to keep from rolling my eyes at her.

"Vivian. Please. If I hear one more 'my flame' today, I am going to combust." Like with the other innkeepers, I had to leave a flaming sigil somewhere, and the bowing and scraping that had accompanied the act had been truly embarrassing, especially since I had been clutching Talon's jacket closed across my bosom at the time, the seamstress not yet arrived with her ready-made options.

"Darling, apologies," she says with a warm smile. "Just know that what I am going to ask you, I ask as House Gryphon and not as your friend."

I nod. "Okay, so what is it?"

"I'd like the opportunity to question Aurora about what she knows about blood magic. Namely, where she got her information. The rituals she's doing, we have no record of them. Elias told me he's been experimenting with what we do know, and, well, he isn't able to come even close to what Aurora can do."

"Isn't that good?" Talon says. "That means no one else can repeat it."

"As long as we burn everything in her hidden workshop in Phoenix Crest," I say, pulling the last bits of meat from a bone with my teeth before dropping it on my plate and wiping my hands on a napkin. My instinct is to say no to Vivian's request, but for some reason I think of Leonetti tossing a book of letters at me when I refused to try to learn how to read when I came to his house.

"All knowledge is worth having, minnow," he'd said. "That's not just for those self-important gryphons. There is nothing so sad as the willfully ignorant. So start practicing those letters if you truly want to be of my house."

"Do it," I say, the memory making me hoarse. I stand with a yawn. "With the gryphon at your side, it should be easy to discover the truth. I'm going to take the innkeeper up on that offer of somewhere to sleep. Talon?"

"Yes," he says, a little too hopeful, and I give him a rueful smile.

"Can you round up Caspian, Elias, and everyone else, and let them know we'll head out for Phoenix Crest tomorrow? We're closer here than if we return to House Dragon, and Adelaide and Gianna will be in Phoenix Crest by week's end. And the last thing I want is to give my sister another reason to be cross with me."

If he's disappointed my request isn't something more carnal, Talon doesn't let it show, simply stands and nods. "Of course. Finn will be at the Crest on a similar schedule, with half my army. Bloodscale will submit."

"And let me know when you're finished with Aurora. I have some questions for her as well," I say, directing that last bit to Vivian. She inclines her head and I head off, upstairs to the room the innkeeper so generously set aside for me.

I pull off the borrowed boots I wear, too small and too stiff to be comfortable, and throw myself onto the bed. I've barely stripped off my goggles and closed my eyes when I hear screaming.

The room is dark, and the phoenix screams in echo to the scream outside, the sound ripping through me so that I have to open my mouth to release the noise. My door flies open and Talon is in the doorway, disheveled and adorable.

"What's wrong?" he asks, and I shake my head, a sob lodged in my chest.

"I don't know—Vivian," I say, pushing past Talon and running out the door, barefoot. He yells that I forgot my goggles, but there's no time. I can feel the anxiousness welling up in me.

The gryphon is in mortal danger.

I'm outside the inn, startling a few townspeople entering. The sun has set, and dusk spreads cool fingers across the land, a gentle breeze chasing away the last of the day's heat. My heart pounds, the kind of feeling one gets when startled from a sound sleep, and that's when I see the gryphon explode out of a barn on the outskirts of town.

"Darling," Talon asks, sensing I know something he doesn't.

"That isn't Vivian," I say, and the gryphon screams, a sound of grief and confusion. "Oh no—Talon, check out that barn. I'm going after Elias." I hastily undo the ribbons securing my day dress, and step out of it.

There are Dragon regulars heading toward us, but there's no time. I can feel the desperation and rage in Elias, but even worse is the taint of blood magic. Vivian had said Elias was experimenting with rituals, but now I realize that means they were casting spells.

They're the gryphon, which means Vivian is dead, but Chaos doesn't like having its children tainted by blood magic. Their screams of pain are because Chaos is trying to cleanse the foulness.

It must feel like having their insides scrubbed.

I launch into the air after Elias, hoping that Talon can take care of whatever he finds in the barn.

And then there is only the chase.

28

TALON

I don't do what Darling says: I know what's in the barn. I left
Caspian there with Elias less than an hour ago. Caspian swore
he'd sleep as a dragon or never sleep again. Elias promised to stay
with him.

Instead I gesture for Dragon soldiers in the inn yard to follow
me around the back of the inn to the storage shed where we'd imprisoned Aurora.

It's deserted. The soldiers on guard must have run toward the
screaming, since it came from the faraway barn. Only one remained behind, collapsed on the ground; he's bleeding out from a
gash under his jaw. One of the soldiers with me kneels and touches
his face, but she shakes her head at me. There's too much blood
pooling under him, anyway. I quickly scan his body and see it: a
smear of blood on the palm of his hand, hidden by the curl of his
limp fingers and the nighttime.

Darling burned out Aunt Aurora's persuasion boon, but blood
magic remained.

I know what I'll find inside. Grimly I stare at the thin wooden
door. "Secure the building, and send everyone out searching for
Aurora. If sighted, kill her instantly. Use projectiles if possible.
Look for blood. Don't let her touch you."

Above, the gryphon screams again, swooping past. My neck

aches with how fast I snap my head up to look. We all look.

The gryphon drops, then catches itself, screaming in pain. It flies raggedly, and there is the burning comet of the Phoenix Reborn shooting toward it. Toward them. Elias.

I clench my jaw and grip my falchion. Then I kick in the storage shed door.

Firelight flickers from four torches set into sconces on the walls. Shadows claw through the shelves of wine and grain, there's a knocked-over chair, and the packed dirt floor glistens sickeningly.

Vivian Chronicum stares dully at me, sprawled dead on the ground. Neck torn open and blood smeared across her mouth. I hold my soldiers back and study the scene. There's no need for my boon to trace what happened. Aurora used her own blood, gouged by her own nails, probably, or freed by tearing her thin wrist skin against ropes and the wooden back of the chair. She escaped, and attacked too fast for scholarly Vivian to fight back. Despite being the Gryphon regent.

I suspect the blood across Vivian's mouth is Aurora's.

She surprised the soldier outside, the moment the gryphon transferred to Elias and they began their commotion, drawing away the rest of my Dragons.

The emotions burning up my chest are too wild and conflicting to parse. Rage, grief, fear, cold killing intent. I push them all down and spin, stepping out of the shed. "Get the Gryphon regent's body cleaned and brought respectfully into the inn. We'll have to beg the owners' forgiveness and take it over for now. This is where I'll set up command. You—" I point to two soldiers—"with me. The rest of you keep searching for Aurora. All the houses and shops and barns, even if the locals don't want you to. Especially if they resist."

I return to the front yard of the inn. The owners cling to each other in the doorway, as well as two of their other guests and servants. They all stare at the night sky.

A roar blasts across the stars. The dragon empyreal has joined the phoenix in the chase for the gryphon.

I let myself watch a moment. It seems Caspian is corralling Elias as best he can while Darling gets a grip on them.

Turning to the innkeepers, I clear my throat for their attention. The woman looks at me. "I need your inn," I say. "You'll be compensated, but it needs to be cleared out for me and the phoenix. The largest room should be prepared for the phoenix and the new Gryphon regent, and we'll take one for funeral arrangements. There are two dead already, possibly more to come. Please prepare as much food as you can manage immediately. I hope we'll be moving on tomorrow."

The innkeeper and her husband bow hurriedly and vanish inside with their people. I instruct one of the soldiers with me to help them. Just then, a soldier dashes into the yard. "My blade! One of the drakes is gone, and a civilian hostler dead."

I bite back a curse. "Direct everyone to focus on that area, and the fastest route out of the city. I don't know which direction she'll take," I say, letting frustration seep into my tone. My boon should be the solution! I have to fix it. Finding out how to negate the spell on my boon should have been the priority with Aurora, not Vivian's research.

Overhead, the gryphon screams. I look up in time to see Caspian whip his tail around midflight, rearing with a huge gust of air, and the phoenix collides with the gryphon, wrapping them in brilliant flames.

They are a fireball nearly as bright as a sun, lighting up the whole village. Everyone is seeing this miracle.

"Go," I manage to command.

The soldiers salute distractedly and disperse again. I can't take my eyes off the fire.

Then the dragon snaps its teeth and pulls in its wings to fall. Right for me.

My eyes widen in alarm, but the dragon twists midair, then lands with a flash, crouching as a naked young man in the center of the yard. Caspian immediately stands out of a small indented crater, neck craned and mouth open as he stares up, too.

The wind is warm, comforting as it wafts down. As we watch, the ball of fire spreads into wings, and lowers slowly.

Darling cradles Elias as she lands gently. The wings flicker, gorgeous flaming primary feathers arcing gracefully.

Caspian darts forward to take Elias from her, but Darling bares her teeth at him and holds tight. "Not yet," she says, her voice echoing strangely.

I turn and grip the sleeve of the innkeeper's husband. Everyone has emerged to stare, awestruck. I tug at him. "Get clothes, now."

His mouth remains parted, but he nods, backing away as the fire of Darling's wings fades.

I don't even have my jacket to offer her. I ran out of my room at the screaming in the middle of getting ready for some rest, and only grabbed my falchion. At least my boots were still on.

As the fire dims, Darling lets herself sink to the yard, Elias with her. Caspian hovers, his hands fluttering over both their shoulders.

The new darkness blankets everything, and my eyes are full of fiery afterimages.

Somebody puts clothes in my arms. I take them and go to wrap the regents up and bring them inside.

The largest room at the inn is the one they gave Darling, so that's where we all end up. I bring in one of my soldiers with a newly awakened light boon, and he sets boonlights very low on several surfaces. It's enough for us to see, but Darling doesn't need her goggles. I help dress a mostly unconscious Elias in loose clothing and Caspian gets them into the bed, then climbs in after and sits with his back to the wall. Caspian drags Elias into his lap.

While Darling dresses and I murmur with my soldiers just outside, ordering water and food and wine brought up, Caspian holds onto Elias like he'll die without them. His fingers are blanched where they press into Elias; his mouth is a tight line.

I return briefly to my room to fully dress and check in with my soldiers and the innkeeper. No sign of Aurora, still, and I order the Dragons to pull back. She's likely far gone already, and attacking her isn't worth it when we can't predict her strength and skills in blood magic other than to assume the worst. I won't sacrifice more people if I don't have to.

The food and drink arrive back at Darling's door as I do, and I help the innkeeper set it all on the little table. Darling is slumped there, staring at Caspian and Elias. She glances up at me, violet Chaos glinting in her eyes.

"Eat something," I say softly.

I take a cup of water to Caspian. "Here." I put it to his lips. He pries a hand away from Elias and makes the barest attempt to drink before shifting to offer it to Elias.

The Gryphon regent shudders as if they have a fever. Their eyes squeeze more tightly shut.

Caspian hugs them more tightly and puts the cup to their mouth. "Elias," he murmurs. "Water."

Elias turns their face away from the cup, pressing into Caspian's chest. Their whole body shivers again. Caspian shoves the water back at me, and then tenderly brushes curls away from Elias's temple.

"Why are they like this?" I ask Darling. It isn't how Caspian or Darvey behaved or looked after the phoenix brought them back to themselves. Maybe because of the violence of Vivian's death?

Darling drops her spoon into the half-empty bowl of stewed vegetables. She pushes the bowl across the table. "They were practicing blood magic. It messed up the transfer, and then I had to help the gryphon clean itself up."

I frown, studying Elias. Caspian continues to bend around them, stroking a finger along their hairline. I say, "They said it was the only way to counter Aurora's blood magic. And it worked."

"It's wrong," Darling says with finality.

"Elias knows that."

"Vivian would—" Caspian starts, then cuts himself off with a small choking sound.

We all fall silent. I move nearer to Darling. She's staring at the two of them, and she looks too young suddenly. Haunting in the dim light, without her smoked lenses. In slightly large clothes.

"Cas," Elias whispers suddenly. They clutch at Caspian's arms.

"I'm here," my brother whispers back.

Darling stands. I take her hand and squeeze it. Her skin is hot.

"Vivian, she—she—" Elias opens their dark eyes and looks up at Caspian.

"I know," Caspian says darkly. "I'm sorry."

Elias chokes on a sob. "I feel—feel awful," they gasp.

"It will get better," Caspian says, but it's difficult to believe his dead tone.

"I didn't—want—"

"I know," Caspian says again. He holds Elias tight, then raises his head. Tears glimmer like tiny sparks in his eyes, and he snarls at Darling. I nearly step back, startled. For a moment, there are fangs in his mouth and his eyes pierce violet. He speaks in a voice too deep for his own, gravelly like scales and teeth crawling up his throat, "It's no wonder we destroyed the phoenix back then."

Darling jolts, her fingers tightening painfully on mine. I tug her closer, shocked at my brother.

Caspian snarls again. "If it wasn't for you—Aurora should have been skewered on Talon's blade this afternoon, and Vivian *alive.*"

"Caspian!" I snap. I drag Darling behind me, though she struggles to free herself from my grasp.

My brother's face *ripples* and I see scales emerging, and I yell his name again. "Stop!"

Darling jerks free of me, glaring at Caspian, who's maintained his human form—barely. "Maybe *you* should have seen this coming, dragon," Darling says, then she storms out of the room.

I shoot Caspian a disgusted look and follow.

In the hallway, I nearly run into Darling. She's frozen just outside, and at my touch she asks without looking, "Where is she?"

Though I'd rather not, I escort Darling to the lower level of the inn, where the bodies are laid out, clean and covered and ready for the morning's various House rituals. Vivian, my soldier, and the hostler. They're each on a narrow table brought in from the kitchen and dining room. I enter first and extinguish most of the boonlights.

Darling walks unerringly to Vivian's body, which is draped in a red cloth. She puts her hand over Vivian's forehead. I watch Darling's face as carefully as I can in the dark. Her big eyes are like pits of Chaos. She stands there, a hand on Vivian, and breathes raggedly.

I wait. Just next to her, trying to radiate my concern, my stability.

"Did I do the wrong thing?" Darling asks very quietly.

I think she's asking Vivian.

Swallowing my own sorrow, I move and put my arms around her from behind. Darling allows it, but doesn't lean back. I hug her, and I say, "I don't know. You thought it was the right thing then, and so did Vivian. She trusted you, and you trusted her. Second-guessing yourself now undercuts that trust between you. Caspian is awful. And grieving. Don't listen to him."

Darling trembles in my arms. Her hand falls away from Vivian, and I feel a tear drop onto my hand as she bows her head.

Without a thought, I lift Darling into my arms. I carry her upstairs, waving off several soldiers. She holds on, tears smearing my neck.

In my room, I sit on the bed with Darling in my lap and hold her while she cries. It isn't long. Darling isn't going to let herself fall apart, and I'm grateful she trusts me enough to allow herself this much.

She sniffles, sighs, and I can feel her gathering herself to push off my lap.

I squeeze gently around her shoulders. "Darling, I need you to do something for me." I hope it will be a distraction.

Darling wipes her face with both hands and meets my eyes from too near. I look between hers—the Chaos shimmers against brown-gold—and I wonder what her eyes are like from this near when she's the phoenix. I hope I get to see it. "What?" she says.

"I pulled my soldiers back to Ashroot. They aren't chasing Aurora."

Her jaw sets.

I continue, "It's too dangerous when we don't know what she's doing. Where she's going. If I could trace her, we'd know. Where, what, and we could prepare. She couldn't catch us unawares again."

"Talon—"

Hearing the denial in her voice, I press faster. "You said you can burn the blood magic out of me. And you did it to Elias."

"They're the empyreal! It could kill you!" Darling pushes at my chest.

I hold on. "It won't. You won't. You didn't kill Elias. Or Aurora, when you took her boon."

"That's a risk, too," she whispers furiously. "I could burn off your whole boon."

"It isn't doing me any good right now anyway."

Darling scoffs angrily.

"It's worth the risk. I trust you."

"Vivian trusted me, and—"

"I know." I hold her gaze. "I told you, she was right to."

"Talon," Darling murmurs, and blinks: a tear falls from each eye.

I loosen my grip to wipe them away. One with my thumb, one with the knuckle of my forefinger. I hold her gaze the whole time.

She shakes her head, expression breaking into grief. But then Darling kisses me.

It hurts.

Lightning scorches through me, along my veins and bones. Blood bursts in my mouth. I clench my whole body, hard, harder, holding myself together against the pain. Vaguely aware of hands on my face, forehead to mine, as I pant against Darling's lips.

The lightning inside me is so bright, turning the room into the surface of the sun. I'm inside it, and it's so hot it's white, everywhere.

It suddenly strikes, and I jerk around Darling, squishing her to me with a cry.

And I see Aurora. I see her racing across the plains outside Phoenix Crest as dawn gently washes against the stars in the east. She's on one of the narrow paths curving toward the rear of the fortress, the back of the mountain.

I come to with a gasp.

"Talon, Talon!" Darling's hands are on my face.

My eyes widen. She's straddling my lap, fingers digging into my hair.

"I'm . . . fine," I say, just as the door slams open and soldiers fight their way to pour in. I look past Darling and somehow pry a hand from her waist to hold out at my soldiers. "I'm fine," I say more loudly. My vision blots with colorful balls, little fireworks, and stars. "But I'm going to—to faint."

Darling makes a little noise, and I grip her wrists.

"She's going for Phoenix Crest, a—a secret way in? It worked." I try to smile, but my teeth feel bloody. I think I bit my tongue.

"All right, Talon," Darling says as she slides off me, and helps me ease back right as I pass out.

29

DARLING

Vivian's death is more of a blow than I am expecting. I've only known her a short time, but I've come to rely on her knowledge more than my own instincts. And she was strong as an empyreal, stronger than anyone else. An excellent second-in-command, and when I think of her last terrible moments, something in me hitches painfully. I've known loss, more than my share, but this one hits differently.

This one feels personal. Perhaps because it's so unnecessary. Or perhaps it's because I haven't even had the chance to properly grieve Leonetti, and now here is another burden to shoulder.

Even the phoenix is grieving her loss. The gryphon lives on, but Elias is weak, the blood magic they did in the past few days making it difficult for them and the gryphon to bond. It will be a while before they can take their rightful place at the head of their house.

I now have not a single empyreal at my side that I can depend upon.

Caspian is spoiled and self-involved, Adelaide is angry, and Gianna and Darvey are too young to call upon in any real way. I'm feeling alone and bereft with a task too big to accomplish on my own, and the sensation sends me back to Vivian's body, hoping that perhaps there is something there that will tell us what Aurora plans to do. There is a nagging feeling that we've all overlooked something, that in our haste and panic some critical piece was missed. The sensation belongs more to the phoenix than to me, and I give myself over to it.

The guard minding the room where the bodies are being stored bows and silently steps out of the way when I approach. I incline my head in acknowledgment. The boonlanterns inside the space are low, and I'm thankful that there is no need for my goggles. But I almost wish I had the protection of them over my eyes, hiding my sadness.

The first time I examined Vivian's body, it was with the grief of someone who had just lost a friend. This time, I approach the remains with the analytical mind of the phoenix and the heart of Chaos, of beings who have existed longer than any one of us, and may hopefully know what is happening.

I pull back the sheet and examine the wounds, pushing back against the wave of pain and anger that threatens to overwhelm me. Aurora will pay for this. But first, we have to know just what she did to Vivian.

That's when I see the sigil.

It's hidden, an afterthought on the inside of Vivian's dark arm. I don't know what it does, but when I use a little Chaos to burn it away, I stumble backward with a gasp.

Vivian's body was mutilated, the true extent of the damage only revealed now that the blood magic hiding the wounds is destroyed.

The few injuries that were visible before were only the beginning. Vivian put up a fight. There are numerous markings upon her body, bruises and the like, but most noticeable of all is the gaping hole where her heart used to be.

Aurora has the heart of an empyreal, and that means nothing good.

The realization sends me out of the inn, past the guard who calls after me, and toward the shadows at the edge of town. My pain, my grief, my anger are too much, and I explode into flames, heedless of my garments. Part of me hopes the seamstress has another dress I can buy.

I give the phoenix control, and the scream that emerges from my throat is a combination of my pain and the empyreal's long-simmering rage. This is what was done to the phoenix long ago, in that place beneath House Dragon. And the fact that it's happening again is untenable.

We will not let Aurora Falleau get away with this.

I fly, farther and faster than I ever have before, the phoenix a comet streaking across the sky. I leave Pyrlanum behind, sweeping out over the open sea, my flames reflected back to me on inky waves. I could fly forever, when I feel it. A tickle of awareness, Chaos reaching out to me.

Talon. His worry runs down the connection of his boon, and I tilt and return back the way I came. The phoenix sends him a memory of a place we soared past while leaving town: trees, a small stream, peaceful and secluded. I need space, and air, and to be away from all the ears and eyes of the soldiers and townspeople.

I need somewhere that I can just be Darling Seabreak, grieving orphan, and not the Phoenix Reborn.

Somehow, some way, Talon gets it.

He waits for me in the copse of trees outside town. When I land, he holds a robe, something fine and embroidered. It doesn't smell of Caspian, though, and Talon smiles in the dark, the small boon-lantern near his feet enough to make the space day-bright but not enough for him to see.

"I wasn't sure it was really you sending me the image," he said.

"You were looking for me," I say, and his eyes are wide with wonder.

"So you can sense when I use my boon," he says.

"Boons are gifts of Chaos," I say, walking toward him. He averts his eyes, trying to give me a sense of privacy, but I want him to look at me, to see that I am still the same girl he fought in that dining room so long ago in Lastrium. "I am the heart of Chaos. I think it sort of comes with the job."

"The guard said you rushed off, and I was worried," he says. He holds out the robe and I take it before tossing it to the side. "Darling, what is it?"

"I don't want to talk about Chaos, or blood, or empyreals," I say, my voice husky. "I just want you."

He opens his mouth to respond, but I'm already standing before him, pressing into him. "Darling," he begins, and I silence him with a long kiss.

"If you don't want me, tell me now," I say, even though if he rejects me, I will fall to pieces. It's too hard, being this thing that everyone looks to, to be everything to everyone and nothing to myself. My sister is angry with me, I haven't even properly grieved my adoptive father's murder, and yet I'm expected to lead an entire country to peace when most of them would have tried to kill me on sight a few months ago. I just want one thing that is my own.

"I want you," he says. And that is all I need.

I press into him, and he responds by kissing me fiercely, passionately. It isn't gentle, but gentle isn't what I need. I answer him back, growling a little as we fall onto the discarded robe. His clothes are an annoyance, and I fumble impatiently with the ties to his trousers until he gently pushes my hands away with a small laugh.

"Are you sure?" he says, his voice thick with his own desire. "I can't . . . I don't want to lose you again."

Flames erupt all around us, my flames, and I press into him. He's all wide wonder as tiny tendrils of fire dance across his skin, and he laughs. "How is this possible?" he wonders. It's just like back in the inn, but this time my flames caress him affectionately.

"You can't burn the heart of the phoenix," I say. It's an answer to a question he didn't ask, but from the way his expression softens, he understands what I am telling him.

I love him, this foolish, loyal, kindhearted dragon. And if the words are too hard to say, and they are, then I will just have to show him instead.

I wake alone the next morning in the room set aside for the Phoenix Reborn. Talon is gone, even though the space where he'd been is still warm. The curtains have been pulled shut and a new dress lies across a chair at the foot of the bed. When I pick it up, a slip of paper falls from between the folds:

Figured you might want actual clothes. Finn and the barghest arrived at dawn. Meet us in the ready room. ~T.

The simple gesture warms me, and I bathe and dress quickly, my stomach growling with hunger. I pull on my goggles and have only gone a few steps in the hallway when I run into a wall of a person.

"Careful," Finn growls, and flames immediately leap from my skin. He holds his hands up in surrender. "Relax, I come in peace.

Talon is overseeing the funeral arrangements since Elias is still in no condition to do so."

I cross my arms. "So why are you lurking outside my room?" I ask. "The last time you were near my rooms, you tried to kill me."

Finn nods, and has the grace to flush a little bit. "I know. And I owe you an apology. In my defense, you did have a pot of poisoned lip tint."

"I never would've used it," I say, and Finn nods.

"I know. That was what Adelaide told me," he says. "Which is why I'm here to apologize. We saw you flying last night, like a shooting star across the sky . . ." He trails off and his eyes go distant. "And after I saw that, I knew I'd been wrong. Chaos wouldn't let a murderer be the phoenix."

The awe in Finn's eyes is a bit much to take, so I change the subject. "Wait, Adelaide? How did you see her?"

"We were on the way down to Barghest when Darvey said we needed to turn back. We found Gianna and Adelaide in a carriage riding toward the village. They said that an empyreal had fallen and we all needed to meet here. I thought it was all just sort of odd, but they were right."

I nod. "Are they all in the ready room?" At Finn's nod, I huff out a breath. "Good, can you find Talon and Caspian as well? Everyone needs to hear this."

I swing by the kitchens on my way, startling a maid who curtsies far too much but burns so brightly with Chaos that I try not to mind.

"Do you have coffee?" I ask, and she pours me a cup of it before offering me a pastry that is so overwhelmingly delicious that I devour the entire plate of them.

"I'm sorry," I say, running my finger across the plate to pick up the last of the buttery crumbs. "But these might be the best pastries I've ever had."

"It's my boon," she says, her pale cheeks flushing prettily. "I used to burn everything, but recently I've discovered I know how to bake perfectly."

"If you ever feel like leaving your small town, come to Phoenix Crest," I say, feeling not the least bit guilty about my offer. What is the point of being the Phoenix Reborn if I can't have the best pastry chef in all Pyrlanum?

I take my coffee with me to the ready room. When I arrive, Caspian and Elias are sitting on a low couch, while Gianna and Adelaide lean against a far back wall, deep in conversation. Darvey is stretched out next to the fire, more hound than boy. Everyone looks up as I enter and immediately begins talking.

"Wait until Talon and Finn arrive," I say, holding my hand up to forestall any questions. "I only want to say this once."

"Well, haven't we taken to leadership quite nicely," Caspian snipes, and my temper gets the best of me.

"Yes, because it turns out that we can't all drink ourselves into a stupor and then pout by a mountain lake when work needs to be done," I snap. Caspian opens his mouth to respond, but then winces as I pull at his Chaos, and settles back into a sulk. I don't know if it's the whims of his empyreal or his own selfishness that has made him unbearable these past few weeks, but I don't have time to ponder the matter, especially when Finn returns with a weary looking Talon.

"Vivian has been sent back to House Gryphon for internment,

and the hostler and Dragon soldier have been burned, their ashes sent to their loved ones." Talon looks tired, both physically and emotionally, and I want to enfold him in my arms, but first things first.

"Good, thank you for seeing to that," I say. "So, you all probably know that Bloodscale has refused to surrender Phoenix Crest without one of the Dragon princes in tow."

"I'd do the same," Adelaide says with a shrug, and I nod.

"That's not our biggest problem. Aurora is. She cut out Vivian's heart."

Everyone explodes at that: Caspian's face twists with scales as Elias moans in pain, Adelaide and Gianna ask what that means, and Darvey darts to tuck himself into the side of Finn. Only Finn and Talon hold their tongues and wait for me to continue.

I wait until everyone falls silent once more, and Talon takes that moment to speak. "Why didn't we see that when we first found her?"

"Aurora hid the worst of the damage with blood magic, most likely thinking it would buy her time. And she's right. I would've gone after her immediately if I'd known. As it is, this changes things. Darvey and Gianna need to be kept far away from Phoenix Crest, seeing as they're the youngest and the weakest of us. Elias as well."

"Wait, what is the deal with the heart? Does it let her see the future, like when she killed my father?" Adelaide asks with a frown.

"No. It will let her deal with Chaos," Elias says, their voice weak. "The heart of an empyreal is a direct link to Chaos. The first empyreals sacrificed their own hearts. Aurora of course would never, but whatever she's planning, it must be big."

"I think she's going to try to become the cockatrice," I say. "She was House Cockatrice before she was House Dragon, and we have no idea where the last empyreal is. She obviously didn't have any plans to become the gryphon, and even if she did, Chaos still chose Elias. The fact that Aurora is heading to Phoenix Crest makes me think there might be a shrine there, like under House Dragon."

"So how do we stop her?" Adelaide asks, and I shake my head.

"*We* don't. I need you and Finn to take Darvey and Gianna out to sea, far away from whatever Aurora is planning. Elias as well, until they are healthy. I'm going to head back to Phoenix Crest to see how the recruiting is going with my Flames. We're going to have to take Phoenix Crest in order to stop Aurora, and luckily, I have two Barbs who are experts at infiltration. Not to mention Brigh and her soldiers. We should be able to go after Aurora once we figure out how she got in."

Talon says, "I can pinpoint on a map where I saw Aurora heading, on the northwestern side of the Crest. Brigh and your Barbs will find the route from there."

"Talon and I will take the castle," Caspian says, straightening. "If Bloodscale wants the Dragon princes, he'll get them. As long as you can stop Aurora."

I nod. "I can. And if I can't, Adelaide, you'll have to take the younger empyreals to the Teeth Islands. They'll be safe there."

"She can't cross the seas as long as I'm there," Adelaide agrees. "But you don't have to do this alone."

"Yes," I say. "I do. I'm going to leave at midday. I'll get there before Caspian and Talon and get everyone ready. Any questions?"

No one says anything. And so, without another word, I head out of the room. But before I go, I stop before Talon and kiss him on the lips, claiming him for my own before everyone in the room. If he minds, he doesn't show it, his arms wrapping around me and holding me tightly before letting me go.

And then I leave to ready myself for the lonely flight back to Phoenix Crest.

30

TALON

We follow Darling toward Phoenix Crest after a brief, informal ceremony relieving Finn of his duties to House Dragon. It's just me, Caspian, Finn, and Darvey there, and I clasp his arm, quietly thanking him for his service and friendship. Finn glares at me the whole time, but it's only because he's holding back emotions. It's difficult to pry my fingers off his forearm. He's been my second since I was fourteen. I've never led or battled without him somewhere at my back.

Caspian is the one to actually say it. "It won't be easy to divest yourself of the instincts and trappings of a Dragon, Finn Sharpscale, but you're free of our House and responsibilities."

Finn slams his fist against his heart. "I will bring my instincts to serve my new House tirelessly."

"Welcome to House Barghest," Darvey says rather too loud. The kid looks overwhelmed: pink-cheeked and shaking a little bit. But he doesn't waver.

Finn goes to one knee and makes his promises to his new House regent.

I swallow and put my hands behind my back to clench them together. Caspian narrows his eyes at Darvey. "Take care of your new dog, Barghest," he says with a small growl.

Darvey slides behind Finn, then scowls ferociously at Caspian. It makes my brother laugh approvingly.

Then I watch Finn take up the rear guard of the empyreal party. Adelaide Seabreak leads, with two carriages between them, and only a handful of her Barbs with her. I mount up on Kitty with Caspian on another war drake at my side. Then I gesture my order for the slice of Dragon army Finn brought to head out.

The journey to Phoenix Crest isn't long. We should arrive before nightfall.

Kitty fidgets under me, turning one big green eye to Caspian any time he so much as shifts. He's riding a slighter drake, and seems to be getting on with her fine, tugging the drake's crest feathers fondly when it chitters at him. But for the most part he seems caught in his own mind, staring at nothing.

I didn't see him bid goodbye to Elias, though I assume they shared some kind of farewell.

Probably nothing as promising as Darling's kiss. When she did that, in front of everyone, I'd felt my weariness burn off like morning dew. Even though we were both fighting too hard, surrounded by trouble, lacking sleep, the kiss made me feel like everything was right. Not only between us, but everywhere. I was exactly where I belonged, doing exactly what I should. Leading House Dragon at the command of the Phoenix Reborn. I'm supposed to love her. It's supposed to be the easiest thing.

It's hard not to think about how awful Caspian has been to her recently. Before he was obnoxious and manipulative of her—of everyone—but I thought he liked her. Now he hasn't said a kind thing to her in days. He's resentful and cruel.

I don't know how to broach the subject. We've never been close that way, mostly because Caspian refused to allow it. Pushing me away as a child, refusing to explain anything to me, keeping me assigned far from Phoenix Crest. "Caspian," I start.

He slides me a knowing look, and although his words are kind, his tone is sneering. "What is it, little dragon?"

"Did the dragon empyreal make you like this?"

"Like what?"

I sigh, and Kitty snaps her teeth at Caspian and his mount. Caspian snaps right back. "Forget it," I say.

We ride on, the road cutting between rough gray boulders and the spearing evergreens found near Phoenix Crest. Behind us the small Dragon army makes a noise like a river of metal and claws.

Eventually, Caspian pulls a flask from his borrowed uniform jacket. He sips, then offers it to me. "It's *tea*," he says.

I accept. It is, shockingly, tea.

"I've always been like this," Caspian says when I return his flask. "Awful. Just ask anyone."

"Darling doesn't deserve it." I flick him a glance, thinking of what Elias said to me before this most recent disaster: *he doesn't love me.* "Neither does Elias."

"Nobody deserves it, Talon." Caspian smiles a mean, toothy smile. "Even Aurora doesn't."

I understand exactly what he means. "She deserves worse."

"That's right. She's taken so much from me." Caspian rubs his fingers down his war drake's spine. The drake preens. "Vivian was my friend. Maybe my only one. And Elias was simply *mine*. She took them from me, too, making them the empyreal. They can't ever be mine again."

There's a shadowy ripple on his face again, the power of his empyreal rolling under his skin. When Caspian flexes his hand, for a moment his knuckles are scaled dark green.

"I should have killed Aurora when I was fifteen," my brother snarls. "When I became High Prince Regent. I should have gutted her with a paintbrush. Stuck another through her pretty lying eyes."

"She won't live past tomorrow," I promise.

Caspian looks coolly at me. "Then what? After this is over? We take back the fortress from Bloodscale for the phoenix; she deals with Aurora. Then what for House Dragon? The War Prince seems to have divided loyalties."

"You get to decide," I say lightly. Ignoring his insinuation about Darling. Staring ahead as the road drops through the foothills. The sun catches threads of water shining between the trees. "You're the Dragon regent."

"Oh, Darling already told you what I'll do. Selfishly retire to my mountain lake and take a nap for a few years. So you get to decide, actually."

"Then I'm going to remake House Dragon into something I can be proud of. Where our strengths serve Chaos and Darling and Pyrlanum, instead of cutting it to pieces. A House where our mother never would have died."

Caspian holds his silence for a moment, then hands the flask of tea back to me. "Hmm, I suppose if you manage that, I'll come visit."

I want to say, *You're letting Aurora take you away from me, too.* But I hold my tongue. It's enough for now to be glad he's alive.

We ride into Darling's war camp set at the edge of the village below Phoenix Crest. True to her word, Darling has not only prepared them for our arrival, but the phoenix already took off again with Brigh and her two closest Barbs.

I close my eyes and reach for Darling. She's moving quickly on foot, heading around the north side of the jutting mountain housing the Crest. I pull back my boon quickly, not wanting to distract Darling. They'll probably travel through most of the night, given Darling's abilities. Rest for a while, and start hunting Aurora's back entrance as soon as they can.

We'll be ready.

I organize the troops pretty quickly. They're nearly all Dragons, most having been under either Brigh's or Finn's command for the previous weeks. Plus a group of soldiers formerly serving in Phoenix Crest who swore themselves to Darling specifically before she flew after Caspian and me three days ago.

I have a full claw of Teeth, too, and I borrow a Teeth uniform for myself. The army has been watching the field leading to Phoenix Crest constantly, and evacuated most of the civilians from the area. Reports show more and more people arriving in the area to join either Bloodscale or the phoenix. Most come for Darling, thank Chaos. Even if Bloodscale digs in and we have to set siege, we'll have twice his numbers. Plus a huge dragon empyreal and Darling burning it down from the inside.

As the sun sets, I join one of the soldier contingents at a fire to eat. To my surprise, Caspian plops to the grass beside me, flicking his fingers in hello to the soldiers around us. He slumps against the rock serving as my seat and drinks from his flask. I doubt it's tea anymore.

It takes a while for the conversation to pick up again, as the soldiers stare at Caspian and either bow or try to ignore him. I offer him the last of my bread, but he says, "I ate half a herd of sheep at the top of the week. Not hungry."

I stare, but it's enough to make the bravest Dragon soldier lean nearer to the flames and ask, "My blade, you . . . will you do battle tomorrow with scale and claw?"

Caspian grins with all his teeth. "Oh yes, if General Bloodscale does not surrender to our War Prince here, I shall do my best to eat him whole."

One of the soldiers laughs, and another claps him on the shoulder. A third lifts her own cup to Caspian. "Regent," she says as my brother lifts his flask in turn.

I take my leave, stacking our used bowls to return them to the temporary kitchens. Then I wander the camp, checking in where I can, and sourcing extra paper for a gift. The moon is high, blotting out stars.

When I make it to the command tent I'm sharing with Caspian, I wash up and put on the underclothes of the new Teeth uniform to sleep. Then I set the stack of paper on Caspian's pillow, along with a bundle of pencils and charcoal tied together with an old bootlace.

I lie down and listen to the sounds of the war camp. I hope this is my last one forever. Or at least a very long time. Or if I have to go to war again after tomorrow, it will be with Darling at my side.

Before I sleep, I look through Chaos for Aurora.

She's a vivid purple trace, deep in the guts of Phoenix Crest. Hunched over a bench, hair tied back, alone. Bruises gouge under her eyes, and she seems exhausted. Good.

I shake off the vision and let myself look for Darling one last time. The phoenix pushes onward in the moonlight, a flickering shadow leading three behind her.

This time, before I break the connection, Darling reaches up to touch her lips with her fingers. I imagine myself warm and confident, and hope she feels it.

When the sun rises, I'm dressed in the full scarlet and white of the Dragon's Teeth, waiting at the front of camp facing Phoenix Crest. As the first rays light up the highest tower, Caspian's old tower, I nod, and soldiers release a sparrow drake that trails long golden and green ribbons, marking it as a messenger from the Dragon regent himself.

The message is for General Bloodscale, commanding him to leave Phoenix Crest and meet me here. He should be prepared to turn control over to me.

The full contingent of Dragon's Teeth waits behind me, and five lines of regulars after that, including a special unit of the phoenix's sworn soldiers who have done their best to mark themselves with fire-colored jackets and purple armbands.

Caspian drifts to my side barefoot with a long robe hanging from his shoulders and loosely tied around his waist in a pretense at modesty. He's come ready to fight, as the soldier last night said, with scale and claw.

My brother doesn't look at me, but offers a folded parchment. I take it, opening it. There's a sketch of a woman, vague and almost ghostlike in the lack of fine details. Except her mouth and the edges of her eyes. Despite that, I know her.

She's our mother.

My mouth is dry. She might look like Aurora a little bit, but her eyes are like Caspian's. I can't see myself in her. Maybe if it were a painting with colors, so I could compare irises or hair or skin tone.

"I know none of this is Darling's doing," Caspian says quietly. I glance over, but he's studying the dark silhouettes of Phoenix Crest's battlements and towers. "The dragon I've become dislikes feeling obligated to the phoenix. It—I—would rather have a partnership. Not give ground. Take, take, take. Hoard, you know, protect what's ours, et cetera. But that isn't how it will happen this time. Too much was poorly done a hundred years ago. For a generation of empyreals, at least, the phoenix will be a queen."

"Not that long, if Darling has anything to say about it."

Caspian's lips quirk up. "Perhaps. She's remarkably stubborn."

"House Dragon *will* partner with the phoenix," I tell him. "And if you stop trying to bloody her heart, you might remember Darling always liked you, despite your behavior. You haven't lost all your friends. You don't have to lose her. And—and you don't have to lose me."

"Ah, little dragon," Caspian murmurs. He sways toward me, touches our shoulders together. "I don't know how to have a future."

"Let's get through today, then worry about how to keep you from being a total monster."

"Ambitious," Caspian drawls.

I grin at him, tucking the sketch of our mother into my uniform jacket. "I know."

We don't have to wait long for General Bloodscale's response. It comes when the far gates of Phoenix Crest swing open slowly, the great chains creaking loudly enough we can hear them across the field.

Bloodscale emerges with a phalanx of green-jacketed Dragons at his back, riding a war drake meaner-looking than Finn's.

I walk out to meet him, Caspian just beside me and the Teeth flanking us. We don't have war drakes, and we don't need them.

Bloodscale is a grizzled, strong man in his early fifties. He served with my father, coming up with him rather like Finn did with me. Bloodscale was my army mentor, more of a father to me from ages twelve to seventeen than my own father could have been. He's hard, scarred, and wearing the same bright red I wear, with gold striping and plate armor across his collar and shoulders, and a massive armored belt of scale mail. His large sword is strapped to his back in the quick-release sheath he always preferred. I only have my falchion and claw.

I stop after a few paces, and wait. He stops his war drake. "War Prince," he says in his most disapproving voice. "Caspian," he adds, angry with disdain.

"Dragon regent," I correct. "In more than name, in actuality."

Caspian tilts his head, but otherwise holds his tongue.

Bloodscale says, "We have heard. But you look the same indulged child as always, Caspian."

"The states are not mutually exclusive," Caspian sighs.

I hold out my hand. "Give control of Phoenix Crest to me, General. It's time. The Crest has always been the fortress of the phoenix; we of House Dragon merely held it for her."

Bloodscale snorts. "Let's find a phoenix more to our liking, then, not an orphan whelp from some unknown house. Kill her, and a new phoenix will rise, yes?"

"Give control of Phoenix Crest to me, General," I repeat. That is all I'm here for. "If you do not, you will be marked a traitor to House Dragon, and killed or imprisoned or exiled from Pyrlanum."

My old mentor curls his lips and shakes his head. "Phoenix Crest belongs to House Dragon, not those who betray our ways."

"Ah, Talon, I'm sorry," Caspian murmurs.

I clench my jaw and draw my falchion. "Either acknowledge your War Prince and first scion and submit, or admit you are a traitor and face me in combat to prove your worth by scale and claw."

Even Caspian startles at the old phrasing. It's a challenge from one Dragon to another. The soldier at the fire last night put the idea in my mind.

Bloodscale stares at me for a long moment, measuring. He's been disappointed in me since all this began, for taking Caspian's side in wishing for peace. "Talon," he begins.

"First Scion," I say, correcting him again. He's done this to us; he no longer has the right to our given names.

The old general scowls. "Very well, First Scion. War Prince. You have lost your way, abandoned your family. I will fight you, though your father would dislike it."

"Aurora has influenced him," Caspian says quietly to me, and I agree. *She* would say we've abandoned family. Only Aurora.

"I am not afraid of you, General," I say. "Father would approve of that."

Just then I feel a strange tug on my boon, as if it's active, but I haven't opened the way. I close my eyes, ignoring Bloodscale as I see a trace: violet, rainbows, flickering tiny flames. Darling. I look for her, and see a narrow door, twisted metal and old wood set between two columns of rock face. They found it.

I open my eyes and to my brother I say, "It's time."

Caspian laughs and immediately throws off his robe.

Bloodscale and the Dragons behind him startle, but before anyone can truly react, Caspian takes two steps forward and in a twist, a flash, he is changing.

A dragon fills out the field, raised onto its hind legs, wings snapped out fully, and the dragon arches its neck and roars.

Even expecting it, even having seen him before, my mouth falls open. He's huge, and shining green-black with those gilded markings, jagged horns, and stretching wings.

Muscles bunch under his scales, and Caspian leaps into the air. He flies, and every eye watches as he gains height. He soars for the ramparts of Phoenix Crest.

Bloodscale motions for archers, but none of the Dragon soldiers tear their eyes away from the dragon empyreal to notice.

Caspian screams, a reverberating sound I feel in my bones.

Then he alights upon the highest tower: his, the one he took over years ago to fill with mad, scrawling prophecies of Darling Seabreak, the Phoenix Reborn. He lands, and then, with a wrenching motion I can barely make out, Caspian knocks the roof off.

Stone and tile fall, silent from this distance, but I witness the destruction. The entire Crest must be trembling.

Caspian roars again. The dragon empyreal has returned to his old throne.

31

DARLING

We've just reached the hidden door when there is a roar that echoes across every hill and dell within a day's travel of Phoenix Crest. The sensation of a nearby empyreal shivers across my skin, and I smile.

"All right, let's move," I say, taking the lead. I shove the door open easily, empyreal strength nearly splintering the ancient wood. The other side is dark, and I strip off my goggles while Brigh, Len and Penna pull out a few boonlights behind me.

I was surprised when Brigh volunteered to come along rather than fight with the Dragon army, but she'd just laughed. "What, and miss all the fun?" she said, and I don't blame her. I'd much rather be skulking under Phoenix Crest than on yet another battlefield.

Once the rest of my party have lit their boonlanterns, the ambient light behind me is more than enough to see by without my goggles. I lead the way toward the shrine. I can sense its terrible energy, and the trip is shorter than I'm expecting.

The cave widens and opens up on an amphitheater just like under House Dragon. But this one is far grander, with a hint of ancient columns and strange glyphs that I can't read. In the center of the space is another inky pool, the water vast and deep, and impossibly, Aurora stands upon it, torches flickering around the edge of the lake. She wears heavy robes that make her seem small, like a lost child. Her hair is wild, and she grins maniacally as we enter.

"I felt you," she sing-songs. "But now you'll feel nothing." Her hands bleed from deep cuts, and when she claps them together a wave of energy erupts toward us. I manage to spread my fiery wings wide, a partial change that is less controlled and more instinctive. The energy, a twisted form of Chaos, slams into me. I scream and fall to my knees, the flames around me guttering suddenly. Penna crumples to the ground and Len is thrown across the room, slamming into the wall with a sickening crunch. Only Brigh manages to withstand the wave of power, falling to one knee before standing once more. Still, blood trickles from her nose.

"My flame," she manages before swaying from side to side and passing out as well.

"That should've killed all of you," Aurora says with a frown. She's distracted, muttering to herself as she takes a step to the side and an altar rises out of the water. "No matter, you can't stop me. I'm the rightful heir, and I'll have what's owed to me!" Her voice is low, and she begins talking to herself again. I can't understand what she's saying, but it reminds me far too much of Caspian's ritual on the ramparts at House Barghest. Then, I became the phoenix. I have no desire to see what Aurora intends on summoning.

I reach for the phoenix, intent on using the empyreal against her, but I feel *nothing*.

I cannot change.

I reach once more for the phoenix, for Chaos, for some sense of that other self of mine. But it feels like the phoenix is far away, and in that moment, I understand what happened. The phoenix took the brunt of the blow meant to kill all of us, saving us, but being knocked out in the moment.

I have a feeling that was how the Last Phoenix met their end, unable to transform and outnumbered three to one.

But I am not that phoenix, and I withdraw my blades. It's not the falchion that Talon let me borrow, but the long knives I've always preferred. If I cannot kill Aurora with flame, then I will do it with steel.

I charge toward Aurora, but an invisible barrier keeps me back. I pound my hands against it, but I am helpless to do anything but watch her blood magic.

"House Cockatrice will return to its glory! You tried to keep me from my rightful place, but I *will* be the cockatrice. And then you will have to treat with me. You stole my boon, but you will not steal my destiny, you uncultured mutt!" Aurora yells. She laughs, the sound wild and unhinged. I think of how Leonetti used to always call those who had lost their minds "Chaos-touched," and I wonder if perhaps there is some truth to the old saying. There has to be a reason the long-ago blood mages turned away from their disgusting craft and toward something more like a partnership with Chaos. I know people too well to think it was the cost, the lives spent in pursuit of their own selfish goals. But perhaps there had been a cost for them, one that they weren't willing to continue paying.

It's clear from Aurora's jerky movements that she isn't well, and I holster my blades before pounding on the invisible barrier. "Aurora, stop! This won't go how you think," I say, because I have some insight into how Chaos works, and it greatly dislikes being twisted to the whims of others. It's like a river, determined in the course it charts itself.

And willing to break through a dam at the first sign of weakness.

Aurora ignores me, pulling things from the robe she wears and laying them on the altar one by one. When she pulls out a heart, Vivian's heart, I realize what she is going to do.

Talon said something about Finn seeing Aurora's dreams, and in that moment the phoenix begins to wake, groggy and still far away. It manages to send me an idea of what Aurora is trying to do, and my stomach turns.

I cannot stop her, but I can be ready to strike when the moment is right.

With my eyes still on Aurora, I go to check on the others. Len is still out cold but breathes steadily, and Brigh is beginning to wake. As she makes to sit up, I push her back down.

"Rest for now. There's a passage not far from where Len fell. I'm going to drag you over there. Once you're steady, we'll escape into the castle."

"What about the blood witch?" Brigh asks, her voice strange, her words slurring just a bit. She's awake, but she's far from good.

"Whatever she's doing, we can't stop her. But we need to be ready to move when the time is right. I'm going to move you over toward Len. Pretend to be unconscious."

Brigh nods, and I manage to heft her onto my shoulders and set her down with Len next to the passage—not the one we came down, but another—before doing the same with Penna. She murmurs as though she's having a nightmare, and I pick her up as well and deposit her with Len and Brigh. They are tucked into an alcove in the rock, and I lay a hand on Brigh's arm.

"I need you to hide us," I say, and Brigh's eyebrows raise.

"How do you know?" she asks, and I shrug.

"The phoenix is the Heart of Chaos," I answer, because that's the only answer I have for her. "We have to wait, and then we'll make a run for it."

Brigh and I watch as Aurora takes a bite of Vivian's heart, just as Caspian did with the phoenix's heart at House Barghest. But there is no column of flames. Instead, a sickly yellow-green smoke begins to billow from Vivian's heart, and Aurora begins to cough and choke on it as it surrounds her.

When Aurora's first scream echoes throughout the cavern, I tap Brigh and gesture for her to make her way up the tunnel, but she shakes her head and gestures back toward the lake.

"Look. I think it's killing her," Brigh whispers near my ear. Sure enough, Aurora clutches her throat, her screams dying away into choked gurgles that echo throughout the cavern, a ghastly sound. I go to help her, and Brigh holds me back.

"She's already killed one empyreal, my flame," she says, and I nod, remaining where I am. I want to do something to stop Aurora, but sometimes the most important part of the battle is surveying the scene. And when Aurora finally collapses, falling backward into the dark lake, I stand and hold out a hand to Brigh.

"Can you move?" I ask. The words have no sooner left my lips than there is an inhuman shriek behind me.

"What is that?" Penna asks, slowly sitting up at the sound, her expression confused and horrified.

I turn, slowly, feeling the nearness of an empyreal. Only this feeling is foul, like meat left to rot. I'm expecting to see the cockatrice when I finally look toward the lake, all scales and feathers and glowing eyes. Instead, a hideously twisted creature stands in the middle of the dark water. It has the body of a hunting cat, much like the sphinx and the gryphon, only the fur is mangy and greasy, huge patches of it missing and revealing a serpent's scales beneath. Aurora's face is where the head would be, her hair matted and her eyes too large, bulging and slit-pupiled. She screams again, a sound that makes me want to roll into a ball and hide, and her open mouth reveals needlepoint teeth. But worst of all is her tail, a fearsome thing bearing a poisonous point, like the sand crawlers that stalk the dunes and the sewers in Nakumba.

"What is that?" Brigh asks, and Chaos supplies the answer.

"Manticore," I say. "An aberration born of blood magic."

The creature begins to lurch out of the water, and the movement shakes me from my trance.

"Go, into the passage," I say, hefting Len on my shoulders before pushing Brigh and Penna ahead of me. They lean on each other, their steps deliberate and slow, and I have just made it into the safety of the stone when I feel the rush of air and turn back to see Aurora's luminous yellow eyes staring at us.

She screams again, the sound making the stone around us shudder, but then we are hurrying along the path. It isn't long before we reach a wall, the lever mechanism obvious, and Brigh triggers it. The stone slides up, counterweights and gears grinding, and we exit into what I know to be the wall surrounding the quarters assigned to House Sphinx.

After all this time, I've finally figured out how Gavin snuck into my rooms what feels like forever ago. It's a bitter comfort.

I carry Len into the rooms, which look to have been ransacked. Most likely people fleeing Phoenix Crest in the wake of a new regime. Years of war have made people very good at fleeing.

I place Len on the bed, and help Brigh and Penna to chairs.

"Stay here, keep your head down. I have to go after the manti-core." I reach for the phoenix, trying to shift since it would be faster to fly, but I still cannot fully reach the empyreal.

"Be careful," Brigh calls. "Talon will have my head if anything happens to you."

I give her a quick nod before heading back the way we came. The trip is much faster without Len's dead weight, but when I arrive back at the cavern, there is a sulfurous smell and a gaping hole where the top of the cavern used to be, blue sky above. Huge boulders litter the lake, the water displaced so that the entire cave is now flooded, and I cannot help but swear long and loud as I pull my goggles from my pocket and onto my watering eyes. Overhead, the dragon circles, calling out a battle cry, and I reach fruitlessly once more for the phoenix.

The manticore has joined the fray.

32

TALON

Every member of the Dragon armies, and those gathered who belong now to the phoenix, watches as Caspian claims the ramparts of the Crest. He roars from the ruins of his high tower, and the roar reverberates through the morning air.

At least half Bloodscale's army sinks to their knees, dropping weapons. War drakes roar back to Caspian, high shrieking cries. The Dragons behind me stand tall. That is our empyreal. We have these traitors trapped between us.

"Walk to my side," I yell. "Come stand with your first scion, Talon Goldhoard! This is the charge of House Dragon! Follow the Dragon regent; be the claws and teeth of a new Phoenix Reborn!"

It's as easy as that for those on their knees. They get up and start for me. A handful of soldiers riding war drakes wheel their mounts around—difficult when the drakes are so keyed to Caspian's hulking figure. Some Dragon soldiers grab their comrades, pulling them along. Others hold each other back, unsure.

General Bloodscale dismounts, boots hitting the bent grass hard. He strides toward me, but not to kneel; he reaches for his great sword and looses it, swinging it into a ready position. "You challenged me by scale and claw, boy," he growls.

"Fine," I say, and as I walk to meet him, I unhook my claw from the back of my belt and slide my left hand into the fingers, strapping it securely around my wrist. Then I unsheathe my falchion and don't pause to bow or give Bloodscale the first move.

I attack.

We're of a height, but Bloodscale is wider in the shoulder and has twenty years of experience over me—not to mention his longer sword. I have to be faster, unhesitating, and use every leverage of my slighter strength. And my boon.

I open to Chaos as widely as I can without triggering a vision, just as Bloodscale blocks my first strike.

This is how I trained my boon since it first appeared when I was nine years old. I see Bloodscale's dark green trace, the shimmering edges of it blurring toward his war drake, and I see it shimmering ahead of him, too: the next steps of his feet, the next swing of his sword, the next turn of his body. It's predictive, it lets me be faster, lets me analyze him instantly.

And it's even more powerful than before.

Bloodscale hits hard, but I block with blade and claw, scraping the claw along his sword to make a horrid shriek of metal. He bares his teeth, swings, but I'm there. I'm wherever he strikes.

He knows this is my boon. He knows he has to trick it.

His next strike is heavy enough I struggle under its weight, though I knew where to be. I fling him back and slice in, turning almost under his arm. He grabs for me with his free hand, but I claw at him, twisting my falchion up under his ribs. Bloodscale shifts so the blade slices his thick scale mail belt, using his bulk against me. My falchion's small size lets me maneuver close like this, where his great sword is too long and awkward, but Blood-scale kicks me far again. I roll, suddenly aware I have no armor against him: one blow from that sword will not only cut me, but break bones.

I see his patterns. I lower and duck in, then dance back, moving around behind him. Bloodscale twists. My claw catches his arm, tearing cloth, but it meets gauntlet, and I have to let go to turn fast on my heel and meet his sword with mine. Bloodscale turns, too, giving me a slighter target: it's sword on sword for a moment. I pant carefully, watching.

Bloodscale is breathing hard, too. His face is red with exertion and fury. Neither of us is bloodied yet.

When he pauses like this, his trace pulls back. He's remembering how the boon works, trying not to think ahead himself.

I smile grimly.

Just then I feel a strange wave in the air. It's like my boon expanding and contracting all at once. Then yelling and shocked cries reach us from the far end of the field, the north near the fortress. I don't take my eyes off Bloodscale, waiting for him to look away first.

Neither of us move until we hear the wail.

It is bloodcurdling and awful. My whole body shivers, and I see Bloodscale blanch. I turn toward the sound and stare at what I see.

A true monster, not an empyreal but seemingly patched together from them. Rotting fur falling off its leonine body to reveal dark scales, a long neck covered in feathers and more fur, with stubby wings of tattered skin and scales flapping as it runs across the field on four huge feline legs, gouging the earth with talons. It screams again, and as it approaches, it seems to get larger.

It's no illusion of closing distance: the thing grows like Darvey the barghest can. A tail curls up over its haunches with a barb on the end that glistens with dark liquid.

And its face. "Holy Chaos," I whisper. This thing wears a stretched and hollowed version of Aunt Aurora's face. Her vivid eyes are wholly blue, faceted with bloody bruised purple like Chaos itself turned to rot.

The sheer *wrongness* of her transformation crawls along my skin. I have to swallow bile. I'm not the only one. I hear retching amidst the gasps and cries of horror.

I can't look away.

She charges through the army, Dragons running in all directions to get away from her.

I tear my gaze away to glance behind me to the Dragons and Flames, who are just as horrified, but holding our ground. "Archers," I yell, then spin back around to the thing Aurora has become just as soldiers yell in new shock, and with a gust of wind Caspian lands on Aurora's huge, disgusting back.

The Dragon regent beats his wings and grabs up Aurora, turning over to fling her fifty paces across the field. He roars, racing after, and Aurora screams that awful wailing cry again. Her mouth is filled with needle teeth. Caspian doesn't hesitate to attack again, ignoring the barbed tail and her wicked talons. They skim off his empyreal scales and he snaps at her neck.

The brush of boot on grass is my only warning: I turn, lifting my falchion just in time to block Bloodscale's strike. But my shoulder wrenches painfully in the tight space. Something tears. I clench my jaw and slash at Bloodscale's face with my claw.

He jerks back.

"Stop this—you see what she's become!" I cry at him. Pain radiates down my arm. I can still lift my falchion, though.

Bloodscale scowls. "This is a challenge. Interruptions don't matter."

"It's over," I yell, catching the eye of soldiers behind Bloodscale.

Archers have run to the front, most heading for the battling empyreals.

"Can't let you off so easily," Bloodscale yells back, and attacks again.

I meet him, grunting with the effort. His strength pushes me back, and I lean in, with all my weight. I glare. "Stop," I say through clenched teeth.

"No," he answers.

I heave everything I can, claw caught around my own falchion blade to give me extra leverage to hold it against his great sword.

Then, I drop.

It hurts, but I fall and roll, jerking at his sword. Bloodscale cries in surprise as he falls with me. He lands hard, groaning. I roll again, free of him, and as Bloodscale tries to stand I lash in and stab him up under his scale mail belt; my falchion guts him.

I jerk it back, nauseated again, for what I've done.

Standing shakily, I stare down at the general grasping at his bleeding stomach. He glares through the pain, but I simply nod, then turn and take in the scene:

Caspian is twined around the thing Aurora made herself, clawing at her belly, but she has scales, too. She snaps needle teeth at him, but he stabs up at her face with the horns cresting along his nose and brow. Her barbed tail flails, and soldiers dash back. War drakes hiss and scream around them like a ring.

I run closer.

Archers stand ready, but there's no way to hit her without hitting Caspian. It doesn't matter; his scales are too strong.

"Fire at her face and eyes," I command. "Where there aren't scales. You can't hurt the Dragon regent."

They set a volley of arrows loose. The arc is perfect, but most of the arrows ping off the creature, and several off Caspian.

The dragon manages to scour the monster's face with his horns, leaving sickly red-purple gouges behind. She shrieks and flails; her tail cuts down and Caspian digs in with all his claws. They roll against the ground, making the field tremble. Dust rises as both massive creatures flail. I stand my ground, but it's difficult. The war drakes dance and scream. One dashes forward to attack the Aurora-thing, but her tail whips out, knocking it back and slicing scales with its weeping tip.

Aurora screams, and Caspian bites at her, but she catches her front talons against his wing, tearing the stretched skin. Caspian hisses and throws her again. He leaps, still half-flying, and the attack is back on.

Talon.

My name sounds amidst the cacophony. I blink. I can't tell if I heard it or sensed it, but I suck in a gasp. Darling.

As the Dragon regent and the twisted monster brawl, I turn and look through the waves of soldiers surrounding them. Here and there a few fight, but most are caught up in the spectacle of the empyreal battle.

I focus on my boon and use it to trace Darling.

She's here, pushing toward me. On the field. The sun shines down on her, on smears of blood at her hairline, on the round smoked lenses of her goggles.

I run in her direction. "Darling!"

"Talon!"

I shift my path, and soldiers get out of my way, parting like water.

There she is. Gasping as she staggers to a halt, having clearly raced here. After Aurora. She flickers in my boonsight, purple flames jagged and wisping out. She's only Darling, looking smaller than she's seemed in months. A long knife hangs loose in one hand.

I reach her, and she grabs at me. My injured shoulder aches, but I wrap my left arm around her, careful with the claw. "What happened, what did she do?" I demand. "What's wrong with you?"

"I need you, Talon," she says, fingers digging into me. She drops her knife and the tip sticks into the grass.

A thrill at her words has me nodding. Anything. Anything she needs.

"I need you," Darling says, "to use your boon and find the phoenix."

My lips fall open in shock. "You—"

"She did something. Talon, listen. The phoenix is here, caught, pushed down, but I can't drag it up, I need—"

"Me to find it," I say it as a vow. I drop my falchion, and pull her closer with the arm around her waist. "I will."

"I know." Darling rips off her goggles. In the broad daylight she stares at me wide-eyed, dark brown eyes haunted by flecks of purple and sudden springing tears. "Do it now!"

In the middle of the battlefield, I tear open my boon and kiss her.

33

DARLING

Talon's kiss burns away the last of the blood magic, his boon seeking and finding the phoenix, and by extension, Chaos. And yet, I linger, not pulling back, letting him continue to kiss me. It's silly, battle rages all around us, but the phoenix agrees with me. We've missed this.

Somehow, I feel the empyreal more fully than I ever have, now that it has returned. I feel as though that has something to do with having my heart back. I pull back a little and Talon smiles down at me uncertainly. "Better?" he asks his voice low. I nod.

The shriek of the manticore splits the air once more, ruining the moment and pulling me back to the matter at hand.

"We have to find a way to stop her," I say, watching as she and Caspian tear at each other fruitlessly. The barbed tail skids off the dragon's hide, searching for weakness.

"I think the best bet would be to target her eyes and her face," Talon says.

I nod, and begin to strip. "I can try to burn her away . . ."

"No, look!" Talon says, grabbing my hand before I can begin to remove my clothes.

The manticore has managed to find one of the soft spaces near the dragon's joints. The monstrous lizard howls in pain before dancing back, moving drunkenly from side to side.

"Whatever that poison is, you won't be immune to it," Talon says.

"You have a better idea?" I ask, feeling desperate. We can't have the manticore ravaging much longer. Here on this place chosen as a battlefield there are only soldiers and other combatants. But less than a league away is Phoenix Crest, a city filled with nothing but innocents, people just trying to live their lives. We have to be able to take hold of her before she turns her rage toward that goal.

"If you can get me on top of her, I can stab her in her eye," Talon says, hefting his sword. He winces and I touch his arm.

"You're injured?" I ask, and at his nod I press Chaos into the wound, just as I did back on the ramparts when I burned his hands. Only this time I can sense it better, the bond with the phoenix and by extension Chaos stronger than ever before. "Better?" I ask, and he nods.

I kick off my boots as the poison finally takes hold of the dragon and the massive empyreal crashes to the ground. The manticore shrieks in what must be triumph, the sound keening higher, like a raptor pulling a fish from the waves. I forgo the rest of my clothes and release the phoenix. "Try to relax," I tell Talon, before stepping backward to give myself space for the change. I know I won't burn Talon, but I'm not sure about the Chaos invoked in the shift.

I soar around the field once before circling low over Talon. He stands utterly still, and there is no fear in his face, only trust. I angle my body so that I can grab him with a single claw, the flames there tamped so that he won't burn. But it's less than a thought. I was honest when I told him the phoenix would never burn its heart. And he is mine.

The manticore screams again, the sound causing me to tighten involuntarily around Talon. *Sorry*, I send down the connection, and the phoenix sends him an image of what I am planning: I will drop him, and he will have to make his way to the head while I distract the monster before us.

Only the manticore launches itself into the air on its damaged, leathery wings, swiping poison claws at Talon. I soar out of range and flip Talon into the air, catching him on my back at the last possible moment.

"Okay, let's not do that again," he says, and I scream in amusement. But I have to suddenly dive and tuck my wings into a full body roll as the manticore's tail comes sailing toward where Talon just was.

I send him an image of the tail and he tightens his thighs on my back in response. "Ready!" he yells, and I circle the manticore tightly, curving around behind her so that Talon has a clear shot at the tail. He's fast and steady, and the blade cuts through the chitinous appendage with a sickening crunch.

"Now!" he yells, and I dive toward the manticore, flying over the creature upside down so that Talon can relax and land on the creature's back.

He manages to make the switch, if a bit awkwardly, but immediately begins to use his claw and falchion to climb toward the creature's head. And while he does, I circle the manticore, reaching for the Chaos wrapped up within the blood magic and pulling. But whatever spell Aurora cast is stronger than even the phoenix's connection to Chaos.

It's up to Talon.

The manticore screams and tries to turn toward Talon, but that just gives him what he wants. She snaps at him once, twice, and on the third time Talon shouts, a Dragon battle cry, and buries his falchion to the hilt in her eye. The effect is instantaneous.

The manticore evaporates in a sickly green smoke, leaving behind both Talon and Aurora plunging toward the earth. Panic runs through me, and I turn back to Talon. I have to catch him. If he hits the ground, he will die.

And I am not ready to lose him when I've just found him again.

I urge the phoenix to speed, and let go. There is a strange hiccup, a feeling of moving through space but not time, and then I am there, impossibly enough, wrapping human arms around Talon while phoenix wings try to slow our descent. We're falling too fast, so I wrap flaming wings around both of us and aim for an empty space in the field, soldiers running to give us a clear spot to land.

It's more of a crash, the ground arcing up around us and melting in the heat of the phoenix wings. The air is knocked out of me, and I feel a few ribs snap, but as I lie in the glass cradle made by our impact, they heal immediately.

I sit up and lean over Talon, and he grins up at me. "Let's do it again," he jokes, and I laugh, climbing to my feet unsteadily.

Talon strips out of his uniform jacket and settles it around my shoulders, and I stand and look across the field. We stand in a glass flower made by my crash, and around us a few Dragon soldiers have fallen to their knees, crying. I'm crying as well, because I have no goggles, until Talon reaches over and miraculously pulls a pair from a pocket within his jacket. "I figured an extra pair might be handy," he says, settling them over my eyes.

I shrug the rest of the way into Talon's coat, securing it over my nakedness and then taking Talon's hand in mine. As we cross the field, soldiers sink to their knees, and I free boons as I go, leaving a chorus of gasps and exclamations behind me. But it's half-hearted, the work I do.

My attention is for the body in the middle of the field.

Aurora lies wide-eyed, Talon's sword driven through her eye. Dark lines crisscross her face, and one of her hands is still twisted into a claw. She is sickening to look at, and the urge to cry nearly overwhelms me. Leonetti is gone because of her, as is Vivian. And House Sphinx, if the truth be told. So much pain and loss, all because of one woman and her lies. And for what? Power? Importance? The heart of a man who would never have been hers? I will never understand.

But all Pyrlanum *must* remember. Otherwise, it will only be a matter of time until another blood mage rises to challenge Chaos.

I turn and realize that the soldiers on the field are waiting, expecting me to make a proclamation of sorts. I take a deep breath and let it out on a sigh.

"This is a new day for Pyrlanum," I call, my voice carrying across the field. "Today is the end of the House Wars, and the end of inequity and greed. Today we begin a path toward a new Pyrlanum, one that is fair and peaceful. Blood magic has no place in our lands, and let any who still practice this foul ritual know this: if you stand against Chaos, I will burn you to the ground."

I toss a bit of phoenix flame at Aurora's body, and she ignites instantly, burning hot and fast. When the flame abates, there is not a speck of her left, just a clear glass pond with Talon's sword in the middle, embedded and sparking with bits of purple Chaos.

The murmur of the crowd is instantaneous, and I pull Talon through the people pressing all around us, who fall back in reverence. There are whispers of "My flame," and "Phoenix Reborn," all around us, but once we've broken free from the worst of the crowd, people give us wide berth.

"I, uh, hope the sword wasn't sentimental," I tell Talon, and he laughs.

"It is now a monument to the Phoenix Reborn's triumph over blood magic," he says with a shrug. "I can't think of a better use."

"Our triumph," I correct him. I pull him to me and kiss him deeply. "Speaking of which, the phoenix is urging me to purge the rest of the shrines across the continent, beginning with the one where Aurora did her ritual. Do you think you can take care of this?"

"Of course, my flame."

I almost correct him, but there's something different about the way he says it. More of a caress than a statement of obedience. So I kiss him once more, tear off the smoked lenses and shrug out of his jacket, and take to the air feeling happier and more myself than I have in forever.

The phoenix has truly returned.

CHAOS

t's been five weeks since the Phoenix Reborn took back her throne, and every morning I wake up beside Darling.

Which is a good thing, because I barely see her otherwise.

Today she groaned and rolled after me when I got up to wash and dress; then, as I headed out the door of the phoenix's royal suite, I felt the kiss of delicate flames against my cheek. I turned and grinned at her.

"Do I have to wear it?" she asked with a little pout from where she wolfed down a quick breakfast beside the hearth.

"No," I said, letting my smile fade into something softer. She doesn't have to do anything she doesn't want to anymore. But she will.

Darling laughed—loud and bright. I left with the joyous sound ringing in my ears.

It'll be hours before I see her again, tonight at her investiture. Finally the phoenix will officially be enthroned in the partially restored Crest fortress, with every empyreal and first scion present to witness. We're celebrating, but not lavishly: a ritual on an open balcony, facing the front of the fortress, so all Pyrlanum can attend. For days people have been arriving, taking up inns and guest rooms, and camping along the entire edge of the field.

They've put up a shrine around the sprawling glass flower melted into the earth where Darling and I landed during battle, and a second one, a tomb, around my falchion where Aurora died. Someone with a floral boon spent days awakening seeds until the field grew wild with bright green grasses and waves of wildflowers. People walk across and children play, but the flowers come back every dawn. From the windows of our suite, it looks like a gently rolling green sea, dotted with color.

Most of the slow recovery has not been so beautiful.

Darling spent the first week gone every day, all day, hunting the remnants of blood magic across the island. She exhausted herself purifying our land and Chaos, tumbling out of the sky at dusk with barely enough energy to eat and sleep. I saved my reports for the early mornings, murmuring to her while she pressed her face to my shoulder and pretended to keep dozing until I'd say something especially outrageous or infuriating about how the cleanup was going.

There were pockets of resistance, of course, but they're few and far between, easily put down by a combined party of Dragon soldiers and the Flames sworn to the phoenix. No, the uglier aspects are the continuing discoveries of just how bad things have been for so many people. My work has always been destructive, I know that, and putting things back together is hard.

It's more rewarding, too.

Miranda Seabreak is here in Phoenix Crest doing the job of organizing just about everything non-military, and we work well together now that we have the chance, leaving only the biggest decisions for Darling herself. House Dragon has the biggest infrastructure left both for communication and movement, and all that has been opened up for Miranda's use, and anyone's. We sent messages out immediately with peacekeepers to inform the people of Darling's heroic actions, inviting everyone to the investiture, and setting up phoenix stations where people could come to make reports and complaints and hear the latest news from Phoenix Crest. Money and resources need to be reallocated, the worst destruction and oppression triaged, and, as Caspian offered Darling nearly half a year ago, reparations made.

Dragon offers the most, of course, but House Barghest and House Gryphon are not far behind in needing to contribute. Fortunately, the regents of both are amenable. Darvey will do anything Darling asks, and the remains of Barghest are rightly cowed by their giant dog of a leader now, despite his youth. Especially with Finn backing him up. Elias continues to recover from the violence and taint of their transformation, but is quietly dedicated to the restoration of Gryphon's reputation.

House Kraken has both gathered their members closer and sent out their tentacles to test various waters. They're reestablishing themselves in coastal cities that used to belong to them, which has caused a few headaches for me when the current residents occasionally resist. But I happily turned Lastrium over to Kraken, wishing that old mayor were still alive to have to suck it up.

Gianna returned to Nakumba with a group of Adelaide Seabreak's Barbs and Darling's Flames, only to find dozens of volunteers hoping to help her restore the house. The last report I received read they've made more progress rebuilding than we have at Phoenix Crest. Gianna is doted upon, and rightly so. I sent the contents from Darling's first room here at the Crest, the House Sphinx–designed gifts and clothing Caspian commissioned for his game with Darling. But we kept the suite here fitted for House Sphinx, and as of yesterday, it's Gianna's for her visit. She arrived with a small contingent of her very own people, hoping Darling will help her name a first scion after the investiture tonight. Adelaide came just behind her, storming and prickly as ever. Though House Kraken has their official suite in the main fortress, Darling gave the newly cleansed lake under the keep to Adelaide, so she doesn't have to be cranky out of water for her entire visit. It makes me—and most of my soldiers, I'm sure—constantly nervous to know there's a massive kraken under our feet at any given time. I'm working on letting go. This is Phoenix Crest, and House Kraken is no longer my enemy.

I sent Arran Lightscale, one of my best Teeth who missed out on all the recent fighting as he occupied Barghest, up to Dragon Castle as my representative there. He's been working alongside Annag Mortooth to weed out any Dragons loyal to Aurora or Bloodscale or our old ways, with the help of a truth-seeking House Gryphon baker kindly lent to us by Elias. Once everything is settled and the muscle of my army isn't needed so much to maintain Darling's peace, I'm disbanding most of it. We don't need a standing army. Some will come to be Flame soldiers instead, others will stay in Dragon Castle as guards and instructors, but most will have to return to other ways: farmers and drake herders, blacksmiths and miners.

That should make it easier when Darling inevitably disbands the system of governing scions and forces us to begin electing leaders. I'd like for Annag or Arran to be chosen, or both, or maybe Bram Featherblade, an old Dragon historian who showed up at Dragon Castle claiming to have been my father's disappointed tutor who'd been hiding in the library at House Gryphon for three decades.

If one of them is elected, then I can just be Darling's consort.

The first time I heard someone hushed for calling me the Phoenix's Heart in my hearing, I nearly perished from embarrassment. But it's a better title than War Prince. Once I can hand over House Dragon, I still plan to take over training and commanding Darling's Flames, if I can convince Len he doesn't want the job, because soldiering is what I know best. The things I do for Darling's heart are nobody else's business.

After a long morning of smoothing the logistical nightmare of so many people pouring into the Crest and the meadow outside, I take my hastily grabbed and very late lunch up to the ramparts. My thoughts are tangled up trying to recall which of the new stewards Miranda appointed to her staff is the one with the whisper boon, and if they can use it to speak across distances to multiple people at once. Darling has awakened so many boons nobody has ever heard of, it's been another layer of mess working through what people can and can't do. Every day more people arrive for Darling to meet—she goes to the nearby camps and villages to let them see her and unlock their boons, before she sets off for distant corners of Pyrlanum she has yet to visit, only to spend the day doing the same. Darling hasn't taken a single hour of a single day off, but I'm hoping tomorrow morning, at least, we can rest.

I'm so caught up, I nearly run into Elias on the tower stairs.

"Talon," they say, just as startled.

Elias stands two steps higher than me, lit from behind by the sun through the open tower door. They step down to meet me. I wish my hands weren't full of food and drink.

"How is he?" I ask. I've barely spoken with Elias since they arrived yesterday for the investiture. They look significantly better than last month, dressed in loose red robes similar to those most of the empyreals wear. Easy to shrug off. Their brown skin is less purple around the eyes, with a healthier glow, but they obviously have lost weight since becoming the Gryphon regent.

"Patient," Elias answers softly, glancing over their shoulder toward the open tower door above us.

That doesn't sound like my brother. *But then again, he's only a little bit my brother anymore*, I think with a frown. "Have you found anything in your library to help?"

"Nothing that contradicts Darling's diagnosis. She is most likely correct, and Caspian isn't willing to take the risk with her cure."

I sigh.

Elias touches my hand, the one clutching the plate of cold meat and bread. Their touch is glancing and feather-light. When I look back to their golden eyes, I see the intensity of the gryphon behind them. "Nobody understands his choice better than me anymore," Elias says.

Grimly, I climb past him and emerge onto the rampart.

It's the largest upper wall of Phoenix Crest, a dark spread of stone between two small but sharp lookout towers. Caspian's old, tallest tower, the one he destroyed, is a crumbled ruin nearby.

In front of me the dragon stretches like a giant lizard in the late summer sun, absorbing heat into his black-green scales. One huge green eye pops open at my bootstep, and when he sees me, Caspian lifts his head.

It's been weeks, and he can't change back to his human form. The manticore's poison fused the forms together, Darling thinks. She could strip them apart, heal the toxin, but the risk isn't burning up or death—that Caspian would allow. The risk is permanently stripping the empyreal from him, and Caspian refuses.

Selfishly, furiously, I think he's doing it because he prefers to be the dragon. He doesn't have to lead or speak or do much, though early on he helped transport a few new cornerstone boulders here, and he has carried soldiers between the Crest and Mount Hoard. But mostly, he soaks up the sun and soars around.

Darling pointed out if Caspian loses the empyreal, it would very likely be mine, so Caspian is sparing me that. I said, *Then we could fly together*. Darling reminded me we already can.

I nod at my huge draconic brother and settle down to eat with my back leaning against the base of his neck. I can feel his sunbaked heat through my uniform jacket and shirt. He allows it, and listens to my report while I devour the food. The water is for me, and the wine for him. Sometimes he lets me pour it onto his tongue, but today Caspian snaps it between his teeth and eats the whole bladder.

As I talk about plans for feeding and sheltering so many people for the next few days—and how we're going to be in trouble if it rains, unless we find several people with weather boons—and go over the ritual Miranda's planned, Caspian harrumphs and sighs, and occasionally lets a whine out between his huge teeth. He can't speak, but he's getting better at communicating. It's a relief. Darling insists he's all Caspian in there, sharing space with the empyreal, instead of being subsumed by the sense of the dragon. When I'm with Caspian like this, it feels a bit more real.

Eventually, I have to get back to work. I put my hand flat on Caspian's sun-hot snout, petting him the way I'd pet Kitty. Caspian rolls his eyes. Something about the movement seems fond.

The rest of my day is spent putting out various fires around the fortress. Nearing dusk, when I really should start getting ready for the ceremony, a young girl with purple ribbons in her hair marking her a Flame runs up to me, eyes huge, begging me to hurry along to Miranda's office just off the Phoenix Hall because there is an emergency.

I run.

Only to hear Miranda and Brigh arguing fast, and louder than either of them usually is, over what sounds like . . . seating arrangements for tonight.

I slow, incredulous, and barge in.

Brigh grins with all her teeth. "Thank Chaos, Talon."

Miranda doesn't do anything as inelegant as resort to sarcasm, but merely says, "Will you be standing with House Dragon or the Phoenix Reborn tonight?"

I drop my mouth open, stunned.

"With us," Brigh says.

Miranda smiles with a hint of the poison she's known to make. "You make it sound like you aren't good enough to represent House Dragon, Brigh, even with the empyreal perched on the roof like a giant lizard."

"I'm not—" Brigh starts in again, scowling just like Finn.

"I'm standing with Darling," I say. "Brigh, you'll do fine."

Miranda smiles. "You'll be standing directly across from your brother," the former Kraken says sweetly.

"This was really the emergency?" I say. Both women turn to me with such a look I raise my hands in surrender. "I'm going to go get ready. Have you heard if the Cockatrice remnants have arrived yet?"

"They have," Miranda nods. "They're being organized into two groups: one related to the little screamer, who will be staying in the Cockatrice suites, the rest for the meadow camps until they can be escorted to Mount Klevon."

"Good." One of the first messages we sent in the aftermath of retaking the fort had been to the known branches of House

Cockatrice where they'd taken refuge across the sea in Saverna. We'd asked if they knew the location of the newborn cockatrice empyreal and welcomed them home. Their response had been disappointing, without any sign of an empyreal, but they promised many of them would rush back for the investiture. "I'll see you all in an hour in the Phoenix Hall," I say as I back out, hoping they don't have anything else to delay me.

I make it away from the public and political section of the Crest and into the private wing, to the rooms Caspian used once upon a time, which now belong to the Phoenix Reborn. And me.

Just as I round a corner, an earsplitting shriek pierces the air.

I clap my hands over my ears, though it never helps. Wincing, I press on toward our rooms. My head rings, aching, and I really hope we can solve this when the Cockatrice refugees are sorted.

A short whirlwind of feathers and claws explodes out of the phoenix suite's doors, and barrels toward me. I crouch, having learned the hard way not to run. "Lilou," I say and brace for the tiny empyreal to slam into my chest.

She's chittering and flapping her wings, dropping pearlescent white and lavender feathers, swiping with her wickedly hooked beak as she tries to talk to me. I hold her carefully, her little heartbeat easy to feel in the delicate bird body. Her tail feathers drape in a cute stubby rainbow.

Behind her comes Darling herself, half-dressed and dashing barefoot, followed by two Flame attendants.

Darling says something I barely hear through the ringing in my skull, and unfortunately the baby cockatrice in my arms screams again.

I definitely pass out for a split second—another reason it's good to be nearer the ground—and snap to as Darling hugs the empyreal to her, arms gouged by flailing little chicken legs. Suddenly there's a flash of fire, and Darling cradles a naked toddler with bright auburn ringlets and happy blue eyes.

I stand shakily and nod to Darling's sudden concerned look. My skull pounds, I can't hear, but the moment Darling passes the kid to the attendants, she puts her hands on the sides of my face. The soft flicker of phoenix fire soothes away the pain and hearing loss, and I tilt forward to kiss her.

"Talon," she says softly, but I can hear it. I smile and stand with her.

"That little brat," I say looking back at the attendants. One is a former Dragon soldier, Marjorie; the other I don't recognize. "The Cockatrice remnants arrived," I tell them. "Lilou's parents must be among them."

"Oh, *good*," Darling gushes. She sends Lilou a playful grin. "You behave, kid, hear me?"

Lilou, being wrapped in a little blue robe, squirms. "Run!"

"I should . . ." Darling says, watching the young Cockatrice regent try to escape her attendants. One holds her wrist tightly while the other makes promises about her mother and father.

Four days ago, Darling suddenly dropped out of the sky, landing before Phoenix Crest with a tiny little girl in her arms.

She'd been out on the western lowlands, meeting people and unlocking boons, when Chaos screamed at her to fly east, east, east. The first of the Cockatrice refugees had returned, and the moment a particular family disembarked from the ship, their two-year-old daughter turned into a gorgeous, vicious, rainbow monster chicken.

We learned the empyreals are literally connected to the heart of Pyrlanum, to the Chaos in our land. Darling brought little Lilou here ahead of her family, who traveled overland as fast as they could.

"You have to get dressed," I say.

"You too." Darling huffs, then grabs my lapel to take me into the suite with her. "She just won't stop; she's too excited," Darling says. "Usually after I turn her back, she can't just pop into the chicken again for at least an hour. That will get us to the ceremony."

"It's still big emotions?" I manage to shut the doors behind us, and start helping Darling into the layers of gown and robes she'd been halfway into.

She hums agreement, fussing with the ties of one underrobe. This is designed with the colors from all houses, layered and recut to fall around her like flames. I have it on good authority that two of the layers were repurposed from Caspian's extravagant robes still intact in the wardrobe.

"Maybe Miranda can make her a tincture to keep her calm until she understands better," I suggest.

Once she's tied in, I take my turn while she binds her curls into a few tight twists. I can't help stealing glances at her arching neck and the movement of her fingers. It takes me twice as long to dress as it should. I'm simply wearing a black coat over part of my uniform, with copper buttons and scale mail over my shoulder and falling down my back like a half cape of fire. It's easy. While we prepare, we trade stories from our day. Darling stayed close, greeting people who only arrived yesterday, then spent time with Darvey and Gianna, before going for a swim in Adelaide's underground lake. It's good for her—for the phoenix—to bond with the empyreals. The kraken is making it even harder than Caspian.

"Adelaide told me the lake is salt water," Darling says as she draws a line of dark purple under my eye, delighted, I think, to be painting me. She doesn't need eye makeup, she insists, because even though the ritual itself will be held with the hall dimmed enough for her to see, the rest of the time she'll wear her goggles. Her hand on my jaw strokes lightly. "She thinks she can make it all the way to the sea from here, deep through the earth."

I suppress a frown at the thought. "It makes sense for all empyreals to have access to Phoenix Crest in their empyreal form."

Darling stops and grins at me. "You hate it."

"I hate it."

"Not as much as I hate the Phoenix Mantle," she says.

I laugh, knowing I was set up. "You don't have to wear it," I remind her.

But Darling goes over to a trunk near the hearth. She lifts the lid. "Help me?" she says breathlessly.

I do.

The Phoenix Mantle isn't a cape, but a huge piece of jewelry that settles around her collar, shoulders, and back. Elias had records of it that included drawings, and they sent copies over for a woman with a metalworking boon to use in creating it. Thin copper and silver twist and lift like small flames, fitted perfectly to Darling. When the two sections are latched and settled where they belong, it looks like she's on fire.

Of course, we've all seen Darling actually on fire, but this effect is lovely. Even though, despite all the finery, the outfit made in every detail for today, she's wearing one of her oldest pairs of smoked lenses.

I help Darling situate the crown, then kneel to help her into her slippers. I glance up to find her watching me with the shadow of fear on her beautiful face.

Standing, I take her hands. "You can do this," I say. "I'm not going anywhere."

"*We* can do this," she whispers.

There's a knock at the door, and Miranda's voice calls that it's time.

I weave our fingers together. Darling squeezes mine, and then together we head for the Phoenix Hall.